THORNFRUIT

FELICIA DAVIN

CONTENTS

For J, who knows everything about me.

1

THE GIRL IN THE MARKET

TEN YEARS AGO

WHEN EV was three years old, a wave had crashed into the cliffs of Laalvur. As the flood waters had drained from the lower city back into the ocean, they'd left a giant dead medusa speared on the splintered wreckage of the harbor. The monster's carcass had lethal tentacles as long as three men lying end to end. It had taken six people to lift its massive bell.

It was a horrible story—medusas killed people, and so did waves—and Papa always made it worse by saying words like *oozing* and *gelatinous*. But Ev still wished she'd been there to heave it off the ground and throw its corpse back into the ocean. Or maybe she could have saved someone from drowning. The heroes in her favorite books were always doing things like that.

Ev was twelve now and her life hadn't offered much in the way of adventure, but she remained hopeful. She zigzagged down the narrow street after her father and their cart, ignoring the slap and clatter of donkey hooves, wooden wheels, and leather sandals against the stone and straining to hear the water instead. A whole ocean of it, her father had promised. But the harbor was still another steep turn or two beneath them on the path, and Ev couldn't see that far down.

Papa said sometimes the sky and the stones of the city were so red that they made the ocean look red, too. Ev had been to Laalvur before, but she could only conjure a vague memory of orange-brown cliffs pierced by dark doorways and people everywhere, even on ladders between the street levels. Her best friend Ajee didn't believe her when she said she'd seen the city. She'd sworn up and down she was telling the truth, but she hadn't come back with any good stories.

"Did you see a shark? Or a medusa? Or a *wave*?"

Ev hadn't.

Ajee said it was dumb to want to be like people in books when Ajee and Ev were just going to live in the village of Orzatvur their whole lives, where there were no sea monsters and no princesses to save.

It didn't matter what he thought. He wasn't here. Now she was old enough to help bring their cart to the market, and she'd walked all the way from the farm with Papa. Her dog Tez had tried to follow her, and some of her cats, too, but she'd shooed them all away at Papa's orders. She had to do what he said if she wanted to come back every week. Then she'd finally see something exciting enough to impress Ajee.

When they arrived at the lowest level of the city, Ev could hear and smell the ocean before she saw it. Even when they pushed their way from the thronged street into the open market —where everyone was unloading carts of ripe cheeses and fruits, vendors were already calling out their wares in singsong chants, and there were pack animals jostling and squawking chickens in cages—the smell of fish and salt was in every breath, and the water lapping at the city's edge was a rhythm beneath the noise.

There weren't many open spaces in the lower city, squeezed

between the cliffs and the water as it was. Laalvur was named after the old god Laal, who'd supposedly laid his body down to make the Dayward side of the world. The cliffs were his right hand, with four rock fingers reaching into the sea and a long stretch of the city curving along the low, marshy coastline like a thumb.

Ev and her father set up their cart to sell fruit in the market, a cove between Laal's middle and ring fingers, which were called Arish and Denan. The inlet and the neighborhood that clung to the cliffs like algae were both called Arishdenan.

Arishdenan held the second largest harbor in Laalvur, after Hahim. Small boats were docked all along the sunny length of Arish and the shaded length of Denan, so the inner harbor bristled with masts. The docks and decks of the harbor and the market had been rebuilt in Ev's lifetime, since the wave nine years ago. The wood already creaked with weathering from salt and sunshine, but the boats bobbing next to it were painted blue and yellow. Fresh, brilliant colors in defiance of the fearsome sea, with lyrical names to match. From where she stood next to her father, Ev could see a small vessel called *Her Heart as Constant as the Sun*.

The sun was indeed constant and fierce, scattering gold reflections on the water and striping the red cliffs with shadows. The water near the city was dark and brownish, not the brilliant red reflection of legend, but even that struck Ev as strange and beautiful. From far back, sheltered between the pillars of Arish and Denan, Ev could only see a slice of sky and ocean, and still, she'd never seen anything grander.

Farther out to sea, there were ships anchored in the water. Ajee had better believe her this time.

"It must go on forever," she breathed.

"It's nothing but salt and poison," Papa said. He'd unloaded half the cart while she'd been staring. "Except for the islands, but those have their own dangers."

"It's not poison." Ev was too old to fall for that. The medusas were poisonous, but not the water itself.

"It is if you can't swim."

Papa had been all over the world, from his home in Adappyr, where it was so hot that everyone had to live in an underground city, all the way to Estva, where it was dark all the time and people built walls out of ice. He used to work on a ship. He'd been as close to the islands as anyone ever got. Ev loved his stories. She'd never been anywhere at all.

"Don't wander off," her father warned. "Or I won't bring you with me next time."

Ev heard people speaking Laalvuri, Adpri, Hapiri, and languages she didn't recognize, and she saw pale-skinned Nalitz-vans and Day tribeswomen in robes, but hardly anyone stopped to buy something. The vendors called out the same chants over and over, and a priest of the Balance gave a loud, droning sermon about how the good, civilized people of Laalvur must root out superstition and let go of their false fears of magic. *It is the Year 764 of the Balance*, he was saying. *The time has come to embrace the truth*. No one was paying attention to him. Sometimes pamphlet-sellers strode through, crying out the latest news and rumors. Her father haggled with a customer over the price of melons and berries.

Food odors thickened the hot, still air. Why did anyone eat fish? Ev didn't care if priests said that eating the flesh of animals was part of God's Balance. It smelled gross.

Ev should've brought her book. Papa didn't like her bringing books everywhere because they were so expensive, but if he didn't want Ev to read them, then he should stop buying them for her.

She was in the middle of a series called *The Sunrise Chroni-*

cles. All the books took place in a magical world where the sun moved across the sky, and Day and Night were times instead of places. In this strange world, people could stand in one place and see the sun at one hour and the stars in darkness the next. Ev had never seen the stars. The only darkness she knew existed in windowless rooms, a luxury manufactured by humans. The sky over Laalvur was always red-gold, and the sun hung in the same low spot all the time. The idea that the sun could disappear—that the whole sky could turn black—enchanted and chilled her. What a changeable, chaotic world that would be.

More importantly, at the exact location of Ev's bookmark, the evil Regent had just locked his niece, Aurora, in a tower for speaking against him, and now it was up to the hero, a clever and dashing wanderer named Vesper, to save her.

Vesper was secretly a prince from another land. Ev knew because she'd read the six-novel series twice already, mostly by the green glow of lamplight in her dark bedroom, hours into the shift of the Honeycreeper when she ought to be asleep. She'd be happily on her way to a third reread if only Papa had let her bring volume two.

Ev sighed and sat down on the stones to sweat in the shade of the cart. She slouched. Her mother would be horrified.

That was when Ev saw the girl.

She thought it was a girl, anyway. It was definitely a kid, a little younger than her and a lot smaller, crouching under one of the other carts. Rags the color of mud. Long tangled hair the color of—well, Papa should stop complaining about how often he had to haul water because his spoiled daughter loved bathing so much.

Ev froze. It wasn't just that she'd been caught staring. The other girl was round-eyed with terror. Trails of sweat cut through the filth on her skin. She was staying so still that she was trembling with the effort of it. Tez had been like that, before

Ev had coaxed him out from under the bush where she'd found him.

Ev put a finger to her lips, and then, when her father wasn't looking, she reached into the cart and stole a handful of thornfruit. Their hard, brown rinds pricked her palm.

She lobbed one—carefully, casually—under the cart, so that it rolled to a stop within the girl's reach. The girl stared. First at the fruit on the ground, and then at Ev.

Ev caught her eye, and then plucked a thornfruit out of her hand and held it up to demonstrate. She dug into the rind with her thumbnails until it split and popped open, revealing its sweet red insides. She pinched the fruit from its casing and ate it.

The other girl's hand snapped out from the folds of her clothing. She snatched the thornfruit from the ground. She brought it so close to her face that her eyes crossed when she looked at it, and she squeezed it until it was nearly flat between her fingers. Satisfied with her examination, she imitated Ev's demonstration, peeling off the outside and dropping it. Then she popped the red part into her mouth and swallowed it.

It was weird, and funny, but Ev didn't want to scare the girl by laughing. Instead, she tossed her another one. It landed a little closer to Ev than the first.

The girl crept forward, still trying to stay hidden under the cart. But she accepted the gift.

Her hand was so thin. Under all the dirt, her face was thin, too. She must be an orphan. She must not have a home. Ev's chest went tight. What had happened to this girl? Who had let it happen? Why hadn't someone protected her?

The priest of the Balance had said something about this in his sermon. He'd told a terrible story of families abandoning their own children on the Temple steps, if the parents feared the child was *Unbalanced*. Some people dreaded that word and preferred to say *touched*. The priest stressed that the Temple would, of course, take care of any children found on its threshold, as the sacred Balance required and as the Temple had always done, but that such action was not necessary—there was no such thing as magic.

Was that why this girl was alone in the market? Had her family abandoned her because they thought she had magic? And if her family had abandoned her, why wasn't she in the Temple Street orphanage?

Ev didn't know if magic was real. The priest had said, "The good people of Laalvur do not live in the grip of superstitious fear." According to him, Laalvuri were not the barbarians across the sea in Nalitzva, who slaughtered all those suspected of magic. The people of Laalvur—proper, decent folk—welcomed all kinds. Some children were strange. Madness was part of the Balance, too.

The priest had said all that, so it must be true, but still Ev couldn't imagine her parents abandoning her, or any parents willingly leaving their child on the Temple steps, no matter how strange.

But she knew from living on the farm that people sometimes left litters of kittens in sacks on the side of the road. Cruelty was part of the Balance.

But so was kindness.

Ev held out her hand with half a dozen thornfruit in it. The girl reached out, but her arm was too short. She would have to crawl out from under the cart. In the shadows, her eyes were wide and dark. She shook her head minutely and pulled back, drawing her baggy tunic around her.

Ev pushed herself to her knees and leaned forward.

It was just enough movement to get her father's attention. He immediately saw the girl and Ev's outstretched red hand, and snapped, "Ev!"

The girl darted out, knocking into both carts, spilling and splattering a fall of ripe fruit all over the stone. Another merchant, seeing split melons and crushed berries on the ground, yelled "Thief!"

Ev stood up and shouted, "She didn't steal anything!" She'd never shouted that loud in her life. But no one was listening, and Ev's father grabbed her shoulder and kept her from running into the fray.

The girl had spindly legs but she was nimble. She wove between the carts, colliding with crates of produce and people alike. A man caught her with one hand. She yelped and stabbed her sharp little elbow into his stomach. He let go.

Then she was off again. Ev wanted to run after her and help her, but her father was still holding her back, and the girl was too far away now. Instead, Ev bit her lip while she watched.

The girl might run down the length of the harbor. From there, she could head around the narrow point of Arish into the next V-shaped inlet, Hahimarish, or she could take the switch-backed path up into the higher levels of Arishdenan and the hills of the city beyond. Either might be enough distance for the merchants to give up on following her. She'd caused some chaos, but she hadn't actually stolen anything, and she was just a girl.

She did head for the upper city, but not the way Ev expected. The girl ran deeper into the market. Then she scrambled up the steep wall to the next street. She moved like a spider, side to side, using her hands and her bare feet to hold onto the rough stone.

A man latched on to her ankle. She kicked him off.

Ev's mouth dropped open. The girl was so small and the man's grasp had been so solid. Ev knew how hard it was to get free of someone's hand, since the boys at school grabbed her all the time. You had to wrench free right at the weak point of their grip, where their thumbs met their other fingers, or else it didn't work.

The girl hadn't done that. And her kick hadn't even connected with his face. The man had grabbed her, she'd jerked her leg, and his hand had just opened. Almost like he'd been shocked by the feel of her skin.

The girl kept scrambling up the red cliff face of Arish. Why was she going *up*? How was she going to get away?

Laalvur was cut into the cliffs, with one street that zigzagged from the top of each cliff to the bottom. Some sections of the path had shortcuts—stairs cut into the stone, when the grade wasn't too steep, or ladders when it was. The cliff faces of Arish and Denan were connected by a network of wood and rope bridges, crisscrossing Ev's view of the sky.

The girl pulled herself up to the street. A few men from the market had run after her, taking the long way around. They might have caught her, except there was a ladder directly in front of her. She jumped on it and started to climb. The men followed. She grabbed the top rung and stomped on the face of the man behind her.

Barefoot, and so small, she couldn't have done much damage. But the man was surprised. His foot slipped, knocking into the man behind him, and all three of them went down in a pile.

There was a lot of shouting. The girl dodged everyone in her path. This time, she was running toward Arish Point, rather than into the V of Arishdenan. Ev twisted to watch her.

They were going to catch her. Someone had to do something. The girl was so far away now, but maybe if Ev ran, she could still get there in time. Ev just had to get free of her father's grip. She stepped forward, and he spoke.

"Evreyet."

Her full name came so often at the end of sentences like *stop bringing animals into the house, Evreyet* or *stop climbing trees in your nice clothes, Evreyet* that her parents no longer needed to say anything but her name. Papa and Mama said "Evreyet," and Ev heard, *Don't sneak out of school with Ajee, Evreyet. Don't read novels all shift after we send you to bed, Evreyet. Don't start fights, Evreyet.*

Her parents had said that last one plenty of times and it wasn't even true. Ev never started fights. She only finished them.

While Ev's father was holding her back, the girl from the market scurried up a second ladder.

Ev's nails were biting into her palms. The girl shouldn't have gone up. The street was narrow and crowded, but now she'd made a scene. She couldn't hide. She was trapped. Any second now, someone was going to catch her. The men from the market were still pulling each other up from the ground, dusting themselves off, but they were shouting at people in the street to stop her.

Above Ev, a bridge was creaking. The girl had dashed to the middle of it.

People waited for her on either side. The bridges were sturdy but small, meant for one person to cross at a time. But no one needed to step onto the bridge to catch her. She had nowhere to go.

The girl clambered to the top of the wooden railing, gripping it with her bare feet, holding her arms wide for balance. Then she raised her arms above her head, placed her palms flat against each other, and dove.

Her tiny form sailed down, slicing into the air between the two cliffs, and cut smoothly into the water.

The ocean resumed its calm sway to and fro.

Ev's heart rattled against her ribcage. She bit her lip. The girl didn't come up for air.

What if it really is poison? Ev thought, and then forced the thought away. That wasn't true. There weren't any medusas in Arishdenan inlet. They lived in farthest depths of the sea.

Behind Ev, the market returned to business. People righted their overturned crates and carts. The men who'd chased her began to make their way back down to the lower city. People grumbled, but life had to go on. There was work to be done.

"She'll be alright," Papa said, and patted Ev's shoulder. "You, on the other hand, have a mess to clean up."

Ev nodded but didn't look at him. Nothing broke the surface of the water. It was only when her father tapped her on the shoulder that she came back to herself. Ev glanced down at her hand, hanging limp at her side, her palm sticky with the pulp of crushed red fruit.

HALF A SHIFT DRIPPED BY, four hours heavy with the odors of the market and the ocean. Ev waited patiently while customers came by and inspected their cart, lifting the melons to see how ripe they were and picking through the thornfruit. She counted their coins afterward.

When no one was buying anything from her, Ev watched the painted boats bob in the harbor. It had been too long now, and the girl wasn't going to burst through the glassy surface of the water. Ev was disappointed not to see her again. She nurtured a secret hope that the girl had slipped away unseen. The alternative was too awful to contemplate.

Ev had seen animals die at the farm. And all her grandparents were gone—Mama's parents had both died when she was little, and Papa's parents had died before she was born. She knew about death. But she'd never seen a person die. She shuddered.

The low chatter of the market crescendoed into chaos and

then went silent. A group of guards in grey uniforms forced their way into the crowd, pausing to interrogate people. The crowd split in two suddenly, as if answering an unheard order.

A woman strode into view. Ev's first impression was a swishing whirl of fabric. The woman was wearing the same type of loose trousers and long tunic as Ev, but the similarities ended there.

Ev's clothes were sewn from plain blue cotton. There was a little scroll of pink-and-green floral embroidery decorating the sleeves and the open V of her collar, because Mama always wanted everything to be beautiful and she was willing to spend hours hunched over her needle and thread to make that happen. The rest of Ev's tunic was simple. It fell straight from her shoulders, short-sleeved and knee-length so as not to get in her way. Like the rest of her, it was damp with sweat. She'd wiped thornfruit pulp on the thigh of her trousers earlier, right under where her tunic had a split seam at the side to allow her to move freely.

Ev didn't usually spend any time thinking about what she was wearing, but just being in the woman's presence made her feel scruffy.

Ev had never seen anyone wear so much fabric—she didn't even know what kind it was. Not cotton. Not even the finest wool. It whispered and glinted in layers of lavender, shot through with strands of silver. The woman's tunic went all the way down to her ankles, flaring out like a dress, and its bottom edge swung with a heavy band of embroidery. The cuffs of her trousers, barely even visible underneath her tunic, had matching embroidery. Ev thought of her mother's painstaking work and wondered how many shifts had gone into these clothes. To wear something so luxurious down into the harbor, this woman must be very, very rich.

She must be a member of the Council of Nine that ruled the

city. The Council had a representative from each of the nine richest Houses in the city. Of these, there were four Great Houses and five Lesser, and the wealthy scions of the Great Houses lived in mansions up on the tips of Laal's fingers.

Which of the Great Houses would have guards with grey uniforms? Mama would know. Papa, fiercely suspicious of Laalvur's rulers and upper class, considered it a waste of time to talk of such details. But Ev knew the names of the four Great Houses despite him: Solor, Katav, Garatsin, and Varenx.

Varenx House was the only one ruled by a pale-skinned woman of Nalitzvan descent. A legendary beauty.

Was the woman really Iriyat ha-Varensi?

How could she be anyone else?

She moved smoothly through the market. Her guards—clearly, the guards belonged to her—held the crowd back. She stopped occasionally to speak to someone, and when her brief conversation ended, she walked forward unimpeded. Even if she'd been dressed in rags, she would still have been commanding—enchanting, even. It was more than her stride, and more than the cleared path in front of her. She seemed to own even the empty air around herself, changing it with her presence.

The woman was covered from head to toe. Ev's mother had told her that this was the latest fashion among wealthy women, supposedly for modesty and protection of their delicate skin. Ev recalled her mother gushing about how Iriyat ha-Varensi had started the trend herself, with her devotion to charitable work at the Temple of the Balance. She helped care for the orphans who were left at the door.

Iriyat ha-Varensi might be religious, but there was nothing modest about the wealth on display in this woman's outfit. All that cloth, and so much of it embroidered so delicately. The woman had even covered her hair and her face, leaving only a strip for her eyes.

When Mama talked about fashions, Papa liked to say that rich people covered their faces so no one could recognize them when they were committing crimes. After taking in the sight of this woman, Ev didn't think that was very likely. She would never forget this.

The woman had eyes the color of an ash plume on the horizon. A warning in smoke from the distant peak of Adap. A dangerous grey.

"Excuse me, young man," she said, and the fall of fabric over her face fluttered as she tilted her head at Ev.

Ev stiffened. "I'm not a boy." Ever since she'd cut off all her hair—braiding and washing it was such a waste of time and boys were always grabbing it in fights—people made this mistake. Usually, when she corrected them, they frowned in disapproval. No one seemed to care that the first snip of the scissors had made Ev lighter and happier.

Iriyat examined Ev again, and then Ev's father. Ev bit her lip, acutely aware of their difference. Ev had grown up on a farm an hour's walk from the city, but she took after her Adpri father instead of her Laalvuri mother, so sometimes people treated her like she didn't belong.

Laalvur was a port city that welcomed everyone. Only sometimes it didn't feel very welcoming. When Iriyat looked at Ev and her father, was she thinking the same things that the Orzatvur village school kids said to Ev? *They say Adappyr's a paradise, and the only people who leave are the ones who get kicked out. The criminals. I bet your father's a murderer!*

But Iriyat's gaze softened. She held up a hand in apology to Ev, then touched it to her heart. Unlike the rest of her, her hands were bare. Her pale skin surprised Ev. Not only because that color, faint peach-pink like the inside of an unripe melon, was rare in Laalvur, but also because it made no sense. Whether Iriyat was covering herself for modesty or sun protection, she ought to include her hands. Where were her gloves?

No other part of her was exposed. She was even wearing leather boots. Her tunic had long, tight sleeves, and the fabric at her neck went right up to her chin. An imposing silver collar ringed her neck. All those layers with all that jewelry on top. Ev was hot and tired in her own clothes, built to be practical in the heat.

Iriyat ha-Varensi showed no sign of discomfort. It was only Ev who was sweating, burning under the gaze of those eyes. Iriyat was no taller than her, but Ev felt as if the woman towered over her. She'd breathe easier if Papa came over. He was taller than everyone.

"I hope you can help me. I'm looking for a girl," she said. "A tiny little one. Black hair. About nine years old. She might be dressed in rags, the poor thing. I had word that she was here earlier this shift, causing trouble."

What was her connection to the girl? Did she want to help her? That would make sense. Someone should help her.

Ev's father came to stand behind Ev. He put a hand on her shoulder. Ev didn't look up at his face, but she guessed he was scowling.

Iriyat wasn't intimidated. "Oh," she said. She had a beautiful laugh. Her jewelry jangled. "You must think me very rude. I'm so sorry not to have introduced myself. Iriyat ha-Varensi," she said, as if it were funny to have to state her own name. Her voice was not unkind.

No wonder the whole market had stopped for her. Ev tried to keep her eyes from widening. It was like meeting a real-life queen. She could have been in a character in one of Ev's novels, or one of the goddesses from the old religion. Varenx House had been founded two hundred years ago by Nalitzvan aristocrats who'd fled religious persecution in their home and established themselves as cloth merchants in Laalvur. Iriyat had come to power at the age of eighteen, after suffering the tragic deaths of both her parents in the wave that hit the city when Ev was three.

None of that impressed Papa. "I know who you are."

Mama would be mortified to hear that he spoke to Iriyat ha-Varensi like that, but Papa was from Adappyr, where no one was richer or more powerful or more important than anyone else. He did *not* like rich people, and he was not afraid.

Mama always said that was because he had no sense.

Iriyat inclined her head. To Ev's amazement, she unpinned one side of her veil and moved it away from her face.

Revealing her face made her even more imposing. She wore a pleading expression that matched her huge, sad eyes as well as her clothes. Age had hardly touched her smooth, unmarked skin and full lips. "Can you tell me anything of the girl?"

"There was a girl," Papa said. "Looked like she hadn't had enough to eat."

Iriyat's lovely face crumpled, and she touched her hand to her heart again. "Poor thing," she said. "She's an orphan, you see. I took her in, but she's a curious creature, given to wild flights of imagination. Sometimes she likes to run away. I doubt she's been able to find much to eat in the past few triads. Can you tell me where she went?"

Papa tilted his head toward the water, and Iriyat's eyes went wide.

"She jumped," Ev volunteered, dissatisfied with her father's silence. He didn't seem to like Iriyat, but she looked so sad and worried. "From all the way up there." Ev pointed to the bridge above them. "I watched for a long time, but I never saw her come up. Do you think she's okay? Does she know how to swim?"

"I couldn't say," said Iriyat, even paler than usual.

"What exactly," Papa said, "does a girl like that do in your household?"

"Oh," Iriyat said. "I know she probably looked terribly ragged when you saw her. I've tried my best to keep her fed and clothed since she's been in my care but she's—" Iriyat paused, searching for a word. "Difficult."

"But you want her back," Obin observed.

"She's in my care," Iriyat said, and there was a hard edge in her voice.

She didn't seem to like being questioned. Ev wished her father would be more cooperative. He was treating Iriyat like she'd done something wrong. All Iriyat wanted was to help the girl, which was what Ev wanted, too.

The slight change in Iriyat's tone had no effect on Ev's father. Obin remained stonily silent.

"I'm sorry to keep you from your affairs. I'll take my leave," Iriyat said, and she reached out toward Obin with one slender, bare hand.

She obviously expected him to clasp her hand in his. He didn't.

Ev stared at her father, mortified. She turned back to Iriyat and said, "What if we see her again?"

Iriyat took a shuddering breath, straightened her shoulders, and smoothed her unwrinkled skirts to calm herself. Then she pulled her veil over her face again, pinning it to the cloth that covered her hair. "Please send word to Varenx House if you do."

Ev nodded, too stunned by the possibility of visiting Varenx House to say anything at all. That girl would get the help she needed, and more. The house sat at the tip of Dar, the lowest of the four fingers, but it was still high above the city. Situated at the tip like that, anyone in the house would be able to see for ages. All that ocean. It must be so beautiful.

The Great Houses sat like glittering gems at the tip of each point, with their thin red stone towers catching the light. Or at least that was what Mama said. Ev had been disappointed that the houses had been so far away early this shift when she and Papa had arrived, and now they were too low down in the harbor to get a good view. But she'd been invited to see one up close! Maybe even to go inside! All she had to do was catch sight of the girl.

Mama said the Great Houses were all dug deep into the cliffs, with their lower floors hollowed into the rock. The richest of the houses, Solor, had more floors than anybody knew, and the lowest ones were all vaults filled with treasure.

Iriyat ha-Varensi left in a bloom of silvery lavender skirts. She parted the crowds just as she had before, and Ev's father watched her go out of sight before swearing, "Smoke and fire."

Papa had grown up with the smoking peak of Adap looming over his home, and he always swore like that. Mama scolded him when he did it in front of Ev. Once, he'd even said *smoke and fucking fire* while Ev was standing right there. But at least he hadn't said it in front of Iriyat ha-Varensi.

"You were so rude to her, Papa," Ev said with quiet horror. She crossed her arms over her chest. They'd met a famous person, an *important* person, and Papa had been even grouchier with her than he was with everybody else. And she'd been so beautiful, and so sad. "We should've helped her more. She was upset."

"If she was so sad about that girl, why wasn't she treating her better?" Papa said. "That girl was desperate to get away from something."

"She said the girl was an orphan! The girl ran away!" In fact, Iriyat had said she'd taken the girl in—meaning the girl must have run *from* Varenx House. But why would she do that?

"People say all kinds of things," Papa said. "Doesn't mean they're telling the truth."

"But how can you know if somebody is lying?"

Papa shrugged.

"So you might be wrong," Ev said. Iriyat had been on the verge of tears. She had a reputation for helping orphans. Why wouldn't the girl want to go back to Varenx House, where she wouldn't have to hide under carts and eat thornfruit off the ground? "She could be telling the truth."

He shrugged again. Ev spent the rest of the shift carefully scanning the harbor, the market, the streets. She did not see the girl again.

2

LITTLE GHOST

THERE WERE TWO secrets in Varenx House, and Alizhan was one of them.

She didn't have to stay hidden away in a locked room upstairs. She could hover at the edges of Iriyat's parties, dressed as a serving girl, perfectly visible. Anyone who wanted to look at her could look at her.

Most people didn't want to.

It was the secret that made them look away, although none of them knew that. People glanced at Alizhan, gathered a vague impression of small-fragile-feminine-delicate and long black hair, and then just as they were on the verge of musing *pretty little girl* and setting her aside as harmless, something about her jarred their thoughts in a different direction: *what's* wrong *with her?*

Some people averted their eyes, and some people covered their reaction, but everyone thought it. Alizhan was accustomed to it.

People were unsettled by the way she carried herself. She

fidgeted and trembled in company, or she held herself apart from people, stone-still. She never looked into people's eyes when she spoke to them—or if she did look into their eyes, it overwhelmed them. She talked far too much or not at all. She answered questions that no one had asked.

Alizhan knew all of these things because people were always thinking them so loudly and clearly. She also knew that Yiran, the other person in the kitchen right now, was concentrating hard on pitting olives so she could pretend Alizhan wasn't in the room with her. A slimy curl of resentment was winding through Yiran's thoughts: Why was Alizhan even in the kitchen, if she wasn't going to help? Why did Iriyat let that horrid little monster lurk around the house? And why was Iriyat always talking to Alizhan and spending time with her? Iriyat never paid any attention to Yiran, and Yiran was actually useful. Yiran was prettier, too. And nobody got chills when Yiran walked by them.

Yiran's knife missed an olive and chopped into the wood of the cutting board.

That was the secret. That was why people didn't like be around Alizhan. Even if they didn't know that Alizhan could feel their feelings, they could sense a strangeness about her. Iriyat had been trying to teach her to behave properly for years. Look into people's eyes, but not too much. Smile, but only at the right time. Ask questions, but only boring questions that you already know the answer to. Talk, but only about the right things. Determining the right time to smile or the right thing to say meant distinguishing a person's inside—their thoughts and feelings— from their outside, the words they spoke aloud and the way they moved their face and body.

People's outsides were not always the same as their insides. Alizhan had trouble telling the difference.

For instance, right now she wanted to say to Yiran, "I'm *not* useless. Iriyat keeps me around because I tell her what her political rivals are thinking." But Alizhan wasn't allowed to say that, because that would be telling the secret. And Yiran hadn't said that Alizhan was useless out loud. She'd only thought it.

At least, Alizhan was pretty sure she hadn't said it.

Instead of saying anything, Alizhan walked over to Yiran's cutting board, plucked a pitted black olive out of the pile, and ate it. It was a fierce burst of flavor, bitter and briny, against her tongue. She chewed, swallowed, and took another.

Yiran buzzed with anger. But she didn't reach out and slap Alizhan's wrist for stealing and slowing down her work. She pulled her arms in close and edged away.

Once, a long time ago, Yiran had tried to be friendly. It had happened when Alizhan had botched an escape after spying on one of the Council members. She'd stumbled home to Varenx House with a twisted ankle, bloody knees, and scraped palms. Yiran had seen her come in and been moved to sympathy. She'd never liked Alizhan, but up until that moment, she'd always felt a twinge of guilt about it—Alizhan couldn't help being the way she was. Some people were just born wrong.

Yiran had insisted on patching Alizhan up. She'd learned the hard way that contact with Alizhan's skin meant instant pain and a splitting headache for both parties at the very least. That time, it hadn't been the very least. Alizhan had blacked out. She knew from Yiran's memory—she always tried to keep the incident away from her thoughts, the way she might distastefully pinch a soiled rag—that Yiran had vomited and then passed out.

A shift or two later, when she next saw Yiran, Alizhan had informed Yiran that she was lucky she hadn't drowned in her own vomit, because it was true. Also, Iriyat was always telling Alizhan to be friendlier. Alizhan thought it was nice that Yiran hadn't died.

Yiran had hissed, "Get away from me, you monster."

She no longer felt guilty about disliking Alizhan.

Yiran had been quick to tell all the other Varenx House servants, too. Not that they'd needed any encouragement to stay away from Alizhan. Alizhan could always feel the fear and revulsion crawling through them. They called her "crazy girl" or "little ghost," as if saying her name would bring them bad luck.

Alizhan wondered sometimes if, as the "little ghost," she was destined to end up like the other ghost. There were two secrets in Varenx House, and he was the other one. No one ever spoke about the other ghost, but she knew sometimes Yiran or one of the other maids had to go up to that room with a bowl of soup. It wasn't really a ghost, of course, but everyone was just as terrified as if it were. Alizhan could feel him every time she passed by one upstairs bedroom. A terrible jumble of anger and confused memories hissed out of that room at all times. It was sickeningly strong. She could feel it through the walls and the locked door. Alizhan avoided the big ghost as much as all the other servants avoided the little ghost.

Neither of them was really a ghost, but they might as well have been. Ghosts were incorporeal. Untouchable.

Is that what happened to him? Is that how he became a ghost— never being touched? Alizhan could be touched. But only by Iriyat.

Iriyat was blank. The only quiet thing in the cacophony of the world. It was a strange kind of comfort, that blankness, since it meant Alizhan could never feel if Iriyat liked her. Iriyat said that was how the world worked for everyone else, that they never knew anything for sure about other people. She said that was what *trust* meant. Trusting Iriyat was worth any amount of uncertainty—when Iriyat touched her, Alizhan felt only the warm skin of her hands.

When Alizhan was a child, Iriyat used to hold her in her lap and stroke her hair. If Alizhan behaved, controlled herself, did what Iriyat asked, sometimes Iriyat would hug her. Alizhan was nineteen now. Those touches had become rare gifts, as if in growing older, she could shed loneliness in the same way she'd outgrown her old clothes.

According to Iriyat, Alizhan was the only one of her kind. The only person touched with this particular madness. Sometimes it was a relief to know that no one else ever had to live this way.

Other times it was not.

Whether she was passing through the halls of Varenx House or Arishdenan market, the yearning pulse of the world thrummed in Alizhan's mind: friends greeted each other with handshakes and cheek kisses, children jumped into their parents' embraces, and lovers longed for each other's bodies. Everyone wanted to be touched somehow. In that one way, at least, she was no different. It must be nice to live in a world full of blank people, where anyone could touch anyone else.

But Alizhan lived in this world, and Iriyat was all she had.

So when Iriyat said *I need your help*, Alizhan said yes. Even if the next sentence was *I need you to come to a party*.

It was Alizhan's least favorite kind of work. Being in a crowd of people was dizzying. All those thoughts and feelings made her tremble and sweat. She could stand it for a few minutes at a time.

The trick was to focus on one person in order to shut out all the others. Alizhan had learned this as a child, during one of her many ill-fated attempts to run away.

Back then, she'd been convinced that somewhere out there in the chaos of Laalvur, her real family was waiting for her. They regretted abandoning her at the orphanage. They wanted her to come home. If she could only get to the city, she'd find them. Her real family would be able to touch her.

Alizhan knew better now. There was no family waiting for her. They didn't want her. They never had.

But one of her attempts to run away had led her to the

Laalvur market, and that was where she'd met the thornfruit girl, who called herself Ev and who warmed with affection every time she saw Alizhan.

No one else ever felt like that because of Alizhan.

It was worth all the sickness and the exhaustion that Alizhan suffered in the middle of the market crowds to bask in Ev's kindness for a few fleeting moments. Alizhan went back to see her again and again. They never spoke, because Alizhan could never stay, but she knew that warmth radiating from Ev meant that Ev liked seeing her, too—a strange, novel feeling. Ev didn't even know Alizhan's name. She thought of Alizhan as "the thief," or sometimes "my thief," but she never stopped Alizhan from palming a handful of fruit.

Alizhan would rather be a thief than a ghost.

She could never stay long, but she never regretted going to see Ev, even at times when she had to dash into an alley and collapse afterward.

Those moments with Ev had taught Alizhan more about how to move through the world than long years of training with Iriyat ever had.

It was thanks to Ev, now, that Alizhan could take a deep breath and do what Iriyat wanted. She plunked Yiran's bowl of pitted olives onto a tray and went out into the party.

As the head of Varenx House, Iriyat spent a lot of time throwing parties for other wealthy and powerful Laalvuri. Alizhan was familiar with not just the heads of the other three Great Houses —Mar ha-Solora, Sideran ha-Katavi, and Ezatur ha-Garatsina— but their families, friends, servants, business associates, and lovers. She knew all the members of the Council of Nine, all the wealthiest merchants, and all the most powerful priests.

It was easier to memorize and recite years' worth of past Council votes, trade deals, and secret affairs than to be in a room with all of them at once.

None of them knew who she was. Perhaps they remembered her face—that pitiful, strange servant girl Iriyat insisted on keeping, from some sense of charity. But as she wove between groups of people carrying trays full of foods to nibble or glasses of sweet yellow wine, people took note of what she was offering, and nothing else.

Although once, three years ago, Iriyat had hosted the Prince of Nalitzva, a young man called Ilyr. He'd sailed all the way across the sea to come visit the Dayward coast, and Iriyat, being of Nalitzvan ancestry, had offered him her hospitality. Alizhan had certainly not expected him to notice her, let alone be nice to her. But when Ilyr had first arrived, he'd been so anxious at the first gathering that he'd been in physical pain. When he'd ducked around a corner early in the party, Alizhan had found herself sneaking after him, tray of glasses in hand.

"Are you all right?"

"I... don't know," he'd said, shaping his syllables with the deliberate precision of a foreign speaker. "Can I have some wine?"

She'd offered him the tray, and he'd taken a glass and said, "Thank you." After a gulp, he'd added, "And thank you for asking," so quietly and with such genuine gratitude that Alizhan still remembered him fondly. She'd never told anyone about the incident, not even Iriyat.

Was it reassuring to know that even a prince could panic? Or was it depressing? Either way, Alizhan had been pleased to discover that sometimes, wealthy and powerful people were nice to servants.

Nobody at the present party would thank her so gratefully.

Staying steady required Alizhan to focus on a single person.

She switched her attention from one person to another after a few minutes, scanning the room for anything of interest. Iriyat always wanted to know what people thought of her—did her parties impress them? what did they think of her work with the orphanage?—but she collected information of all kinds, even things that Alizhan found inconsequential, like *Sideran thinks the Prince of Nalitzva is very handsome.*

Sideran, head of Katav House, was a beautiful woman, according to Iriyat. She was tall and slender and dressed in a teal tunic and trousers, with her black hair in a long braid down her back. Sideran didn't thank Alizhan for offering her a glass of wine because she was far too busy talking at Ezatur, the head of Garatsin House, to notice Alizhan.

Normally, beautiful women were only invited to Iriyat's parties if there was no conceivable way to exclude them. But Sideran, in addition to being the head of one of the four Great Houses and thus difficult to exclude, had a flaw that Iriyat found useful: she never stopped talking. She'd spent her life surrounded by people who'd never dream of interrupting her or telling her no. A stream of complaints flowed constantly from her mouth. She rarely said anything that wasn't about herself, unless it was to disparage someone else. Her company was so unpleasant that Iriyat, possessed of social graces, instantly seemed radiantly beautiful by comparison.

Alizhan found Sideran tolerable. Because she always said everything that was on her mind, she was a much quieter presence than many of the other guests, who both talked out loud and also kept up a private running commentary in their heads. It didn't bother Alizhan that the contents of Sideran's mind weren't particularly interesting. She was straightforward, and that kind of simplicity was rare at Iriyat's parties.

Sideran's conversation partner, portly and bearded Ezatur ha-Garatsina, had spent most of the conversation contemplating ways to exit it without upsetting her. He wanted to use his time more profitably. Ezatur was always thinking about money. He had two daughters, and he wanted desperately to marry them off. It was his fondest hope that Mar ha-Solora, head of the wealthiest of the four Great Houses, would accept one of his daughters. Every time he came to one of Iriyat's parties, he always wanted to trap Mar into a conversation about marriage and get him to change his mind on the subject.

Alizhan, who had access to Mar's thoughts, found that supremely unlikely.

Mar ha-Solora was Alizhan's favorite party guest. He had an organized mind. He was a clever and serious man, always considering trade deals and political alliances. He also disliked parties, which immediately won him Alizhan's sympathies. Mar always wanted to put in the briefest possible appearance, or to find a dark corner where he could drink alone. Alizhan always did everything in her power to help him achieve these goals, although he'd never asked for help, and she didn't have much in the way of power.

Iriyat seemed to like Mar despite their occasional political differences, although with Iriyat, it was always hard to tell. Alizhan knew for certain that Mar adored Iriyat. He thought she was sweet and innocent. She had just enough intellect to make her company enjoyable. He took any excuse to come over. In a moment of distraction after a few glasses of wine, Mar had once thought *those would fit perfectly in my hands* while his gaze had drifted toward Iriyat's breasts, a detail that Alizhan had dutifully shared and that Iriyat found endlessly entertaining. After every social event, Alizhan was now required to report whether Mar had spent any time appreciating Iriyat's figure.

The answer was always yes.

It pained Alizhan a little to give these reports, since she'd formed a kind of secret solidarity with Mar. Lots of people thought Iriyat was beautiful, or wanted to sleep with her. No one else exercised Mar's subtlety on the subject. But subtlety was no protection against Alizhan, and her loyalty was, first and foremost, to Iriyat.

Besides, if Alizhan ever felt conflicted about Mar, it helped to remember what else she knew about him. Mar found Iriyat's religious inclinations less tedious than other people's. Indeed, tolerating Iriyat's displays of faith made him feel magnanimous. The poor little thing couldn't help it, he thought; the tragedy of her parents' early death had marked her so strongly. Mar had never really thought of Iriyat as a rival. He didn't think she was smart enough.

Iriyat never corrected his assumption.

From the way Yiran and the other servants tittered when Mar was in the house, he was probably good-looking himself. Whatever that meant. Alizhan could never tell what anyone looked like. She could see perfectly fine, but faces eluded her. Most people had two eyes and a mouth and a nose. Why was everyone so concerned with minute differences? Alizhan's inability to describe anyone's physical appearance frustrated Iriyat. Even when Alizhan saw faces in other people's thoughts, she couldn't distinguish them. It was a bad quality in a thief of secrets.

Alizhan could tell that Mar had brown skin and black hair, but so did she and most everyone else in Laalvur. He was tall and broad-shouldered and a great deal bigger than her, but that was true of most everyone else in Laalvur, and probably the rest of the world. So she didn't know what Mar ha-Solora looked like in any useful sense.

At this moment, Mar and Iriyat were standing on the balcony together, taking in the view of the sea and the golden sky. It was early in the party for the two of them to be alone together. Iriyat usually waited until after the meal to engage

Mar, if he was still present.

Alizhan padded across the thick patterned carpets and the smooth red tile floor, trying not to step on any trailing hems as she did so. When she reached the other side of the room, she didn't immediately step over the threshold onto the balcony. Her slippers were on a rack by the door downstairs, a long way from this salon, and Iriyat would scold her if she went out on the balcony barefoot. Alizhan trooped down to get them, then swung by the kitchen to pick up a fresh tray of wine glasses. Having good manners was exhausting.

"Wine?" Alizhan said, approaching Iriyat and Mar.

Iriyat nodded and accepted a glass, her long fingers curling around its stem. "Mar?" she prompted.

He was unusually distracted. *Take it*, he thought to himself, grabbing for a glass. *Keep her talking until the boy gets out.*

Alizhan started, making some of the glasses clink together and slosh their contents. She had to steady the tray before it all went crashing to the floor.

What boy? Keep Iriyat talking? What did that mean?

For Alizhan, a person's present thoughts and feelings were as obvious as the bells announcing the shift change from all the towers in Laalvur. She didn't always understand what she sensed, and sometimes perceiving someone's inner state was more like smelling odors or touching textures than hearing speech or seeing images. Not all thoughts were words. Some people—and some thoughts—were louder and clearer than others. With very few exceptions, people couldn't hide their current mental and emotional state from her.

Skimming the surface of someone's mind was effortless, but digging into the depths required more concentration. Iriyat was always encouraging her to practice this skill, since it was hard to catch people thinking of their most guarded secrets while chatting at a party. If Alizhan wanted to be a good thief, she couldn't be satisfied with snatching whatever had been left out on the windowsill. She had to learn to pick the lock on the door and sneak inside to find the real valuables.

Alizhan followed the thread of worry in Mar's thoughts. At the center of a web of suspicions, there was a boy—wiry, short-haired, rough—and his story. It started with an orphanage. Not the one in Temple Street where Alizhan had been abandoned as a baby, which Iriyat funded and frequently visited. The boy insisted there was another, secret orphanage, where the priests sent all the children who were too malformed and Unbalanced for the house in Temple Street. Mar had no proof that such a place existed, and no one else could confirm the boy's wild story. The boy, Kasrik, said this second, secret orphanage also belonged to Iriyat. Kasrik said he'd been held captive and tortured there before his escape. Mar didn't believe it—the poor, addled boy also claimed he could read minds—but the boy was eager to investigate, and it struck Mar as an opportunity to solve another nagging question.

A boy who claims he can read minds. That detail, nothing more than superstition for Mar, rang out like a bell for Alizhan. She sucked in a breath and nearly came back to herself. No, no, she wasn't finished yet. She had to focus. She delved back into Mar's mind.

Kasrik had obviously been mistreated by someone. Mar would find out who was responsible and take care of it. And, in doing so, he'd clear Iriyat's name of any ugly rumors Kasrik might have spread. If this got out, even in just a few of the most salacious and untrustworthy pamphlets that circulated the city, it would be damaging. Iriyat was a lovely, kind person who didn't deserve any more suffering. Her life had been marked by tragedy, and instead of letting it ruin her, she channeled all her efforts into helping others. She did so much good for the city, and Mar respected her work and valued their relationship.

She'd never be his intellectual equal, but she had wit. Iriyat was a gift indeed. But she didn't possess the ruthlessness necessary to protect her own reputation from these rumors, so Mar would do it for her.

Mar had explained all of this to the young man, but Kasrik was difficult to reason with and dead certain Iriyat was responsible. Concerned that Kasrik would take matters into his own hands without guidance, Mar had given him a task. It was a bit of misdirection, unrelated to the boy's wild and horrifying allegations, but it would keep Kasrik busy and lay things to rest.

Mar had asked Kasrik to sneak into Iriyat's library and steal volume eleven of *A Natural History of the World*. He'd warned Kasrik that the book might be in Iriyat's study instead. That was the source of his interest in what would otherwise be a dull volume listing the quakes, waves, and eruptions of two centuries ago. Mar had seen this very book lying open on Iriyat's desk on two separate occasions in past months. Iriyat wasn't a slow reader. Could she really be so interested in natural history that she'd reread the *same* volume within a matter of months? Mar didn't think so. The book must be a cover for some other text.

A small part of him wanted it to be a journal. To his knowledge, Iriyat had never taken any lovers. Why was that? Was it religion alone? Or did she have some secret reason for abstaining? She must know by now that she could have Mar if she wanted him. He'd never said as much to her, but she was no fool. Women, in his experience, were attuned to such things.

It would probably come to nothing. Perhaps the book was exactly what it seemed. But Mar was curious, and Kasrik was eager to find evidence, and the theft would be simple enough. Mar would have Kasrik return the book after a triad or two, hardly any time at all, and no harm would be done.

When Alizhan came back to herself, Iriyat was removing the tray of glasses from her hands. "You look a little ill," Iriyat said,

caressing Alizhan's cheek. Iriyat was as soothingly blank as
always. A rivulet of sweat ran down the back of Alizhan's neck.
Her heart drummed against her ribs. "Perhaps you should go sit
down. One of the other girls can take over for you."

Behind Iriyat, Mar felt tight with concern.

Alizhan had other things to think about: the boy, the book,
the library. He was there now. Stealing the book. Reading minds.
She turned on her heel, still wearing her slippers, and ran.

POSITIONED in the center of the house and built without
windows to protect the books from the elements, the library was
a grand space lit only by the greenish glow of lamplight. Candles
and books were a dangerous mixture, and Iriyat was wealthy
enough to get her light by other means. Shelves of leather-
bound books, some handwritten and some in more modern
print, lined every wall. There was a large, round table in the
middle of the room and two upholstered chairs in opposite
corners.

The room shivered with the eerie quiet of a place that had
just been disturbed but now lay vacant. Books were strewn
across the floor. A few had fallen open, spreading their white
pages in the gloom. Alizhan knelt, closed them, and turned
them over to check their spines: fourteen volumes of *A Natural
History of the World*. Volume eleven was missing.

Sloppy, amateur work. Alizhan rarely stole tangible objects,
but when she did, she strove to leave no traces.

If neither the thief nor the eleventh volume was here, then
she had to check the study. A small wooden door tucked into the
corner of the library connected the two rooms. Alizhan pulled it
open as silently as possible, then slipped inside and found
herself surprised.

It wasn't possible for people to sneak up on her. She could feel them coming, thinking about their families, their plans, their ailments, their desires, their next crushingly witty retorts. Even through walls, Alizhan could feel if other people were near her.

Except if those people were blank.

Before she'd been slapped with the sight of this person—this boy, Kasrik—Alizhan had thought Iriyat was the only blank person in the world. But she felt nothing from Kasrik. And yet he was indisputably there. He was skinny, with the too-long limbs of adolescence and black hair sticking up from his head in wild tufts.

She could read neither his thoughts nor his expression. Alizhan didn't usually feel her faceblindness so keenly. Reading faces, as opposed to minds, had always struck her as a primitive, inferior practice. But now that the book of Kasrik's thoughts was closed to her and her only option was to decipher his face, she found herself illiterate. Stranded in a foreign land.

What was Kasrik thinking? Had he seen her? He hadn't moved. The book was open on the desk under his hands, and he was reading it, his fingers tracing across the lines of text.

If Alizhan couldn't feel Kasrik, could he not feel her, either? She hovered in the doorway and held her breath. He must be able to hear her heart beating. How could he not know she was there?

There was nothing unusual about the book. Volume eleven looked like its fourteen siblings, bound in brown leather with black printing-press letters marching in formation across thin, cream-colored paper. It wasn't even a one-of-a-kind manuscript, but a printed book with many other duplicates in the world. How important could it be?

Kasrik was on the opposite side of the desk from her. She could leap forward, wrench the book from his hands, and run back into the library. He might chase her. He had longer legs than she did. But she had the advantage of knowing the house.

He exhaled, slammed the book shut, and looked up.

From the length of his stare alone, Alizhan would wager that Kasrik was as surprised by her presence as she'd been by his. More evidence that he was like her. She darted forward, put both hands on the book, and tugged.

Kasrik let go. "You're one of us," he said. "Why are you working for her?"

Alizhan couldn't make him understand all that Iriyat meant to her, so she said nothing. She clutched the book to her chest and backed toward the door.

But *one of us*. What did that mean?

"I can't let you take that," Kasrik said. He vaulted over Iriyat's desk and suddenly Alizhan was up against the wall and his hands were on the book. Very close to her hands. Her stomach churned with anticipation. If they touched, would it hurt?

"Mar's playing you," she said. "He doesn't think this book has anything to do with your story."

"I know," Kasrik said. People usually protested more. But Kasrik must already have known what Mar thought. "He's lying to himself. Iriyat's playing *you*." He pulled, and Alizhan clung to the book. "She hurts us and has us killed. You're a traitor if you keep working for her."

A traitor? Who exactly was Alizhan betraying? She hadn't known there was anyone else like her in the world until a few moments ago. And how did Kasrik know she was like him? Was Alizhan blank, too?

Her whole life, Iriyat had let Alizhan believe she was alone. And yet here was Kasrik, saying *us*. Alizhan wasn't alone. She was just like Kasrik.

Kasrik, who could read minds. Kasrik, who was blank.

Was it possible? Was blankness how people like her—*people*

like her—recognized each other? Even the possibility was a punch to the gut.

"Iriyat *is* one of us," Alizhan said. She didn't mean to say anything. The words and the thought were simultaneous.

Kasrik was almost as shocked as she was. "Wha—"

Alizhan had to know what was in the book. She jerked it out of his grasp, slid to the side, and dashed into the library. Her jaw slammed into the floor a second later as Kasrik tackled her and she went sprawling into the pile of *Natural History* volumes. The pain rattled her bones. But there was no skull-splitting bombardment of thoughts and feelings. It was sharp and startling and new: a normal kind of physical pain, the pain of being hit and trapped between the corners and spines of books and the bony weight of a human body.

There was no time to reflect on the novelty of touching a stranger and remaining conscious.

Alizhan clutched the book beneath herself and tried to crawl forward and buck him off. He held fast. She could feel him reaching to the side, and an instant later, something heavy hit the back of her head.

LIGHT HURT. Air hurt. Existing hurt. Alizhan was in bed. She kept her eyes shut. What had happened? How had she gotten here? It felt like her bed. She couldn't remember coming to her room.

Where had she been last shift?

"You got hit on the head." Iriyat's voice.

Of course. There was someone sitting on Alizhan's bed, and everyone else would have been thinking loudly.

She was safe, in that case. Alizhan exhaled, and Iriyat stroked her fingers through Alizhan's hair. The gentle pressure of fingers playing over her scalp was a comfort so simple, pure, and rare that Alizhan would've let herself get hit on the head much sooner if she'd known this could be her reward.

"What happened?" Alizhan remembered standing in the kitchen with Yiran and stealing an olive. If Yiran had been preparing food, there must have been a party. Alizhan opened her eyes and looked at Iriyat, who was still dressed for a party in purple silk and heaps of jewelry. Had she not slept?

"You went after a thief," Iriyat said. Between her thumb and her forefinger, she rolled a sprig of tiny purple flowers back and forth. Lavender shadebloom, one of Iriyat's own breeds. Behind the blond crown of Iriyat's bent head, a mottled burst of green leaves—six towering potted plants—dominated Alizhan's bedroom. All the Great Houses had fabulous gardens, signals of wealth and taste, but only Iriyat took such a passionate interest in hers.

"And the thief hit me on the head," Alizhan guessed. The void in her memory scared her. She'd never forgotten anything so completely. "I'm sorry. He must have gotten away."

"Shh," Iriyat said. "You're hurt. I'm sorry he hurt you. One of the guards heard a noise in the library and found you on the floor. He says he thinks you were only out for a moment or two, but it was long enough for the thief to get away. I had the guards bring you here. I'm afraid the stress of being touched caused you to pass out, and then I let you sleep. The shift of the Honey-creeper just started."

Iriyat's parties always took place near the end of the Lyrebird shift, which meant Alizhan had slept through the shift of the Rosefinch. Eight hours.

A thief could get a long way in eight hours.

Still. Shouldn't Alizhan be able to recall what had happened an hour or two before she'd been hit on the head? The time in between being in the kitchen with Yiran and getting attacked?

Not knowing was an itch in her mind. She'd never catch the thief if she couldn't remember him.

Something Iriyat had said nagged at her. *I had the guards bring you here.* None of the guards liked to touch Alizhan. The feeling was mutual. Iriyat was a small woman, but Alizhan was even smaller. Iriyat could have carried her. That would have been safer and easier, since Iriyat was blank.

Blank. Yes. That was important. But why?

Iriyat had said they'd found Alizhan in the library. From these details, Alizhan began to trace the outline. There'd been a boy and a book and a fight. He'd said something. What had he said? Why couldn't she remember?

"You look like you're concentrating," Iriyat said. "Take your time. You need your rest. I don't want you to exhaust yourself."

Alizhan didn't want rest. She wanted to remember. She wanted to catch the person who'd left this dark hole in her memory. Her body could still feel the sharp points of his elbows and knees from when he'd tackled her. Alizhan searched for something more useful. A name. "Kasrik, I think?"

"Kasrik," Iriyat murmured. "He hit you on the head with volume fifteen of *A Natural History of the World.* An index to the whole series, a list of every known quake, wave, and eruption and their dates—quite a thick book."

The incident came back to her in pieces. Another detail leapt to the surface. "He was working for Mar."

Iriyat sighed. "Of course he was. You know Mar's never had any sense when it comes to me. He probably thinks this is a great game. I will tell him that I do not appreciate him hiring street urchins to break into my home and attack my staff. All for an inconsequential book."

"I'll get it back," Alizhan promised.

"When you're feeling better," Iriyat said. "You should rest first."

Alizhan had broken into Solor House before to spy on Mar's business dealings or his mistresses. The house sat at the tip of Hahim. It was a challenge, scaling the Nightward side of the cliff and then climbing up to the second story balcony, but she could do it. It wouldn't be any different than the other times.

Except—

"Iriyat," Alizhan said, a detail suddenly coming back to her. "Kasrik. I think he was like me."

Iriyat's hand stopped moving through her hair for a moment, and then resumed its steady pattern, stroking from the crown of her head on down. "That vicious, conniving rat? No, my little shade-blooming flower, he wasn't anything like you at all."

3
___

TOUCHED

E V'S THORNFRUIT THIEF FLITTED INTO the Arishdenan market, put a finger to her lips, and slid under Ev's cart.

In ten years of visits, she'd never done anything like this.

Ev thought of them as "visits," although she supposed that, technically, they were robberies. They'd happened every week for ten years, and Ev had never reported a single sighting to Varenx House.

Her second encounter with the girl had echoed the first. The girl had passed by their cart in the market, still dirty and ragged and small and shivering, but not hiding under another cart this time.

She'd skimmed her hand over the top of the basket of thornfruit, and before Ev could catch her by the wrist, she'd stolen a handful and slid out of reach. No one else had noticed her.

The girl had smiled at Ev—so wide and toothy it was nearly feral. She'd let Ev witness the theft. The whole thing had been on purpose. Ev was sure of it.

Every encounter after that was as fleeting, as silent, and as secret, by some unspoken pact. Ev and the thornfruit girl were participating in something illicit and thrilling.

Ev could've caught her. Ev could've said something—asked the girl's name or offered her own. Ev could've grabbed her or chased her. The girl was fast, but Ev had longer legs. And Papa had been teaching her to fight with a staff, so she could've tripped the girl.

Ev never did. It was the only exciting thing about going into the market in Laalvur, wondering if her thief would show up. They'd developed a strange kind of friendship.

She never told Papa or Mama or Ajee about the girl. They wouldn't have understood. And Ev liked having a secret. Something she didn't have to share. None of the other girls in Orzatvur had a thief-friend. None of the boys who spit on her and called her father a murderer had anything that exciting in their lives. And their parents, the shopkeepers and bakers and blacksmiths and cobblers and priests of Orzatvur, the ones who shook their heads and said *can you believe her mother lets her wear her hair like that* and *what do you expect, look who she married* when they thought Ev couldn't hear them, not one of them knew the first thing about Ev's little mystery.

The girl was often as Ev had first seen her—filthy and dressed in rags—but not always. Over the years, she grew less terrified: more controlled in her movements, more sure in her expression. As her fear lessened, her hair and clothes became less unkempt.

Ev tried very hard not to think of taming a wild animal, but the comparison was so easy. She'd lured cats and dogs into friendship with the promise of food. But it wasn't nice to think of the thief like that. She was a person. A strange and intriguing person, but one who made her own choices, not a creature to be domesticated.

Still, Ev was pleased and honored every time the girl came back.

She never stole from anyone else, or if she did, Ev never saw it happen.

Even when the girl no longer looked starved or terrified, Ev worried about her anyway. Her appearances were always brief. They never spoke. Who was she? Was she an orphan? Did she live on the street? Or had she gone back to Varenx House? And if she had, what was she doing out in the world?

But when the girl—a young woman now, and taller, but only just barely—slid under Ev's cart, Ev didn't have time to ask any of these questions. The young woman put a finger to her lips and then disappeared into the shadows.

Ev stacked the last wooden crate in her cart. Her donkey was already hitched. If he sensed the woman under the cart, he didn't show it. Ev drew the sheet of burlap cloth over the cart and grabbed her staff.

Two men, so heavily armed that they clanked when they walked, approached her just as she was turning around. "We're looking for a girl."

It had been a decade since Iriyat ha-Varensi had said the same thing to Ev. A decade since Ev had watched the girl dive into the water and disappear. Papa wasn't with her this shift, but she remembered his cool disdain for Iriyat ha-Varensi's questions.

"I've seen a lot of girls. The market is crowded," Ev said. She didn't like the way the two men raked their gazes down her body. Laalvur had a city guard, but it was a small force. The Great Houses and other wealthy citizens employed their own men to keep the peace, or so they called it. House guards started fights more often than they ended them. Regardless of the insignia on their tunics, they never made Ev feel any safer. These two men wore blue tunics embroidered with the insignia of Solor, the

Great House that sat at the tip of Hahim. Not Varenx House, then.

What did Mar ha-Solora—or his guards—want with Ev's thief?

"She's small. Wouldn't even come up to your shoulder."

"Hardly a helpful description," Ev said. Most women were smaller than her, and the world took every chance to remind her. It hadn't even been a triad since Ajee had spluttered his objections. *What man wants a wife who towers over him?* Not Ajee.

Still, being tall had its advantages. She could look these two men in the eye while they questioned her. The first guard stepped closer to her. Ev could smell fish sauce on his breath. Ugh. She wanted to recoil, but there was no space. The wood of the cart brushed the backs of her legs.

"She's got long black hair and light eyes, but she might be wearing a disguise," he said. He was broader than Ev, but not as big as Papa. He would still fall hard with one precisely aimed strike. Ev's grip on the wood tightened. It would be easier if she had more space, but there was nowhere to move. She would slam her staff between his legs if she had to.

Brutal, and brutally effective. Papa had been very clear on that point.

"She's a strange one, got a real unsettling way about her," the other guard said. He spoke in the clipped, rapid way that characterized people who'd lived in Laalvur all their lives. He was a little leaner than the first guard. He might be faster in a fight. Even if she took out the first guard, the second one would have time to draw his sword.

He stayed a step back, smirking at how Ev leaned away from the first guard.

"What's in the cart?" the first guard said.

Four empty crates under a sheet of burlap. Ev stepped to the side, shifting away from the guard, and drew back the cloth.

They peered into the crates for a moment, and then exchanged a glance. Ev held her breath. Then the first guard crouched down to look under the cart.

Smoking hell. Ev lifted her staff. She could slam the butt of it into his head. No. That was panic talking. She couldn't knock out a Solor guard in the middle of the market. The other guard would have his sword at her throat in an instant.

But the first guard just shrugged and stood up. "No sign of her," he said to his partner. Satisfied, they took their leave.

A sigh rushed out of Ev once they were out of sight. How had they missed the thief? When she was sure no one was looking, she ducked down to check under the cart. There was nothing there.

Then she squinted into the shadows. She'd expected the woman to be crouching on the ground, and when she hadn't seen that, her gaze had passed over the scene without incident. But the woman was clinging to the bottom of the cart, bracing her feet against the corners and flattening her small body against the wood.

The men were gone. Ev made a great show of rearranging her burlap sheet, spreading it wide like a curtain and shaking it out. The woman dropped from her position without a sound, and Ev covered her as she crawled into the cart. Ev had to pack the wooden crates around her and then lay the sheet over the top of everything.

After she checked the donkey's harness, Ev peeled up the corner of the sheet one last time to check the cart. The woman's grin glinted in the shadows. She was wedged between the crates, curled into a tiny ball. Ev's bones ached at the sight, but the woman looked perfectly pleased with herself. She put her finger to her lips again.

Ev nodded once, a little offended at the reminder. She knew how to keep quiet. She let the sheet drop.

Ev wanted to hurry out of the market, but she forced herself to take her time. It was a long, slow trip through the narrow switchbacked street that led up and out of Arishdenan. The donkey seemed torturously slow this shift. Ev tried not to look at the cart, but there was nowhere else to look. If she so much as breathed in the direction of one of the young men hawking pamphlets, they'd be in her face offering her their curious and ghastly mixture of politics and pornography, featuring members of the Council of Nine—*Slutty Sideran's Secret Affair!*—for the low, low price of two kalap. Ev never wanted any part of what they offered, but she especially couldn't afford to spend money or time on that now.

Was the woman hurt? What had she done to make Solor guards follow her? Was anyone else angry with her? Was Ev being followed? It was impossible to tell in the city with so many people around. The back of her neck prickled.

Her path back to the farm wound through the terraced hillsides. Ev kept to the light as much as possible, dodging the pools of shadow on the road. It would be easy for someone to hide in these hills. The sun-facing sides had been denuded of trees so that no shade spotted the farmland beneath, but the other side of the road was rocky and wild. Ev walked with her staff in hand.

Her father rarely talked about Adappyr, and he never talked about why he'd left, but Ev knew the Adpri abhorred violence. And yet her father knew how to fight. He'd insisted on teaching her. If she was going to get into fights, he said, she ought to win them. He'd taught her to fight with her fists and with a staff, and at first he'd treated it like an art. There were stances to learn, forms to follow, sequences of movements to memorize. Later, he'd taught her a desperate, cornered kind of fighting—in those lessons, he said things like *go for the eyes, use your teeth, kick him in the balls.* Ev's imaginary opponent was always a *him.*

Where had he learned all this? Why was it so important to

him for Ev to know all of it? Were the whispers about her father being a murderer true? She'd asked him about it between drills, and he'd only said *Don't hurt anyone you don't have to.* And then he'd swung his staff at her and they'd gone back to sparring.

Ev carried her staff to the market when she went by herself. Men were less likely to ask her to smile if she was carrying a big stick.

She wondered if men asked the thief to smile. Ev had never seen her with a weapon, so men probably said all manner of nasty things to her. Ev clutched her staff, twisting the smooth wood in her hand. It was stupid to feel protective of a stranger.

For all she knew, the woman could be lying in wait and planning to kill her.

Probably not, though. And she was so little. Ev could take her.

They were far enough out of the city, and this stretch of road was empty. It was still a long walk back to the farm.

"My name is Ev," Ev said aloud. She'd been waiting to say that for ten years.

Nothing in the cart stirred. The woman didn't answer.

"It would be nice to know your name, that's all," Ev said. She thought about pointing out that she was taking a huge risk by trusting the woman and smuggling her out of Laalvur, but that seemed obvious, and she didn't want to be rude.

There was a shuffling and snapping of branches in the undergrowth at the side of the path. Ev grabbed her staff in both hands and whipped around. Someone burst forth, barreling toward her. Ev lifted her weapon high, stared down her assailant —black cloth over face, leather jerkin, dagger in hand—and slammed the end of her staff into his forehead.

He thudded to the ground. Ev took a half step forward. He was unconscious. His face was covered, but he wasn't big enough to be one of the guards from the market. He wasn't wearing

Solor colors or Varenx colors. So who was he? And why in the smoking hell was he following her? If he was a robber, he could have picked richer targets in the city. Was he a rapist? Or was he after her thief? Ev glanced over her shoulder to make sure the woman was all right, and a second man leapt up from behind the cart.

The corner of the cart was between them. She thrust her staff across the distance. He dodged nimbly, surging forward and drawing a knife from his belt. Ev took a step back and began whipping the staff in a figure 8 in front of her body. He only had a knife, so he'd need to be close before he could hurt her.

He darted in again and she struck him in the side before he could touch her. In the instant of his stunned reaction to being struck, she plunged her staff toward his head, but he was too fast. He slipped out of her way. He took another step toward her, and Ev backed up again, her staff still spinning. He'd come around the corner now, and the cart no longer stood between them. Ev lifted her staff, whirling it above her head and then bringing it down until it cracked against his skull.

He stumbled, and Ev meant to hit him again, but she heard leather shoe soles scraping against the packed dirt of the path—the first man had gotten up again. He was behind her. She needed more space. She needed to get away from the cart so that she could swing freely and have a chance at hitting both of them. No—the first man was too close, and he had a knife. Ev gripped the staff in both hands and rammed it backward without looking. He grunted. She'd caught him in the abdomen.

But now the second man was slashing at her, drawing his blade in a hot line of pain from her ribcage to the front curve of her hipbone. Ev grit her teeth. It was a shallow cut. She thrust her staff forward, trying to spear the second guard in the gut. She got him, but the blunt end of her staff wasn't enough to stop him. Ev was attacking both of them savagely now, hitting with as much force as possible, but there were two of them, and there was no space.

The thief erupted out of the cart and bashed the second man in the face with an empty vegetable crate. The sturdy wooden crate withstood the assault, and Ev had to dodge the wild swing herself. The thief went for the first man after that, smashing the crate into his face with abandon. It was enough of a distraction for Ev to sweep her staff under the second man's feet and trip him. Once he was on the ground, she put the end of her staff against his windpipe and her foot on his knife hand.

"Don't move," Ev said. She looked over at the thief. "Everything okay over there?"

"Great!" the thief said breathlessly. Sweat ran down the sides of her face. The man was unconscious and bleeding from a cut over his eye. The thief, her little grey-gloved hands still clenched around her weapon, had a sickly pallor, but she looked directly at Ev and forced a smile.

Ev knew from experience that hurting another human being for the first time was upsetting. And the woman must have been terrified before that, trapped in the cart. But hurting people should be emotionally difficult, so it was a mark in the woman's favor that she looked ill.

"Oh, that's not why—" the woman started, and then stopped to watch Ev bind the hands and feet of the other man. Whatever she'd intended to say, she let it go. Her hands unclenched and she dropped the wooden crate. It nearly hit the unconscious man in the face, but instead fell harmlessly to the ground next to him, kicking up a little puff of red-brown road dust.

"Are there more of them, do you think?" Ev said.

The thief's mouth twisted in contemplation for a moment. "Let's not find out."

Ev had to sacrifice her scarf and rip a strip from the bottom of her tunic before both men were adequately tied up. It took much longer than she wanted. Her cut wasn't bleeding badly, but the fabric of her tunic was sticking to it and every time she moved, it pulled sharply. "So now we just... leave them here?"

"Well, I don't want to kill them," the thief said. Her nonchalance alarmed Ev, who hadn't expected to end up discussing murder so casually when she'd set off for her weekly trip to the market. "And I didn't really enjoy their company, so I don't want to bring them with us."

With us. As if they had a plan to go somewhere together.

With exaggerated dignity, the thief picked up the crate from the ground and set it back in the cart. Then she walked to the front of the cart and prodded the donkey—who'd remained calm throughout this ordeal—into walking forward.

She seemed to cheer up as they got farther away, and with her cheer came chatter.

"You were *spectacular*," the thief was saying as they walked. "I loved how quiet you got. Everyone is so loud all the time, and I was hoping you wouldn't be like that, but then on the way here you were being so noisy, all full of doubts and questions—"

Ev narrowed her eyes at the woman. She'd said two sentences on their long walk out of the city. That hardly qualified as "noisy."

The cut on Ev's side stung. She'd just been taking her usual path home. She could have led these men straight to her parents' farm. There might still be others following them. Fiery fucking hell, what a monumental fool she was. She had no idea what she'd gotten herself into.

"Don't be mad," the woman said, interrupting the flow of her own story and startling Ev. The woman wasn't even looking at her.

Ev wasn't mad. She was tense. Apprehensive. Uncomfortable. The distinction wasn't worth mentioning, as was generally the case for Ev's feelings, so she said nothing.

The instant passed. The woman launched back into her retelling. "Those men showed up, and you went so quiet, it was like there was only one thing in the world: the fight. It was so clean and calm and perfect. I get that feeling, too, sometimes. People are crowding you and chasing you and all of a sudden, you can focus. You know exactly what to do."

"Do people chase you often?" Ev said. She didn't like to interrupt, but the question struck her as urgent.

The woman shrugged. "I don't know. How much chasing is normal? Does it matter? I wish I could feel that way all the time. So sure of everything. Not distracted and confused." The thief sighed, and then said, "Oh! My name is Alizhan, by the way. I wanted to tell you earlier, but you were being so loud and I could tell those men were there, and it didn't seem like the right time. I'm sorry I never told you before. I wanted to. You were always happy to see me. No one is ever happy to see me!"

Everything she said came out in the same quick, light tone. *No one is ever happy to see me—what a funny world we live in!* That lightness was a decoration, a distraction enclosing the hollow loneliness of what she was saying, and it was as fragile as a painted eggshell. One or two taps, and it would crack. Ev said nothing, and she meant her silence as an act of kindness.

"I like that feeling, the one you get when you see me," the woman was saying. "That's why I came to you. I knew you'd help me, and I knew you had a staff, but I never knew you'd be so *good* at it." Alizhan grinned at Ev, as wide and bright as a caricature drawing in a pamphlet. There was something goofy and endearingly *off* about her. Ev was beginning to get the impression that Alizhan didn't spend much time with people.

Despite everything, Ev couldn't stop herself from smiling back. Monumental fool or not, she was in it now. She had to find out what kind of trouble this strange girl was in.

"Oh," said Alizhan after they'd been walking for a little while. "You're not mad. You're in pain."

"It's just a cut," Ev said reflexively. What an odd way for Alizhan to phrase it. How could she tell, anyway? Ev wasn't complaining.

"No, don't be like that. You're hurt, I can tell. Do you want me to look at it? Maybe I should look at it," she said. "You probably shouldn't let your tunic stick to it like that. Hey." The last word was directed at the donkey, who stopped when Alizhan tugged on his harness. Her attention returned to Ev. "Sit in the cart."

Ev sat. Alizhan took a deep breath, as though being near Ev required preparation, and then lifted up the bottom hem of Ev's tunic with no warning at all. The cut ran diagonally along Ev's left side, from her lower ribs to the top of her hipbone.

"Wow, you have... a lot of muscles."

Ev sighed, and then regretted it, since the movement pulled at her cut. "You don't know what you're doing, do you?"

Alizhan was holding Ev's tunic up with one hand. Her other hand, still gloved in grey leather, hovered close to the cut, one finger extended.

"Don't!" Ev said. She had no idea where those gloves had been. They were probably as grimy as the rest of the girl. She grabbed Alizhan's bare wrist to keep her hand away.

Something jolted through her. Shock lit Alizhan's wide eyes. She wobbled in Ev's vision, a grimace of pain on her face. Ev fainted.

4

LYREBIRD SHIFT, 30TH TRIAD OF ORSHA, 761

I DO NOT WANT TO tell this story, and yet I must.

I am not a liar by nature, only by necessity. Still, it is a trait I have cultivated for many long years, and having trained and trimmed myself into this shape, I find it difficult to fight free of the habit. But I want there to be truth between us, tangled and thorny as truth always is.

I know it has not always been easy between us. If you are reading these words, know this: you are the one thing in this world for which I care.

Everything I have done, all of it, has been for you.

There. I shall try to recount the whole of it now. Were these words destined for other eyes, I might put them in better order, but this text is mine and yours alone, so I will let my mind's seeds take root where they fall. I trust you will understand me.

I will start with Arav. I wish I could say I noticed him as soon as I boarded the ship. (It was called *In the Shade I Saw My Love Go Walking* after a song I hated at the time. Following tradition, the crew had nicknamed the vessel *Shade*.) I wish I could say our eyes met and our hearts sang and we were drawn to each other. But that is not how it happened. I am sure I was rude to him in

those first shifts, although I cannot remember a particular incident; I was rude to everyone on the ship. I was sixteen and I did
not want to be there.

I had prayed for sickness, eruptions, waves, war—anything
so I did not have to cross the water to meet Rossin Tyrenx, the
wealthy lord in Nalitzva who was to be my husband. But calm is
crueler than chaos: the rowers were strong and the sea was
peaceful, and I was my parents' gamepiece.

When I was a small child, I would sometimes ask my father
for something while implying my mother had already given me
permission, or vice versa. This is not a special or precocious
behavior, but a crude bit of manipulation many children
employ. It almost always fails. That is not my point. When I tried
it with my father, he made no attempt to dissuade me from the
tactic. He was charmed, and even proud: "We may teach you
statecraft yet, little one."

He was not in the least duped, or threatened, by my clumsy
negotiation, and he reacted much the same way to my potential
future husband's request to see my face—and my hips—before
signing any marriage contracts.

My future husband was no clumsy child. He had inherited a
title, but his fortune was of his own making. He owned a fleet of
ships and a vault of gold bars. He was rumored to have poisoned
two of his rivals, but no proof had ever been found. He was
unlikely to stand trial for any accusation, since he had half the
Nalitzvan court in his pocket. By all accounts, he was a
formidable man. But he was not wealthy, powerful, or calculating enough to be a threat to my parents.

There were no rumors about my parents. They were benefi-
cent, beautiful, beloved.

I must pause here, and digress. I will not apologize for it. The
seeds take root and their shoots unfurl in all directions.

Growing up in Laalvur as a young woman of wealth and

class, I struggled to find pastimes that did not bore me. I did not like dancing or drawing, novels or needlework. My singing voice is best left unheard. I learned fashion only as a necessity for appearing in the world suitably dressed, and even that was a late revelation for me. I was a charmless and unappealing adolescent, mystified by my fellow young women and utterly ignorant of young men. But if young men had no interest in me, I was equally uninterested in them. There was only one acceptably feminine hobby that sparked my interest, and even that, I pushed to the very limits of propriety: I loved gardening.

I owe my knowledge of gardening to an old woman who worked for our family. I call her an old woman now, although in retrospect she was perhaps fifty-five. Her black hair was lined with silver and she seemed ancient to me at the time. Parneet was a former Priest of Doubt who had given up the mysteries of the priesthood for the certainties of digging her fingers into the dirt. She did not care that I was a sullen and ill-mannered girl; she was stern and rather ill-mannered herself. Parneet, silent, solid, and dressed in shapeless clothing, cared only that I was interested in plants and would do what she told me.

My parents soon gave up sighing over the number of tunics and slippers that I ruined by kneeling in the dirt. When they kept me from my garden, I was moody and difficult and of little use to them. We arrived at a compromise: they would allow me to garden, and I would behave as they wished otherwise.

Perhaps my parents perceived that gardening offered me something I could find nowhere else, although I doubt it. Gardening is a type of creation that no art can achieve. What is a song or a painting compared to new life? And not just one life, but generations of life. There was a whole world available to me in our garden, one that I controlled as I could never control anything else in my life.

Parneet taught me many things, and that knowledge has

been the gift and joy of my life. But for now, I will name only one. She was my parents' chief gardener, and it fell to her to keep our house garden in the most prized Laalvuri style. This required choosing an aesthetically pleasing distribution of shade-growing flowers and sun-growing flowers, planting them in their appropriate habitats in an arrangement that was carefully curated to look natural and wild, then letting their roots and tendrils uncurl and climb over the house and its grounds, judiciously clipping a vine or uprooting a weed here and there. She hated order, neatness, and symmetry, but there was a composition to her work, a balance. Untrained observers cooed over the lush, fragrant wilderness that surrounded our house; God's Balance had blessed us with fertile ground. More perceptive guests could appreciate the masterpiece, but they knew better than to credit the master.

Parneet worked hard to render her own work invisible. As the saying goes, *the gardener's hand should not be seen.*

My parents were gardeners in their own way, and they cultivated their reputation. Like Parneet's vines, my parents' reputation appeared to spring naturally from their youth, beauty, power, and virtue. All their ruthless cutting and weeding went unseen.

In Nalitzva, they impose a ghastly, unnatural order on their gardens, planting in stark rows and clean grids and cutting their trees into geometric shapes. I suppose they think it matches their neatly gridded cities of white stone. It is a plodding, hamfisted way of abusing the natural beauty of our world. Trust Nalitzvans to use brute force, even in gardening.

You see now why my betrothed was no match for my parents.

In my youth, I did not care for any of this. Childish attempts at manipulation aside, I resisted all of my parents' efforts to educate me about politics, social graces, and the ways of the world. I did not want to live in their world of quiet dinner conversation, all trade agreements and tedious compromise.

And yet they had uprooted me from my garden and plopped me on the deck of a ship. It had taken me a whole triad to stop feeling sick, and I had only just emerged. Laalvur was a smudge on the horizon. Even the red Dayward coast was receding from sight. My gloved hands gripped the wooden railing. Certainty took firm hold of my heart: I would wither and wilt in the cold light of Nalitzva. What my parents called a betrothal was a death sentence. I could only flourish in the red earth and warm air of Laalvur. Our ship rowed Nightward, and I turned my face toward the Day one last time.

I am not proud of it: I began to cry.

It seems foolish now, that I could not think my way out of even the simplest of traps. But to tell the truth—as I strive to do in these pages—I did not truly become myself until I met Arav. Parneet had shown me what it was to dig my fingers into the earth, to sow seeds, but the earth is a beginning. It is the sun that calls life to the surface, bursting forth, unfurling, reaching its fullness.

I did not know that when I met him.

"I hope you can swim, crying girl," he said. "Because I'm not jumping in after someone whose name I don't know."

He leaned one large, callused hand against the railing. He did it so casually, with such confidence and ownership. For sailors, a ship is more than home. It is a part of them. Arav's arms might as well have been sculpted from the same warm brown wood as the oars. He was very, very beautifully made.

"You know my name," I said stupidly. Everyone on the ship did. They were charged with delivering me safely to Nalitzva, and I was precious cargo.

"But you don't know mine," he said. "It's Arav."

"I'm not going to jump," I said, although the thought had

crossed my mind. I was a sixteen-year-old girl weeping over a ship's railing.

"Good," he said, and grinned. Arav had a full mouth and an extraordinarily prominent nose. The beauty of his body was readily apparent, but the beauty of his face revealed itself in the quirks of his thick eyebrows and the quickness of his smile. He was always in motion. "Because I'm not fighting off a medusa over some girl I just met."

"You couldn't."

"I could and I have."

"They have poisonous tentacles as long as this ship," I retorted. "Besides, there aren't any around."

"Which one of us do you think has seen more medusas, crying girl? Me or you?"

"Stop calling me that. I'm not crying anymore."

"Well," he said. "Look at that."

He smiled again, and I understood his purpose at last. It was pure generosity on his part. The other sailors knew better than to try to befriend someone so high above their station, and they teased Arav about social climbing. Their mockery was tinged with jealousy. Young men do the backbreaking work of rowing and sailing in the hope of clawing their way out of poverty, and perhaps eventually captaining a ship. The others thought Arav was trying to skip the hard part by flirting with a rich girl.

Perhaps, in the same way that a sixteen-year-old girl weeping on the deck of a ship cannot help but briefly contemplate jumping, a poor boy speaking with a rich girl cannot help but contemplate her fortune.

I try to look at these facts with a cold eye, but for once, they are unnecessary. They do not capture what happened. Arav saw a crying girl and he wanted to make her smile. He was that simple. He was that sweet. He was the opposite of my complicated, calculating parents, and I liked him immediately.

Arav had big dark eyes and his shiny black hair constantly flopped into his eyes and had to be brushed back—to no avail— while he talked. Even when he was at home in the city, a clean sea-salt scent misted his brown skin.

He stayed and talked to me for hours. Our conversation began as a way for him to distract me from my troubles, but he had excited my thirst for knowledge. Arav, who had joked so easily about having fought a medusa, was curiously reluctant to tell me the whole story. I had to ask him all kinds of questions, circling around my real goal of hearing him describe the encounter.

I learned from Arav that there were dozens of different kinds of medusas, from the smaller ones that drifted through the water in huge, glowing colonies, which were harvested for lamp fluid and came in all colors, and the rarer, massive ones that floated alone. In five years on the sea, Arav had seen only one.

Once he began to tell the story, he could not stop. It poured out of him in one long rush.

Their ship had been close to the Nightward coast, and the water had been dark. A ghostly shape glinted deep beneath them. Was it a reflection from a lamp on the ship? A trick of the light? The other sailors and Arav had argued fiercely. If it was a medusa, it was the biggest one any of them had ever seen.

Medusa venom, extracted with precise care and tempered with other ingredients, can be made into a liqueur that brings burning bliss to drinkers. Some believe that in the perfect blend, in the right dose, it can be a cure for pain. In the wrong dose— or the right dose, depending on your purpose—it is lethal. Whatever uses it can be put to, people in all the cities of the world pay handsomely for the venom.

Unlike lamp fluid, which comes from smaller and less dangerous medusas, the giant's venom is a rare commodity. Only the islanders know the true secrets of hunting giant medusas, and they live in isolation and protect their knowledge by sinking any ship that ventures too close. They do business with a select few trusted traders in Nalitzva, Laalvur, and Adappyr, and that arrangement has made everyone involved very rich.

Mainlanders have been trying to learn to track and catch giant medusas for years, with little success. Arav and his friends knew all this, but they were young. Dazzled by the promise of wealth and glory, they thought none of it mattered. Other people had failed, but they were not other people.

The Balance had swung in their favor and brought them a medusa.

A monster, if it caught them.

A prize, if they caught it.

Arav and five friends lowered two rowboats into the water. They took every spear and blade they could find, along with the sturdiest net. Giant medusas can weigh as much as four men.

Lamplight medusas float together by the dozen, or some-times by the hundred. Aimless, they go where the water takes them, trailing tentacles. To our knowledge, they do not possess sight or hearing. They are predators, but they hunt by ambush, waiting for prey to wander into their tentacles so they can sting and swallow it whole.

Arav and his friends thought that giant medusas must hunt like their smaller cousins: deaf and sightless, drifting and waiting.

Something bumped the underside of their rowboat. It began to rock.

"An accident," Jai said. "It can't see us. It doesn't know we're here."

It thudded against the boat again, and the boat tipped side to side. Cold water splashed over the side and hit Arav's hand. He only caught a glimpse of the thing moving, stretching and compressing its gelatinous body to propel itself through the water. Mushroom-shaped, transparent green, the medusa pulsed with silent power, ropes of tentacles slithering with each thrust. It was huge. Arav looked to the second rowboat, where Tsardeya, Katvar, and Rahal had a clearer view. Their faces were lined with terror.

"It knows," Arav said. His heart was wild in his chest, a rhythm at odds with the rocking of the boat. But he was not yet afraid. The thing in the water could still be his salvation. Money to keep his family in silk and silver for all their lives. "Spear it next time you see it. Right through the bell."

The next time the medusa knocked into their boat, Arav was waiting with a spear in hand. So was Tsardeya, standing in the other rowboat.

Arav punctured the bell, but not before Tsardeya threw his spear with such force that the second rowboat rocked. He missed. Spears and beast disappeared under the water.

They waited, staring at each other across their boats. Arav could hardly think of anything except the next surfacing, but the empty readiness of his mind was threaded through with one question: how could it know? How could the medusa know they were there?

"It's wounded," he assured the others. "We'll get it next time. One spear all the way through, and we're rich."

The medusa shot up from the depths and slammed into the second rowboat. The boat flipped. Tsardeya, Katvar, and Rahal were dumped into the water. Into the tangled nest of tentacles.

They screamed. They stopped screaming.

Their bodies seemed to vanish into the water, into the monster's body. An arm would bob up, and then a leg. Only after long moments of horrified staring did Arav comprehend that the thing's poison was dismembering them, dismantling their flesh, dissolving their bones.

Death had been instant. Decay was nearly as fast.

Jai and Hoshekur picked up their oars in horror, intending to get back to the ship and as far from the water as possible.

Arav picked up another spear.

Jai grabbed his shoulder. "Are you crazy? Didn't you see that? No fortune is worth that, Arav."

Arav shoved Jai's hand away. "I'll sleep better if that thing's dead."

He would not let them die for nothing. Bloody foam scummed the surface of the water. The monster feasted on his dead friends in full view of his living ones. A trail of luminescent fluid leaked from its wound in a glimmering dribble of green, tainting water and viscera with its touch.

Anger had spurred Arav to grab the spear, but it was the thought of returning to their families in Laalvur that kept the weapon in his grip. Like him, all three of them were from the Marsh, where parents, children, grandparents, aunts, uncles, and cousins, young and old alike, slept side by side on straw pallets in single rooms, crowded into creaky wooden houses stilted over the water. Tsardeya was married. Katvar was barely seventeen years old. Rahal was the elder brother to four siblings. Arav did not want to climb the stairs to their families' doors with only bad news in hand. *Your husband, your son, your brother is never coming home.* Even if he himself never took home a kalap of profit from this creature, he would drive the life from its body and sink the worthless remnants of its corpse to the depths of this watery hell. At least then, he could offer them this reassurance: *I killed the thing that killed him.* He would do this so he could say: *It will not take anyone else's life.*

It would be a small comfort, but Arav could offer nothing else.

He did not consider his own life. Only the death of the monster mattered. There was rage in Arav's veins, and that was its own kind of lethal venom.

For a moment, there was only the water lapping at their boat and the wind wafting over their skin. Arav ignored the chill. Perhaps the medusa was sated and no longer cared about three little humans in a boat. Or perhaps it had stopped sensing them because they were not rowing.

Arav forbade Jai and Hoshekur from dipping their oars in the water. He stood perfectly still.

The boat drifted closer. Closer.

Arav struck. Swift, decisive, he pierced the bell with force. Ripped his spear out, its deadly tip now glowing green, and thrust again.

The medusa did not move.

Jai and Hoshekur stared, and then Hoshekur said, cautiously, "Is it dead?"

Arav rocked the boat experimentally. The medusa remained still. He nodded at Jai and Hoshekur.

The problem of collecting the monster's carcass was a difficult one. Even before broaching that, Arav wrestled with whether it was worse to profit from the monster that killed his friends, or to leave a potential fortune floating dead in the water.

The thought of touching the corpse, stained with his friends' blood and leaking green lamp fluid, made him shudder. He wanted to leave it in the water, to forget it forever. But forgetting was impossible. The alien wrongness of the creature—a thing with no bones and no blood, a thing that belonged to another world or another time—and the nightmare of his friends' deaths, their blood bubbling on the surface, would haunt him no matter what he did.

Jai and Hoshekur were right: no fortune was worth this.

But they owed their friends' families whatever they could offer them.

Capturing the thing's bell in netting and rigging it to float behind the ship was the effort of eight sailors over the course of an entire shift. Even in death, the medusa was a formidable enemy, its tentacles still spiny with venom. The luckiest of the sailors who worked that shift were hauled back up to the ship sickened and exhausted, with whiplike thin black scars wrapped around both forearms. The unluckiest was Hoshekur, who died after two shifts retching and writhing in pain. Jai lost his left arm up to the elbow, the tissue blackened and dead.

I had never heard such a horror story, and I was left open-mouthed and speechless.

"I'm sorry about your friends," I managed to say, after a moment.

He nodded.

I could hardly grasp the reality of it—had he really lived through that?—until he held out his palms to show me the strange tangle of scars on each arm. They were so thin that I had not initially noticed them, but once my attention was on them, I could not resist tracing the latticework with the tip of my finger. Wavy lines crossed his wrists and the backs of his hands, and whorls of black marred the skin of his arms up to his elbows. Where the scars were, he had no sensation in his skin.

I could not really touch him, of course. I kept my gloves on.

"It changed me," Arav said. Witnessing such horror would change anyone, but that was not what he meant. "Part of me died when it touched me."

"You mean your skin," I said. I was still exploring, and Arav was patiently holding out his arms for examination. Even with gloves, touching anyone was a novelty to me. I had never been so close to a man.

Arav shook his head no, but refused to explain further. It would be months before I took his meaning.

After a while, it dawned on me that I was behaving inappropriately. I was keeping Arav from working or resting, and the other sailors were directing baleful looks at us as they passed. I should not have been so close to him for so long. Our conversation, and thus our touching, had to end.

"Will I see you again?" I asked.

Arav raised his eyebrows comically high and looked pointedly around the ship, and I blushed at the foolishness of my own question. I tried to put my head down to hide it, but Arav put a finger under my chin to tip my face up toward him. For the first time since telling his story, he was smiling again.

I had never wanted anyone to kiss me before.

Arav's mouth quirked. He dropped his hand, turned, and walked away whistling.

5

A NATURAL HISTORY OF THE WORLD

THE TASTE IN EV'S MOUTH was sour and acid when she woke up. Her back was against the rough wooden planks of the cart. Everything about her body felt wrong, and it wasn't the nausea, or the cut, or any physical discomfort, but a slithering, soul-unsettling feeling of being in the wrong skin.

Ev sat up. She looked at her hands and touched her own face. The same hands. The same face. Ev was herself. Her hands didn't sting, because she hadn't scraped her palms sliding down a carved column at Solor House. Her throat wasn't raw, because she hadn't been sick in the garden at Varenx House.

But Alizhan had. And while Ev was unconscious, she'd dreamed she was Alizhan.

Had it been a dream? Or had it been a memory?

ALIZHAN'S LIFE would be a lot easier if she could just wander up the switchbacked streets of the Jewelbox, knock on Mar ha-Solora's front door, and say "Hello, you stole something from my employer, and she would like it back."

She was wandering those very streets right now. She'd finally convinced Iriyat to let her out of bed so she could investigate. Kasrik had already had hours to get the book back to Mar. Alizhan just had to pray that the damn thing was still in Solor House.

The Jewelbox, Laalvur's richest neighborhood, was nestled in between the rocky promontories of Hahim and Arish. It extended along the Dayward side of Hahim, and it had gotten its name because of the way the sun lit up the colored glass windows that all the bankers and merchants put in their homes. A lacy filigree of shadows from the high wooden bridges connecting the two cliff faces overlaid the streets below. The scattered reflections over the red stone, and the yellow and purple flowers in windowboxes, and the green vines curling up trellises and over doorways studded the neighborhood like gems. Alizhan could grudgingly admit that the place really did resemble a jewel box, something precious to be tucked away safely.

But the neighborhood, patrolled by Solor guards and distinctly unfriendly to strangers, was a real pain in the ass. Alizhan was in a hurry to get out.

The streets of the Jewelbox were as narrow and steep as all the other streets in Laalvur, but they tended to have fewer piles of donkey shit. Property close to the water was slightly less expensive than homes on the upper streets, nearer to Solor House, her destination.

Alizhan wended her way up through a few more Jewelbox streets, hiking as high as she could before she had to scramble around the end of Hahim and cross into the shadows. Hahim, the land form that would have been Laal's index finger if anyone still believed in the old ways, jutted diagonally into the water, with one of its sides forming a wall of the Jewelbox and the other facing Nightward. The city continued beyond Hahim down into a large, open harbor. Beyond Hahim Harbor, along the coastline that would form Laal's thumb, lay a sea-level neighborhood called the Marsh. It was a sprawl of ramshackle houses on stilts, all in constant shade and perched precariously close to the water. From this high up, if she turned her head, Alizhan could see the steady green glow of lamps in a few windows, as well as fires burning bright and dangerous. But the Nightward side of Hahim had only scruffy mosses growing on its shadowed rocks.

There was a path up the cliff face if you knew how to climb. Years of long practice had given Alizhan the strength and the patience for it. Her hands were good for something other than causing pain: she found handholds and footholds like a creeping vine. Even in shadow, she could cling to the rock like lichen. *My little shade-blooming flower,* Iriyat called her.

Alizhan did not normally steal *things*. She was a thief of secrets, not objects. She shuffled through shadows, collected conversations, and fished in people's feelings. Stealing an object presented an exciting change of pace. It would be easier to sneak into a house and filch something than wander through one of Iriyat's parties, observing her guests. Picking locks and scrambling through windows never made Alizhan so dizzy that she had to bend over and retch.

Solor, the oldest of the Great Houses, had constructed their home on the first and highest of the city's rocky promontories that extended into the sea like grasping fingers. Its red towers watched over the city, and rumor had it that generations ago, crafty old Kos ha-Solora had hollowed out the entire end of Hahim, from the water all the way up to the cliff peak where his mansion sat, for secret vaults full of treasure.

It was nonsense, of course. Alizhan had broken into Solor House before, whenever Iriyat had some whim to spy on Mar, and there were only two underground levels. That was more than most people could afford, but still, the distance from the water to the top of the cliff was twenty stories. Not even Mar ha-Solora had that much wealth. And if he did, he'd never have spent all of it hollowing out the end of Hahim. Alizhan had spent a great deal of time eavesdropping on Mar, at Iriyat's parties and in his own home, and she knew he preferred to spend his money keeping his mistresses in silks and perfumes.

Mar's tenderness toward Iriyat was a secret buried under a mountain of pragmatism. Mar might hope that Iriyat was refusing all other lovers as she slowly warmed to him, but he wasn't awaiting her change of heart with priest-like chastity. For as long as Alizhan had been eavesdropping on him, there had been a succession of beautiful women in his bed, mostly well-off widows or unattached actresses and dancers, but he didn't say no to the occasional unsatisfied wife.

Mar might not have carved out the whole cliff to store his treasure, but he did think of his home as an unassailable fortress. He never had enough guards to keep her out because he didn't expect anyone to climb up the dark side of the cliff. He expected even less for that person to be a little ghost who could see people's insides better than their outsides.

Alizhan reached the top of the cliff and was confronted with the Nightward wall of Solor House. A few rooms had carved stone screens to allow the cool Night air to pass into the house, but the majority of the wall was solid, windowless stone. She paused. Sensing people through stone walls required concentration. Moments passed before she felt a guard on patrol. He was bored and hungry—there was nothing of use in his mind. The book's location wouldn't be common knowledge. Alizhan would need to find Mar himself in order to know where it was. Kasrik might still be in the house, but she couldn't read him, which left only Mar as a possibility.

The bells had just rung for the shift of the Lyrebird, so Mar was likely awake. He was likely to be awake during any shift; he hadn't doubled the massive fortune of Solor House by sleeping. He might be anywhere inside his enormous house. It would be easiest to get inside by climbing up to the second-story balcony and unlocking a window or a door, but the balcony was on the Dayward side of the house.

Alizhan inched toward Hahim Point, scrabbling along where the cliff edge met the rough-hewn stone of the wall. The Point itself was narrow and exposed. Her hand scraped a loose pebble and it tumbled free, jouncing up and down as it struck the rocky ledges.

She didn't hear it hit the water. The distance was too great.

Heights made other people feel cold with fear. Their stomachs lurched when they looked over a precipice. But for Alizhan, that grand, dizzying drop sparked something hot and bright inside her. High places were a threat and a thrill all at once. The focus required by a long climb was a kind of bliss.

Alizhan didn't look down. She didn't look over her shoulder, either, although the air changed temperature as she pulled herself around to the Dayward side. Anyone down in the Jewelbox who happened to squint up at the Point right now might see a brownish smudge clambering over the rocks. There was nothing to be done about that. What mattered was not being seen by the guards.

It was brazen to enter Solor House like this, but it was no more brazen than what Kasrik had done at Varenx House two shifts ago while Mar himself had been drinking wine on the balcony.

The Dayward side of the house was open to the light in classic Laalvuri style, with an arcade of carved red stone columns. Boosting herself up to the balcony required hardly any work.

Up on the balcony, Alizhan flattened herself against an outer

wall of the house. The same guard that she'd felt earlier—
Boredom—was passing by again. With her shoulderblades
pressed painfully close to the stone, she waited.

Another guard. Itch.

Itch's thoughts were slightly more useful than Boredom's.
There was no hint of a small leather-bound book, but he had
seen Mar ha-Solora recently. It was hard to get a clear image out
of his mind—people were always a riot of feelings and impulses
—but Mar seemed to be at work. Dayward light. A desk. He
didn't want to be disturbed. That was all Alizhan could be sure
of. But a new problem arose.

If Mar was in his study, he might be looking at the book.

She couldn't steal the book while he was reading it. She was
a superb lurker, an expert sneak, but her craft was based on
avoiding notice. On the occasion when that tactic failed, Alizhan
resorted to running away.

As Kasrik had demonstrated, she wasn't always good at
running away. Her bruised head was still sore from their
encounter.

She didn't have a plan for confronting Mar. But Itch and
Boredom had both circulated to other parts of the house by now,
giving her an opportunity to slip into the second story. She crept
through the house until she sensed Mar.

He was in his study. Alizhan hovered outside the closed
door. She recognized the feel of his mind. He was concentrating
hard, and he was deeply troubled.

The shape of his thoughts was geometric, as though he were
weighing some foreign object in his hands, touching its surface,
sliding his fingers over it in search of a latch to pop it open. He
was looking for patterns, rearranging elements until their edges
fit together, solving a puzzle.

Alizhan suddenly understood: he was reading the book, but
its importance eluded him. In truth, its importance eluded

Alizhan, too. Like the other volumes of *A Natural History of the World*, volume eleven was a modern, printed book, not a unique manuscript. Mar could buy himself a hundred copies if he wanted. Alizhan's memory was fragmented, but she'd seen the book when Kasrik had held it open on the desk, and she couldn't recall anything special about Iriyat's copy.

But Iriyat wanted the book back.

Mar didn't know that, but he was studying the book with dedication. He'd seen it on the desk in Iriyat's study too many times to assume that it was simple pleasure reading. Mar still refused to believe the boy's wild stories that Iriyat was some kind of ruthless, murderous mastermind—to what end?—but she had secrets. Iriyat was sometimes a friend, but sometimes a rival, and knowing her secrets could only be to Mar's advantage. Besides, it was always wise to keep a watchful eye on one's fellow Council members. Ezatur and Sideran were self-important fools, but there were sharper minds among the minor Houses, people looking to move up in the world.

The text caught his eye again, and Mar scanned the descriptions of historical natural disasters, running his fingers down the page. Trying to read the text through the image in Mar's mind proved impossible for Alizhan. He was distracted by his own thoughts.

What if Iriyat really was a student of natural history? Wine-blurred memories surfaced: conversations about quakes and eruptions, the conditions that preceded them, the destruction that followed. Iriyat never liked to talk about waves, and Mar never pressed her on the subject. She had good reason to hate the sea, which had taken her parents from her. She'd even refused to sail to Nalitzva when the royal family had invited her.

Curiously, for a woman with such an overpowering fear of water, Iriyat was also fascinated by the islanders, especially their methods for tracking and trapping giant medusas. Indeed, Iriyat had introduced Mar to the Prince of Nalitzva three years ago, and it was at her party that Prince Ilyr had first dreamed of undertaking his voyage to the islands.

No. All of that was a distraction. Mar flipped another page in the book, then stopped to rub his fingers together. They itched.

His thoughts wandered back to Kasrik. The boy claimed someone was rounding up children for some sick purpose, hurting and killing them, and he insisted Iriyat was behind it all. He might be addled, paranoid, or mad. But someone had hurt him. Mar intended to find out who. Laalvur was his city, and if someone was hurting children, he was going to stop them.

Besides, if the boy really could read minds, he could be of great use. It might benefit Mar to have Kasrik in his debt.

Mar was a man of great determination. If Alizhan was going to wait for him to leave the book unattended, she'd be waiting a long while.

There was one thing she could try.

For years, Iriyat had tried to train her to use her touch as a weapon. It had never quite worked. Alizhan always hurt herself —puked or collapsed or both—in the attempt. Every time, she had head-splitting dreams, or visions, or memories, for shifts and shifts afterward.

But sometimes the other person collapsed too.

Alizhan had to keep herself conscious and functioning long enough to get the book out of the house. She wouldn't be able to climb back down the cliff afterward.

A sound in the hallway interrupted her considerations. Alizhan looked up and saw Kasrik.

Stupid! She'd forgotten he could sneak up on her. Sensing Boredom and Itch make their rounds through the exterior stone wall of the house had made her complacent. Overconfident. No one could sneak up on her in a hallway.

God damn it. With Kasrik in the world—and maybe more like him—Alizhan would have to learn to be more careful.

She was never supposed to be seen outside Varenx House. There was no time. He could shout or tackle her at any moment. Unless she overpowered him some other way.

Alizhan tore her gloves off. She shoved her palm against Kasrik's face and pushed him against the wall. Squeezing her eyes shut, she focused. Touching him still felt blank and neutral, just her hand against the jut of his nose, the hair of his brows, and the skin of his forehead. For the first time ever, this blankness was not a relief. Alizhan wasn't seeking comfort.

She hadn't been able to read Kasrik during their first encounter. Now, aided by contact, she dug into his mind with ferocity. And there he was: angry, aghast, and in agony from her touch. His pain became Alizhan's, but she bit her lip and kept her hand in place. She could feel his eyes moving beneath his eyelids, but he was frozen, unable to resist or retaliate. She held her hand against his face until he swayed and fainted.

Only an instant had passed, but it felt like an age. Alizhan's skull rattled with new information—thoughts, feelings, intentions, fears, fears, *fears*. A vessel fit to burst. Darkness spotted her vision. It was only the salt tang of blood from her lip that brought her back to herself, bleeding and sweating and trembling in the hallway, towering over an unconscious boy like the monster she was.

One ragged breath later, Alizhan slammed into the study and slapped her hand against Mar ha-Solora's shocked expression. Compared to Kasrik, he was easy prey. The world went black for an instant, and her stomach lurched. She ignored it. Mar slumped over his desk. Alizhan grabbed the book, shoved the spine between her teeth, bit down, then half-flung herself out the open study window, slid down a column, and ran.

THE CARVED STONE column had scraped her palms raw. Alizhan held the book gingerly. Her ears were ringing. Her head was a bruise. It hurt to look at anything, and her mind swam with images her eyes had never seen.

A windowless room. Whimpers. A grim, silent man. Other children. Iriyat's sweet voice. A glass bottle of clear liquid. A stripe of pain down her back—no, not Alizhan's back. Kasrik's.

What had happened to Kasrik to cause him that stinging pain? What were these memories? Had he really heard Iriyat's voice, or was that Alizhan's own memory swirling into the fog of his confusion? Who were those children? Were they all blank? Were they all like Alizhan?

Alizhan crouched in a corner of Varenx House garden, hidden in a thicket. She'd already been sick once. Breathe, *breathe.* She had the book. She'd done what Iriyat wanted. Iriyat wouldn't be happy that Alizhan had been seen, but she could fix it. They could fix it together. Iriyat was resourceful and resilient, and she'd always forgiven Alizhan before. All Alizhan needed to do was to go inside and give her the book.

But Kasrik's memories gave her pause. His fear was still coursing through her. Iriyat's voice echoing in her mind.

Kasrik was like Alizhan. That meant Iriyat had lied. If she'd lied about one thing, why not lie about others? Why did Iriyat want the book back so much?

Alizhan was careful not to get any dirt or blood on the pages when she opened it. She saw what Mar had seen: the first pages revealed nothing. It was simply volume eleven of *A Natural History.* There was nothing distinguishing about it at all. Identically neat characters crowding every page. The opening pages were a very dry account of the quake that had happened between Nalitzva and Estva in 579, and the wave that had hit Laalvur shortly after.

She ran her fingers over the pages, as though they might reveal something her eyes couldn't see.

Shit! Her hands were bare. She'd left her gloves on the floor of Solor House. She'd have to get another pair from her room before delivering the book to Iriyat.

It wasn't a book worth stealing. In Alizhan's opinion, it was hardly even a book worth reading—it was no *Sunrise Chronicles* —but Iriyat had infinite patience for dull histories. The book's spine wasn't stiff, and the thin pages turned easily. Iriyat had obviously read this more than once.

Alizhan flipped to the back of the book, where she discovered a list of dates handwritten on the flyleaf. It was an index of significant natural events—volcanic eruptions, waves, quakes—and it was as boring as the rest of the book. Except that it was in Iriyat's hand.

Alizhan studied the list, but nothing about it made the book worth stealing. Mar ha-Solora had jeopardized his friendship and political alliance with Iriyat over a list of dates?

Alizhan closed the book and then closed her eyes. The world was still flickering and shifting in her vision.

Her skin stung with remembered pain, and she retched again, her throat raw. She could still feel Kasrik's panic, churning with her own. Someone had hurt him very badly. Then Alizhan had come along and hurt him again.

There was nothing to be done. Alizhan took a breath and forced herself to stand. Carefully, quietly, she went inside. She avoided the other servants. People were so complicated, always overflowing with feelings. Alizhan couldn't take any more. She hated showing up in front of Iriyat shaking and sickly.

At least she wouldn't be empty-handed.

Iriyat was in her study, but unlike Mar, she wasn't bent over a book in frustration. The closed door muffled her conversation, but Alizhan—her senses ill-used and tingling—recognized that the man in the room was Vatik, the captain of the guard. He was distressed. Resistant. Even horrified.

Iriyat, as always, was unreadable.

Blank.

All hells. Why hadn't Alizhan made that connection before? If Kasrik was blank, and he was like Alizhan, then what did that make Iriyat?

Or had Alizhan made this connection before—and then been hit on the head? Maybe it had disappeared from her memory along with those missing few hours.

Alizhan crept out of the house. The Nightward side of Varenx House wasn't a solid stone wall. Certain rooms, like Iriyat's study, had perforated stone screens for decoration and air circulation. The screen would hide Alizhan while she tried to discern what was happening inside.

She wasn't betraying Iriyat, the only person who'd ever taken care of her. The only person in the whole world who liked to touch her. She wasn't. It was curiosity, a whim, an absurd hunch that would lead nowhere. Alizhan only felt sick because of her earlier misadventure.

Alizhan was careful not to rustle her clothes when she crouched down. Inside, Iriyat was sighing. Squinting through the elaborately carved stone, Alizhan could make out that Iriyat was standing with her back to the screen, and Vatik was facing it. She knew Vatik was a big man with a beard, from the way everyone else thought of him, but she recognized him from the way he crackled and sparked with rage at everything around him. Now, in Iriyat's study, Vatik was even angrier and more disgusted than he had been.

"It's very tiresome, the way you protest every time," Iriyat said.

"Every time? What do you mean, every time? This is the only time this has ever happened. I am loyal to you, my lady, I always do what you ask, but *this*—"

"Yes, yes, I know, you always do what I ask, except when you don't," Iriyat said. She sighed with irritation again. Then she cupped her bare hand around Vatik's face. It was an intimacy that neither Alizhan nor Vatik expected. Vatik and Iriyat were not lovers; Alizhan would have known. The gesture wasn't affectionate, but abrupt.

And Iriyat was barehanded. Where were her usual gloves?

"I'm sorry," Iriyat said in a very different tone. Vatik's eyes were wide. "Forget that."

For just a moment, he went blank.

Iriyat removed her hand. She wiped it on her clothes, a reflex.

A moment later, Vatik's tumble of emotions rolled through him again, but it was tempered with puzzlement. He calmed. "What was it you needed, my lady?"

"You know how much I value you," Iriyat said. Alizhan couldn't see, or even imagine, the beauty of Iriyat's face, but she knew the beauty of Iriyat's voice. Clear, slow, sweet like honey. Alizhan focused on the sound of it even as her heart skittered against her ribs. "I need you, Vatik. I need you to protect me. Can you do that?"

"Of course, my lady."

"It's a difficult matter, I know. You know I'd never ask you to do something like this unless it was absolutely necessary. But I can see no other way out." Iriyat sighed, and the rush of air conveyed none of her previous annoyance. It was the sound of despair, of resignation, of a hard decision.

It worked on Vatik.

Alizhan had spent a lifetime watching Iriyat's craft. She knew it was only words and gestures—and the occasional mind-altering barehanded touch, though Alizhan couldn't think of that, not now, not yet—but it was a power that Alizhan could never comprehend, let alone possess. Iriyat inspired trust, loyalty and love in almost everyone she met.

Alizhan was no exception.

Did she touch me like that? Is that why I forgot so much of the past triad? What else has she lied about? No, no, Alizhan couldn't think of that now. She had to listen.

"Remember, he's very clever and very dangerous," Iriyat was saying. "Too clever and too dangerous to be taken captive, I'm afraid. There's no saving this one. Don't be fooled by his youth. He's a threat to us and everything we've worked for. You have to find him and *stop* him, do you understand?"

Was Iriyat talking about Kasrik? Was Iriyat talking about *killing* Kasrik?

Vatik nodded. He turned as if to leave the room.

"Vatik? One more thing."

Vatik turned back toward Iriyat. Alizhan often knew what people were about to say, but never with Iriyat. Still, she had a terrible, stomach-dropping premonition.

"Don't let him touch you."

Alizhan jumped up from where she was crouching and ran.

Solor House was a risk. Alizhan had been seen. She'd stolen the book. She'd attacked Mar ha-Solora himself. They'd be looking for her. But if Kasrik was Vatik's target, then Alizhan had to find him and warn him. She scrambled away from Varenx House, down the terraced streets and across a bridge over Denandar inlet. Alizhan was breathing hard by the time she got across the city and back to the Jewelbox. Her second trip up the cliff was miserable—her scraped palms stung, her lungs screamed, and she couldn't stop shaking. The stupid book was keeping her off balance.

Alizhan hid in the garden, watching and waiting, checking

every passing guard's mind for thoughts of Kasrik. Where was he? Didn't he ever go outside? Maybe he'd left already. Alizhan kept an eye out for Vatik, too. Would Vatik really kill him here, on the grounds of a fellow Council member's House? Maybe he'd wait to catch Kasrik somewhere else in the city.

She waited. And waited.

A whole shift passed. Alizhan shivered with fatigue and hunger. She couldn't stay here. She'd have to find Kasrik some other way. But it had been long enough now that Iriyat would have noticed her absence. Iriyat would notice the absence of the book, too.

There would be guards from Solor and Varenx searching Laalvur for Alizhan. Her options were dismal. She was homeless and friendless, alone in the world.

Alizhan only knew one other person in the whole city—the girl in the market.

EV TOOK A DEEP BREATH.

That dream—it had been a memory. Alizhan's memory. That was what the world looked like to Alizhan. People were a constant writhing mass of wants and needs, only half-decipherable. In stories, people talked about *mind-reading*, but it was nothing so clear as a book. It was sight, sound, and sensation. She could feel what other people felt.

All the faces in Alizhan's memory had been indistinct: eyes, noses, mouths, but with none of the precision necessary to identify someone. There was a bewildering sameness to the features. Was that how Alizhan saw her?

More importantly, if Ev had seen something from Alizhan's mind, what had Alizhan seen? Had Alizhan been able to see inside her all these years?

Ev clenched the side of the cart.

Alizhan stirred from her position on the ground. How long had they been out? An instant? A shift? A whole triad? They were too far from the city to hear the bells. Ev wasn't hungry. The donkey, still hitched to the cart, was waiting patiently. It couldn't have been that long.

At least the road was deserted. They needed to get somewhere safe. Ev needed to clean and bandage her cut. Alizhan needed—well, Ev hardly knew. Evidence of some kind of wrongdoing? A way to understand the importance of the book? A way to find Kasrik? Protection from everyone who was trying to kill her?

"Food."

Even with Ev's new understanding of how Alizhan perceived people, her comment came out of nowhere.

"I want food. But wait—you understand—you dreamed you were me?" Alizhan's eyes lit with surprise. "That's never happened before, at least not that I know of. Usually I get other people's memories instead of the other way around. But I don't touch people very often." Alizhan pulled herself up, squinting and blinking, rolling her shoulders and shaking her head. Ev was grateful to be able to look at Alizhan's face, to see the dark arches of her brows over her wide grey eyes and the strong, straight line of her nose, even if she had only a vague idea what was swirling behind all that. It was so much easier.

And Ev could touch and be touched by anyone she wanted.

Ev's gaze slid toward Alizhan, but she stopped herself from looking and stared at the road instead. She had to avoid thinking about that. The walk home was going to be even more difficult and uncomfortable than she'd thought. Ev got out of the cart and set off. Alizhan followed.

"You're afraid of me now," Alizhan said with heart-breaking resignation. "Because we touched and I hurt you."

Ev kept walking. That wasn't how she would have described her inner state, but she didn't want to discuss it with Alizhan. In truth, Ev had no idea what she was feeling—a stinging where her cut was, and an ache, a rush, a tumult inside herself—so how could anyone else possibly know? She didn't want Alizhan to look inside her or even *at* her.

One thought dominated all the others in Ev's head: *there are things in my head that I don't want her to know.*

Lots of things. Everything.

Or maybe just one in particular. One that Ev hardly even allowed herself to think about. It had something to do with women, with the way they moved, with the way Ev always felt a little breathless if they smiled at her.

"Please don't leave me yet," Alizhan said. "I know you don't like being around me, now that you know. No one does. But I've never been out of the city before and I don't know where to go or what to do and it's been at least two shifts since I've eaten anything and—well, you know the rest."

The "rest," presumably, being the number of men searching the city for Alizhan and her stolen book, or the discovery that Iriyat was keeping secrets. Ev didn't want to feel Alizhan's desperation, poorly disguised with lighthearted cheer, on top of her own mysterious feelings. It was too much.

"Alizhan," Ev said, taking a breath. She needed the moment to think more than she needed the air. "We have a lot to talk about, like who is trying to kill you and how we can get them to stop, but I can't have this conversation until we get this clear: you have to try not to respond to things in my head that I don't say out loud, and you have to stop telling me how I'm feeling." Ev took another fortifying breath. "I don't like it."

It was hard to be honest and gentle at the same time. But since Alizhan was some kind of visionary, or touched in the head, or both—and regardless of all that, she had recently bashed a man into unconsciousness with a judiciously aimed wooden crate to the face—Ev had to tread carefully.

"Maybe you can't help *knowing*, but pretend that you don't. For my sake."

"Why, though?"

The answer seemed so obvious to Ev that she had trouble putting it in words. For a mind-reader, Alizhan seemed to have very little grasp of how people felt. "It makes me feel naked," Ev said. "Vulnerable. The things in my head are supposed to be private, unless I say them out loud."

"Everything's going to take forever if we do it this way," Alizhan grumbled. "No one ever wants to let me be myself."

For one sharp, resentful instant, Ev wanted to say *I rescued you without knowing your* name *and you haven't even thanked me!* but she wasn't given to outbursts, and she considered her response for a moment too long, since Alizhan was already talking again.

"Fine," Alizhan said. "And sorry. Wait. Am I allowed to apologize, or is that breaking the rules? Would a normal person know that you're frustrated? You are, right? You feel kind of... scratchy. Spiny. Like something with bristles. I don't always know what people are feeling or thinking. Sometimes I sense something, or hear or smell something, and I just have to guess what it means, and Iriyat says I'm very bad at it because I've had so little human contact in my life, but I don't see how I can *get* more human contact when—well, anyway, *bristles*. I know you don't want me to talk about your feelings. I'm not doing a very good job apologizing.

"No, not bristles," Alizhan interrupted herself. "*Thorns*. Like a thornfruit!"

Ev didn't find this amusing.

"Are you upset because I didn't say thank you? Because I meant to, but then you were hurt and I got distracted and then we *both* got knocked out—which is my fault, sort of, but also a little bit your fault, since you're the one who touched me, but it's okay, you didn't know, so I forgive you, and anyway, the point is, I *am* grateful. Very grateful. And I also hope you'll stop being afraid of me, because I like you, and I think you used to like me, before you found out that I'm some kind of monster, and I wish I wasn't this way, because it was nice when you liked me. It felt good. I'll try to follow your dumb rule if it means you'll be friends with me. I'm not always very good at knowing what's outside and what's inside, but I'll learn. I've never had a friend, but I'd like to. Okay. I'm done. Sorry. Thank you."

Ev had repressed a sigh for most of this full-speed monologue, but she was overwhelmed by the end, so a little sound slipped out of her, a sigh and a laugh all at once. Resignation and recognition. Maybe a little charm, too. "Apology accepted."

"Oh, good. I was ready to keep going, if necessary, even though—"

"Alizhan?"

"Yeah?"

"You're not a monster."

And with that, they had reached Ev's farm.

6

ONE SMOKING HELL OF A MESS

L ONG HOURS AFTER SQUIRMING UNDERNEATH Ev's cart in the market, Alizhan's heart was still wild in her chest, an animal scrabbling to get free of its cage. As their walk ended and Ev's family farm came into view, it occurred to Alizhan that her feral, frenzied heart might be trying to tell her something.

Other people's feelings could be so overwhelming. Her own were communicated through the enigmatic code of her body. Her heart tapped out messages that her brain was slow to decipher.

That sharp, cold streak down her back and in her gut when she'd slipped under the cart. Had it been fear? Excitement? And what was she feeling now?

It was easier to turn her attention outward. Ev was buzzing with worries and doubts and pains as they walked up the path toward a collection of single-story buildings in brown stucco and red tile, feelings Alizhan wasn't supposed to know, or wasn't supposed to say she knew, and which she didn't want to know in the first place. Ev had said *you're not a monster* and that was all

Alizhan wanted to think about. Just the words. Not the lingering doubts.

The tips of Alizhan's fingers itched inside her gloves.

A large dog came bounding up to them, its coat brindled black and brown and its tongue lolling, and for a moment, Ev was brilliant with happiness, kneeling on the ground to give the animal a belly rub. "This is Tez."

Tez jumped up and conducted a thorough and enthusiastic investigation of Alizhan with his nose. She took off her gloves for a moment to scratch behind his ears, and then in a sudden sign of trust and approval, he flopped on the ground and offered her his belly. Alizhan obliged him.

Ev was pleased.

That warmth from Ev made it all worth it. For an instant, there was nobody hunting her. There was no Iriyat, no Kasrik, no Mar, no journal, no chaos threatening to consume her world. There was just Ev and her striped dog wiggling in the red dirt.

And in truth, it had nothing to do with the dog. Alizhan liked animals just fine. She could touch them, and they made the world less lonely. But being able to touch animals was a poor substitute for the real contact and comfort she wanted.

Tez turned and loped up the hill toward the house, drawing both of their gazes.

The sight of Ev's home brought her no calm, even though it was charming. The main farmhouse was built in traditional Laalvuri style, its rooms organized around three sides of a square courtyard with a garden and a shallow pool to catch rainwater, that rare treasure. The house was oriented so sunlight fell directly on the open side of the courtyard. Opposite the open side was a wall of stone columns, leaving the kitchen and the parlor open to the warm air. The other sides of the house were enclosed, so they must contain bedrooms. It looked like a nice place to grow up.

It wasn't the sight of the house that made the air turn sour with Ev's feelings, but the young man who walked out of it to greet them. Ev thought his name with such dread that Alizhan had no trouble learning it. Ajee didn't look worthy of such an intense reaction to Alizhan, but people never looked like much of anything to her.

He was a little shorter than Ev, so he was still a head taller than Alizhan. His black hair was pulled into a short braid, and he was wearing a tunic and trousers in red with black embroidery at the cuffs and collar. The clothes meant nothing to Alizhan, but both Ev and Ajee thought about them for a moment as he came into view. *Wedding clothes.* His feelings were as unpleasant and prickly as Ev's, and then there was sharp note of surprise.

"Who's this? What happened to you? You're hurt!"

It was his voice—rich and warm—that called the memory to the surface.

OF COURSE I LIKE YOU, Ev, but not like that.

Alizhan had dreamed this, after Ev had touched her. Ajee's face sparked no recognition, because faces never did, but his voice echoed in her head. Such a lovely voice, but not at all the words that she—no, Ev—had wanted to hear.

Ev and Ajee had been sitting together on a smooth patch of sun-warmed rock at the top of a hillside, looking down at the farm where they'd grown up together. In a moment of silence, Ev had brought up the future. "Maybe we should just get married."

They could join their neighboring farms into one property. It had never been Ev's dream to stay here—at least not without seeing the world first—but she was twenty-two years old now and it was time to put away her foolish childhood dreams. It made sense to get married, didn't it?

Ev had known, distantly, that this proposal was dull and practical and not at all romantic. It was nothing like how Vesper had proposed to Aurora after carrying her from a burning building. It was nothing like any of the books Ev had read. But grand passions were reserved for people with grander lives. Wasn't Ajee always telling her to stop paying so much attention to stories? It was sensible and simple to marry someone she knew and liked. She could be happy here on the farm. She and Ajee were friends. They'd grown up together, sharing their lives up to this point. They could keep going.

She hadn't expected Ajee to say no.

She hadn't expected him to say that she was being *ridiculous* and *ruining our friendship*. He'd grown agitated, gesticulating and starting and stopping sentences without ever getting to the end. And then he'd choked out a short, dry laugh and said *Think how absurd you'd look in a wedding gown!* and *Would you stomp up to the altar with your staff in hand?*

He'd treated her idea like a joke.

The joke wasn't just that he might marry her, but that *anyone* would. His cruelty had caught her by surprise. Ev had always known she wasn't beautiful—too tall, too broad, too different— but it had never seemed to matter before. They'd spent years working and playing together, sparring and racing and wandering all over the farm. As kids, they'd often slept in the same room, talking to each other long after their parents had shut the door and told them to go to sleep. She'd taught him to fight with a staff last year, and in return, he'd stolen a bottle of wine from his parents. They'd drunk the whole thing up in the barn loft, dissolving into dizzy laughter over nothing. He'd kissed her up there, and more. She remembered it with warmth.

Maybe he didn't.

Ajee had strode away from her without saying goodbye, and it wasn't until two or three triads later that he'd found Ev in the barn and said, "I've been meaning to tell you this, but it only just happened. You see, there's this girl—"

"Seliman," Ev said immediately. Orzatvur was a small village, and there were only a few neighboring farms. There weren't that many girls. One in particular had always drawn Ajee's eye. Ev didn't care about Seliman so much as the fact that Ajee hadn't bothered to apologize for anything he'd said.

"Yes," he said dreamily. "She said yes. We're getting married."

"Oh."

"Isn't it wonderful?"

And here was the strangest part of the memory. Alizhan had *been* Ev, and had felt the hollow in Ev's stomach and had known exactly how much Ev had wanted to yell *no*, or burst into tears, or maybe hit Ajee in the face. Her fist had tightened. But instead, she'd blinked once, forced her fingers apart, smoothed her tunic, and said, "I'm very happy for you."

And *smiled*. Ev had smiled.

<hr />

ALIZHAN WAS ANGRY NOW, just thinking about these memories. Ajee was standing in front of them, waiting for an explanation, and Alizhan wanted to reach over and grab Ev's staff so she could whack him.

"I'm fine," Ev said in answer to Ajee's questions, which wasn't true, and then said, "Get everyone—no, on second thought, just get my parents. I'll explain inside."

He turned and went inside, and Alizhan said, "I don't like him."

Ev's voice went high with surprise. "Why not?"

Ev had asked Alizhan not to talk about what she could see in

Ev's head. The rule was a nuisance and it was going to make life difficult for both of them. But Ev had also smuggled her out of the city and saved her life. Ev knew the truth about her and had still said *you're not a monster*. So instead of explaining, which would have required breaking Ev's only rule, Alizhan huffed, spat on the ground, and strode into the house after Ajee.

————

Ev's normally calm and cheerful mother gasped at the sight of blood on Ev's tunic. Neiran covered her mouth with her hands and set all of her jewelry jangling. One deep breath later, she'd lifted her long black braid over her shoulder to get it out of the way, taken firm hold of Ev's wrist, led Ev into the bathroom as though Ev were still a small child in need of direction, instead of a twenty-two-year-old woman who towered over her mother.

Neiran began to rinse out Ev's cut and wrap her abdomen in clean linen. Ev didn't protest. She was grateful to be taken care of, and to be given a mug of bitter pain-relieving tea, and she was just about to start explaining everything to her mother when she heard people talking in the kitchen.

Alizhan was in the kitchen with Papa and Ajee, and who knew what someone might say or do to her? From the other room, Ev heard her father introduce himself as Obin Umarsad, and Ajee gave his own name as Ajeekar Chatragat, to which Alizhan replied, "Alizhan... Alizhan."

She didn't say *Alizhan Varenx*. But she wouldn't have. She was a servant, not a family member. Still, she might have had some other family name. How lonely, to be not only an orphan, but an unknown.

Neiran finished tying off the linen wrap with the professional ease of a tailor and the long practice of a mother whose child had scraped herself raw too many times to count. "Who is that girl, Evreyet, and how did you get hurt?"

"She needed help, Mama."

Ev waved her mother's fussing away with one hand and went into the kitchen. Her father wasn't scowling at Alizhan, but he also wasn't doing anything to make Alizhan feel at ease in a strange place among strangers. And he was a wall of a man, imposing even when he smiled, which he only did for Neiran and Ev. Obin couldn't help but loom over Alizhan, making the kitchen feel cramped. He believed firmly in equality and justice for all, but it was hard to tell from his demeanor.

Ajee's arms were crossed over his chest. All three of them were standing around the round wooden table, rather than sitting. The room was silent.

"She said you could explain," Obin said.

Ev told them about the Solor guards in the market and the masked men on the road, but could not bring herself to mention the stolen book, the dream-memory, or Alizhan's particular skills.

Obin's eyes narrowed as his gaze settled on Alizhan. Ev wondered if Alizhan ever noticed things like that, people squinting at her, or if she perceived their scrutiny in her own way. "I remember you," he said. "You're barely any bigger than you were. You were in the market—it must have been a decade ago—and Ha-Varensi came looking for you. You jumped off a bridge into the water. Ev was upset."

Alizhan nodded once, slowly. "I was... a difficult child."

Alizhan might not be a child any more, but Ev privately thought the present tense might be more appropriate for *difficult*. Then she remembered there was no such thing as thinking anything privately, and grimaced.

"You still work for Varenx House?"

"I did until very recently," Alizhan said. Perhaps it was

because she saw faces so indistinctly and could never study anyone else's expressions in order to train her own, or perhaps it was simply her large and lively features, but Alizhan's expressions always seemed too big for her face. They didn't fit. Her eyes were wide with uncertainty. After a moment, she said, "Ev left out some parts of the story. There's a book. It belongs to Iriyat, but it was stolen by Solor House almost two triads ago. I broke in and stole it back, but unfortunately, I was seen."

"That explains why Solor guards were looking for you, but what of the others?" Obin asked.

"They were from Varenx House."

"Your own employer?" Alizhan simply looked at Obin until he said "Ah." It was a rare sight, someone taking on her father like that. Ev loved him fiercely, but when he looked his sternest, even she found him imposing.

"So you pissed off two of the Great Houses and then you came *here*," Ajee said.

"I wanted to warn you," Ev said.

"What were you thinking?"

Obin put a hand on Ajee's shoulder and stopped him from saying anything else. "Alizhan, you must have had a reason for doing what you did."

"Yes, but it's... hard to explain."

Now Obin stared at Alizhan. "You brought danger to our door, so you'd better come up with an explanation."

"We don't know everything," Ev cut in. "Someone came to Ha-Solora with accusations against Ha-Varensi. That prompted him to have the book stolen. And we—she, I mean, Alizhan— intended to get the book back to Iriyat, but it's not clear if we can trust her, either. Alizhan overheard a conversation where it sounded like Iriyat was plotting to have someone killed."

Obin huffed. He seemed to take it as a given that neither

leader could be trusted. Ev's mother put her hand on his to quiet him. Neiran had always worried about his politics.

"And what is this book?" Obin said.

"Volume eleven of *A Natural History of the World*. We don't know why it was important to Mar," Ev said. "Or Iriyat. Mar suspected it might contain some secret, but he didn't understand it."

"This is one smoking hell of a mess."

"Obin," Ev's mother chastised, just as Ev said, "I know, Papa, but—"

Her father looked pensive, and Ev stopped talking. "How do you know Mar ha-Solora didn't understand it?"

Ev knew because Alizhan knew, and Alizhan knew because —well, that wasn't Ev's secret to share.

"Can I see it?" Obin said.

Alizhan hesitated, then shrugged and handed over the book, which now looked a little worn around the corners. Obin accepted it, then sat down at the table. He opened the book to the first page to study the text, as though the secret might reveal itself if only he stared hard enough.

"I can't prove it to you," Alizhan said. "I can't prove anything. I need to investigate. I need to get back into the city—"

"You need safety from all the people who are trying to kill you," Neiran interrupted. Mama hadn't introduced herself to Alizhan, and she didn't bother now. "You need food and rest and —forgive me—a bath and some clean clothes."

"They can't stay here!" Ajee interrupted. "Solor guards are searching the city for them, and it's only a matter of time until someone searches the outlying villages."

"Are you suggesting that I throw out my own daughter?" Neiran said coolly. Ev's mother was a small woman whose round face was marked with faint lines from laughing and smiling so often. Ajee looked suitably taken aback by her tone.

"He's right, Mama," Ev said.

"Oh, they're not trying to kill me," Alizhan said, with the tiniest emphasis on the word *kill*, in the way someone else might say *oh, I don't think that shade of blue suits me*. A minor correction. Ev stared. What did Alizhan think they wanted with her, in that case? If Iriyat was willing to have Kasrik killed over this book, why would she balk at killing Alizhan? But these thoughts were pushed aside when Alizhan continued, "They would've killed Ev, though. But she kicked their asses!"

Ajee and Neiran both frowned at this addendum. Obin's expression remained neutral, but Ev thought he might be trying not to smile. He was a good teacher.

"You can sleep a shift here," Neiran said, responding to Ev instead of Alizhan. "We can handle ourselves." She spoke these words without even glancing at Obin, who was still intent on the book, but Ev took her meaning. It was not Neiran who would be answering the door with a staff in hand, as fierce as she might be with needles and pins.

"There's a space under the floorboards in the pantry where Alizhan can hide if anyone in uniform demands to search the house." Obin looked Alizhan up and down. "You'll fit."

"There's a *what* where?" Ev had lived in this house her entire life and never encountered any such thing.

"Your father likes to take precautions," Neiran said. "He doesn't trust anyone."

"And neither should you," Obin said. He closed the book and slid it across the table toward Alizhan, who took it back.

Ajee looked like he was about to protest, and Ev understood his doubts. If Obin was preaching general mistrust, then why shelter Alizhan? It was a risk. But Papa and Mama trusted Ev's opinion of Alizhan.

Her opinion wasn't enough for Ajee. No part of her was.

It was stupid to get upset about a few cutting remarks when

mere hours ago, someone had tried to cut her open. And yet Ev looked at the floor and swallowed around the lump in her throat.

"Even if the guards don't find her, what then?" Ajee said. "You're mixed up in something you know nothing about."

"We'll solve that after we eat," Neiran said lightly. She went into the pantry. Alizhan followed her, book in hand, and her bare feet made no sound against the floor.

THERE WAS a bathroom adjacent to the kitchen with a white-tiled floor and a copper soaking tub. Unlike the kitchen, it had no windows open to the light. It was walled all around for privacy, so the only light came from the green glow of the lamps, glass globes filled with the luminescent fluid drawn from medusas, and their reflection in the smooth tiles.

Ev filled the tub for Alizhan and handed her an old set of clothes. It was a tunic and trousers in goldenrod yellow with matching embroidery, all Mama's handiwork, the cotton soft and worn. The trousers had been too short for Ev for years now, but the outfit would fit Alizhan like a tent. Still a vast improvement over the filthy rags she'd been hiding and sweating and bleeding in for God knew how long.

Alizhan stared at the clothes for a long time without saying anything.

"You don't like them?" Ev ventured.

"Oh, no, it's not that. I don't care about clothes. But it's easier to get around in Laalvur if people ignore me. People don't really like to look at me anyway, of course, because they can tell there's something wrong with me, but dressing like a beggar gives them an easy explanation for why they don't want to look at me. It's better for me that way." Alizhan's gaze darted from one side of the room to the other. She chewed her lip. "So it's on purpose, now, the rags and the dirt and all that. Because it makes life easier. But it didn't use to be. When I was a kid, I mean. It wasn't on purpose, back then."

"Because no one took care of you?"

"No, no, they tried. At least, after I got to Varenx House, they tried. So many servants tried to dress me or bathe me or brush my hair. But you know how it is when people touch me." Alizhan held the clothes in one arm and started gesturing with her free hand. "There was always a lot of screaming. Kicking. Fainting. That sort of thing. And so after a while, they stopped trying, and by the time I could do all those things for myself, I didn't like any of them."

"But now it's on purpose," Ev said. She didn't really need clarification. But her heart ached for a little girl who couldn't be clothed or fed or cuddled, and what she really wanted to say was *why didn't Iriyat do those things for you?* and that felt intrusive.

"Oh, Iriyat," Alizhan said, waving a hand in the air and completely forgetting their new rule about mind-reading. "Yes, she could have. But she's always busy. But anyway, yes, now it's on purpose, so stop being sad."

Ev wasn't sure whether that command was meant for her or Alizhan herself, but either way, Alizhan obviously wanted to move on from this conversation topic. "So you... want the rags back?"

"No, no, that's okay, I... don't need them." Alizhan clutched Ev's old clothes tight to her chest. "There's always more rags, you know? They're not hard to come by. This is fine."

"Okay," Ev said. Navigating a conversation with someone who could see into her head and hear everything she didn't say out loud was taxing. Ev hadn't missed Alizhan's reaction, and the way her thin fingers had clamped folds into the fabric, but they obviously weren't going to talk about it. *Stop being sad,*

Alizhan had said, as if Ev's feelings were like the water gushing into the tub, and one turn of the faucet could stop them.

When Ev shut the bathroom door behind her, Ajee was waiting for her, and he drew her into the far corner of the parlor, as far away from Neiran's work in the kitchen as they could get. The open design of the house left few possibilities for private conversations. Ajee didn't sit, so neither did Ev.

"You have no business messing with whatever she's involved in," he said. "Varenx House? Solor House? Don't treat it like it's an adventure from one of your books. You grow thornfruit and muck stalls, Ev. You're not prepared for this. And there's something wrong with her. Did you see how twitchy she was in the kitchen? She can't look anybody in the eyes. She's not right in the head. She's a goddamn Unbalanced mess who'll get you both killed."

Ajee was never very religious, but apparently he'd gone to enough sermons to take all the warnings about "touched" people to heart. *Superstitious garbage* was Ev's first reaction. Except now she knew it was all true. Alizhan possessed an ability beyond normal human senses—the simplest word for it was *magic*. If magic was real, then the Temple of the Balance was no longer preaching superstitious garbage, but prejudice.

"You have to get rid of her," Ajee said, as if Alizhan was a thing that could be thrown on a refuse heap.

What would Alizhan sense, if she were standing here? Could she sense them both through the wall? Was Ajee really so concerned for Ev? Why was he raising his voice?

"You grow thornfruit and muck stalls, too," Ev pointed out, unaccountably hurt by this description, as accurate as it was.

"Yes, and I know my place!"

Ev opened her mouth but had no idea what to say to that. She'd offered to stay on the farm with him and get married, and he hadn't wanted that, either. Eventually she said, as neutrally as possible, "You think I should have left her in the market."

"Yes," Ajee burst out. "She's a thief! Let the Houses sort it out between themselves."

"If Alizhan's suspicions are correct, people will die for what's in that book," Ev said. "People might already have died."

"And soon you'll be one of them!"

"She needs help, Ajee."

"So she's another one of your little rescues?" Ajee said. "She's not a kitten, Ev. She's a person. A person you don't know."

Ev had nothing to say to that. She didn't know everything about Alizhan, but she knew enough. More than she could explain to Ajee.

He shook his head and made a sound of disgust. "I can't believe it. All this time, I thought you were sensible."

All this time, I thought I was in love with you, Ev thought and didn't say. It had only been four triads since she'd brought up marriage, but it felt like years. Ajee was still wearing the red-and-black wedding clothes he'd greeted them in. Mama must have been taking his measurements. Ev could see now that some of the embroidery was unfinished, black threads dangling from his wrists. His trousers were unhemmed. Still, it was fast work on Mama's part. Unless she'd already known that Ajee was planning to propose.

Had Ev been the last to know?

She huffed. The sound wasn't quite a laugh, but more importantly, it wasn't a sob. Had Neiran been protecting her by keeping this secret? It didn't feel much like protection.

Maybe it was for the best that Ajee had rejected her. Even if Ev had been Ajee's wife, she still would have helped Alizhan. And in that case, she'd have brought Alizhan home and Ajee would've thrown her out.

Ev didn't want to be sensible. She wanted to do the right thing.

The thought was like a deep breath. It made her feel grounded, settled. She didn't need to say it out loud to Ajee, to hear him scoff at her, because she didn't care what he had to say anymore.

When Ev said nothing, Ajee stalked out through the courtyard. Ev stayed still for an instant. Winning an argument ought to come with a sense of triumph. Instead, a question hovered in the back of her mind: had they ever been friends? Ev didn't want to answer that, so she went back to the kitchen to help her mother, and then she heard her father call her name.

He was no longer in the kitchen, but the Nightward wall of the kitchen was set with wood and paper screens to let the cool air flow through, so Ev could hear him. She went outside and found her father sitting in the shade of the house. In contrast to his usual stillness and self-possession, one sandaled foot was scuffing at the scrubby ground.

"Are you angry with me, too?" Ev asked.

A pause. "No," he said. "I just want you to be careful."

"That's why you called me out here?"

"She's very pretty," her father said. He wasn't looking at Ev, but at the shadow cast by their house. Only a few hardy shade-growing flowers dotted the rocky ground. "Alizhan."

Ev hadn't been expecting the subject. It made her seize up with fear. Before he could delve any deeper, she shot back, "What does *that* have to do with anything?"

He regarded her in silence for an uncomfortably long time. "Maybe nothing," he said, as if it were a concession. "Just be careful."

"You said that already."

"It means don't trust her, Ev," Obin said. "Her, or anyone else, but be extra careful with her. I remember that girl from your first time working in the market, and that means she's been working for Varenx House for a long time. Keep that in mind. And I see the way you look at her."

"I look at her the same way I look at everyone else! With my eyes!"

He held up a hand, and Ev quieted. "I know you're trying to do the right thing. I won't tell you what to do. I wouldn't know what to say. But I want you to have this."

He pulled a coinpurse out of the pocket of his trousers, slid a ring off his finger, and handed both to her. The purse was heavy. Ev had seen the grey ring before because he always wore it, but had never examined it in detail. It was angular, two pentagon-shaped bands connected by a zigzagging line of metal. She slipped it over her index finger experimentally, but it was too big.

"You can put it on a chain if you want," he said. "I don't know if you'll need it. But if you need to get out of the city, you can go down to the harbor and find a ship called *And There Still the Curling Vines Do Grow*—just ask around for *Vines*. Show that ring to anybody on the crew and tell them you're my daughter. Don't let them scare you off. They might not be friendly, but they'll help you. But keep that to yourself if you're ever in Adappyr."

This was as close as her father had ever come to saying anything about his past. Ev's brows drew together. "Why would I be in Adappyr?"

He shrugged. "Just in case."

"That makes no sense. Whatever this is, it's contained in Laalvur. We just have to find someone who can decode the book, and then go from there. We'll have to be careful. There might be a trial. But I can't imagine needing—" Ev looked inside the purse. No white palaad coins, just a pile of brown kalap tinged with green, but it was more money than she'd ever held in her hand. Where had all this come from? Had her father hidden it in the space under the pantry floor? Did he have other secrets? The ring implied that he did.

"Just take it, Ev," he said. "Set an old man at ease."

"I don't see any old men around here," Ev said with a smile.

Her father flapped his hand in dismissal of her joke, but said nothing. After a moment, she nodded and pocketed the treasure.

"We'll understand if you have to leave and not come back for a while," Obin said. "Well. Your mother won't be happy about it, but she'll understand."

Leave? Ev had never even been to the villages on the other side of Laalvur. Was it fear or excitement at the idea of leaving that set her heart beating faster? "Are you talking about going into exile?" she asked. "Like when you left Adappyr?"

"No."

That sentence shuttered the conversation, and Ev was disappointed, but not surprised. She should never have asked. But he'd been the one to bring up the past. Sometimes talking to her father was like navigating a maze with a dead end around every corner. Ev kept her face expressionless and said, "I should go check on Alizhan."

She turned to go.

"Ev."

Her father stood up and wrapped her in a hug. Enveloped in darkness and enclosed in the circle of his arms, for a moment, Ev felt as if nothing could hurt her.

7

LYREBIRD SHIFT, 12TH TRIAD OF HIRSHA, 761

M Y STAY IN NALITZVA AT the home of Rossin Tyrenx was a dull misery. I have lived through deadlier horrors, now, than the fetid breath and coarse beard of a man four times my age trying to kiss me, and yet it still makes me shudder to think on it. Had I not been myself, I might have worse things to remember.

But I am my parents' daughter. I had ways of slipping out of his grasp and redirecting his attentions. So I returned to the decks of *In the Shade I Saw My Love Go Walking* disgusted and exhausted but mostly unharmed.

I was not sad to see the white stone of Nalitzva fade from view, although the motion of the ship made me sick again. We sailed home, rather than rowing, since the winds blow from Night to Day. It is much faster to get from Nalitzva to Laalvur than the other way around. As much as I wanted to escape Tyrenx's clutches, I was in no rush to return to my parents'.

I lay wretched in my bunk for a triad, and when my seasickness receded, I walked unsteadily to the deck for some fresh air. There, I had time to reflect on what my parents would say when I arrived. They would not care that I hated Rossin Tyrenx, who spoke to me like a child and tried to grope me with his knobby fingers.

It was not long before Arav found me. "Crying girl," he said. "We talked about this."

I had not realized that I was crying, and the sight of his smile —the soft, sad way one smiles at a weeping person, tempering cheer with sympathy—made me cry harder.

Heedless of the danger, I threw my arms around Arav's neck and sobbed into his shoulder. He took it with grace. I could not breathe enough to explain myself to him, but he did not ask me to. He stroked a hand down my back.

This is what I knew: my parents would force me to marry Tyrenx. He would force himself on me.

Never. I would force my hand against his face until he forgot his own name.

They kill our kind in Nalitzva. That is why my family fled so long ago. Our people had grown careless and shed their secrecy, and they paid for their mistake in slaughter. After that, we kept our secrets, even in warm and welcoming Laalvur. As soon as our family arrived, we set about erasing ourselves from history.

In our modern era in Laalvur, it is considered backward and uncivilized—the height of absurdity—to believe in magic. That is no accident. That is the work of my ancestors. They did it so that we might live. They destroyed evidence and laid hands on witnesses. They soothed the terror of the truth into a rumor. In dining halls and parlors and temples and harbors, everywhere, they made a great show of laughing and saying: *how could there be people in the world who could make memories disappear with a touch? Has anyone ever seen such a person? Is there any proof?*

Years and years my ancestors worked at this, their masterpiece, their own disappearance. They succeeded. They saved themselves from being hunted to extinction. It is the greatest erasure of memory in history—except it is nowhere in history.

After all, what good is a power like ours, if people know?

There are other kinds of magic, but ours is the most hated. The oldest tales portray our kind as untrustworthy, deceitful, manipulative, cheaters and betrayers by nature. Or they did, until they were forgotten.

Nalitzvans are right to fear us. Laalvuri are fools to dismiss their fears as old wives' tales. There used to be many names for us in all the languages of the world, but my favorite is the Old Nalitzvan: *smaroi*. Lacemakers. Lace is a delicate art, an arrangement of absences all strung together with fine thread. As Lacemakers, we construct nothing from something. We make holes.

My ancestors must have thought it a great joke to go into the textile trade.

Like true lacemakers, our craft depends on our hands. I have heard that in the islands, they call our ability touch-magic, *uheko*, from their word for *hand*. There is no dexterity involved. Simple contact is enough, bare skin to bare skin. The fine control is mental rather than manual.

As an adolescent, I resisted the tedium of training. For years, I frustrated my parents by only being able to perform the simplest of erasures, wiping away the last few moments of someone's memory. But I discovered in Nalitzva that with untrained raw force, it was possible to knock a man unconscious with a touch.

This experiment of mine had two trials, both borne of panic. In the first, I deliberately tore off my glove and swatted Tyrenx's hand away. In the second—unintentional—he approached me from behind, slid his clammy hand under my braid to touch the bare back of my neck, and then dropped like a stone. Until that moment, I had thought only my hands could have that effect, but terror and revulsion amplified my powers. Had I paid attention to my training, I would have known this to be true of all intense emotions. In any case, both times, Tyrenx woke up confused, but not permanently damaged. He attributed his collapses to too much wine.

Gifted Lacemakers can reach back into someone's memory and steal any moment they like. Those of us with the most perfect technique are not limited to moments. We can vanish people, places, words and ideas from the mind, although it is time-consuming and tiring to do so.

The highest degree of control, though, is to touch someone's skin without touching their memory.

Startled out of my sobbing, I looked up at Arav. His stare was foggy and unfocused. I dropped my arms and leapt away from him, putting my hands behind my back.

"Arav?"

He blinked. Then smiled. "Yes, crying girl?"

"I told you not to call me that."

"But how else can I get you to make that face, with your eyebrows all scrunched together?"

I rolled my eyes.

"No, not like that, like this," he said, and imitated my scowl with exaggerated ferocity.

I laughed despite myself, momentarily reassured that I had not damaged him, and Arav broke into a grin. I knew then, with rare clarity, that the right thing to do was to turn away. Every moment Arav spent in my company, he was in danger.

And yet I stayed.

For him, I thought, I would learn the control I had always lacked. Until then, we would both have to wait. I did not touch him again on the ship, not even with my gloves on, and he did not try to touch me. That stretched my willpower to its furthest limit. I could not stay away. I learned which shift he slept, and which he worked, and I adjusted my schedule so we could spend every waking minute together. We knew without speaking of it that our time together was precious, that we both wanted an impossible thing, and we were similarly determined to reap what we could from such a paltry harvest. Even in each other's company, we were always left wanting more. I lived in hope of getting what we wanted, which is the sweetest torment.

We did not stop when the voyage ended. I was able to use my parents' distaste for the dirty work of gardening against them. I claimed to be spending all my time there, and as I had to sneak back into the house through a path I had worn into some bushes, I usually had the dirt and scratches on my clothes to prove it. Parneet knew I was up to something, since she and her staff had to do the work that I was leaving unattended, but she did not like to involve herself in matters outside the garden. She claimed to be indifferent to my affairs, but none of her staff mentioned my absences to my parents, for which I was very grateful.

It was then that I learned to cultivate loyalty. Had the gardeners not kept silent at Parneet's orders, I could have manipulated their memories, but I found it more pleasant to manipulate the household finances to their benefit instead. When I made a public fuss about how we did not pay our gardeners enough, my parents simply acquiesced without examining my motives more closely. I had always manifested such a distaste for politics, after all, and I had been perfectly compliant with their wishes of late—why should they not grant me this one small service? Sometimes it is easier to operate in light than in shade.

Arav and I carried on this way, meeting in secret whenever his ship was docked in Laalvur, for months. When I was not with him, I worked fervently on my control. I shook hands with our guards, with priests in the temple, with vegetable sellers in the market. I stumbled into strangers in the street by practiced accident, brushing my bare hands against them. If they made indignant exclamations, if they looked at me with clarity afterward, I knew that they remembered our exchange and that I had succeeded.

It took half a year before I would put my bare hand in his. Other young men would have pressured me for more, or lost interest. Arav possessed surprising stores of patience.

"Don't be scared," he told me, intertwining his fingers with mine.

"I'm not," I said, but I was. I had still never explained it to him. My parents had drilled into me that our survival depended on secrecy. But my silence was motivated by something other than the protection of my fellow Lacemakers. It was selfishness. I worried that Arav would not love me if I told him the truth.

"You're so worried all the time. It's just hands, Ya-ya." No one else called me that, but Arav had always liked to give me nicknames. Doubling a sound in a child's name is a common endearment. My parents had never done this. They were not much for endearments.

Ya-ya brought to mind shouting or laughing or singing. It was an absurd, childish nickname that did not suit me at all. I loved it.

Arav held our hands up between us for a moment. "No harm will come of this. But I'll stop if you want to."

"I don't want to stop," I said. I wanted more. I wanted to tell him everything. But the words would not come, so I closed my mouth.

"I would never hurt you."

"I know," I said. Arav was always so strikingly honest, so overwhelmingly sincere. I believed him in a way that I could never believe anyone else. Have I ever known anyone so pure? Even now, thinking of the way he gripped my hand and looked into my eyes still makes my heart full to bursting. "That's not what I'm afraid of."

"Then what are you afraid of, Ya-ya?"

That I *will hurt* you, I thought. I said, "Volcanoes. Waves. Medusas."

"Sensible," he said. "And here I thought you were afraid of getting caught walking the streets of the Marsh hand in hand with a poor boy."

My parents would be angry if they knew. Even if Arav had never touched me, if anyone recognized me with him, it would jeopardize my marriage to Tyrenx. I had taken to covering my hair to prevent this. My skin was not so distinctive, since people of many different colors come to make their way in Laalvur, but blond hair remained a rarity.

Because I covered my hair, Arav's family thought I was very religious. His parents and siblings lived in the tiniest house I had ever seen, a little wooden room stilted above the water and creaking in the wind, but they welcomed me warmly.

I loved them, and yet I put them at risk. Arav had identified my real fear—discovery—but he had no idea what consequences it would bring for him and his family.

Entering their home, I understood why Arav had been so motivated to catch the medusa and sell its venom. Money would have vastly improved their lives. But Arav had been the only sailor to come home whole from that disaster—or perhaps not whole, but still able to work—and so he had made sure the earnings from their catch had been divided up among the families of the others. I loved him for it, and yet I still wished he could have been more selfish.

At first I was stiff in his family's presence, hesitant to return their hugs, but they embraced me so readily that it was hard not to love them. They had given me Arav, after all.

I was especially thrilled to make the acquaintance of Arav's sister, Eliyan, who was two years older than him. I had been starved of female friendship my whole life, and she accepted me with warmth. She was much quieter and more serious than

Arav, and it was strange to see his mobile, expressive features on such a reserved face. But the two of them were close despite their different temperaments. Her approval meant the world to me.

They did not know who I was. I was already behaving recklessly by befriending them in the first place, but telling them my real name was too great a risk even for me.

Arav told them I had grown up in the Jewelbox and that my name was Ya-ya, and they never asked for more. They talked as though Arav would marry me, as though I was already their daughter and sister, even though they knew as well as we did how unlikely that was. It was exhilarating to spend time in their world, where we could all pretend.

My own family would lock me up if they knew. Arav's concern that I might be afraid to be seen with him was well-founded. In my heart, I knew exactly what my parents would do to Arav, to his mother and father and Eliyan and their four younger siblings if they ever found out, but I could not bear to think of it. Down here in the shady, salt-scented mud streets of the Marsh, the threat felt very far away.

And Arav had just asked me about my fears and told me I was being "sensible."

"I'm sensible, but not that sensible," I told Arav, and it was all too true. He laughed. We kept walking, our interlaced hands swinging between us.

I turned seventeen, and my marriage loomed on the horizon. It might not be the end of everything, but it was an end nevertheless. Once married, I would live with Tyrenx in Nalitzva, and I would only see Arav if he could discreetly get word to me that the *Shade* had docked in Nalitzva, and if I could escape Tyrenx's mansion, and if we could find somewhere out of the way to go in an unfamiliar city with strict laws against adultery. The obstacles were almost insurmountable. And for what? A handful of stolen hours a few times a year.

We both wanted more, and it was this heady mixture of doom and desire that made me grow reckless.

The Marsh is strung along the coast in the shade of Hahim, and the neighborhood connecting the sea-level Marsh to the height of the Point is an ancient warren of steep streets and sloping staircases called Breakneck Hill. Arav and I used to walk the length of the Marsh and then loop through Breakneck Hill. The streets there were so narrow that Arav could spread his arms wide and touch the buildings on opposite sides. It was almost always possible to find some little side alley where no one was around.

It had been more than a year, and we had hardly done anything. I trusted Arav's self-control more than my own. He would not touch me unless I invited him to, so it would have to be my choice.

The first time it happened, he had just come back from a weeks-long voyage to Nalitzva. I had spent his absence alternately sulking and practicing my control. I had missed him so much that I could hardly contain a little bounce of excitement when I saw him in the harbor.

We went walking. It is a long, arduous walk from Hahim Harbor up Breakneck Hill, and I am sure Arav spent the whole time cheerfully telling stories about his time at sea—he was rarely silent—but I remember none of it. He brought me seeds and seedlings as gifts, knowing I preferred them to cut flowers. That I do remember. As soon as we found a modicum of privacy in an alley, I pushed him up against the wall. It might have been a funny image, if anyone had been watching. I was so much smaller than him. But he went willingly.

I had to go up on my tiptoes. By that time, he had divined my intentions and was already leaning down to meet me for a kiss. I wish I could say that it was exactly as I had always imagined, that it was better than I had always imagined, that it was wonderful beyond imagining. It was not. I was seventeen and I had never kissed anyone before—common afflictions, easily cured—and I was terrified that I would slip up somehow and permanently ruin his memory.

But I could not live the rest of my life without knowing what it was like to kiss him.

I was rigid and direct. The kiss was over an instant after it started.

Luckily, Arav was both more experienced and less encumbered by fear. And he was Arav: sweet, easygoing, pliant. He always possessed an astonishing ability to intuit what I wanted even when I could not communicate it. It was Arav who pulled us together and made us fit. He curved a broad hand around my waist and let it span the small of my back to press us together. He was warm and solid under my hands, and I relaxed against him. My arms rose up to wrap around his neck as though that was where they had always belonged. He slid his other hand under the cloth covering my head, knocking it to the ground, and knit his fingers into my hair. He angled his head to deepen the kiss. I could think of nothing but the feel of him.

There was more: lips and teeth grazing neck and shoulder, hands slipping under clothes. But all that matters is that when we broke apart, he looked right at me with those clear brown eyes, tucked a stray lock of hair behind my ear, grinned, and said, "Iriyat."

8

HALF-TRUTHS

A LIZHAN'S LIFE WAS UPSIDE DOWN. Entering Ev's home and meeting her family was an alien experience, as strange to Alizhan as if someone had given her the power to breathe water and explore the darkest depths of the sea.

They were strangers, but she knew exactly what they felt: caution, sympathy, fascination.

What did Iriyat feel for her?

Alizhan sank down into the hot water of the tub until even the top of her head was immersed. Her whole life, she'd thought she was alone in her nature. Some people were just born wrong, and Alizhan was one of them. Iriyat had cared for her anyway. They were meant to be. Iriyat's blankness, her emptiness, was a defect that countered the over-full nature of Alizhan's own deformed mind. The two of them were misshapen but symmetrical, balancing each other out.

But Iriyat had lied to her. Iriyat was not merely blank. Iriyat was like Alizhan. Or not exactly like her, but close enough: her bare hands were a danger to other people. And they were not alone together against the world. Kasrik was like them. He'd said there were more.

Alizhan surfaced, sheets of water sliding over her shoulders.

Was Kasrik alive? What if Vatik had already killed him? It would be her fault. She needed to find him. But what then? How would they hide from Iriyat? And how would Alizhan figure out what was in that book?

A priest in the Temple of Doubt might have insight. They studied for years and years to earn their robes, although they disavowed all certainty in their search for truth. Their black robes were decorated with feathers, a symbol of their founder, who'd supposedly made all his choices by throwing a feather into the air and letting it fall to one side or the other.

Priests of the Balance were also highly educated, but Alizhan didn't want to go near that temple. Iriyat spent too much time there, and Kasrik's nightmarish memories echoed with voices talking about *restoring God's Balance.*

Why would that be?

According to official Temple decree, there was no such thing as magic, and therefore it was foolish to fear it. There was only God's Balance, the sacred equilibrium of Night and Day that made life possible between certain death in the frozen wastes and the scorching desert. The Balance was fragile, and both extremes were necessary. Were the desert not so hot and bright, nor the ice so cold and dark, the thin belt of the world where light and dark mixed—that perfect twilight where fish swam in the water and plants grew in the soil and people built their homes—might be as desolate and dead as the rest.

God's Balance included eruptions that rained fire and poisoned the air, quakes that buckled and rent the earth, and waves that crashed and drowned cities. Destruction was necessary for creation. Death was necessary for life. Pain was necessary for pleasure.

Officially, it was right and good and sacred to the Balance to care for the old, the sick, and the mad. Unofficially, sometimes a

strange and difficult little girl unsettled her family and neighbors by wailing in pain when anyone touched her, and by
knowing things she had no business knowing, and so she was
marked as an aberration, a horror, a monster, a disturbance to
the Balance, and dropped at the threshold of the Temple to
become someone else's problem.

Alizhan didn't remember that part of her life, for which
she'd always been grateful. She remembered only Iriyat, who'd
taken her in when no one else would, who'd fed her and sheltered her and tended her hurts.

Was that a lie, too?

Alizhan couldn't stand to think about the question. Real
heights didn't scare her, but within herself, there were plenty of
ledges she wouldn't approach. What if she slipped and fell into
those depths? How much anger was down there? How much
pain? A fall like that would break her open.

Better to think about something else.

Kasrik had told Mar there was a second orphanage—not the
one on Temple Street, but a different, secret one. Maybe he'd
gone back there. Maybe if Alizhan went looking, she'd find
Kasrik and the secret orphanage. It was her only lead. She could
take the book to the Temple of Doubt to find out if any of the
priests could read it, and then she could lurk near the
orphanage until someone had useful thoughts.

But first she had to get back into the city without being
noticed.

There was a knock at the door. Alizhan stood, sloshing water
out of the tub, and grabbed for a towel. "Come in."

When Ev opened the door, Alizhan was wringing water from
the length of her hair and wrapped in a towel. Ev had such a
deafening avalanche of contradictory feelings that Alizhan
winced.

One of Ev's feelings soaked through all the rest, a cold splash of mortification. Ev *hated* that Alizhan knew what she was feeling. But it was different from the miasma of fear and suspicion among the other servants in Varenx House: Ev hated it because she liked Alizhan.

It was time to say something. Alizhan had no hope of getting it right.

"I know you don't want me to talk about your feelings, but I should just tell you now," she said. "I know you think about me sometimes—not just about what I'm going to say next, or if I'm trustworthy, or the kind of things your family wonders about me. You think about my face or my body or my hair or the way I walk or how it would taste if you kissed me. It's buried under all your other thoughts most of the time, but the thread is always there."

Ev took a deep breath, but she didn't deny it.

"It's okay," Alizhan said. "I don't mind."

"Oh," Ev said, and the air in the room cleared a little. Alizhan had never understood why it wasn't okay for two men to like each other, or two women, or two people of any kind. She knew exactly how common those attractions were. Ev was relieved that Alizhan didn't care. Unfortunately, their conversation wasn't over yet.

"I know you can't help it," Alizhan said. She always wanted to talk as fast as her thoughts went. But she slowed down here, because that was how Ev talked, and Ev was kind, and Alizhan wanted to be kind in return. Whatever was between them, it was fragile. If she said the wrong thing, Ev would stop wanting to be friends with her. "People just feel things sometimes, whether they want to or not. So I won't tell you to stop. But don't hope for anything, either." Alizhan knew Ev wasn't going to say anything, but she paused anyway. "Please don't be mad. I'm not saying this to hurt your feelings. I like you and I think you might be the only person in the world who likes me. And it's not that something is wrong with you, with your face or your body or your hair or anything. But you know what happens when people touch me."

After a slight hesitation, Ev gave a slow nod.

"So I can't feel that way about anybody," Alizhan said. It wasn't true. Desire took root and budded in her the same way it did in so many others. But it was a delicate plant, one that could never bloom in the cold, dark climate of Alizhan's life. There was no reason to plant the seed for something that could only shrivel and die.

Alizhan wasn't accustomed to lying, and she didn't like the way the words tasted. But it was better this way. Safer. For both of them. "I just want to say that now, so you don't get your hopes up. I hate disappointing people."

Ev was hurt, but a little hurt now was better than a broken heart later. And she was trying her best to understand, because that was what Ev did.

And if Alizhan thought about Ev sometimes—her body or her hair or the way she walked or how it would taste if she kissed her—well, no one would know except her. Those stray temptations grew like weeds, tenacious and unwelcome. There was nothing to do but uproot them. No sense in letting things get any further. "I'll try not to talk about this anymore."

"There's food," Ev said, after a silence. "If you want to... get dressed."

"We have to go to the Temple district."

"Fine," Ev said, and left immediately.

Neiran had cooked rice and stewed leafy greens with onions, almonds, currants, and cream. The dish was spiced so fragrantly and Alizhan was so hungry that she almost cried tears of gratitude when Neiran handed her a bowl. She barely got out the words "thank you" before she was grabbing a piece of bread and shoveling food into her mouth.

Neiran was impressed and a little concerned by how much she ate, but she didn't say anything, so Alizhan didn't say anything, either. Neiran was also worried—about Alizhan and whether she was lying, about Ev and whether she was making a mistake, about Ajee and Ev's fractured friendship, about her family and whether they were in danger and distantly, about Ajee's upcoming wedding and whether she would finish sewing in time—but following Ev's rule, Alizhan commented on none of these subjects.

The meal was over almost as quickly as it began. Alizhan tried to wash up, but she was shooed out of the kitchen and into the bedroom, where she found Ev sitting on a mattress on the floor with Tez and two cats, an orange one taking up as much space as possible, and a grey one curled tightly into a circle.

"That's Vesper and that's Aurora," Ev said, indicating the orange cat and then the grey one. "They're not supposed to sleep in here."

"Vesper and Aurora—like in the books! And I won't say anything," Alizhan promised. She was getting good at that.

Ev warmed with a mixture of fondness and embarrassment. "You've read *The Sunrise Chronicles*?"

Of course Alizhan had read them. The novels had occupied a huge portion of young Ev's thoughts, exciting Alizhan's curiosity. She'd begged Iriyat to add the series to her library. Ev wouldn't like that answer, so Alizhan nodded vigorously. "All of them. But I think the first one is my favorite."

Ev's embarrassment evaporated once she knew Alizhan also liked the books. "But when they get separated in book two and have to find their way back to each other—"

"I hate it when they're separated."

"Me too," Ev said. "But they fight through so many obstacles to see each other again. And they get reunited. I love that part."

"Yeah," Alizhan said. She already knew which parts Ev

loved, and why, but for some reason, she still wanted to hear Ev talk about it. But sleep was calling.

The only light in the room came in through the door with Alizhan. True darkness—an enclosed room with no exposure to the sun and no lamps—was the only luxury Alizhan cared about, and she would have been pleased to discover that Ev shared her taste for it in other circumstances. But the air in the room crackled with nerves—Ev's fatigue was no match for her anxieties about sleeping next to Alizhan. Alizhan was accustomed to sleeping alone, safe from the distraction of other people, so the artificial dark wasn't as peaceful as it could have been for either of them.

She lay awake and tried not to scratch at her fingers, which were itching again.

Still, it was a moment of relative calm and safety in her newly upside-down life, and Alizhan was grateful: for Ev, for Ev's family, for the food, for the bed, for the three little furry bodies curled up next to her and the steadiness of their breath in sleep.

Alizhan woke up to a man leaning over her.

She must have been exhausted to have slept through his approach. He'd been so silent that not even the animals were stirring.

How had he gotten in? Had he killed anyone?

Ev was alive and asleep next to her. Alizhan concentrated for a moment and felt Neiran and Obin in another room, alive, their sleep undisturbed. She couldn't feel Ajee, but he slept in one of the neighboring houses.

Ajee had been right. She never should have come here. She'd brought danger to all of them.

The man was vaguely familiar to her, and after a moment, Alizhan recognized him: Boredom. So Mar had sent someone after them. Boredom wasn't bored now.

He also wasn't touching her. Mar had warned him. It was too dark to see what kind of weapon he was carrying, and his thoughts were all strategy. How could he get the girl and the book to Solor House with the least amount of damage? He didn't want to wake anyone. Could he knock her unconscious and carry her away? If he did that, he might not find the book.

Alizhan had declined Obin's suggestion of the crawlspace under the pantry floorboards. One of them creaked. It was too obvious. Instead, she'd buried the book at the bottom of a barrel of salt.

Boredom, whose real name was Zenav, noticed that Alizhan was awake. Should he incapacitate her? Or would she cooperate? He couldn't go back to Mar without that book. Mar wouldn't be angry, but he might never give Zenav anything interesting to do again.

So Zenav wanted Mar's approval. Alizhan could work with that. He wasn't planning to hurt or kill anyone. At least not yet.

"I'll make you a deal," she whispered.

He was surprised, but silent.

Alizhan jerked her head toward the door. She slipped from the bed as gently and silently as possible. Zenav followed her out of the bedroom. Once outside, she faced him. Sunlight glinted off the sword hilt at his side.

"You tell me what you know about Kasrik, promise not to hurt anyone here, and I'll get the book and come with you," she said, keeping her voice low.

"What?"

"Which one of us just got abruptly woken up? Pay attention, Zenav. I said I'll make you a deal. This is the deal."

"How do you know my name?"

"Does it matter? You can't find that book without me. Do you agree to my terms or not?"

"Kasrik's a common name."

She sighed. He was stalling, and she was no good at describing people. "A boy. Not a little kid, though. Somewhere between the ages of eleven and sixteen, probably. Not done growing. Skinny. He has black hair. He would've been hanging around Solor House these past few triads."

"Everyone has black hair," Zenav protested, but the description was enough to bring a memory to the surface. Alizhan couldn't be sure if he was picturing Kasrik or some other adolescent boy.

"Yes," she said, taking a guess. "How recently did you see him?"

"He comes and goes," Zenav said. He was still bewildered, but answering her questions implied an acceptance of her terms. For a man who'd been sent to kidnap her from her bed, he was fairly agreeable.

She was cooperating. He had a sword. Zenav had every reason to be agreeable. "It's important. When?"

"Saw him last triad, I think. Honeycreeper shift," he said, getting closer than she wanted him to. Mar had instructed Zenav not to touch her. Zenav wasn't an attentive listener.

By Alizhan's estimation, it was currently the Honeycreeper shift of the twenty-ninth triad of Pyer. Zenav had last seen Kasrik on the twenty-eighth.

Was that enough time for Vatik to find him and kill him?

"Do you know where he goes?" Even as Alizhan asked the question, she could tell that Zenav knew nothing more. He wasn't sure why she cared so much about the boy. Mar had instructed the guards to let Kasrik into the house whenever he wished, but had said nothing else about him. Zenav assumed Kasrik was some kind of charity case, a kid from the Marsh looking for work or money.

"Somewhere in the city. Probably the Marsh. Maybe Breakneck Hill. Hell, maybe he robs houses in the Knuckles for kicks, what do I know? None of my business."

Alizhan led them into the kitchen. Interrogating Zenav with spoken questions in addition to reading his mind had the benefit of proving to Alizhan that he was honest. Zenav wasn't even lying by omission. He simply didn't know enough to help her.

Maybe Itch would have been more useful.

"I know Mar told you to bring me back unharmed. He wants to talk to me," Alizhan said. There, that was one truth. The trick with lying was to remember that no one else could see inside her. All she needed to do was keep cool on the outside. Everyone else lied all the time. And she wasn't even really going to lie. She was just going to remark on a few, select, useful truths. "Mar and I, we're... on the same side. Investigating the same problem. We just had a... minor disagreement. But I'll go with you, and I'll bring the book to him."

Zenav tensed. He knew she was about to make more demands.

"Mar and I have a problem. We know there's something important in this book, but we can't tell what it is. We think there's some kind of code."

"Why tell me this?"

"Take me to the Temple of Doubt," Alizhan said. It was close enough. Zenav would get her into the city, and then she could figure out how to ditch him and find Kasrik. She would go to Mar when she decided it was time, and not before. "Let me talk to a priest about the book."

"You haven't even proved that you have the book yet."

Alizhan turned on her heel and went into the pantry. She pried the lid off the barrel and plunged her hands into the salt, digging. She hoped Neiran would forgive her for the mess cascading onto the floor. She was trying to save lives.

She hit something solid about halfway down. She pulled the book out, shook salt from its pages, then held it up to Zenav. She was keeping her promises so far.

"Yeah," he said, in slow acknowledgement of what she was saying. "So why didn't you go talk to the Doubters yourself? Why are you all the way out here? Why tell me?"

"There are some other people in Laalvur looking for me," Alizhan said. She had Zenav's interest now. Without suggestion from Alizhan, he was imagining bringing Mar not only the girl and the book, but also the cipher. "And for this book."

"And if they find you…"

"I'd rather have you with me," Alizhan said.

Zenav was flattered. *So small*, he was thinking, eyeing her collarbone, her shoulders, the width of her wrists. *She can't possibly defend herself.* He'd already forgotten Mar's warning not to touch Alizhan. Zenav probably didn't believe in magic. But he did believe Alizhan, and that was all that mattered.

"Take me through the city gates as your prisoner."

The feeling in the room changed, sharpening with anger, and it took Alizhan a moment to understand that it wasn't Zenav who was upset, but someone else. Ev was standing on the opposite side of the kitchen from the pantry door, her anger so smoky and acrid that Alizhan swallowed to get the taste out of her mouth. It didn't work.

Zenav hadn't noticed Ev standing behind him, dressed but barefoot, leaning casually on her staff. How could he not know she was there? But he was only focused on Alizhan's suggestion that he take her as a prisoner. He'd grabbed the rope he'd brought before Alizhan had even finished saying the words. He reached for Alizhan's arms, and she yanked her hands away.

"You don't want to do that," Ev said from behind him, and surprise shot through him. "Not until she has gloves on."

Her voice was so calm and even, at odds with how she felt.

Why was Ev so angry? Alizhan wasn't supposed to know that. Ev had asked her not to look inside her head. But it wasn't really "looking inside." The feelings were just *there*. Ev might as well have asked Alizhan to walk around with her eyes closed all the time.

Alizhan couldn't do that. She peeked. And down at the bottom of the well of Ev's emotions, she touched something cold. It slithered away fast, too fast for Alizhan to be sure of what it was. Fear?

There was no time to think about that. Zenav was waiting for her to say something, making discontented noises. Adding another person was not part of the plan. He didn't yet trust Alizhan, but he felt as though he had the upper hand with her. Zenav didn't know what to make of Ev.

"She's right," Alizhan said. "Trust me." How funny to speak the words *trust me*, when Alizhan never had to take anyone on faith.

Except for Iriyat, and look how that had turned out.

"You left these in my room," Ev said, holding up a pair of gloves.

Alizhan crossed the room to take them from her, put them on, then walked back to Zenav and submitted herself to have her wrists bound. Zenav was wary. He worried more about Ev and her staff than he did about Alizhan. Still, he tied Alizhan's wrists behind her back without making contact with her skin.

Ev was still fuming, but her anger was fusing with resolve. She wasn't going to let them leave without her. She remained firm on this point, even though she also thought Alizhan's plan was foolhardy.

So what does that make you? Alizhan wondered but didn't say. Instead, she gave Zenav her most reassuring smile and said, "And you have to let my friend Ev come, too."

9

ROSEFINCH SHIFT, 20TH TRIAD OF
HIRSHA, 761

I SEE NOW THAT I should have married Rossin Tyrenx.
Certainly, it would have been briefly unpleasant. But it would also have kept my parents content and distant, and in time, I could have owned him. After that first triad, he could never have touched me again. I could have had his fortune and my own, with estates on either side of the ocean. I would have had to endure some separation from Arav, and some secrecy, but hardly more than what Arav's work and my family already demanded of us. And then in the future, when Tyrenx's memory had frayed to lace and the thread of his life had unraveled, I could have married Arav. I could have raised our children in all the comfort and security they deserved. Who could have stopped me?

Perhaps it would not have happened that way. Perhaps Tyrenx would have discovered my secret and had me killed. Perhaps Arav would have met some other girl as soon as I left. Perhaps our love would have faded, as young love does.

I cannot know any of this. All I know is what happened.

It was my idea. Arav resisted at first. He wanted to do it *right*, as he said: marriage first, then sex. I will never forget his expression when I told him he had to ruin me.

"*Ruin* you," he repeated, staring. Those wide brown eyes. He had such a wonderful face. I will never be able to convey in words how emotive he was. How quick. How unguarded. There was something novel in every expression. Arav's surprise, his outrage, his happiness, they never looked like anyone else's. Every time he experienced an emotion, it was as if it was the first time; as if he had only just learned how his own face worked and he was trying out every possibility. Things passed in an instant: my suggestion offended him, but then he grinned wickedly, leaned in so close that his nose touched my cheek, and said into my ear, "I hope you'd enjoy it at least a *little*."

"Arav." I was trying to make a plan.

"I don't want to 'ruin' you, Ya-ya." He paused, and his tone turned sly. "There are other things we could do, you know. Things I've read about in… books. Things that aren't so risky."

"The risk is the point," I said. "Rossin Tyrenx will break the betrothal if I am no longer a virgin. A pregnancy isn't necessary, but it might be useful as proof."

"A pregnancy." No more wicked grins. He was upset again. "As 'proof.' That's a baby you're talking about. A child."

"You don't want one?"

"Of course I *want* one! I want a dozen! But right now we're still sneaking around in alleys because you're terrified of your parents finding out about me. I want to fix that problem first. And I want to get married. And I want you to talk about it like *you* want to be the mother of my children, instead of talking about whether it's 'useful' or 'proof.'"

"I do want that," I said, more quietly. "I want to marry you —*you*—not some vile old monstrosity in Nalitzva. I want to have your children, not his. And in some other, better world, we could do those things in the order that you want. But that's not the world we live in. My parents are going to ship me off to Nalitzva in less than a year. We have to do it this way to break my betrothal. My feelings aren't going to solve this problem. Planning will."

"Sometimes I miss that crying girl," he said. "I knew what to do with her."

I smiled. "I heard you know exactly what to do with me. I heard you've been reading *books*."

He laughed. That was as close as we ever came to fighting. Everything was easy with Arav. Our next few times together were happy. I had never understood, until then, how uncomplicated love is. My family's love—if it was that—had always come with contingencies and requirements. They would be happy *if*, they would be proud of me *if*... and so on. Attaining their love felt impossible. Meanwhile, Arav and I were in love, and that was simple, and everything else seemed simpler for it.

With all my planning, it took until the beginning of the new year to find an opportunity. For the weeks of the festival of the New Year, even the streets of the Marsh were strung with garlands of red, white, and yellow *uzet* and *yezhem* flowers. There was drumming and dancing in every open space and song and laughter in the air. Arav's whole family went out of the house for hours. We always went with them at first, because Arav loved the festival and didn't want to miss it. He wanted to dance, to buy sweets drizzled with honey for his siblings, and to drape flower necklaces over my shoulders. But after a few hours, we would find some excuse to slip away. The first time, we went back to the house. I cherish the memory and can still describe every breath of that encounter, but I understand that you might rather not know the details of what we did. I will say that I am sure Arav had to pick crushed red petals out of his pallet for a week afterward.

"There's something I should tell you," he said as we lay

together on the rumpled sheets. His head was resting on my chest and he was drawing his fingers through the loose strands of my hair. "I hate keeping secrets from you."

I had not known that he was capable of keeping secrets.

"I tried to tell you once before," he said. He lifted his head to look me in the eye. "But I couldn't. I was worried about what you'd think of me. But this is serious now. I love you and I want you to know. And I hope... I hope this doesn't change what's between us."

"It won't," I said, still convinced his secret must be some trivial, innocent thing.

"When I said a part of me died when I fought the medusa, you thought I was talking about my scars. But I was talking about my mind. I used to know things that I don't anymore."

I could hardly breathe. I didn't fully understand what he meant, but my thoughts were elsewhere. What did this mean for my own secret? Did I owe Arav the truth?

"Like what?"

"I used to know what people were feeling or thinking," Arav said. "I know it sounds impossible. But it's true. Just by being around people, I could sense what they weren't saying. And then after the fight, I couldn't anymore."

Something about the medusa had changed him. Was it the trauma of the fight? Or was it the venom? If it was the venom, could it change me? Could it change my parents? These were all questions I couldn't ask without revealing my own secret.

"I know you probably think I was Unbalanced," Arav was saying. "And maybe I was."

"Do you miss it?" I kept the question quiet, worried it would give away my thoughts.

"When my friends went into the water with that thing, when it devoured them, I felt every sting. I knew their last thoughts. I felt them die."

The horror of that was unspeakable. I shivered and stroked his hair.

"At first I was glad to be rid of it. I never wanted to feel that way again, and I knew it was safer to be like everyone else. But after a while... it's hard, not knowing what people are thinking. Maybe it's wrong to miss it—to miss knowing things I had no right to know in the first place—but I do."

"It's not wrong. You were never wrong. You were just different," I said, and kissed him. "This doesn't change anything for us."

"Good," he said. "Good. I'm so glad. It was killing me to keep that from you. I wish I'd had the courage to tell you before, but I didn't."

If I'd met Arav before his encounter with the medusa, he might have known my secret. I wouldn't have had the choice of whether to tell him the truth. I could have told him right then, as he had chosen to tell me. But Arav wasn't a Lacemaker. He didn't take memories from people. His hands weren't a danger.

His hands were already traveling down my body again. Then we were kissing instead of talking. The moment was gone. I hadn't told him.

Next time, I thought to myself. *Next time.*

There were many next times.

In retrospect, his parents must have known what we were doing. Still, we worried about them returning home and finding us, so we soon switched to going out in Arav's rowboat. He knew every little hidden cove in the coast, where the water was calm and the sand was soft. We carried on like that for weeks.

And then I came home one triad and my parents were waiting for me in the garden. The shift of the Honeycreeper had been called just as I left Breakneck Hill, so my parents should have been asleep. Yet I emerged from the bushes, brushing dead leaves from my hair, and there they were.

The first thing I noticed, even before their expressions, was that they were not wearing gloves. It was strange to see my own parents bare-handed.

It is possible for one Lacemaker to manipulate another, but it is extremely difficult. We have strong natural defenses against our own kind. Lacemakers often marry other Lacemakers, for many reasons, but one is that touch between us tends to be safe. It requires a great deal of power and control to create a hole in another Lacemaker's memory. It does not happen by accident.

My parents had not said a word, but I recognized the threat.

To this moment, I do not know if a gardener betrayed me, or if my parents put the pieces together on their own. Perhaps it is one last remnant of childish optimism that I prefer to believe I was discovered, rather than betrayed.

However my parents had found my secret, there might still be missing pieces. They might not know who Arav was. They might not know I was already ruined.

And because I had told no one—not even Arav—they could not possibly know how well I had trained myself in the use of my own power. They still thought of me as their inept, undisciplined child.

That was an advantage. I had learned, starting with the moment that Rossin Tyrenx tried to touch me, that appearing powerless can make one powerful.

"Please," I said. I did not have to fake desperation. "Don't hurt him."

"We won't, we won't," my mother promised.

My father's hard expression said otherwise.

"This happens sometimes," my mother said. "People make mistakes. It's fine. It hasn't gone too far yet. We just have to correct it. It won't hurt at all. Everything will be fine."

It had gone too far, by my own design. But they did not know that, and I did not intend to let them. Not yet.

"Both of you will be happier when this is over," my mother said in the kindest of tones. She took a step toward me, the silk of her tunic whispering against her knees. She looked soft and sophisticated in grey and lavender. "It will only take a moment. You won't feel a thing."

We tell each other that Lacemaking is painless, but this is only because no victim ever remembers the experience.

"We'll never see each other again, I promise. Don't take him from me," I begged.

"Your promises mean nothing," my father said. He did not bother to disguise his anger as concern or kindness. "How can we trust you? I will have his name!"

So they did not know. I could still protect Arav.

"Merat," my father said, addressing my mother. So she was the one who would take Arav from me. Was she stronger than my father? More skilled somehow? Or did my father ask her to do it because despite everything, he loved me too much to hurt me like that? How can I possibly credit such an unbelievable thought, after all these years? And yet the idea haunts me. The words appear on the page. A most unwelcome ghost.

I digress. Her given name was all the instruction my mother required. She raised her hands.

There are things even Lacemakers like to forget. Our craft is violent. It hurts to have your memory altered. It hurts more if you resist.

My mother cupped my face in her hands. From the outside, for anyone who did not know what we were, it must have looked like a gesture of comfort. A mother soothing her weeping daughter. The two of us were a matched set of beauties, pale and soft and golden-haired, dressed in delicate silks. A lovely veneer.

And an unspeakable violation underneath.

Tears sprang to my eyes as her fingertips touched my temples. My mother's touch was physically gentle but mentally vicious: the hard, sharp edge of a spade digging through my memory. I shrieked and sobbed and made no effort to restrain myself. I knew my father would hate it—even born and raised in Laalvur, he was Nalitzvan enough to despise any display of emotion as weakness. *Let him hate this*, I thought. *Let him suffer even a fraction of what I am suffering.*

My mother was looking for a name and a face in my memory, and she found one easily. I thought of Jai, the only other sailor who had survived the encounter with the giant medusa, the one who had lost his arm. Jai lived in the Marsh, not far from Arav's family, and we had met several times. It was wrong to set my parents on his trail, but I could not feel sorry for it. Even now, I know I would make the same choice. I had to sacrifice someone to save Arav. It would cost Jai only a moment of pain—instantly forgotten—to lose all his memories of me. When my parents found him, as they surely would, my little trick would become obvious. I hoped that my parents would see that Jai was innocent and leave him alone. I hoped they would save their real fury for me. More importantly, I hoped that by the time they discovered Arav's identity, I would have had a chance to warn him so he could leave the city.

You will note that I am writing of both Jai and Arav, evidence that my memory of both of them remains intact. My mother could not take anything from me. My practice had paid off. I had grown strong enough to withstand her. But the pain was real, and it was easy to pretend she had succeeded. I knew exactly the reaction to imitate: the blinking, wobbling daze that marks victims of our craft. It is exhausting, having one's memory altered. My fatigue was genuine.

My father did not wait for me to recover. He simply grabbed me by the arm and led me to my room. I went willingly, thinking all the while about how I could get word to Arav. Parneet or one of the other gardeners might be able to help me. I would have to be discreet.

My father shoved me toward my bed and left the room without a word.

I did not panic. Then, outside my door, I heard a bolt slide into place.

10

DOUBT IS PRAYER

A LIZHAN WAS A FIERY FUCKING reckless fool, and Ev was the twice-burned dope who kept following her into trouble.

The worst part was that Ev had never been so angry as when she'd realized that Alizhan was standing in the kitchen with some sword-wearing stranger, making plans to slip out of Ev's life forever.

Ev should have clonked Zenav on the back of the head at the first opportunity. But her father was always in her head saying *don't hurt anyone you don't have to* and Ev hadn't known what to do.

That instant of hesitation had won her a rope around her wrists and a long, silent walk back to Laalvur. Zenav was hovering behind the two of them, carrying Ev's staff. She couldn't say anything important to Alizhan in his hearing.

Not that she wanted to talk to Alizhan.

Zenav obviously didn't consider them worthy adversaries, these two young women who'd willingly made themselves his captives, as he'd only bothered to bind their hands and not their feet. Ev twisted her wrists, rubbing them against the rope. The binding wasn't painfully tight, but it was well knotted.

Zenav was using her staff as a walking stick. Would he use it in a fight? Or would he drop it and unsheathe his sword instead? If she got in close enough, he'd have to fight hand-to-hand. He was bigger than her, and more experienced.

Ev had overheard most of his conversation with Alizhan, so she understood that Mar had sent him. He was looking for Alizhan and the book. Alizhan's questionable plan seemed to involve stopping at the Temple of Doubt.

They entered the city walls in the foothills outside the cliffs of Dar. The guards let Zenav and his two prisoners pass. Just like that, Ev and Alizhan were back in the city. Ev had, at least, had the foresight to tuck her father's gifts into her pockets. Zenav hadn't bothered to search her.

From the outer walls, they climbed up into the hilly streets of a neighborhood called The Knuckles. Then they turned toward the coast, and Zenav marched them down the zigzagged street on the city-facing side of Dar.

Varenx House loomed above them at the tip of Dar. Ev looked down at the inlet of Denandar instead, at the Temples carved into the Dayward side of Denan, and still her skin prickled.

The Temple of the Balance, the wealthiest temple in the city, was high above the water on the light side of Denan. The Temple of Doubt, a newer and far less powerful organization, had ensconced itself two levels below, still on the more prestigious Dayward side of the inlet, but at much greater risk of destruction by wave. Zenav herded Ev and Alizhan across a narrow wooden bridge high above the water. Alizhan wobbled on her feet. She was sweating. Their walk hadn't agreed with her, and Ev knew from Alizhan's memories that crowds never did.

What did Mar ha-Solora want with them? Were Ev and Alizhan going to end up in a cell in the bowels of Solor House? Did Mar intend to move against Iriyat? How could he, if she could erase memories with a touch? How could anyone? Perhaps Ev would end up in a cell in Varenx House instead. A cheery thought.

Or maybe Iriyat would touch her and make her forget all of this. Even better. Iriyat would put Alizhan back to work, most likely, and nobody would ever know what was in that book. And if they never found Kasrik, would anyone remember him?

The bridge creaked under Ev's foot, startling her out of her worries. When she looked up to step carefully off the bridge and into the crowded stone street, there was a pair of eyes watching them.

A tall, solidly built man dressed in grey. His curly salt-and-pepper beard was neatly trimmed to show off the hard line of his jaw. He wore a sword. This man might be the one from Alizhan's memory, Iriyat's head guard. Vatik. Ev was able to notice physical traits that Alizhan missed: the scar through the outer edge of his left brow, the pale blue of his mismatched right eye, and the grim set of his mouth. Ev had never felt so hated, and Vatik wasn't even looking at her. His stare was all for Alizhan.

Vatik kept his hair short and wore no rings or earrings. Nothing to grab. His grey clothing was loose enough for easy movement but not so billowing that it would trip him in a fight. What could Ev do against a man like that, who wore a sword with such practiced ease? Zenav still had her staff.

"Alizhan," Ev hissed. Zenav was listening, but she couldn't let the moment pass without saying something.

Alizhan glanced at her. She looked a little unfocused, maybe even ill. It must be the crowd affecting her.

There was an idea. Could Ev just... *think* the words and not say them? But she'd asked Alizhan not to peek inside her head. "We're being watched," Ev said quietly.

"By about fifty people," Alizhan said, not bothering to whisper. "I can hear them all."

Ev pressed her lips together and raised her eyebrows, then tilted her head in Vatik's direction. He was weaving through the crowd, his pace leisurely, but he was clearly keeping an eye on the three of them.

Alizhan looked in that direction, puzzled. She was probably on the verge of protesting again that *everyone* was watching them, so how could she possibly single out anyone?

"Oh," Alizhan said. She stopped so suddenly that Zenav almost ran into her back. He grunted at her to quit gawking and keep moving.

So much for discretion. Now they were even more conspicuous than before.

Alizhan's realization couldn't have come from scanning the people on the street, since she was staring into the distance as usual. She must be examining someone's mind.

"That's Vatik," Alizhan said, confirming Ev's suspicions.

"He's watching us, right?"

"Zenav," Alizhan said, addressing their captor and not deigning to answer Ev's question. "Remember how I said there were some people looking for me?"

"You mean to tell me they're here," Zenav said. They stopped in front of the columned facade of the temple. He gestured for Alizhan and Ev to go through the door. "No one draws a blade in a temple. If they're still here when we come out, I'll take care of it."

Zenav would be more evenly matched with Vatik than Ev. His hands weren't bound, for one. Both men had swords. Zenav was smaller and younger, but he might be more agile.

Ev didn't want to be anyone's prisoner, but given the choice, she'd take Solor House over Varenx House. As far as she knew, Mar ha-Solora couldn't touch her and make her forget her own name.

With that reassuring thought, she crossed the temple's threshold.

The oldest structures in Laalvur were built into caves in the cliffs. The caves had been expanded and smoothed through human effort. Because the rooms of the temple followed the shape of the original cave, the ceiling of the entrance arched high above their heads. Even with the sunlight streaming through the door, it still felt dark and cavernous. The eerie effect was, if not entirely deliberate on the part of the Temple of Doubt, then certainly desired.

Ev had never set foot inside before. Her father's suspicion of authority encompassed religion as well as politics. Papa might not have been impressed by the enormous entrance hall, but Ev was.

The hall was bustling. People came to make inquiries of every kind, since the priests devoted their lives to the knowledge of all subjects. The edges of the hall were occupied by a series of desks separated with wooden partitions. At each desk sat a black-robed priest, face marked with a stripe of kohl from temple to temple, symbolizing both their fallibility and the darkness that obscured their quest for truth. The makeup was meant to remind everyone of the difficulty of knowing anything for sure, and to keep the priests humble in their eternal education, but Ev could remember Obin muttering many times that no makeup could do that.

Each priest was surrounded by stacks of books and papers, working in the soft green glow of a lamp. Under the murmur of conversation in the room, if Ev listened, she could hear the rustle of feathers when the priests shuffled in their robes.

There was an uneasy truce between the Temple of Doubt

and the Temple of the Balance. The division between them wasn't a difference of religion, but a difference of perspective. All things, including doubt, were contained in God's Balance. Most people on both sides of the division acknowledged that. But priests of the Balance often wondered aloud if it was necessary to dedicate a whole *temple* to doubt. Those who dedicated themselves to doubt thought so, and furthermore, they thought it was foolish to worship God's Balance without being able to understand or explain it. Doubt, they said, guided them in their quest for truth. Studying God's Balance was one way to worship it.

Ev, Alizhan, and Zenav were ushered to a back corner. The priest in front of them glowered at their unwelcome interruption to his work, but when he realized that two of the three people in front of his desk had their hands bound behind their backs, he granted them his full attention.

Zenav dumped the book on the table. "These two tell me there's some kind of hidden information in this book."

The priest was frowning. Zenav's cavalier handling of the book must have displeased him. Although given the deep creases in his bearded face, frowning was his habitual expression.

"My name is Ivardas," the priest said. His tone was a rebuke for something, but whether it was Zenav's handling of the book, his failure to introduce himself, or the three of them disrupting Ivardas's research, Ev couldn't tell. Perhaps his name itself was supposed to impress them, but it meant nothing to her.

He examined the spine and cover of the book, and then opened it carefully, scrutinizing the edges of the pages, the flyleaf and the inside cover. He flipped through all of it, noticed the handwritten notes in the back, and lingered on them.

Ivardas handled the book with practiced expertise. Rumor had it that all the other rooms beyond the entrance hall were filled with books. The Temple also possessed a printing press for the distribution of pamphlets and new books, if any of the priests happened to overcome their doubts long enough to write such things.

A Natural History of the World was exactly the sort of treatise that an initiate might produce to win the right to wear those trailing feathered robes. The study of waves, quakes, and eruptions was of particular interest to priests of Doubt. These disasters, supposedly a natural part of God's Balance, shook the world at its foundations and made it seem very Unbalanced indeed.

Ev didn't have time for these grand questions. She was her father's daughter, a practical girl. The sight of Vatik watching them in the street had given her an idea. Perhaps she could set Vatik and Zenav against each other, and escape from both of them. She was only concerned with one thing: could she and Alizhan get free?

Alizhan had agreed to come back to the city as Zenav's prisoner, but Ev couldn't believe she intended to remain that way. Alizhan hadn't gone to Solor House for help last triad. She'd hidden in Mar's bushes for a whole shift, waiting for a sign of Kasrik, not daring to approach Mar.

When Alizhan had needed help, she'd come to Ev.

Ev was with her now, and they were going to get away.

Zenav was still standing behind Ev and Alizhan, but his attention was on Ivardas. Stretching her fingers painfully far, Ev examined her bonds again. Could they be loosened? She might not have another opportunity.

"What kind of information?" Ivardas asked Zenav.

"We don't know."

Ivardas flipped back through the pages. "What are these strange blue smudges?"

"What smudges?" Alizhan said, and Zenav glared at her for speaking up and ruining the illusion that he was in charge.

In the lamplight from Ivardas's desk, faint coloring was visible over the black print. The paper was marbled with ghostly streaks. It didn't look like writing.

"That wasn't there before," Alizhan whispered, as if she hadn't been able to keep the thought private but wasn't ready to say it at full volume.

"That looks like some kind of washed-out stain," Zenav said. "Not like writing."

"If you leave this book with me, I could examine it more closely," Ivardas offered. They'd intrigued him, and now that he found them worthy of his time, his demeanor improved.

"No," Zenav and Alizhan said immediately.

Ivardas gave them a sour look.

"We were hoping you could help us figure out why this particular copy of the book might be worth stealing," Ev said, hoping to soothe Ivardas with flattery. She needed the conversation to keep going. She couldn't undo the knot in the rope, or slip her hands free. The rope would have to be cut. "Since you know so much more about books than we do. Does that list of dates mean anything to you?"

"What do I know?" Ivardas murmured. It was a refrain so common at the Temple of Doubt that it had been carved on the inside lintel. The outside lintel said *DOUBT IS PRAYER*.

Priests of Doubt were meant to remain humble and eternally skeptical of their own knowledge. Still, they were human, and not immune to compliments. Mollified, Ivardas read the list of dates again. "It is simply a list of events—quakes and things. All public knowledge. Nothing secret. This information can be found in any copy of this book."

In addition to the *Natural History* volume, lying open, there were three stacks of books on the desk. A few loose pages. A quill. An inkwell. A glass lamp filled with bioluminescent fluid. Could Ev use any of that? She looked again. Those pages. They were letters. A more careful scan of the desk revealed a carved wooden handle sticking out from under one of them.

A letter opener. It had to be. Not as good as a knife, but it would do. How could she get it into her hands?

"And the rest?" Alizhan pressed. "Do you have another copy of this volume, for comparison? Or maybe something stands out as unusual?"

"Do I look like Prince Ilyr?" Ivardas snapped. "I am a scholar, not a magician. I will need time to solve this puzzle. Perhaps if you left the book with me."

Alizhan shook her head vigorously.

"In that case, I suggest you read it yourself," he said. "That is the first step with most books."

Alizhan looked so mutinous that if her hands hadn't been bound, she might have hauled back and slapped him. In an effort to redirect the conversation, Ev put aside her own embarrassment at such an ignorant question and said, "Who's Prince Ilyr?"

To her surprise, it was Zenav who answered. "The prince in Nalitzva—you know, the only man to ever come back from the islands alive? He learned their impossible islander language, too. Supposed to be some kind of genius. People say he can read any language, even one he's never seen before."

Ivardas snorted derisively, and then said, "But what do I know?"

"Well, I never met the man. But I guess I don't know much either." Zenav laughed humorlessly. "Maybe I'll join the Temple. Become a Doubter like you."

Ivardas didn't welcome this suggestion or the nickname that accompanied it. For a man who'd devoted his life to the fallibility of human knowledge, he placed a lot of value on formal titles.

"He stayed at Varenx House about three years ago," Alizhan said, though neither man took notice of her. Then, in a louder voice, she asked Ivardas, "You think it's impossible for someone to read a language they've never seen before?"

"Who am I to say what is possible or impossible?" Ivardas said. Ev supposed they should've expected that answer. He closed the book, brushing his thumbs over his fingers and then wiping his hands on his robe. "I cannot be certain. But I must remain skeptical of such a rumor. If Prince Ilyr did possess such an ability, he would be marked for death in his own city. Belief in magic is strong in Nalitzva—and the punishments for those who possess it are swift and fatal."

As Ivardas continued speaking, Ev craned her head to get a better look around the temple. She needed a diversion. Enough time to get the letter opener into her hands and saw at her bindings until she was free. She had no idea what she would do after that. She couldn't fight both Zenav and Vatik. Could she outrun them? Would she need a head start? What would Alizhan do? Would Ivardas get involved? What about the other people in the entrance hall? One step at a time.

There were people asking questions of the other priests, going about the usual business of the temple. Ev wondered if all the priests were so cranky, and all the answers so unsatisfying. Her gaze traveled the length of the room one more time, and then she sucked in a breath.

Vatik was lurking by the door, watching.

Ev said and did nothing. Zenav was behind her, still holding her staff, and Alizhan was to her left. Alizhan's body language indicated that she was paying attention to Ivardas. She hadn't fidgeted once since Ev had caught sight of Vatik.

Unusual. Deliberate, perhaps. Was it a sign? Ev hoped so.

Ev looked directly at Vatik, then glanced at Ivardas's desk, with its stacks of books, its tall column of illuminated glass, and its little wooden-handled letter opener lying half-hidden under a piece of paper. She thought very, very clearly about what needed to happen next.

"Ilyr's reputation as a scholar is more likely the result of careful, continuous effort and study," Ivardas was saying. "Common rumor has elevated his intellect to something supernatural. A dangerous risk, for the prince. He is popular for now, but public opinion could easily turn against him."

"Earlier, you said 'for those who possess it' about magic," Alizhan said. "You believe?"

"I observe."

"Have you ever heard of someone being able to erase memories with a touch?"

Ev didn't need Alizhan's senses to see that this line of inquiry surprised and troubled Zenav.

"There are all sorts of magic rumored to exist, and there is very little proof of any of it," Ivardas said. He paused for a long time, weighing his words. "Some rumors strike me as more plausible than others."

"And?"

"That is one of them."

There was a silence, and just when it seemed the conversation might be over, Alizhan gasped. Ev followed her stare toward the temple entrance. Vatik was no longer silhouetted in the light of the doorway. He was marching toward them.

"Zenav!" Ev said. He needed no more prompting to stride toward Vatik.

Two large, armed men walking toward each other in a crowded public space was enough to alarm anyone. Visitors scattered, and a few priests rushed forward, hiking up their

black robes. The low murmur of conversation heated into argument. A promising beginning, but not enough.

But Vatik's hand was on his sword hilt. Ev twisted toward the
nascent conflict, pitched her voice high, and yelled, "That man is
about to draw a blade in the temple!"

And then Vatik obliged her by doing just that. His sword
flashed in the darkness as he struck at Zenav.

"How dare he," Ivardas said with a quiet rage that made Ev
shiver. His voice pierced through the roar of priests crying blas-
phemy at Vatik and onlookers screaming and scrambling to get
out of the temple. "He will pay for this." Then he stood up and
strode into the fray, and his steady walk belied the deep wrinkles
on his face.

Zenav stepped away from Vatik's first few strikes, dodging
and dancing out of range, his hands raised. He hadn't drawn his
own blade yet, reluctant to commit such a taboo act. From his
movements, she guessed he was trying to talk his way out. But
Vatik advanced until Zenav was backed against a wall. The
crowd encroached on all sides. Zenav was forced to unsheathe
his sword to defend himself. A shriek of metal on metal sliced
through the noise.

She cringed. This was a sacred space. People might get hurt.
She hadn't been the one to draw a weapon, but Ev couldn't
escape the feeling she'd played a role in the transgression.

Black-robed priests were trying to force their way closer so
they could separate Vatik and Zenav. The crowd obscured the
fight, the two men caught in a knot of bodies, shouts and shoves
drowning out the scrape of swords. There was no time to watch.
Ev needed this moment to execute her plan.

Alizhan collided with Ev's back. With their hands bound,
they were unable to right themselves, and they both stumbled,
banging their hips into the desk.

Ev put just enough weight on the edge of the desk that the

whole thing tipped toward her. The glass lamp fell to the floor and smashed, leaking fluid everywhere. Papers fluttered. The letter opener slid into her cupped hands.

There was such commotion that hardly anyone noticed them knocking over the desk. Alizhan stood close behind Ev, shielding her hands from view while Ev sawed at her bonds.

Chaos consumed the hall. Were Zenav and Vatik still fighting? Had they been driven into the street? That didn't matter yet. One thing at a time.

The rope parted. Ev's hands were free.

Alizhan was already in position, holding her wrists out behind her back. Ev cut her bonds with the letter-opener—so much for not drawing a blade in the temple. Alizhan grabbed the book off the table.

There were a hundred people between them and the door, pushing and shoving and trying to spill out into the street. How could they get through? And even if they could, would Zenav and Vatik be waiting?

Before Ev could even shape the words *we need another way out*, Alizhan's gloved hand was grabbing hers and they were dashing away from the grand entrance and toward the back of the room. Alizhan pulled Ev through room after room full of bookshelves and writing desks. No wrong turns. No missed steps. She was as quick and as sure as if she'd spent her whole life there. They skidded over stone floors and shoved past shocked priests and servants. Then Alizhan yanked Ev's arm and veered into a narrow spiral staircase cut into the stone, and they went down into a kitchen, a cellar, and out into an alley.

The angle of the light was different. They were in the shade now. They'd crossed all the way through the cliff and come out on the other side of Denan, and below them was Arishdenan Harbor.

Ev took quick, shallow breaths. They weren't safe yet. They

needed to move. Ev turned to ask Alizhan some unformed question—either *how did you do that* or *what next*—and was struck by the bright red trail of blood leaking from Alizhan's nose. She was shivering and sweating, one shoulder pressed into the wall for support.

Ev reached forward, intending to wipe up some of the blood with her sleeve, and Alizhan collapsed into her arms.

11

HONEYCREEPER SHIFT, 2ND TRIAD OF PYER, 761

ORGIVE THIS INCURSION OF THE present into my
story, but it is important. His Royal Highness Prince Ilyr of
Nalitzva is traveling the world, and his journey has brought him
to Laalvur. Supposedly, the Prince does not travel as a diplo-
matic representative of the crown—does anyone really believe
this?—but for his own education. He is preceded by his reputation as a brilliant scholar.

Naturally, I played hostess.

You remember these events, no doubt, but I record the fullness of my observations so that you might compare them with
your own.

Ilyr is barely twenty-two years old, golden and lovely, and
exactly as well-mannered and charismatic as one hopes a prince
will be. Nalitzvans love portraits and statues, and most princes
compare poorly with theirs, but Ilyr transcends his. His jaw
could easily have been carved from marble. He is athletically
gifted, an excellent rider and dancer, curious about the world
and passionate about establishing a lasting peace between our
two cities. An idealist. A sweet young thing.

There are some good qualities that I have left out of the

above list, and a fearsome intellect is one. Ilyr is not by any means stupid. I enjoyed our talks very much. He does have a passable grasp of Laalvuri. But left to ourselves, we conversed mostly in Nalitzvan, as I was more comfortable in his language than he was in mine. He had much to tell me of his travels to Estva and Adappyr, and I was eager to learn his impressions of our city as compared to his own.

You will probably find this knowledge distasteful, but I write so that you may understand my methods as well as my purpose. So I will divulge that I welcomed Ilyr into my home with the intention of using him. A connection to Nalitzvan royalty could serve me in so many of my endeavors, but one in particular, which I am sure you will come to understand as I describe my encounter with the prince and finish telling my story.

Were I not so publicly committed to my faith and modesty, I would have ordered the most revealing gown imaginable for our meeting. But as I have made quite a show of my devotion, I had to exercise some restraint in that respect. Low necklines, high hemlines, slits and tight fits, these things were all out of the question. Still, it was a stunning ensemble, as my tailor is worth double her considerable weight in gold: a slippery-soft silk in lustrous red, opulently draped to flow over my figure. Nothing was revealed, and yet much was suggested.

I went without a face veil, and I left my hair uncovered as well. Even a modest woman may do so in the privacy of her own home, among friends, and there was no more precious accoutrement for my dress than the burnished gold of my hair, that rare color that is a sure sign of Nalitzvan ancestry. Mine may be the youngest of the four Houses, but the prince had chosen to accept my hospitality rather than theirs.

The prince is blond, and I had heard rumors that his betrothed shared this quality, so I thought it might be a preference of his. Uncovering my hair would signal our closeness before I even began. These preparations are half the battle. Happily, it is not usually necessary for me to sleep with men to get what I want from them. Suggestion suffices.

Such conquests, if they even deserve that name, are predictable. Surprises are a rare pleasure for me. Ilyr was a pleasure indeed. A young man obviously and utterly immune to my charms. I welcomed the challenge.

Everything became clear on the second triad of his visit, when I hosted the heads of the other three Houses, Mar ha-Solora, Sideran ha-Katavi, and Ezatur ha-Garatsina, their families, and a handful of other notable citizens at a party. Ha-Solora is, of course, a beautiful man—how it pains me to give that condescending brute any credit at all—and Ilyr did a poor job of hiding his interest.

You declined to tell me Ilyr's secret on the first triad of his visit. I think perhaps you took a liking to him and wanted to help. You are admirably kindhearted, my little shade-blooming flower, but protecting Ilyr will require more than one person's silence, and his secret is so plainly observable that it hardly deserves the name. I did not need your help to discover it, and neither will many others.

Nalitzva is not an easy place to live for those with his inclinations, and I pity him. If he is ever to accomplish anything as king, he will need to learn to disguise his desires.

Once I knew what he wanted, the matter was simple. I had to distract that fat old boor Ezatur, and the insufferable chatterer Sideran, both of whom had cornered the prince with their hopelessly unsubtle machinations. Ezatur was talking about his insipid daughters, as though the prince might be persuaded to throw aside his life-long betrothal for dull girls who can barely string together two thoughts. Sideran was rather obviously harboring the even more futile design of sleeping with him herself. Even if Ilyr had been attracted to women, Sideran is as unpleasant in personality as she is beautiful. Her late husband thought he could accept that compromise, but I am quite sure she talked him to death.

Ezatur and Sideran sorely tested the prince's diplomacy, and I let them go on for a time just to see how long he could keep smiling. But I am not unduly cruel, and I did intervene.

"Ezatur, doesn't Sideran look lovely this shift?"

Trapped by good manners, he had to agree.

"Oh, well," Sideran started, turning her attention toward him. "I don't know, this tunic doesn't fit me quite as well as it should, and I told my tailor..." She continued, and Ezatur did his best to look interested.

"Let me get you a glass of wine, Your Highness," I said, offering a hand to Ilyr, which he accepted gratefully. He slipped out of the corner, and I led him to the balcony, where we would be able to have a more intimate conversation. Mar was already seated in one of the chairs, drinking alone, as I knew he would be. He avoids social gatherings unless there are beautiful and charming women to chat with. If Mar has noticed that I am the only such woman present at my own parties, he has never mentioned it.

I gestured to the chair next to Mar's, and then picked up the glass pitcher of honey-colored wine from the low table so I could pour Ilyr a glass. "This comes from some vineyards I own, near our western border with Hapir," I said. I oversaw breeding of the varietal myself, but I could not mention that; my interest in cultivating new plants was a sin against God's Balance. The Temple remains unaware of it, but it pleases me to share the secret here. I digress. Hapiri wine is sweet, delicious if you like that sort of thing, but its most useful quality is that its flavor disguises its strength.

Ilyr had not yet taken his seat. He was standing and staring at the view of the sun suspended over the glittering ocean. I was glad he appreciated it, since I was dressed to match in red and gold.

"The sun is so much higher in the sky here," he said. "The light is so much warmer than in Nalitzva."

"So are the people, if you listen to stories," Mar said.

"Oh, but how can that be true, when His Highness has been nothing but warm and generous since his arrival?"

"You flatter me," Ilyr said.

And how easy it is. I sat down on the couch that was positioned opposite their chairs, with the table between us. I poured myself a glass of wine to sip, but left the dishes of olives, almonds, bread, thornfruit, and pink *jiyar* slices untouched. I needed to focus.

I moved some pillows so I could partially recline on my side, folding my knees and spreading my skirts just so. The effect might have been lost on Ilyr, but at least Mar was there to enjoy it.

Once the three of us were comfortably ensconced in conversation, I pressed Ilyr on the subject of his travels.

"It is quite impressive, this mission of yours," I said. "What a pity that you will be unable to explore the hidden cultures of our world. Wouldn't that be daring, and noble, to bring to light something truly unknown?"

"The islands?" Mar said, understanding immediately. He is sharp. Not as sharp as he thinks he is; just sharp enough that I can depend on him to serve my purpose without fully understanding what is afoot. "Are you mad?"

"But think," I said. "Who better to finally breach their deadly waters than a charming royal diplomat, promising a peaceful exchange of knowledge?"

"Perhaps you could," Mar said, addressing Ilyr contemplatively. He was reluctant to admit my point, but equally reluctant to offend the prince. "Still, it would be almost impossible. You'd have a hell of a time finding a willing crew. It's suicide to sail anywhere near the islands."

"But imagine what gifts you could bring to the world if you succeeded," I said. "And I am ever so interested in the culture of the islands, since they keep themselves isolated. They say—well, it would not be proper to speak of it."

"We all know what they say about the islands," Mar said.

"You'll have to excuse me," Ilyr said. "I'm not sure that I do."

As I suspected. His royal education had left out certain subjects. "They say," I began. I looked away for a moment and managed to conjure the daintiest of blushes. "They say the islanders do not always wear clothes. And they say—they say—"

"Women lie with women," Mar supplied, growing tired of my hesitations. "And men with men."

"Oh," Ilyr said. I paused for a moment to see if he would continue, to say *what* or *why* or *how strange* but he said nothing at all. His face stilled into an expressionless mask.

"It happens here, too, of course," Mar said blithely. "But not in the open. Supposedly the islanders see nothing wrong with women lying together, or a man lying with two women, and so on. It is a subject of much speculation in—well, certain books." Mar cleared his throat. He looked uncomfortable at mentioning pornography in front of the prince and me, which I relished, but I wore my most naive and uncomprehending expression. Ilyr was wide-eyed as well, but I suspect his surprise was genuine. At twenty-two years old, even having grown up in strictest Nalitzva in the shelter of the royal palace, Ilyr had doubtless encountered *certain books*; he just did not expect foreign leaders to bring them up at parties.

Mar continued quickly, "But of course, we don't know that for sure, just like we don't know anything else about them, because they slaughter anyone who gets too close. They see nothing wrong with *that*, either."

"Perhaps they do, though," I said, shifting our conversation from sex to violence. There was no need to linger. That work was done. "Perhaps they regret it, but they have some reason to mistrust us. We can never know unless someone brokers a peace. Imagine how the world would change. Imagine what we could learn from them." I smiled at Ilyr. "Your bravery would be remembered forever. More wine?"

"It's a bold idea," Ilyr said. He held out his glass, and I poured. I don't recall him looking at me once during the conversation. It was perfect for planting the seed as unobtrusively as possible.

"The trade in medusa venom would be radically different," Mar mused. "Instead of going through one merchant in Laalvur who happens to have their blessing, we could trade with the islanders directly."

"Or perhaps," I said, "we could learn their secrets for hunting medusas and extracting their venom, and begin to do it ourselves. I am sure we could hunt far more than they do, since we know right now that demand far outstrips supply."

"You're right," Mar said with a laugh. "I always forget what a head you have for business."

Do you, now. I smiled prettily and said nothing.

"That would be the way to do it, though," Mar said. "Promise your crew riches beyond their imagining, and a place in history, and maybe you'd get somewhere."

"My crew would sail anywhere with me," Ilyr said, a bit stiffly. "They are not common mercenaries, but loyal servants of the crown."

"Of course, Your Highness," Mar said, in the same tone he might have used to say *sure, kid*. He does behave perfectly sometimes. He had taken up my cause by this point in the conversation, although knowing Mar, I have no doubt he assumed it was his own brilliant idea to persuade the young prince into doing him a service. "The real challenge would be finding a way in. Not merely surviving their attack, but winning their trust."

"How would you do it, if you were to attempt such a thing?" Ilyr asked.

"We know so little of the islanders, you would need to tread carefully," Mar said.

"Listen to them," I said. "First, before anything else, you must discover what *they* want. Once you know what a man wants, it is not so difficult to persuade him to do what you want instead." Oh, delicious irony. I control my expressions, but I had to lift my wine glass to my lips to prevent either of them from seeing my smile.

"I see," Ilyr said. "But you make it sound as though we'd be at odds, when really, they could benefit from this exchange as well. It would be an *exchange*, after all—I would offer them our knowledge and resources in return. That's only fair."

"I can tell you will be a just ruler, Your Highness," I said. "But this would be a most delicate matter. They obviously do not trust us. *If* you could get to the point of speaking with the islanders, rather than simply having them sink your ship, you would need to prove your good will to them."

"No one else has managed to get to that point in two hundred years," Mar pointed out.

"It is merely a thought experiment, my lord Ha-Solora," I said. "Do you not find His Highness gallant and charming enough to be the one who brings about this change?"

Mar cast a long, dark-eyed glance at Ilyr.

Ilyr, being so pale and blond, blushed a darling shade of pink at Mar's attention. He probably possessed the same endearing innocence in bed. Such sweetness is a weakness of mine—a weakness that I do not often feel. It was a pity that Ilyr would never enter my bed or Mar's.

But sex is a tawdry prize. The game offers far more lasting satisfaction.

"I do," Mar said. "But charm and gallantry will not save him from their cannons."

"*Temperance* will not be troubled by their cannons," Ilyr insisted.

In Laalvur, there is a rather whimsical custom of naming ships after lines from poems or songs. In Nalitzva, they frown on whimsy. They name their ships *Temperance* or *Chastity* instead. Perhaps it is because of his youth, but Ilyr struck me as less dour and rigid than some of his countrymen, which would serve him well in the islands.

"Well," I said, with some cheer to ease Ilyr's wounded pride. "In that case, I would advise you to speak only of your appreciation for their culture, your desire to live among them, and never mention trade. Do not speak of bringing our ways to the islands. They have gone to great pains to avoid contact with us."

"Good advice," Mar agreed. "A light touch is what's needed."

"I'm sure His Highness has a *very* light touch, my lord Ha-Solora," I said. "If you'll excuse me, I must see to the rest of my guests."

I stood carefully, attending to the fall of my skirts. Had Ilyr been interested in me, I might have let them flutter behind me in my exit, but instead I slipped out as unnoticeably as possible. Not that it mattered; he only had eyes for Mar.

And now that the seed is planted, I wait. Contact with the islanders would bear so many sweet fruits.

12

A DOG AND A WOLF

A LIZHAN WAS A LIMP WEIGHT in her arms. Ev carried her through the streets of Arishdenan, wending her way to the innermost point, the back of her neck prickling the whole time. She'd never felt more conspicuous in her life. They had to hide. Ev needed to get Alizhan somewhere safer.

Ev picked the inn with the fewest people gathered around its entrance. The paint had flaked off its faded sign, but between the image and the faint remains of lettering, Ev could see it was called The Anchor. The wooden door, dry and brittle, hung crooked on its hinges and groaned when she opened it.

"Too much to drink," the innkeeper said, surveying Alizhan and handing Ev the key to the room. He made a noise of disapproval. "Don't let her filth up my floors."

Thanks to its thick stone walls, the room was dark and silent and cool, and Alizhan began to breathe more steadily as soon as Ev laid her on the bed and closed the door. A moment later, her eyes opened.

"Should I leave?" Ev asked. "Would it be easier for you to be alone?"

Alizhan waved a hand in the air. Ev couldn't tell if she was being dismissed, or if her idea was. After a few deep breaths, she said, "Stay."

Alizhan lay on the bed in exactly the way she'd been laid there, as if rolling over or sitting up was beyond her powers. Ev tried to exist as quietly as possible, not moving or thinking or feeling anything in particular.

"You saved us," Ev said. "Thank you."

A long silence. There was only the sound of their breath to disturb it.

Then Alizhan scratched idly at her fingertips, rubbing them together. She was still wearing gloves. The gesture was familiar.

"Do your fingers itch?" Ev said. She didn't have time to ease into the question.

"You think it's from the book," Alizhan said immediately. Ev would never get used to having her questions answered before she'd asked them. Alizhan didn't move, but there was excitement in her voice. "You think there's something coating the pages that makes people's fingers itch."

"Ivardas was scratching his fingers after touching the pages," Ev said. "So was my father."

"I had my gloves off when I stole the book," Alizhan said. She pulled them off, lifted her hands above her face, and scrutinized her fingertips. She scratched at them again, and said, with surprising detachment, "Maybe it's poison."

"Maybe it's ink," Ev countered.

"What kind of ink gives people rashes?"

"Those blue smudges only showed up after you stashed the book in salt for a few hours. I think we need to put the book back in salt, let it sit, and see if those smudges get any easier to read."

"I guess the salt can't hurt," Alizhan said. "And it might work! And it's not like we're overflowing with better ideas."

"You don't really think whatever's on the pages is poison,

right?" Ev said, concerned. "Or maybe you think that's what's making you sick?"

Alizhan shook her head. "That's me. That's how I am. How I've always been."

"But we were in the city for half a shift before you got sick."

"If I really need to focus on something—getting away, finding a path through an unfamiliar place, touching someone —to survive, I can grit my teeth and do it. But I pay the price later. When we ran through the Temple, I ransacked the mind of every priest and servant in our way. It was too much. As for walking through the city, I can handle that for a while, some- times," Alizhan said. "If I focus."

"So that's what you were doing while we were walking to the Temple? Focusing? What about all those times you came to steal from me in the market?"

In answer, Alizhan lifted one shoulder and let it drop. When it became clear that Ev hadn't magically intuited the meaning of this gesture, she explained, "I was listening to you, mostly." And then she added, "You're my landmark. I can always find you. Focusing on you makes it easy to shut out other people. I don't think I could walk through the city at all if not for you."

Nothing had ever made Ev feel so naked, as if Alizhan could see right through her clothes and her skin to the rapid beat of her heart beneath it all.

Which, in a way, she could.

Ev tried not to think about Alizhan's fierce grip on her hand as they ran through the Temple, or how terrifying it had been to cradle Alizhan's unconscious body in her arms. Could they only touch if their lives were threatened? Would they ever be able to touch each other again?

"You're afraid again," Alizhan said. "You were afraid back at your house, too. And so angry."

"I was woken up mid-shift because a stranger with a sword

broke into my house. Being angry and afraid is a perfectly logical response."

"Yes," Alizhan said. "But I don't think you were afraid of him. You weren't afraid when those two men attacked us on the road —and Zenav was only one man. I don't think you were angry at him, either. You were angry at me."

Ev crossed her arms over her chest and said nothing. The gesture was one of irritation, but also one of protection: she wanted to cover herself. As if that would help. But Ev couldn't complain about Alizhan eavesdropping on her, not really, because otherwise they'd never have been able to get away from Zenav. And Alizhan had saved both their lives by finding a way out of the Temple, even if using her power had nearly killed her.

Still. Ev didn't have to like feeling so naked.

That was the last of their conversation for some time. The ensuing silence loomed over both of them until Alizhan curled up on the bed and squeezed her eyes shut. Ev went out for a walk.

WHEN EV RETURNED to the room hours later, lugging a bag of salt, Alizhan was sitting up on the bed, awake and acting as though nothing had happened.

"We need to find Kasrik," she said. "The salt is a good idea, too."

"Finding Kasrik is going to involve spending a lot of time lurking in the city," Ev said. What if he was already dead? Did they have any hope of discovering what had happened to him?

"I'm fine."

"Right." Ev split the bag of salt open at the top and packed the book inside. "You know Vatik will still be looking for you. Zenav, too."

"I can't stay hidden in this room forever."

"Who said anything about forever? Lie low for a few triads. Let me find Kasrik."

"How are you going to find him? You can't hear what people are thinking."

"I can see faces and walk through a crowd without collapsing, so I'll start there." Ev had only meant to point out the obvious, but Alizhan's silence said she'd gone too far. "It's dangerous for you," she continued, trying to defend herself. Walking into her kitchen to see Zenav looming over Alizhan with his hand casually resting on the hilt of his sword had sent a stab of fear through Ev's gut. How small she'd looked. How defenseless. Watching Alizhan waver and faint in the alley had been worse. At least Ev could do something about a man with a sword. Whatever sickness was seeping through Alizhan's body was beyond Ev's control.

She never wanted to feel that way again.

"I am small," Alizhan said. She was staring at the wall and her head was cocked. "But now seems like a good moment to remind you that my touch knocks people unconscious, so you don't have to think of me as *defenseless*."

As if Ev could possibly have forgotten that. As if Ev didn't think of that every time she looked at Alizhan's face, or the line of her neck, or the slender width of her hips. "Zenav's sword would have cut you open the same as anyone else."

"But it didn't, because I talked him into doing what I wanted! I'm not helpless, Ev. Stop acting like I'm fragile and useless," Alizhan said. Then, flatly, "Besides, you can't make me stay in this room. And if you don't like what I'm doing, you can leave."

"I just don't want you to get yourself killed!" How did that make her the villain? How could she and Alizhan work together so well in life-or-death situations, only to fall to bickering when it was just the two of them? Not even one full shift had passed since Ev had volunteered to have her wrists bound behind her back rather than risk never seeing Alizhan again.

Ev liked Alizhan. Alizhan was reckless and impulsive and deliberately difficult, of course, and she never followed Ev's rule about not peeking inside, not to mention that she was strange and intrusive and the cause of almost all of Ev's problems, but—

What, exactly? Why *did* she like Alizhan?

It had something to do with the way Alizhan looked at Ev. Not with her actual gaze, since that wandered aimlessly or fixated on nothing most of the time. Everyone else looked at Ev and wanted her to be someone she wasn't. Someone prettier. Someone more feminine. Someone who got in fewer fights. Someone who spent less time daydreaming about books.

Alizhan looked at Ev and saw *Ev*. Too much of Ev, sometimes. But Alizhan liked Ev for who she was, not for who she could be.

Ev owed it to Alizhan to treat her the same way. To let her be herself. Her frustrating, foolish self. But Alizhan was also funny and fearless. Cute, too. And she thought Ev was loyal and heroic and kind, and knowing that made Ev want to be those things.

Ev sighed. She didn't want to fight. "Please don't look for Kasrik by yourself."

"So we'll do it together, then."

"And you promise that if I sleep for a shift, you won't run off and get captured by Vatik or whoever else is after us?"

"As if they could catch me," Alizhan said. "But fine. We'll rest."

Ev nodded, and though sleep fell soft and heavy as soon as she laid her head down, she went to bed feeling lighter.

THEY DIDN'T FIND KASRIK.

What they did find, instead, was a buzz of conflicting rumors about what had happened in the Temple of Doubt. Pamphleteers were crying every possible headline in the street: a man had been murdered in the sanctuary; a riot had broken out; there had been a fight but no deaths; guards from some of the Great Houses were implicated; a guard from Solor House had broken the sacred law of the Temple and drawn his blade—

"That's not true!" Ev said under her breath, frustrated. "We *know* that's not true."

"They don't care," Alizhan said. "They're just trying to sell pamphlets. Most of them make things up wholesale. Lots of them are being paid by one Council member or another. Or sometimes a priest. Iriyat knows at least a dozen of them."

"What?" Ev cried. Obin had always said as much, but she hated to think it was true. Maybe the priests of Doubt were right: there was no way to know anything for sure. But no. She knew what she'd seen.

"A few of them are trying to tell what really happened," Alizhan reassured her. "Nobody's paying them to tell a particular story. They never get much attention, though, and they can be wrong, too."

"How can we find out if Vatik or Zenav survived that fight?" Ev would feel terrible if she'd gotten Zenav killed, even though deep down, she'd always known it was a possible consequence of her plan.

"I expect we'll see them again, if they lived," Alizhan said and shrugged.

Ev bought a few more pamphlets as they walked, anyway. None of them seemed to match the details she remembered from the events in the Temple. One of them contained an interview with a priest of the Balance sniffing that no such chaos had occurred in *his* temple. There was a portrait beside the article labeled with the name "Anavik"—a thin, bald man who looked like he had plenty more divisive and condescending comments waiting behind his pinched frown. Representations of people were a sin against God's Balance, so the priest had not consented to this caricature. Staring at the portrait made Ev uncomfortable. She wasn't devout, but it still felt wrong. Pamphleteers had no respect for rules, whether human or divine. And a small portrait of a man was nothing compared to the images available in other pamphlets. She sighed and kept moving.

"No one's paying that one," Alizhan said, indicating a pamphleteer. "He might still be a crackpot, though."

Ev bought his pamphlet and skimmed the text. "Look," she said, shoving it under Alizhan's nose. The article contained an interview with "A Priest" and there was a tiny printed portrait of a bearded man who was clearly Ivardas.

"I assume that's supposed to be Ivardas," Alizhan said, not looking at the paper.

"Oh," Ev said, embarrassed. A drawing of a face would mean nothing to Alizhan. She ought to know that by now. "Yes." And then, before Alizhan read her mind instead of the pamphlet, she said, "In this interview, Ivardas says nothing happened and it's all a big hoax. No one drew a blade in the Temple. He says, and I quote, 'I would be incensed if anyone had broken that taboo and I would be doing everything in my power to bring that person to justice.' But we were there. He *was* incensed."

"If he's not angry anymore..." Alizhan began.

"Someone made him forget," Ev finished.

No wonder it was so hard to find the truth in Laalvur. Iriyat was constantly erasing the facts.

Alizhan and Ev went out looking for Kasrik every few hours. Ev wanted to be strategic, to search different neighborhoods in an orderly manner, returning at different shifts in case Kasrik was keeping a different schedule. Alizhan wanted to lurk outside the Temple Street orphanage and listen to people's thoughts for as long as she could physically tolerate it. Ev didn't like loitering and watching sweat bead on Alizhan's temples. They were vulnerable and conspicuous. Every time Alizhan began to droop, Ev insisted they retreat back to the solitude of their room. Alizhan protested that this extreme caution was hindering their progress, but they wouldn't make any progress at all if she collapsed.

Their plan bore no results, but it was better for both of them to be doing something. At first, they'd pulled *A Natural History* out of its bag of salt every shift, but they soon switched to checking the book every triad. As the book's pages desiccated, the bluish ink darkened. Perhaps by the time they reconnected with Kasrik, the text would be readable.

Ev hoped that time would arrive soon. The longer they spent in one place, no matter how careful they were, the more likely it was that Iriyat would find them. Would she kill them? Make them forget?

Strangely, Alizhan seemed less troubled by Iriyat's absence from their lives than Kasrik's. Or at least, she mentioned Kasrik more often. "What if he's dead, Ev? What if this is all for nothing because Vatik already killed him and hid his body somewhere? Do you think Iriyat has had other people killed? And if Kasrik is dead, is it my fault?" she'd said. "He did call me a traitor."

"You can't betray people if you don't know they exist," Ev had replied, because she didn't know how to answer any of the other questions, and Alizhan had said nothing.

And then there was the comparatively simple problem of money. Ev slid a handful of coins across the bar in exchange for the tray of food she'd take back to eat in the room with Alizhan: two mugs of beer, a plate heaped with the spicy fried onion dumplings that Alizhan loved, and two pieces of soft flat bread wrapped around a mixture of lentils, potatoes, and fried cheese.

Not a leafy green in sight. Ev hadn't minded the tavern food the first time, or even the second, but it was wearing on her. And it was expensive. Her father's purse had struck her as a fortune, but it wouldn't last long if they kept living in a rented room and buying tavern food.

They'd arrived at The Anchor three triads ago. They had money for perhaps five more, depending on how much else they bought. Ev hated wasting her father's carefully saved money. She ought to be doing something grander with it than buying dumplings. What if they needed to bribe someone? What if they needed to buy bandages or medicine?

She pushed open the door to their room and found Alizhan seated cross-legged on the floor, gingerly turning the pages of *A Natural History* with her gloved fingers.

Ev sat down next to her and put the tray on the floor. It was that, or eat their meal in bed. They couldn't afford a room with chairs and tables.

"Dumplings!" Alizhan said, as if they were a treasured childhood favorite that she hadn't seen in years, rather than what she'd eaten for her last eight meals. She chucked her gloves onto the floor and dug in.

Ev ate her own food with considerably less excitement.

"You want one?" Alizhan proffered the dish of dumplings. This time, it had to be a joke.

"What are you going to do when I finally say yes?" Ev said. "If you keep asking me that question, eventually I will. Do you like me enough to share those?"

"I wouldn't ask the question if you were going to say yes," Alizhan said through a full mouth of food. She swallowed and licked her fingers. Then she pointed at Ev. "And some time, after I cheat everyone in that room out of all their palaad, I'll buy you all the raw leafy greens you want, you little rabbit."

Nobody had ever called Ev *little* or *rabbit*.

Alizhan teased her at every meal. Like many Laalvuri, they

were both vegetarians. But Ev liked her vegetables recognizable —still green, or even a little crunchy—and Alizhan preferred hers browned in butter, seasoned with the entire contents of a harborside spice warehouse, and hotter than the smoking crater at the peak of Adap.

"And fresh fruit," Alizhan continued. "I'm gonna win enough money to pay you back a whole lifetime of stolen thornfruit."

"Those were gifts."

This argument, like the teasing, happened at every meal. This fantasy of winning at cards was Alizhan's solution to Ev's concerns about money. Alizhan's first suggestion had been theft, which Ev had rejected. This second suggestion was hardly better. Alizhan had no idea how to play cards. She planned to learn from the other players—without asking. *You'll get caught cheating and get your ass kicked*, Ev always said. *You'd never let anyone do that*, Alizhan always responded, with utterly unjustified faith in Ev. Ev had to worry for both of them, since Alizhan never did.

"I'll buy you a new staff to replace the one that Zenav took," Alizhan said, in between shoving food into her mouth.

"That might be useful," Ev allowed.

"So you agree that I should go clean out the pockets of every card player in this tavern. Maybe the whole harbor."

"No," Ev said. "But I also don't see how else we're going to get any money, and we're no closer to finding Kasrik."

"I knew you'd come around eventually."

"By that logic, you should stop asking me if I want any dumplings."

Flush with victory, Alizhan laughed, and the crushing weight of the world lifted.

IT WAS the shift of the Honeycreeper. The call had rung out from the tower of the Temple of the Balance, bells ringing in imitation of birdsong, not long ago. No cities ever truly slept, and Laalvur was no exception, but some neighborhoods kept more of a schedule. Wealthy, fashionable Jewelbox residents preferred to work and play during Lyrebird and Rosefinch. Arishdenan Harbor was most crowded during Lyrebird and Honeycreeper. But it was never quiet. Ships arrived from Day and Night at all times, so people worked and drank and visited brothels during all three shifts. The taverns were always open. There were always card games.

Ev and Alizhan had been sharing a bed, catching a few hours of sleep here and there, trying to make sure their search for Kasrik was as thorough as possible. Sharing a bed with someone so beautiful might have sounded tantalizing to Ev in the past, but the reality was miserable. Ev woke from sleep with a stiff neck and shoulders from holding herself taut for hours, as though she could rein in her thoughts by controlling her body. A futile attempt—her dreams were full of brilliant, guilty color. Mostly the bronze of Alizhan's skin, the black of her hair, and the rose of her lips. Ev woke up mortified every time. But at least she got some sleep.

As far as Ev could tell, Alizhan rarely did. Ev was probably keeping her awake with those lurid dreams. How could she possibly fix that?

If something didn't change soon, Alizhan's restlessness would drive her to go out and cheat some sailors out of their hard-earned money without Ev at her back—if she didn't have an attack and fall unconscious on some tavern floor first.

So Ev had promised to accompany her to a tavern this shift.

Alizhan was vibrating with excitement. She was standing on the other side of the bed, facing away from Ev as she pulled her new tunic over her head. New clothes had been a necessary but painful expense. Alizhan's nosebleed had ruined her tunic when they'd first arrived at The Anchor, and bloodstains didn't fit into Ev's ideal, inconspicuous aesthetic.

Ev wrapped a length of fabric around her breasts. It was easier to move unnoticed through the city if people thought she was a man, so she'd stopped correcting people who made the mistake and started encouraging them instead. It had rankled at first, but it rankled more to be propositioned for sex, which happened when she was dressed as a woman.

Men and women's clothing in Laalvur differed mostly in color and in detail, not in cut. Most people wore loose tunics and trousers, and their sex was only evident if their shape could be distinguished under their clothes. Ev's disguise was minimal: loose clothing, short hair, and Alizhan by her side. People who saw the two of them together naturally assumed they were a couple. Since petite, long-haired Alizhan was obviously a woman, strangers tended to address Ev as a man.

No wonder Ajee hadn't wanted to marry her.

The thought no longer stung. It produced a dull ache, like poking an old bruise. Ev hadn't really wanted to marry him either. She'd been searching for something—a future, a purpose —and she'd mistaken Ajee for the answer.

Alizhan, still facing away from Ev, said, "You're much too pretty to be a man." Her hands continued their quick work of braiding her hair.

"You have no idea what my face looks like," Ev retorted, pulling her tunic over her head.

"Well, *I* don't know what your face looks like, but I know what everybody *else* thinks, and that's it. Besides, you wanted somebody to say it, so I said it."

"Stop peeking," Ev said, and they both knew she wasn't talking about nudity. "You don't think men can be pretty?"

"I wouldn't know," Alizhan said. Of course. It had been a silly question. "The whole concept is mysterious to me. A few of them are nice, I guess. I don't really know very many. But sometimes men in the street look at me and think obscene things as I pass by. Did you know that?"

"Unfortunately, they rarely keep those thoughts to themselves."

"That's most of what I know about sex," Alizhan said, painfully honest. "Well. Not just that. People think about it all the time. But I can't imagine it. There's so much *touching*."

That wasn't fear or disgust in Alizhan's voice. It was yearning. And yet she'd told Ev not to hope for anything.

Alizhan was still talking. "So sex never made sense to me—it seemed absurd and disgusting and sometimes terrifying—until I remembered kissing Ajee in the barn loft. That was nice. Until he was an asshole, I mean."

"Alizhan," Ev warned. It made Ev squirm to think of Alizhan possessing—experiencing—her most intimate memory. The worst part was that it wasn't an entirely unpleasant kind of squirming. Alizhan must already know that by now, too.

Ev changed the subject slightly. "And Ajee's not an asshole. He's in love with someone else. That's not his fault."

"I'm pretty sure it is," Alizhan said. It was surprising, but sort of sweet, that she had taken Ev's side so fiercely on the subject. "You still like men, though," she added, obviously intrigued by the idea. "You think they're pretty, or whatever word you want to use. Attractive. Beautiful."

Ev tried desperately to avoid thinking about who, exactly, was beautiful. But she was confronted with the sight of Alizhan ten thousand times a shift. It didn't matter how careful Ev was. Alizhan knew. She'd always known. Mercifully, for whatever reason—Alizhan rarely respected Ev's request not to talk about Ev as if she were an open book—she'd refrained from commenting on that particular subject.

But lately, it came up all the time.

Ev hadn't done anything to encourage strangers in thinking that Alizhan was her lover. She never touched Alizhan in public or in private. But Ev wasn't oblivious. *Alizhan* was encouraging strangers' perceptions: leaning in close when they were together in public, smiling at her, laughing too much, sighing dreamily, biting her lip, tucking her hair behind her ear.

Because Alizhan wasn't especially good at appearing natural even when she wasn't acting, the whole performance had an over-the-top, cheap-street-theater quality to it that made Ev uncomfortable. Alizhan knew that, as she knew everything, but Ev never asked her to stop, and she never offered. It was a useful lie.

Ev said nothing else on the subject of attraction, and Alizhan let it drop. They left their room, passing the empty, shabby common room at The Anchor. Even if it had been lively with card players, they wouldn't have played there, just in case Alizhan got caught cheating. After they'd walked up the street and Alizhan had examined each place they passed, she finally selected a tavern that struck Ev as identical to all the others: dirty, noisy, packed. It was called The Red and Black, and the sign hanging outside was carved and painted to look like a pair of playing cards, the Ten of Suns and the Ten of Smoke. Whatever it was called, this tavern was just as likely to make Alizhan sick as all the others, which meant Ev didn't like any of them.

Alizhan treated her symptoms and fits far more cavalierly than Ev ever could. This, Ev reflected sourly, was because Alizhan had never had to witness herself collapse. Her pupils got huge and her breath hitched and she crumpled instantly, as though her body had been held up by an invisible force that suddenly had winked out of existence. It was hard not to think of that invisible force as *life*, and the collapse as a kind of death.

No matter how Ev explained it to herself, it was fiery awful to watch.

Alizhan was undeterred. She had to work hard to keep her composure in rooms full of people, but she insisted on accompanying Ev anyway. If Alizhan was focusing on Ev's thoughts and feelings in order to block out everyone else's, as was her habit, she'd stopped mentioning it. Ev preferred it that way.

Ev bought them both beers and then ensconced herself at a table with a good view of the card games, where she planned to stay and glower at anyone who approached for the rest of their time here. "Don't piss anyone off too badly. Act natural."

"Of course," Alizhan said, even though they both knew she had no idea how to do that. They both expected this adventure to end in total catastrophe. The difference was that Ev was resigned, while Alizhan was exhilarated. "I'll listen for mentions of Kasrik, or the fight in the Temple of Doubt, or Varenx House or Solor House."

"I'm sure you'll make lots of friends."

"Don't be grouchy," Alizhan said. "Ev?"

"Yeah?"

"You have to give me some money so I can buy in. I think that's how it works, anyway."

Ev handed Alizhan some coins, giving her a pointed look she undoubtedly couldn't see.

ALIZHAN SAT down at the table without being invited. As long as she had a task, she'd be fine. She could focus on a few select people and ignore the rest of the bar. No panicking, no getting sick, no nosebleeds, no fainting, no fits.

The old man across the table from her grunted, "It's ten."

Alizhan dropped ten kalap on the pile of money in the

middle of the table, and they clinked against the other coins. The pile was mostly the brown metal of kalap, dull and tinged with green, since betting hadn't gone high enough yet for anyone to put in a shiny white palaad.

The dealer dealt her a hand. Alizhan studied her five cards as if they meant something to her, although they didn't. Iriyat liked card games, as she liked all games, and she'd mentioned once that Nalitzvan cards included jacks, queens, and kings. Proper Laalvuri cards used only numbers. The suits were the same in both cities: two drawn in red and black, Sun and Smoke, and two drawn in white and black, Snow and Stars. This particular deck had an intricate green pattern curlicued all over the back of each card.

Alizhan's cards were mostly Smoke: Two, Four, Five. The illustration of black smoke wound, calligraphy-style, across the red field of the card. She also had the Seven of Snow and the Ace of Stars, both with little white symbols picked against black backgrounds. She had a vague idea that the suits were ranked in worth: Sun was the most powerful, followed by Stars, then Smoke, then Snow. Other than that, she didn't know if there was anything of worth in her hand.

But Alizhan knew how the woman to the left of the dealer felt. She wanted to stay in the game. Her hand was strong—a Night and Day, meaning three Star cards and two Sun cards. The other men at the table were still sober enough that they'd fold quickly, and the wide-eyed little slip of a thing who'd just appeared at the table out of nowhere radiating foolishness couldn't possibly be a threat.

Alizhan, accustomed to encountering other people's brutally honest opinions of her, didn't react.

Night-and-Day was a stout woman wearing red and yellow with her grey-streaked black hair pulled into a tight, high bun. She dropped twenty kalap in the pot—a whole palaad's worth.

The bearded man to her left was assessing the rest of the table very carefully and thinking *face like a stone*. He smelled like stale sweat. Stoneface wasn't sure what to make of Alizhan yet, except he'd thought *shame about that gigantic nose* when he'd first looked at her. But he hadn't formed any opinion of her skill at cards. Like Night-and-Day, he wasn't impressed by the other men at the table. He liked the look of Night-and-Day, though, and might offer her a drink if the game didn't go too badly for either of them.

Stoneface had the Eight of Snow and the Eight of Stars. Not a terrible hand. But not as good as Night-and-Day's. He didn't behave as Night-and-Day predicted: he called her bet, dropping twenty kalap in the pot without hesitation.

To the left of Stoneface was another man. A sailor, although that was hardly a distinguishing feature in this tavern. Thin and worn out, but not as hairy and unkempt as Stoneface. He thought very clearly about his abysmal hand—a random assortment of low numbers, not enough matching values or suits— and then waved his hand and pushed his cards forward, still face down. He was folding.

Then it was Alizhan's turn. She didn't know the exact value of her own hand, but she knew she couldn't win against Night-and-Day. She folded. Ten kalap wasn't much of a loss.

To the left of Fold was a lanky man, probably also a sailor. Older than Alizhan, but young compared to the other players. His skin was the same deep, rich brown as Ev's, and his black hair was cropped short. Both his hands were branded between thumb and forefinger with the cross that marked him as an exile from Adappyr. Night-and-Day thought he was handsome, if irritatingly talkative. Until the moment that Alizhan focused on him, she'd thought of him as quiet, but then she realized her mistake. The man was vivacious, whistling and humming and chatting with the people at the table and other tavern patrons about nothing at all. She hadn't been listening to his voice.

But his mind was quiet.

It wasn't the seamless, eerie blankness of Iriyat or Kasrik. He radiated a happy warmth. But it felt very distant, and there was no buzz of thoughts beyond it. No stray secondary feelings.

Was blankness something people were born with, like height or hair color? Or was it a habit? A choice?

Was this man like Iriyat and Kasrik? Was he like Alizhan? Was she a blank person, too?

Alizhan wished she could read his face, since his mind was closed off. She couldn't tell if he was faking his cheer, or if his hand was genuinely good. He called the bet, and then said, "You know what? I'm feeling good this shift," and dropped in ten more copper coins.

Now it was the grey-haired dealer's turn. He shook his head and folded, leaving only Night-and-Day, Stoneface, and the blank man in play. The blank man started to whistle a vaguely familiar tune. Alizhan never knew the words to anything. Like most songs, it was probably about lost love. The melody was nice. Night-and-Day, on the other hand, thought *he's not hand-some enough to justify that nonsense*. Stoneface surprised Alizhan —he had a soft spot for the song, and the words came to his mind: *in golden Laalvur by the sea so low, my love lives high on a red stone hill, and there still the curling vines do grow.*

Night-and-Day called the bet. Stoneface folded. There were 150 kalap in the pot. That kind of money could buy Ev a new staff and keep them fed and sheltered for a couple of triads. Too bad Alizhan hadn't had the cards to win it. But she'd lost interest in the game. Her attention was on the whistler.

Night-and-Day flipped her cards. Three Stars, two Suns. The Adpri man fanned his out with a flourish. They were all red and all Suns: a Scorch. He had won.

Scorch took a little bow and then immediately took up whistling again, hooking his arm around the pile of money on the table to draw it closer. The rest of the players slid their cards toward the center and the grey-haired dealer collected them and began shuffling the deck. Night-and-Day was unhappy. Stone-face was downright suspicious. Apparently he'd seen Scorch win several very large pots.

Scorch said, "Buy you a drink if you want."

It took Alizhan a moment to realize he was speaking to her. What did he want? Impossible to tell. He felt the same as he had during the card game. Cheerful, but distant. Muted.

"You gotta remember to look at people's faces," Scorch said, very quietly, and that startled Alizhan even more.

"You *know*," she said. Her heart quickened. She'd never had a chance to talk to someone like herself. Iriyat had never shared anything with her, and Kasrik had called her a traitor and then run. But here was this man, standing here, who might be just like her. He might answer her questions. He might understand. Alizhan had never wanted anything more.

"One or two things, yeah." He shrugged. Then he said, "I think I want some air."

Alizhan searched the bar with her gaze. Ev was still at their old table. She'd watched the first round of poker with worry. Now she was regarding Scorch with suspicion and interest. He was probably Adpri, or Laalvuri and Adpri, like Ev.

Satisfied that Ev had seen her, Alizhan followed Scorch out the door. He walked just like he felt: an easy kind of saunter, not rushed, as if he was enjoying every step. They went around the tavern into a shaded alley, and he sat right down on the ground with his legs crossed. Alizhan sat next to him.

"This the first time you've been down here to cheat at cards?" Scorch asked. He sounded friendly enough. He took out a little pouch of dried dreamleaf, pinched some into a piece of paper, and rolled himself a cigarette. Alizhan liked the sweet, fragrant smoke, but when he offered it to her, she shook her head. She needed her concentration now, and she had enough trouble sleeping without smoking something that would give her strange dreams. Scorch lit the end with a match and began smoking the cigarette.

Alizhan didn't bother denying her intention to cheat. She didn't know if he could read her or not, but the lie didn't seem worth the effort. "Yeah."

She felt a swell of warmth and amusement from Scorch. "Lucky I was there to take those winnings, save you from getting your ass beat."

Ev would have saved her. She didn't need any strangers offering to do the same. But Alizhan had more important questions. "How are you *doing* that?" she interrupted.

"Playing cards? I think you know."

"No, the other thing. The thing where sometimes you're quiet and I can't read you at all, but sometimes a little bit slips through. Am I like that? Am I quiet?"

"As a little temple mouse," he said. "Our kind, we got natural shields. Thing about a shield is, you can lower it if you want to. Then again, sometimes you trip and your shield goes flying, does you no good at all." Scorch took another drag of his cigarette, holding it between two long, nimble fingers. Alizhan's stomach turned over.

"You're not wearing gloves."

"And you are," he said.

Was he purposefully slow at answering her? "Scorch," she prompted.

He laughed out loud. "Did you just call me 'Scorch'?"

"Well, I don't know your name and I can't read you."

"Nah, I like it," he said, still laughing. "My name's Djal, though, if you ever want to use it. Anyway, earlier I said you were quiet like a temple mouse, but that ain't it. Not exactly. See, you've been thinking we're the same. And we got something in common. I got just enough of this," Scorch paused to tap his temple with his ring finger, the cigarette still pinched between his middle finger and his index, "to be real unnatural good at cards.

"But I ain't got that hand magic. Nobody hurts if I touch 'em. I'm a little fluffy yip-yap lap dog. You, little sister," Scorch—Djal —turned to give her a big white smile that she had no idea how to interpret, "you're a wolf."

Alizhan frowned. She wasn't sure how to be a normal human being, one with a family and friends and a home and a life, and here Scorch was telling her that she was something else entirely. "What if I don't want to be a wolf? What if I'd rather be a temple mouse?"

"That ain't the kind of thing we get to choose," Djal said. "I don't know much about wolves, but I imagine they're smart enough that they only bite people they *want* to bite."

"That doesn't help. I keep hurting people. And myself. I need someone to teach me."

"I don't know that I'm the one for that, little sister, and I'm sorry for it. But I might know somebody who could, if you could come with me." He sighed. "I'm too Adpri to believe much in sin. But it's fiery close to sin, the way Laalvur and Nalitzva treat us. In Adappyr, we teach our children. *All* our children, not just the easy ones. This city does make me considerably richer, though. Nobody'd play cards against me in Adappyr."

Alizhan didn't know what to say to that. Djal seemed content to sit in the alley and fill the silence with smoke, but she had no way of knowing what he really wanted. It was awful, not knowing how people felt.

Maybe not as awful as the alternative.

"You're chewing your lip," Djal said. "Got something to say?"

"Wouldn't I say it if I did?"

Djal laughed. "I guess you would, then." He put out his cigarette. "We should go back in. Bet your girl's worried."

"She's always worried." He wasn't supposed to know Ev was a girl. Alizhan hadn't accounted for other mind-readers in her planning. That was beside the point. She still had questions. "Were you serious about knowing someone who could teach me?"

"I was."

"Can I see you again? Can you introduce me?"

"Maybe," he said. "I'm a sailor. I'm in town for eight more triads. We leave on the twelfth of Alaksha, at the call of the Rosefinch. You ask for Djal in any tavern in Arishdenan, they'll know me. They might spit on the ground, but they'll know me."

"That's not much time."

"Not enough for you to learn everything, but there's never enough time for that. It's better than nothing. Go find your girl."

"She's not my girl."

"Mm-hmm."

Djal walked her back to The Red and Black's door. When Alizhan found Ev, she was in the company of two angry men. An instant later, Alizhan recognized Zenav and Mar ha-Solora.

13

LYREBIRD SHIFT, 15TH TRIAD OF PYER, 761

L ET ME NOW RETURN TO describing the events that occurred sixteen years ago. It was the year 745, near the end of Alaksha, only a few weeks from the mid-year festival of Yahad.

None of that mattered to me at the time.

My parents, meticulous planners, had been through my room before locking me in it, and they had removed anything of use. The window was too high above the ground to provide an escape route. The servants who delivered my meals opened the door, slid in a tray, and shut the door. They never left enough food, but they never stayed long enough to hear me asking for more. No one spoke to me for triad after triad.

I slept. I lay awake worrying about Arav. I waited.

Eventually, something would change. Someone would slip up and enter my room. I would have a chance to talk my way out. I would alter memories if necessary.

Instead, my parents came.

The heavy door swung open, and suddenly the two of them were standing in my room. I was in my sleeping gown, barefoot and disheveled. My hair was uncombed and unbraided. Locked in, I'd had no reason to make myself presentable. I had not yet learned to greet my enemies wearing armor. Perhaps I did not yet fully understand that my parents were my enemies.

There was also the matter of my wardrobe. My clothes had begun to fit very snugly around the waist. My sleeping gown, as vulnerable as it left me feeling, was loose enough to conceal the curve of my belly—slight, for the moment, but noticeable.

For their part, my parents were wearing finery and expressions of grim satisfaction.

A cold bolt of certainty lanced through me. They had found Arav. They were here to gloat.

"You made him forget me," I said.

It was the logical thing for them to do. People ask questions about dead bodies. My parents, following a long tradition of Lacemakers, preferred not to leave traces. Still, as long as Arav was alive, I could live with myself. I might never be happy, but at least he had a chance.

And deep down in the soil of my heart, locked away from the light, there was a tiny seed of an idea: I could help him remember. I just had to get out of my parents' house and find him. If I could talk to him, if I could get him alone... We might have to run. We could do that. What did I have in Laalvur? Parents who imprisoned me in my own room? I would sail anywhere with him. Nalitzva, the islands, the wild lands beyond. And even if he never remembered, we could make new memories. We had fallen in love once. We could do it a second time.

As long as Arav was alive, anything was possible.

My parents were silent, and I kept that seed in the dark, far from my expression and my thoughts.

Then I realized my mistake.

"You remember him," my father said, surprise in his voice. He paused for a moment, and his struggle was evident on his face. I was stronger than he had expected, and he was pleased and relieved to know that I was not as useless as he had previously thought. But I was using my strength to defy him, and thus as disappointing as I had always been.

"Of course she does," my mother said. A smile slithered across her beautiful face. Her anger had always been cold. I had tricked her, and she would not forgive that easily. "She sent us on a chase after the wrong boy. An impressive maneuver, but not impressive enough."

"If you had ever listened, all of this could have been avoided. If you had ever practiced Lacemaking for any purpose other than being a lying slut, you would have seen early on that this marriage is a *gift*, not a punishment." My father sighed. "Rossin Tyrenx is not one of us. He could never make you do anything you did not want to."

"And if you had ever paid attention to what we taught you, you would have known how to cover your tracks," my mother said. "People all over the Marsh and Breakneck Hill had seen you with that boy."

"You think I should have erased the memories of everyone in the neighborhood?" It was so wrong—and so daunting in scale—that it had never even occurred to me. That much Lacemaking would be an enormous undertaking, invasive and fraught with risk. It would be exhausting and painful for everyone involved.

"Instead of putting everything we have worked for at risk? Yes."

"Still thinking small, I see," my father said. He sighed, and then addressed my mother. "As long as she remembers him, she can't be trusted outside of this room. Even once she forgets, we will have to watch her."

I trembled. They were going to touch me. I was afraid—if they worked in concert, they could overpower me—and I wanted them to know. Let my fear be visible. If either of them still harbored any affection for me, they should feel sick. What monsters would make their own child tremble in fear at their touch?

My hand almost strayed to my stomach at the thought: *I will not treat my child the way they treat me.* But I kept still. They could not know. I was increasingly certain that they could never know.

But if they thought I was afraid, perhaps they would under-estimate me yet again. What could it hurt to quiver a little?

Bells rang out from the city. The call was neither Lyrebird nor Honeycreeper nor Rosefinch. Of course not; it was not the hour of the shift change. It was a melody I had never heard, hardly a melody at all, but a frantic clanging. I thought that sound was my salvation—my parents froze. They exchanged panicked, blanched glances.

"All hells," my father swore.

"There hasn't been one in twenty years," my mother whispered.

"They don't ring the bells by mistake," my father said. "*The Hour* just docked. We have a goddamned fortune sitting in that harbor and it's going to get smashed to bits and then looted by those lower-city animals."

The Hour and Instant Our Eyes Did Meet was one of my father's ships. It had just arrived in Laalvur loaded down with Nalitzvan gold, having sold richly dyed and embroidered silks to the wealthy inhabitants of the Nightward coast. My parents thought the urgent bells were a warning about an incoming wave. I knew such a warning existed, but had not heard it in my lifetime. My mother was almost right: the last wave was nineteen years prior, in 726, the year before I was born.

"They'll be evacuating," my mother said. "You can't go down there, Orosk."

"Damn it." My father turned on his heel and strode out of

the room. My mother hurried after him, trying to talk him down. The door slammed behind them.

I waited for the sound of the bolt. And waited.

The door was open. There was no time for changing clothes. I slipped out of my room and ran down to the garden. The path I had so carefully worn through the bushes was overgrown, but I plowed through it. Thorns ripped at my hair and skin and dress, and I let them. I had to find Arav. I couldn't go back.

My chosen path into the city involved scrabbling up and down walls and darting through private gardens to avoid contact with guards from any of the Houses. It required me to be agile and furtive, but I had never encountered another person, so it was worth all the difficulty. I had launched myself halfway into someone's garden before I realized my bare feet were bleeding. It didn't matter. Arav would bandage my feet.

Two gardens later, I ran into someone climbing in the opposite direction. His head popped up over the wall and his eyes went wide. "You're going the wrong way," he said, panting. "There's a *wave* coming."

I saved my breath and jumped down into the garden. If citizens were overrunning gardens, the city must be in chaos. There was no point in taking a secret path. I made my way to the street.

A crush of people swarmed me, shoving each other to get uphill faster. I wove through the crowd. I was the only one heading down toward the sea.

I have always been small of stature, and it was difficult for me to see through the crowd. But when I did catch a glimpse of the lower city, I stopped so abruptly that I was nearly trampled.

The sea was *gone*.

It is a common expression among our people to refer to an impulsive fool as a *shell collector*. People hardly ever say the phrase, which is *shell collectors make bone offerings*. As a child, I never understood: were shells not a kind of bone? We do not normally make physical offerings at the Temple of the Balance, but in the old religion, people used to. Why not offer shells? Or bones, for that matter?

I did not grasp the truth of this expression for years, and when I did learn it, it was not from a dictionary or a learned priest of Doubt. The ocean taught me. I hope to God's Balance that it never teaches you.

Right before a wave comes, the sea draws back hundreds of feet from the shore. The newly uncovered red rocks and sparkling sand are a lure for Laalvuri who have not yet seen a wave. A forbidden mystery, exposed. There are always those who scramble down the slippery wet rocks to dig their toes into the sand or stroll farther out to gather perfect, unbroken seashells.

I saw them, those poor fools, before the sea came back.

"Came back" is no way to describe it at all. I thought, having read *A Natural History of the World* and its explanation of waves, that it would be a curling crest of water, a peak that folded back into itself and collapsed as it flowed toward the shore. Naively, I thought it might be beautiful.

Crushed together and sticky with sweat in the street, straining to move uphill through a solid mass of bodies, the crowd watched the ocean. I remember keeping my hands clenched in the fabric of my sleeping gown, my arms tight to my body, trying not to hurt anyone. As if it would have mattered. We would all have been lucky to forget that moment.

There is no verb that can describe the water's return, brutal and sudden. It was as if the rest of the world had moved. The sea was simply there again, where there had been land and air and no sea at all.

Unsatisfied with its former shoreline, the sea devoured the harbor and doused the lower levels of the city. Buildings flooded. The harbor splintered. Those poor shell collectors, invisible under the water, were dashed against the rocks. They made their bone offerings to whatever lived in that watery hell.

Broken planks bobbed to the surface.

I thought of Arav's family's little wooden house on stilts in the Marsh. All the little stilted wooden houses in the Marsh, so much driftwood now. Had they run uphill? Had they gotten away from the water in time?

And Arav. Arav.

The crowd, like a beast with a single mind, began to move uphill again. I wanted to go downhill, toward the water, toward the Marsh, toward Arav.

I didn't realize I was screaming until strangers put their hands on me and asked me to calm down. A couple of men helped me kneel and catch my breath, right there in the street, and the crowd flowed around us—gentler than water.

I must have looked hysterical. Unbalanced. Tangled hair. Scratched arms. Bloody feet. Streaks of dirt on my ripped gown.

Eventually, they moved me inside someone's empty home. It was out of the way of the crowd. I babbled about finding Arav's family.

I know, from reports, that the wave struck on the 28th Triad of Alaksha. I stayed in that house—abandoned by its owners, but occupied by a dozen new residents—for several triads after that. No one was ringing the shift-change bells. Camps formed in the upper city. The water receded from the lower city, but too many people had been displaced. Kind strangers brought me water and food. Everyone was searching for word of someone.

I was, in a way, lucky. Survivors from the Marsh drifted through the upper city, and one of them happened to be Eliyan, Arav's older sister. She heard that I was searching for Arav Matrishal, and she came to sit with me.

I started to cry before she said a word. Her bleak expression told me enough.

"*Shade* had just departed Laalvur when the wave hit," she said. "They were only a few hours out. Not far enough."

Eliyan had always been serious, but her tone was dead flat. A report in someone else's words, since she had not yet come up with her own. She did not say the rest: *there were no survivors. Arav is dead.* It was not necessary. No ship could have withstood that wave. I wanted to reach for her hand. I did not. I will never forget how she looked, standing there limned in loneliness and empty air, her own arms wrapped around her body. There was no one to touch her or comfort her. I tucked my bare hands into my lap with guilt, too horrorstruck to look at my own body.

Arav had promised me that he would stay in Laalvur, knowing there was a possibility that I might be pregnant. He had promised to stop working aboard *Shade* for a while. He had said he would search for work in the harbor, closer to home. Closer to me.

He should not have been on that ship.

He would never have been on that ship if my parents hadn't touched him. But they did, and now Arav was dead. It was my parents' fault. It was *my* fault. Arav was dead.

I never had the chance to tell him. *I never will*, I thought, and went from weeping to sobbing to heaving up what little I had eaten since the wave.

"I'm sorry," Eliyan said. "Whoever my brother was to you, it was obviously important. I wish he had introduced us."

I had nothing to say to that. Perhaps it was for the best that she did not remember me. I curled up on the ground in misery. Eliyan left at some point. Some time passed—an hour, a shift, a triad, a week, who can say—and I did not die. Then guards in Varenx livery found me in the city. They lifted my body off the floor and brought me back to my prison.

14

TEETH OUT

A LIZHAN PICKED THE WRONG MOMENT to walk out of the bar with a stranger. Zenav burst in right after she left, his left arm pushing the door open and his right arm cradled in a sling next to his body. So he was alive after all! Zenav was with a well-dressed, handsome man Ev could only assume was Mar ha-Solora.

Her suspicion was confirmed by the murmur that rippled through the tavern crowd. No one said anything outright, or even looked directly at him. This tavern was a place for drinking beer and playing cards, not gawking at the rich and powerful. Still, they noticed.

Ev had only ever seen Mar in Alizhan's memory, so the details of his face were new to her: the high, skeptical arch of his brows; the few short locks of black hair falling across his forehead, while the rest of it was tied in a single braid down his back; the neatly kept goatee with just a hint of silver.

A scarf of finely woven, lightweight burgundy wool was draped artfully over Mar's shoulders. The fabric was wrapped to show off its borders threaded with an intricate pattern in golden yellow. His tunic and trousers matched the scarf's rich color.

Laalvur was always the same warm temperature, so he wasn't dressed to protect himself against the cold. A man of Mar's looks could hardly be blamed for indulging in fashion—or vanity— but his clothes were more than that. They signaled his wealth and power, and they were enough to make everyone in the tavern keep both their distance and a careful watch.

Zenav, not blessed with Mar's strong jaw or proud nose, slouched next to him looking scruffy and angry, staring down at his wounded arm. What had happened in the Temple of the Balance after she and Alizhan had run?

Both of them stared at Ev like they'd found her at last, and neither was happy about it.

Understandable. She wasn't exactly delighted to see them, either. When would Alizhan come back inside? Ev didn't want to do this alone.

"What do you want?" she asked before they could start.

Mar spread his hands wide. "I mean you no harm."

Ev glared at Zenav and crossed her arms over her chest. "You sent one of your guards to break into my home while we were asleep."

"Your... friend stole something from me."

"She stole it *back*."

"That implies that she returned it to its original owner," Mar said, "and I don't believe she did." Ev opened her mouth to protest and Mar continued smoothly over whatever she might have said. "While intriguing, that fact is, of course, no concern of mine."

"What do you *want*, Mar?" Ev said. If he was shocked to hear his first name, it didn't show. But Ev still found satisfaction—and a little thrill—in disrespecting him.

If he took offense, Mar could order Zenav to unsheathe his sword and kill Ev on the spot. It wasn't exactly legal, but only the other Council members could try one of their own, and they were unlikely to care. If the incident ever came to their attention, Mar could argue that he was defending himself against slights to his honor, and that defense would be accepted. But the case would never advance even that far—there would be no witnesses to report it, despite the two dozen people in the tavern around them. They would all claim to be too drunk to remember the incident, and Ev would be too dead to argue.

Alizhan might kick him in the balls, though, if he killed her. Ev took some solace in this imaginary retribution for her hypothetical murder.

"If the answer is Alizhan, you can't have her. She doesn't belong to anyone but herself. We're not giving you the book, either."

"The little thief?" Mar asked. It hadn't occurred to Ev that he wouldn't know Alizhan's name. Alizhan was at the heart of everything. But to Mar, she was just a servant—a criminal one, at that. "Fine," he said tightly. "That's not why I came here."

Ev's gaze strayed to the doorway, where Alizhan was standing, flanked by her new friend. He was a long, graceful calligraphy stroke of a man. By his features—the rich, dark brown of his skin, the beautiful symmetry of his face, the fullness of his lips—he was Adpri, like Papa. She'd met so few Adpri in her life.

He leaned against the doorway for an instant, observing Mar and Zenav facing Ev. There was something in his steady brown gaze that reminded Ev of Alizhan, though he could hardly have held himself more differently. Then, as Ev watched, he said something inaudible to Alizhan and laid a hand on her shoulder.

Alizhan didn't flinch or cringe. She nodded, smiled to herself, and walked forward.

From across the room, the stranger's eyes met Ev's. There was a white flash of smile and a wink, and then he slid out of view.

Ev could hardly blame the man. Mar ha-Solora's presence in this tavern could only mean trouble.

Alizhan, of course, walked right up to him.

Before Mar could say anything else in answer to Ev's questions about why he was here, Alizhan broke in. "Mar wants our help because Kasrik is missing."

Mar directed his attention at her. "So he was telling the truth —Iriyat did keep one for herself. Why you, I wonder?" A moment's pause. "I've seen you before, and not just when you attacked me. I suppose you've been spying on me all these years."

"Yes."

Ev might have sidestepped the question, or at least couched her answer in some kind of justification or apology, but Alizhan did neither. Both the attack and her years of spying were facts.

Mar sighed and went to sit down at a table in the corner, as far from all the other occupied tables as possible. Zenav followed him, and she and Alizhan were supposed to do the same. Ev sat. Alizhan never really sat so much as she hovered. She twisted in her chair and bounced one knee up and down and then the other.

"You can't know that Kasrik was captured. Maybe he got tired of you not believing him and left," Alizhan said. She omitted that Kasrik might be dead.

"I see we hardly need to have a conversation at all," Mar said sourly. As if infected by Alizhan's restlessness, he drummed the fingers of his right hand on the worn wood of the tabletop. "You can just pluck it all from my thoughts. What delightful company you are."

"What makes you think Kasrik was captured?" Ev asked. She didn't want to play the role of placating the rich man with the armed guard, but Alizhan clearly wasn't going to. And Ev didn't want to be responsible for both of them getting killed. Somebody had to behave with a thimbleful of caution.

"Oh," Alizhan said. Her rigid posture softened, and she slouched in her chair. Her gaze flitted from one edge of the stone ceiling to another. She'd angled herself away from both of them in her fidgeting, but she was obviously addressing Mar. "You care about him."

Mar didn't look happy to have these words spoken aloud, and he continued as if they had never been said. He spoke to Ev, not Alizhan. "Why would Kasrik leave? The boy has nowhere better to go. There's a bed and plenty to eat in my house. I don't ask for anything in return. He's never been gone this long since he came to me."

"And you regret bringing him to Iriyat's notice," Alizhan said. "You feel guilty. And you don't like that I know that, but you shouldn't care. I'd much rather help you find Kasrik now that I know you feel some kind of fatherly affection for him. If I thought this was all about your personal, political gain, we'd be gone already."

Ev hoped to God's Balance that Alizhan was right about Mar. If it was true that he cared about Kasrik, and not just crushing a political rival, that was a good sign.

"But what makes you think we can help?" Ev asked.

"You got away from Zenav when you needed to," Mar said, and Zenav scowled at the tabletop. "And she successfully broke into Solor House. And if Iriyat is to blame for this, who would know better than her?"

Very quietly, Alizhan said, "Iriyat didn't want him captured."

At last, Mar gave her his full attention. "How do you know? Can you read her?"

Alizhan shook her head. "No one can read her. But stop thinking that she could still be innocent. Stop thinking this is all some terrible mistake. I know what I heard."

Mar regarded her in silence, and Ev had a sudden, strong memory of how his mind had felt to Alizhan when she'd been lurking outside his office: geometric, methodical, almost mechanical. He was fitting pieces together. "When did she give that order?"

"I wasn't supposed to be there. I stole the book and I just... I didn't know what to do. So I waited and listened."

"You robbed me on the twenty-eighth triad of Pyer. It's the fourth triad of Alaksha now." Mar paused to compose himself, and then said, "Kasrik is resourceful. He could easily hide for six triads. Anyone trying to kill him would have to find him. Did you give the book to her?"

"No. I haven't spoken to her since before I stole the book from you."

"And attacked me," Mar said. He probably brought it up because he expected an apology, but none came. He ended the ensuing silence himself. "If you never gave the book to Iriyat, she knows you're missing. She might think you suspect her."

"Or she might think something bad happened to me at Solor House," Alizhan said. "Although she wouldn't suspect that you'd resort to violence. She thinks you're soft."

Mar's eyes widened. "She thinks I'm what?"

Soft was not a word that anyone else in Laalvur was likely to apply to Mar ha-Solora. It wasn't just the broad shoulders and the massive fortune. Even here in this dingy tavern, seated and unarmed, he was a powerful presence. He held himself with authority.

One by one, his ideas about Iriyat were going up in smoke. The sweet, innocent woman of his dreams had smiled at him to reveal a mouth full of fangs.

"She thinks you're in power because you inherited it, and that you won't be ruthless enough to hold it if anyone ever provides you with a real challenge."

Mar laughed, or almost laughed. It was more of an incredulous huff. "Does she intend to provide that challenge?"

"I don't know. I don't know what she wants," Alizhan said, and then chewed her lip in thought. "Well, from what she said to me, she wanted the book back. But I think she also didn't want anyone to know that she wanted it back. And Kasrik knew too much."

"But now that the book is missing—and you along with it—capturing Kasrik could be a good source of information, and since he's an orphan, it lets her work in the shade," Mar said.

"So he might still be alive," Ev said.

Alizhan nodded. Then, for a fraction of an instant, her eyes met Mar's. "Kasrik said she hurts people like... us. He said she kills us."

"He said that to me, too. I don't know if it's true."

"But why—" Alizhan started, and the end of her question hung in the air. Ev had never seen her look so lost. "She told me I was the only one."

"She's always been very religious," Mar said, half-apologetically, as if he could soothe away Iriyat's behavior with explanations.

"Lots of people are religious," Alizhan protested.

"You're right. It doesn't make sense. All the more reason to find Kasrik and get that book decoded so we can get to the bottom of this."

"We," Ev repeated. Alizhan trusted Mar already, but Ev couldn't know his heart. She trusted Alizhan, but it was hard to switch instantly from thinking of Mar as an adversary.

"You're not seriously considering taking on Iriyat ha-Varensi by yourself," Mar said. "Everyone loves her. She's wealthy and powerful. Who will believe a crazy orphan and her foreign peasant friend who dresses like a boy?"

Mar wasn't making it any easier for Ev to like or trust him.

"I'm not foreign. I was born here and I've lived here my whole life."

"I know. But that won't matter if you accuse Iriyat of... what, exactly? Murder? Conspiracy?" Mar said. "She'll use everything she can against you. She'll blanket the city in pamphlets."

Alizhan cut in. "I don't think she will."

"Weren't you just trying to convince me she's ruthless?"

"She is. But you're thinking of what you would do, or what Ha-Garatsina and Ha-Katavi would do if someone publicly accused them. Iriyat is different. She won't have to do those things. Not yet, anyway. Her first plan will be to find us and touch us."

Mar had been keeping up a cool, steady front. He didn't like that Alizhan had more information than he did, and he definitely didn't like having his mind read. But his expression and tone had mostly remained neutral. For the second time in only a few minutes, his control slipped. "What?"

"Kasrik didn't know," Alizhan said. "I didn't either until I saw it. Iriyat can touch people and make them forget things."

Mar stared at her. Ev didn't need to have Alizhan's abilities to know what he was thinking. He'd known Iriyat for a long time. At some point in their years-long acquaintance, she must have touched him. "That's not possible."

"You believe Kasrik and I can read minds, but you won't believe this?"

Mar shook his head, then touched his fingers to his temple. "No, I know, you have a point, but..."

"I know," Alizhan said.

She didn't add *I loved her, too*, but perhaps Alizhan couldn't think of it in those terms. Ev, whose gut twisted every time she remembered Alizhan's memory, absolutely did. Iriyat might not have given birth to her, but she was the closest thing Alizhan had to a mother.

"The fight," Zenav said. It was the first time he'd participated in the conversation. "This is why Ivardas can't remember the fight in the Temple."

Mar nodded. "I thought he was just afraid of some kind of political retaliation. I thought he'd decided to stay out of things. But if he genuinely can't remember, this would explain it."

Zenav looked at Ev and Alizhan. "After you *left* me to fend for myself in the Temple, Vatik slashed my sword arm. Luckily, the crowd was pulling us apart by then, so he couldn't finish the job. But Ivardas saw the whole thing, and he was blazing mad. He knew I'd been defending myself, so he swore to me that he'd go after Vatik and bring him to justice for breaking the rule." Zenav sighed and shook his head. "But when I went back to the Temple a triad later, he didn't remember me at all. He told me to stop stirring up rumors."

"But a hundred people must have witnessed that fight!" Ev said.

"It doesn't matter," Mar said. "Rumors are easy to start and hard to stop. If you're right about Iriyat, she has an advantage in this arena, but it's possible to accomplish the same thing with money instead of magic. A few well-regarded, authoritative witnesses swearing that nothing happened, that's all it takes to make people doubt the account of any layperson who happened to be passing by at the time. There are so many different pamphlets on the subject now that no one knows what to believe. But it'll all be forgotten as soon as something else grabs the public's attention." He paused. "I'm sure the Doubters appreciate the irony that Iriyat has mastered spreading doubt so well that she can use it against them. Or they would, if they could remember."

"What a mess," Ev said with a sigh. She hadn't liked Ivardas, but she wouldn't wish this on anyone.

"We'll need even more evidence to take Iriyat down. We have to find all her secrets," Mar said.

"Oh."

Mar looked to Ev, as if she could translate this single syllable from Alizhan.

"It might be nothing," Alizhan said. "But I was one of Iriyat's secrets for a long time. And I think I know another. There's a… ghost. In Varenx House. A person locked in one of the upstairs rooms who never comes out. He—I think it's a man, but it's hard to tell—he's confused all the time, and angry."

"You don't know anything else about this person?"

"Iriyat keeps him alive but never talks about him. There are two or three servants who care for him and feed him and clean the room. They don't know anything about him. No one likes going up there."

"That's a secret, certainly," Mar said. "But I'm not sure where it gets us. Can this man speak?"

"I don't know," Alizhan said. "His mind is a jumble. He hardly remembers anything."

"Ah," Mar said.

"Iriyat must have done that to him," Ev said. "But why keep him alive?"

"She needs him for something," Alizhan said. "Iriyat doesn't keep people around unless they're useful to her." There was a lifetime of anxiety simmering under the lid of that statement.

"It doesn't matter," Mar said. "Whoever he is, he's not enough for us. We need proof. Something irrefutable. Something people can stare at. Something people can never forget."

"Like a written record that incriminates her somehow?" Ev asked.

"Or testimony from Kasrik, if he's alive," Alizhan said. "And me."

Could Alizhan stand in front of the Council and testify

without passing out? Ev bit her lip instead of voicing this concern, but the thought was already there. No matter. She would do whatever it took to make sure Alizhan got through.

Mar nodded. "But you and Kasrik aren't enough. One orphan won't do it, and neither will two. We need the whole orphanage. There must be other people involved—priests, Kasrik said. If we can find them and force them to testify, that'll help. If we can figure out what's in that book, even better."

"We'll find Kasrik," Alizhan said. "And the orphanage."

"Will you let me look at the book, or can I expect to be knocked unconscious for asking?"

"If we're going to work together, we're going to work *together*," Alizhan said.

"What does that mean?"

"I've examined your motives, and I think you're mostly doing this for the right reasons, but you still stand to benefit politically if Iriyat goes down. You can't just do this for yourself, or for yourself and one kid you happen to care about," Alizhan said. "This doesn't end with Iriyat. If we find that orphanage, and if there are children there—no matter how many, and no matter how damaged or strange they are—you're going to make sure they get taken care of. Then, after that, we change things in Laalvur."

"I'm so flattered to have been judged 'mostly good'," Mar deadpanned. "You know it will take more than a few words from me to change the whole city's attitude toward magic."

"I know."

"Well," he began.

"I don't need you to promise, or swear on God's Balance, or say anything at all," Alizhan said.

"I suppose you don't."

"I'll give you the book," she said. "You know I can get it back whenever I want."

Mar had learned, by this point, that his participation in the conversation wasn't necessary. His restrained, neutral expression was shadowed with unhappiness. At his side, Zenav was watching in astonishment.

"We need money, too," Alizhan said.

Mar simply nodded.

As they walked away from the table and into the street outside the tavern, with heavy pockets and new purpose, Alizhan said, "You want to know what Djal said to me." It wasn't a question.

"Djal? Is that the name of the man you were with earlier?"

Alizhan didn't even dignify this with a nod. He was the only possible answer. "He said 'get those teeth out, little wolf.'"

EV HAD ALMOST as many questions about Djal as worries about Mar, and that was saying something. Ev imagined dozens of improbable hypothetical scenarios—Mar was tricking Alizhan somehow, or still in love with Iriyat and bound to turn on them —to torture herself when she ought to be sleeping. Alizhan had her own troubles going to sleep. She didn't need anyone else's.

But that was her whole life. Everyone else's troubles in her head left no room for her own.

Alizhan didn't answer Ev's questions about Djal, because Ev didn't say any of them out loud.

They were perched on a low stone wall outside the Temple. Alizhan was eating thornfruit and dropping the rinds in the street, and Ev wasn't sighing out loud, but she *was* planning to pick up the rinds later and deposit them in a refuse heap like a decent person.

Alizhan could spend a lot longer out in the city when she focused on Ev. It was hard to focus on Ev *and* listen for any strangers' thoughts that might lead them to the orphanage. But

Alizhan couldn't admit out loud that they weren't making any progress, because Ev would drag her back to their room at the first sign of failure. Ev worried too much.

Alizhan dropped another rind on the ground. When Ev was annoyed, she had less time to think about how ill Alizhan looked.

With the tip of her sandal, Ev discreetly pushed the rind into a pile with all the others that Alizhan had dropped.

"You're adorable," Alizhan said, and popped another fruit into her mouth.

Ev didn't understand that at all—she thought Alizhan meant it as a joke—and Alizhan was about to explain when Djal strolled up the street whistling. He had his hands in his pockets and he paused next to them and leaned one shoulder against a column.

Alizhan said, "How did you find us?"

"I looked."

Ev didn't like his answer, but she did like the way he looked. Alizhan hadn't given his appearance much thought at their first meeting, since she'd been far more interested in what she couldn't see. But just like Alizhan was excited to meet another mind-reader, Ev was intrigued by the idea of meeting another Adpri.

It wasn't just Djal's skin that that she noticed. In particular, Ev's gaze was drawn to his arms, their impressive musculature bared by his red sleeveless shirt.

She also took in the narrow width of his waist, the breadth of his shoulders, the exposed hollow of his collarbone and the masculine line of his throat. Then Ev moved on to appreciating his face, and Alizhan was lost.

Bodies were less mysterious than faces, and she supposed that the appeal of Djal's was clear enough, but gawking was a waste of time. Ev should be thinking about their mission. And

Djal should leave them alone and go off to do whatever sailors did when they weren't at sea.

"Shouldn't you be cheating at cards?" Alizhan said.

"Well," Djal said. He didn't sound mad or surprised.

Was Alizhan even capable of hearing emotion in someone's voice if she couldn't read their mind? Being cut off from Djal's thoughts made her doubt herself. She dropped her last thorn-fruit rind on the ground and crossed her arms.

"That's not the sort of welcome I expected after our last conversation, little sister. I came to check on you."

"I'm fine."

"That friend I mentioned, she's just down the street, and I think she might be willing to teach you a thing or two, if you want."

"We're busy."

"What friend?" Ev interrupted. "What would she teach Alizhan? Who are you?"

"I'm sorry," Djal said. "It was rude of Alizhan not to introduce us." Okay. Maybe he did sound a little mad. "My name is Djal," he continued. Why did he suddenly sound so friendly? What was he thinking? It was awful, not knowing. Alizhan squinted at his face as if staring hard enough might makes his features give up all their secrets, but instead of transforming into intentions and desires, they remained eyes, lips, and teeth.

Djal had said hardly anything, but Alizhan harbored a fierce suspicion that he was flirting with Ev.

He was being respectful, unlike the men who talked to Alizhan in bars. And he was offering to help. There was no reason to be rude to him. And yet she couldn't shake the feeling that he'd interrupted her conversation with Ev, which he hadn't, and was intruding, which he wasn't. None of this should have ruffled her, which made her even more agitated, and this was all Djal's fault, and she wished he'd leave.

"Ev," Ev said, introducing herself, and inclined her head.

Djal did the same. Then he said, "And just down there is my friend, Mala." He pointed down the street. Following the direction of his gesture down into the crowd was useless, but Alizhan gathered from Ev's thoughts that he was pointing at a woman. "I think she'd like to meet you both."

"*Appri u go?*"

Alizhan didn't understand the words, but she could guess that Djal was asking if Ev spoke Adpri. The question embarrassed Ev, who shook her head and held up a hand with her index and thumb very close together. "*Fi.*"

"That's alright," Djal said. "You grew up here then?"

Ev nodded. There was a frisson of fear in her thoughts, a concern that Djal might ask why her father didn't live in Adappyr any more, and if he was a criminal like all the other exiles. But then Ev realized that Djal, probably an exile himself, would be sensitive about that topic, and she relaxed. Djal was Adpri. She'd had so few chances to meet her father's people. She had to take this one.

"That song you were whistling when you walked up," Ev said. She hummed a few bars softly, and then recited: "In golden Laalvur by the sea so low, my love lives high on a red stone hill, and there still the curling vines do grow."

Djal nodded.

"Is *Vines* your ship?"

"Well, I wouldn't say she's mine, exactly," Djal said. "There's a whole crew of us. Laalvuri, Adpri, Hapiri, Ndijan, even a couple from up Nightward. Why? Who wants to know?"

Ev's excitement spiked so suddenly that Alizhan had to suck in a breath. She resisted the urge to rub her aching temples. But before either of them could answer, a woman appeared at Djal's side. She was taller than Alizhan, but still short. Her round figure was wrapped in a bright blue-and-white printed dress, and she wore a scarf in matching fabric over her hair. She said something to Djal in Adpri, and he replied in kind.

Alizhan had no idea what either of them was saying or feeling. The woman had shields just like Djal. Was this how it felt to be other people? Completely cut off? She hated it.

Ev didn't know what was going on, either, so Alizhan couldn't rely on her. A whole city full of people thinking and feeling and wanting and needing at full volume, and Alizhan had managed to find two more she couldn't read. She didn't know what their faces looked like and she had no idea what words they were saying and their minds were *silent.*

In other circumstances, it might have been a relief. Right now, it was irritating.

Just to remind herself that she wasn't totally useless and isolated all the time, she scanned the crowd in the street. A rush of thoughts mobbed her—a man in a hurry to get down to Arishdenan, a woman worried for her sniffling child, a priest striding toward a house in Gold Street, and so many more—and Alizhan reeled. It was vertiginous, like peeking over the edge of a cliff and realizing just how far down the ocean was. Except heights never bothered Alizhan. But crowds did. Her heart gave a sickly flutter in her chest. She closed her eyes. She shouldn't have peeked.

A man going to the market. A sailor finally back at home. A man going to the Temple. A woman going to the Temple. A woman going to see her tailor. A man going to meet his lover. A priest, hiking up his robe, hurrying into the Temple.

When Alizhan had let go of her focus on Ev, she'd slipped over the cliff's edge. She was falling, and the ocean was rising up to meet her. People were all around her, and she would drown in them.

"Ye," someone said. Or something like "ye." A long, drawn-out syllable of distress. Had people been talking this whole time? It was so loud in Alizhan's head. "What's this?" Those words were in Laalvuri, but the accent was foreign. "This one is sick. She shouldn't be here."

A child marveling at her first sight of the city. A woman going to visit her mother. A boy looking for pockets to pick. A man prodding at his donkey to pull its cart faster. A woman feeling sick to her stomach. A woman pushing her way through the crowd to cross the bridge.

"I know." That was Ev talking. "She's very stubborn."

Something in the whirlpool of thoughts had flown past Alizhan. Something important. The thoughts kept swirling by— a girl grabbing her father's hand, an old man spitting on the cobblestones—and Alizhan tried to catch her breath and find the one she wanted. *A priest, hiking up his robe*—no, not that one. *A priest striding toward a house in Gold Street.*

Where was he now? Had he gone too far?

She didn't bother to open her eyes. Seeing him wouldn't help. It was his mind she needed to find, not his body. Gold Street. Gold Street. Why was he going up toward the Knuckles, instead of into the Temple? Surely he didn't live in such an expensive neighborhood. Was he making a house call?

There he was. Full of purpose and determination. Panting slightly as he went uphill. Thinking *that damn house full of Unbalanced little monsters.*

Alizhan's eyes flew open. There was something wet and warm running down her face. Then everything went dark.

ALIZHAN'S sudden nosebleed was only one of her symptoms. Her trembling had worsened. She looked dazed, dizzy, unsteady. Her eyes rolled. Her jaw clenched, and then her face spasmed.

Ev stepped forward just in time to catch her and keep her head from cracking against the stone as she fell.

"Smoke," Djal said. "Mala?"

His friend nodded, and motioned for Ev to hand Alizhan to her. Ev shook her head.

Mindful that touching Alizhan could make things worse, Ev laid her gently on the ground, clearing away the little pile of thornfruit rinds first. It was hard to step away. Alizhan's limbs jerked. Froth bubbled on her lips. Her eyes were open and white, circling wildly.

Mala sat down next to Alizhan immediately, and just as Ev said, "Don't touch—" Mala laid her branded hands on either side of Alizhan's face.

Alizhan's limbs stopped flailing. Her eyes closed. Gradually, she stilled.

"What are you doing," Ev said, too panicked to do anything but spit out her question as fast as possible.

Mala gave her a steady look. "Magic," she said, as though she was daring Ev to interrupt. She did not remove her hands from Alizhan's face. Alizhan would never let anyone touch her like that if she were conscious.

"Are you hurting her? She can't be touched, she—"

"I didn't hurt this girl," Mala said. "Whoever it was who didn't teach her how to cope with her gifts, they hurt her. And she can be touched. By me."

Djal put a hand on Ev's shoulder. "Mala's a healer. Mostly she does what all healers do. Cleans wounds, stitches 'em, sets bones. Always wants herbs for teas and tinctures when we stop in cities. But she's got that touch magic, same as Alizhan. When she lays hands on you, you feel better. Even if you didn't feel bad in the first place. It's something else."

"She can heal with a touch?"

Djal shook his head. "Nah. If a man's bleeding and she touches him, he'll keep bleeding. But he won't hurt so much."

"That's not like Alizhan at all, then."

"It's all hand magic," Djal said, and shrugged. "Mala's got more of a chance at teaching her to control it than any of us. And *somebody* has to, before the next attack does real damage. Or until she touches one of us and makes us go crazy."

"That's not what happens," Ev protested. "You just—see into her head, sort of."

"And it was all totally painless, mm?"

Ev had nothing to say to that.

"Besides, you only know what happened when *you* touched her," Djal corrected. "Think you might be a singular case."

Alizhan now looked like she was asleep. She didn't wake when Mala lifted her body from the ground, and she didn't even stir when handed to Djal.

Ev could have carried her. Watching someone else do it made her ache. To stop herself from reaching for Alizhan, she clenched her fists at her sides.

"Now," Mala said. "Where are we going?"

15

LYREBIRD SHIFT, 6TH TRIAD OF ALAKSHA, 761

HERE IS THE PART OF the story I am most loathe to tell. I do not regret anything but this: I awoke, groggy and naked and bruised, on the cool stone floor of some underground room in Varenx House, and as my dazed mind reassembled my fragmented memories, I concluded that my parents intended to kill me. *Fine*, I thought, *let them.*

I knew then as I know now that Orosk and Merat Varenx, the despicable monsters who raised me, killed Arav Matrishal. It will never be written in any court document or street pamphlet or official history, so let it be written here. They murdered him. They might not have called that wave from the deep themselves —the waves persist in keeping their secrets from me, but I will own them in time—but they killed him all the same.

They had killed Arav. Let them kill me, too.

I let my head loll back against the stone. I had been drugged, I think, or perhaps it was malnutrition. My head throbbed. Sick and starved and aching, I waited for some poor unlucky servant to enter the room and carry out the duty of ending my life. It seemed to me at the time that it would be a great relief to be rid of it. My parents would be doing me a service. What reason did I have to keep living, if Arav was dead?

And then I felt you move.

Just a flutter. But it was enough. You, the last remnant. The seed. Letting myself die would mean killing you, and I could not do that. I hated you for keeping me from joining Arav in death, but I loved you for keeping some part of him alive.

It was not a servant who came, but my parents themselves. They could not trust anyone else with the task. They were, of course, barehanded. I did not understand what they intended at first. My father was holding a length of stiff, thin metal wire with a curved end. His arm was hanging down at his side, nonchalant, as though he always went about his domestic business with such an object in hand. My mother cupped a steaming mug in both hands, as though she was bringing me a comforting cup of tea. My eyes watered at the sharp, cool scent of the steam. The fragrance was so overpowering that it took me a moment to recognize it, although the leaves had come from my own garden. A plant called *kalaprish*, so named because its round leaves look like kalap coins.

I had heard stories of desperate young women taking *kalaprish*. It is a toxic herb, and most of those stories ended with dead young women. But women still brewed tea from the leaves or took a few drops of its oil on their tongues. Other methods of ending a pregnancy were far riskier. Suddenly the length of wire in my father's hand made sense: a safeguard, in case they could not force me to drink the tea.

My parents did not want to kill me. They wanted to kill you.

They must have visited my cell while I was unconscious. They were clearly expecting me to be unresponsive. Perhaps they planned to tip my head back and pour the tea down my throat. It was not part of their plan for me to leap to my feet and launch myself at them, shrieking.

I don't remember a moment of decision. No one had said a word. Did my mother take a step forward? Did my father's slack grip on that wire tighten? Or was it my own realization that caused me to react? I do not know. I have never felt so much like an animal, naked and enraged. I flipped the mug into my mother's face, splashing her with hot tea. She screamed. The mug shattered against the wall behind her, shards clattering to the floor.

I lunged for the wire with one hand and I slapped the other against my father's temple. He tried to sidle away from my grip, but I pressed my thumb into his eye socket. My fingers scraped through his hair. He struggled, and then ceased struggling. I was only thinking of that poison, that wire, and how they meant to murder you before you even lived. How they had murdered Arav. I had no room left to think of practicing the delicate art of Lacemaking. I do not even know what I would have aimed to take from him. There was no direction. No precision. My touch was not a scythe but a fire. I swept through and left smoke and ashes, scorched and blackened ruination behind me.

I took everything from him, as he had taken everything from me.

It is possible for Lacemakers to kill with a touch. The body is so vulnerable. The lungs forget to breathe, the heart forgets to beat... I did not do that to my father, but it was a near thing. I do not know what stopped me. Some last remnant of sentiment. Or perhaps it was that he ought to have killed me, rather than leaving me alive to feel the rage and fury of grief. Perhaps what I did to him was crueler than the simple finality of death. I left him breathing, and little else.

He crumpled to the floor when I removed my hand from his face. Only a moment had passed. I was standing there, naked but for a thin sheen of sweat, with the metal wire in my hand. My mother was not even an arm's length away, blotting her red face with the hem of her tunic. She was crying—gasping raggedly, at least. It was hard to tell if she was producing any tears, given the state of her face. I doubt she felt any genuine sadness.

"You killed him."

At that moment, I was not entirely sure whether I had. Either way, I had no regrets. Out of breath, with my heart drumming in my chest, I remained on my feet and focused on her through the force of my anger. Words felt trivial and distant. Instead of saying anything, I reached for her. She put up no physical resistance. She put up no resistance of any kind, other than a very small, soft, "No." I ignored it, as she had ignored my wishes all my life.

She folded under my touch even faster than my father had.

I should have known, then, that she was using my own favored tactic against me: appearing weak and defeated in order to survive to win another fight. But it looked for all the world like I had just destroyed both of them and left their bodies prone on the cell floor, and it was all I could do to stumble into the hallway and call for help. Then I retched and collapsed.

I awoke in my own bed, with the green glow of lamplight all around and the welcome scent of all my potted plants coloring the air. Parneet was at my bedside, waiting. I did not know what shift it was and had no sense of how much time had passed.

"The other servants called me in when they found you," she said. She was sitting as she often did, with her elbows resting on her knees, which were spread at an unladylike width. She looked at a wall, feigning disinterest. Her greying hair was in a messy bun at the nape of her neck—I have no doubt she would have shaved her head if she thought my parents would have accepted it. The thought made me smile. What did it matter what they thought now?

There were streaks of dirt ground into the knees of her loose beige trousers. Even surrounded by death and destruction, Parneet was still herself: always in the garden, never dressing up for anyone, no matter how rich or powerful. It was so reassuring that I almost cried. But she would not have liked that, and I needed to save my tears for more politically expedient moments.

Parneet sniffed. "They seem to think I care for you."

"You would never be so foolish," I said, even as I was touched that she had waited for me to wake. Parneet might not have raised me, but I enjoyed her company more than I had ever enjoyed my mother's, and we had come to an understanding. It was an unspoken understanding, as Parneet preferred that most matters of importance, especially those adjacent to the marshy depths of sentiment, remain unspoken. That suited me. I changed the subject. "Are they dead?"

"They?" she said. "Your father has a pulse. He breathes. But he does not appear to see or hear anything around him. We sat him upright in one of the upper bedrooms."

"And my mother?"

"Was she in the cell, too?"

All Unbalanced hells. She was gone. I had no way of knowing what she remembered—everything, nothing, something? Had her collapse been a ruse? Why would she have run? Who could be sheltering her? She would resurface if I did not stop her. I had to think fast. The chaos of the city served me well in that.

"Listen, Parneet. Both of my parents died tragically in the wave."

Parneet gave me a hard stare, and for a moment I thought she would protest that my father was alive—or at least breathing—only a few rooms away. My mother was alive, too, for all we knew. But instead she merely said, without a trace of feeling, "How sad."

"I am heartbroken, but will assume my duties as the head of

Varenx House despite my grief," I continued. "There will, of course, be a period of mourning of several months, and I will not be able to go out in society. The other Houses will understand that I mean no disrespect by declining invitations and refusing visitors. My betrothal to Rossin Tyrenx will be broken immediately, as I cannot bear the thought of boarding a ship when the watery hell so recently claimed both of my beloved parents."

"Naturally."

"I need the names of everyone who knows about what happened." It would be necessary to determine who was loyal to my parents, and who could be persuaded to help me instead. Anyone who had seen me locked in the cell might be inclined to pity; I could work with that. Most urgently, I needed to find out who trusted me enough to help me hunt down my mother.

"You'll have them," she promised.

I paused. "Since it is now up to me to manage this household, I will need help. Perhaps you—"

"No," she said, and stood up. "I understand what you need to do, and I support you, but you need someone else for that. There is only one way that I like to get my hands dirty." She brushed her hands on her trousers, as if I hadn't already understood that she was talking about literal dirt.

"Of course," I said. And, skirting dangerously close to an admission of feeling, I added, "You know I am grateful for you."

"Wouldn't help you if you weren't," she said shortly, and left the room. This behavior would have been utterly unacceptable in other servants, but Parneet could do what she wanted and she knew it.

I dressed and got out of bed and went down to address the household that now belonged to me.

16

BAD HABITS

A LIZHAN WOKE IN WARM, STIFLING darkness, with the faint familiar scent of their room at The Anchor in her nostrils. She was in bed. Ev wasn't in the room. She shut her eyes. She wanted to dissolve back into the darkness, to shuck off awareness of her body—the ache in all her limbs, the piercing pain of being conscious—the way a snake shed its papery skin.

Even with her eyes closed, Alizhan knew that the woman who'd touched her was sitting on the floor, her gaze level with Alizhan's body, staring. Djal's friend felt a little like Djal—warm, but distant. Unreadable. But not blank like Iriyat.

"Ah, so that's what you want," she said. She spoke Laalvuri with an Adpri accent, slow and musical, lingering over her vowels.

And suddenly Alizhan was invited in. Inside, the woman wasn't like anyone else. She wasn't a crashing wave of thoughts and feelings, a thousand little awarenesses all at once, sloshing over some deeper pool of memories and intentions and beliefs. Her mind was calm and orderly.

My name is Mala.

Alizhan let out a little breath of laughter in surprise. It was so different to be welcomed, instead of breaking and entering. Although most people hardly guarded themselves at all. It wasn't breaking in if the door was swinging wide open. It wasn't trespassing if the residents dropped all their possessions out the window into the street outside.

Shh, Mala thought.

Alizhan had never encountered anyone who could hear *her*. Except maybe for that one time she'd touched Ev by accident, and then Ev had dreamed her memory. But that had been so painful. This was easy. Alizhan knew exactly what Mala wanted her to know: she'd had some sort of fit, and Mala had touched her to help her get through it, because Mala was *uheko* just like her, and now she was going to teach Alizhan to control her powers.

Out of habit, Alizhan went snooping. Where was Mala from? Was she an Adpri exile, like Ev's father? What did she do to get exiled? What secrets was she keeping? What did she want in life? Then she found herself gently shooed out of Mala's mind.

"What's *uheko*?" Alizhan said, opening her eyes. Even the tiny amount of light in the room made her squint. Getting invited to read Mala's mind had almost made her forget how much pain she was in.

"I'll show you if you give me your hand."

Alizhan regarded Mala's outstretched hand as if the older woman was holding a knife. With great caution, she reached for it. She let her own hand hover for a moment, trembling, and then Mala closed her fingers over it.

The pounding in Alizhan's head receded. Her bruises and aches calmed. Relaxed, she breathed deeply. The world went quiet. Alizhan couldn't remember feeling so safe or happy in her life.

"You said we were both *uheko*," Alizhan said, after a stretch of silence. Her voice was slow and sleepy. "This isn't what happens when I touch people. I can't do this."

"I can't read minds," Mala said. "*Uheko* is an islander word for touch-magic. We both have it."

"But your mind is so nice," Alizhan protested. *Nice* wasn't the word she meant to say, but she couldn't think of any other words, and she felt too good to care much.

Mala laughed. "Thank you, little sister."

Alizhan remembered something else important: a priest. Gold Street. *House full of Unbalanced little monsters.* "Ev," she said, too foggy to put the words in the right order. "Tell Ev. Kasrik. The priest. I have to go. I have to find—"

"You're not going anywhere," Mala said. "You've been killing yourself. Next time you collapse, you might not wake up."

Kasrik might die, too. He might already be dead. But it was hard to make her tongue move to say those words, and everything seemed far away, like it was happening to someone else. Was any of this real? Mala had both her hands wrapped around Alizhan's hand now. It didn't matter if this was real. It was good. Everything was so quiet. Alizhan was floating.

She liked Mala. Her mind was so neat. Nobody else had ever invited her in. But Alizhan had tried to go somewhere she hadn't been invited in Mala's mind. Was Mala angry? She didn't *feel* angry. But Alizhan couldn't tell what she felt. What had Djal said? Shields. He'd talked about shields. This was a time when a normal person would look at her face, but it was dark, and Alizhan could never tell the difference between a real smile and a fake one, and her eyelids were so heavy.

"We'll talk about this later," Mala promised. "You should rest."

Nothing had ever sounded like such a good idea.

THE NEXT TIME Alizhan woke up, she refused to let Mala touch her until she could see Ev. She sat straight up and crossed her arms over her chest, because that was what people did when they were feeling stubborn. Mala sighed and relented.

Ev arrived quickly. Djal came in, too, carrying a lamp. He stood next to Mala. Ev sat on the other side of Alizhan's bed.

"Before I collapsed, I found a priest who knew about the second orphanage," Alizhan said. "It's in Gold Street."

Ev must have told Djal and Mala some of the story, because they didn't ask any questions. "So I'll go to Gold Street," Ev said.

"It's a long street. You need my help to figure this out."

"Why don't you tell us what the priest looked like?" Djal said, and Alizhan gaped.

"You can recognize faces?"

Being a little fluffy yip-yap lap dog sounded better and better all the time. Djal could see people's faces and tell them apart. He could read their expressions. He could touch people and be touched without hurting anyone. But he could still look inside people if he wanted to. How come he had all of the good parts of Alizhan's life, and none of the bad?

"You can't?" Djal asked.

Alizhan just looked at him. At his indistinguishable eyes, nose, and mouth that Ev liked so much.

He nodded. "That must be hard."

"It never bothered me until I met people I couldn't read," Alizhan muttered. "Anyway, obviously I have to be the one to find this house. It's the only lead we have, and I'm the only person who can follow it."

"You're also the only one who's mortally endangered by leaving this room," Ev said, forcing a calm into her voice Alizhan knew she didn't really feel.

"I'm not going to die." Alizhan clenched her arms tighter. It was easier to say it than to believe it. Mala had sounded serious on that point.

"Give me some time," Mala said. "I'll teach you a few things to help you. Then you can go."

"We've already wasted too much time! Kasrik might be dead!"

"So might you, if you try that trick again," Mala said. "Ev and Djal will look for your friend. I will stay here and teach you some sense."

"Good luck with that," Ev murmured, and she didn't laugh, but Alizhan knew she wanted to. Did that make things better or worse?

Alizhan dropped her arms to her sides and let herself fall back into the pillows. It was the wrong move, because it made Ev feel sorry for her. Alizhan could feel the slow, cool drip of Ev's pity, and she hated it. Ev didn't usually think of her like that—a thing to be pitied—and it was too close to how everyone else saw her. An uncanny, uncivilized creature. A tragedy. A horror.

Even Djal and Mala, both of them just as Unbalanced as Alizhan, thought there was something wrong with her.

Djal spoke into the silence. "We'll be back soon."

———

"Why are you helping?" Ev asked as soon as she and Djal were outside The Anchor.

Djal blinked once, but her sharp tone wasn't enough to vanish his smile. "So suspicious, little sister," he said, and took one long-legged stride toward the street, as if they were both going to go along with this plan regardless of how he answered her question.

Ev didn't move.

"You were excited to meet me only a few hours ago," Djal

reminded her. "You want to know about Adappyr. You want to know about *Vines*. You especially want to know about your father."

Ev hadn't said one fiery word about her father, and she hated that Djal already knew all her secrets. Alizhan reading her thoughts had almost become tolerable, but this stranger was definitely not invited in.

"You want me to stay out, you'd better learn to keep me out," he said amiably. He didn't seem to be taking her concerns seriously at all. He hadn't made any attempt to answer her.

Wait. "I can learn to keep people out?"

"It astounds me what people here don't know," he observed. "You might not ever be able to keep *Alizhan* out. But you could probably learn to keep me out, most of the time. You could certainly learn to be a little quieter."

Ev relaxed a fraction. Someone who was out to get her wouldn't have told her that. "Alright," she said. "I'm still not going anywhere with you until I know more."

"There's more than one answer to your question. I don't like how this place treats people like me, and I like to help them when I can," Djal said.

So he wanted to help Alizhan. Ev could understand that— but of course, he would know exactly what Ev would find sympathetic. He could see into her head. "What are the other answers?"

"Your family," Djal said shortly.

"You know my father?" Ev said. She tried not to sound too eager or surprised, though the effort was futile around Djal. She'd thought he'd only mentioned her father a moment ago to needle her, to give her a nasty little reminder that he knew everything, but maybe she'd been wrong. Maybe Djal had mentioned her father for some other reason.

Ev's father had once been a sailor, but as long as she'd been alive, he'd worked on their farm. Djal was a few years younger than her father. It was unlikely he'd ever sailed with Obin.

"I know of him," Djal said.

"And that's enough for you to help me?" When other people mentioned that they knew about her father, it was usually people in Orzatvur implying that they knew he was a foreigner, an Adpri exile, likely a criminal. No one had ever said *I know about your father* and meant anything good by it. Until now.

"Not exactly. He told you about *Vines*, but he didn't tell you everything," Djal said. "It's not really my story to share. I hardly know it, anyway. Let's just say we have a friend in common."

That little bit of an answer was almost more frustrating than knowing nothing. She crossed her arms over her chest.

For some reason, that made Djal smile even wider. "Smoke, you look just like—well, anyway, it's delicate, you understand? None of us like to talk about why we left. I don't want to go telling other people's secrets. I'm sure you'll learn soon enough." He paused and smiled. "Oh, now I see you want to know what *I* did to get kicked out. Your head's loud, little sister. You got to work on that."

Ev didn't like any of that, but she supposed he'd given her as much of an answer as she was going to get. Alizhan trusted him. And he and Mala had saved Alizhan. There wasn't time to deliberate. He'd offered to help find the house in Gold Street, and they needed to go now. Ev took off, heading uphill.

It was a steep hike out of the inlet, and wherever possible, Ev took the shortcut ladders between streets. Djal followed her in silence. If she were like him or Alizhan, she'd know the character of that silence—was it companionable? Resentful? Scheming?

But if she were like them, there'd be no real silence in her life at all. The din of the streets would be doubled by the roar of thoughts underneath it all. Ev was glad not to hear that.

As they climbed farther from the sea and into the hills surrounding the city, the streets grew sparser, quieter, and less breathlessly steep. Ev had to slow her pace in the Knuckles, which was not as familiar to her as Arishdenan.

Luckily, the aptly named Gold Street was in a wealthy quarter of the city. The richer a neighborhood was, the more likely it was that the streets were marked with written signs. Poor neighborhoods had no signs, since Laalvur, as a city, was only semiliterate. Ev had heard many of her father's tirades about this sad state of affairs. In Adappyr, everyone could read.

"Everyone can eat, too," Djal said, "or at least, they could before things started to go wrong."

When Ev glanced over her shoulder, he smiled, spread his hands wide in apology, then pointed one finger at his temple. "This is what you meant about me being loud," she guessed.

"You're real easy to read. Always thinking and feeling a lot and never saying any of it."

"That's what everyone does."

Djal laughed. "Trust me. It's not."

"You think I could fix it?"

"I think you'd be quieter on the inside if you were louder on the outside," Djal said, with a shrug of one shoulder. Then he took off, heading up a street to their right, leaving her no choice but to follow.

"You don't even know where we're going."

"Sure I do," he said. "I'm in a city full of people who know their way around."

"When Alizhan tried to find us a way through the Temple of Doubt by reading everyone around her, she collapsed afterward."

"Are you worried about me, Miss Umarsad?" Djal said. "I'm touched."

Ev didn't bother to respond to that.

"Alizhan has no training, so she doesn't know when to stop," he explained. "She doesn't pay attention to her own feelings, including physical signals like pain. And in that Temple, she was rushing through a situation where she and everyone around her were shocked and in a panic. I, on the other hand, am just strolling through this lovely neighborhood, looking for other people strolling through this lovely neighborhood who are thinking about where they're going and where they've been. Big difference.

"Also," he added, grinning, "there are street signs. I'd never win at cards without such excellent powers of observation."

"You don't win, you cheat." Ev hadn't told him any of the details of their escape from the Temple. She ought to be used to this by now.

Ev wasn't thrilled to see that the street he'd chosen was, in fact, Gold Street, but she had to admit he was useful. As its name suggested, the street was not all residences. The beginning of the street was occupied by banks and money changers, but as they made their way further up, the businesses were replaced by neatly kept houses built right up against each other.

"Slow down," Djal said quietly, ambling by her side. "Stop looking so determined. Gawk like a tourist."

These houses weren't open to the light like Ev's family home, but narrow and upright and enclosed. They faced the street, but they were set back from it, protected by walled and gated courtyards.

"We have all the time in the world," Djal said. He slung an arm around her shoulders.

"Kasrik doesn't."

He leaned in so close that the tip of his nose touched her skin. "Especially not if we get caught."

She couldn't dispute that. She tried to relax her pace, admire more, and assess less.

In the lush, low light of Laalvur, these courtyard gardens flourished and flowed across their boundaries, sending tendrils over the tops of the walls. Ev wondered what Alizhan might have made of these homes with large windows and vines draped from their balconies. They looked easy to break into.

"They all have hired guards," Djal said, keeping his voice so low that he might as well have been one of her thoughts. "That's how rich people live."

"Those two have all their windows latched, at least," she said, pointing.

Djal nodded, and Ev suddenly felt foolish for pointing. Djal stopped outside the next house.

Alizhan did that sometimes. He must be sensing something that she couldn't.

"Don't look," he murmured.

As soon as Ev was instructed not to look at the house, looking away became almost painful. It was as if she'd always wanted to see those huge blocks of red-brown stone that made up the lower level, and the red tiles of the roof. The garden in the front was as lush and as manicured as all the neighbors'. Ev could see nothing different about this house.

On second glance, she saw it. None of the vines reached the upper balconies. Someone was tending to the garden in one very particular respect. She never would have seen it if Djal hadn't stopped. What did he sense?

"Look at me," Djal said. He grabbed her hand to get her attention. "We're having a conversation."

Ev's gaze darted back to the house despite his instructions. There were lamps in the second-story windows, and the red paint around the bottom of the wooden door was flaking where the corner hit the doorjamb. The path from the door to the courtyard gate was clear of growth, and the gate wasn't rusted or hanging from its hinges. People lived in that house. People came and went frequently.

"I know," he said. "I see those things, too, and more. But we're not looking. We're just pausing here in the street to talk about where we might stroll next." He lifted her hand up and kissed her knuckles, so that they might seem like a couple.

Smoke, but the two of them made a conspicuous pair. The last person they'd passed in the street had disappeared from sight minutes ago. And they both appeared foreign, to anyone who cared to make such categorizations.

They weren't alone. The door to the house creaked open. From the pointed way Djal stared into her eyes, whoever came out of the house was important. She couldn't afford to turn in that direction and put them in danger. Her heart picked up its pace steadily.

With his free hand, he cupped her cheek. She barely registered the kiss, except that he murmured "Don't be mad," and "Laugh," and in between, his mouth brushed hers.

Ev did laugh, but it was less of a lovelorn giggle and more of an exhalation of shock.

What was he sensing? Who'd just come out of the house? Had they found Kasrik?

Djal's grip on her hand tightened, but in his usual, cheerful tone, he said, "Come on, let's go!"

Then he led her down the street, away from the house. She glanced over her shoulder as they left and saw a thin, bald man narrowing his eyes at them. His angry expression made it easy to recognize him—he looked just like his caricature in the pamphlet. Anavik. A priest of the Balance.

———

TRAINING, it turned out, was not nearly as pleasant as having

Mala touch her. Mala's touch had made her a little stupid, but Alizhan would rather be stupid than suffering. And Mala's training regimen left ample time for her to catalogue her complaints, since all they did was sit facing each other in silence.

Ev and Djal were out in the city finding that priest—and Kasrik—and Alizhan was here, doing nothing. Unbearable. Maybe if she laid her hands on Mala and really focused, she could knock Mala out and go find Ev. Ev would be worried, but Ev was always worried, and she and Mala and Djal were all over-reacting. It had only been a nosebleed. And a loss of conscious-ness. But Alizhan had woken up. She was fine now. She just had to pick the right moment to reach out, touch Mala, and force all of her will into her hands.

"I don't think you're clearing your mind," Mala said. "You're not breathing the way I told you to, either."

"Can you read people *and* do the thing with your hands?" Alizhan asked. Djal had all the good parts of her ability and none of the bad, and now Mala could ease pain with a touch *and* read minds? The world was profoundly unfair.

Mala huffed with laughter. "You could stand to use your other senses every now and then, little sister. You're fidgeting."

"Oh."

Mala shook her head at Alizhan, then reached up and adjusted her yellow headscarf, although it was wrapped and pinned impeccably over her hair. She resettled herself on her chair, smoothing the skirt of her matching yellow dress. Her presence wasn't threatening—she was maybe forty years old, of average height, with excellent posture—but she was very commanding. She seemed to know exactly what she was doing all the time. She also seemed like she'd remember an insult until she was a mound of ashes on a funeral pyre.

Alizhan wondered, not for the first time, what such a neat,

prim woman had done to get exiled from her home, and what she was doing in the company of a sailor who cheated at cards. But she knew better than to ask.

"How do you normally deal with a crowd? Even if it only works some of the time."

"Ev," Alizhan said. "I focus on Ev."

"A bad habit," Mala said with disapproval. "You should rely on yourself. Know yourself."

"There's nothing there to know," Alizhan said. She was an empty vessel. Other people's feelings poured in and washed out. There was no room for anything else inside her.

"Just because you don't know it yet doesn't mean there's nothing there to know. What did you do in crowds before you knew Ev?"

"Pass out, mostly."

"And how long have you know Ev?"

"Either ten years or about a week, depending on when you want to start counting."

Mala said nothing, which was one of those conversational cues that Alizhan never had to interpret on its own. Sometimes people said nothing because the conversation was over and they wanted to stop talking, but sometimes people said nothing because they were giving you an opening. The only way to know was to read the other person's mind.

Did Mala want her to keep talking? Did she want to hear the story? It wasn't a very good story, at least not until Ev showed up, but given the choice between sitting in silence in a dark room and telling the story, Alizhan picked the one where she got to talk.

"I'm an orphan. This woman took me in as a servant, sort of, when I was really young. I don't remember much of my life before that. I spied for her, or stole things, and I got to live in her house and she fed me. But it was hard living there sometimes, and I was lonely, and she wasn't always around. Sometimes I left. I had this dream that I'd find my real family. It's dumb, I guess. Iriyat says—that's her, the woman who took me in—well, she said they threw me out because I was *touched*. That I scared them and they didn't know how to deal with me and they left me at the Temple orphanage.

"I can't read Iriyat, so I don't know if that's true. But other people at the house said the same thing, and they always felt like they were telling the truth. Anyway. As a kid I never wanted to believe that. Who wants to believe their real family would abandon them? So sometimes when I got frustrated or upset about something, I'd run away to look for them.

"And one time when I was about eight or nine—nobody really knows how old I am, comes with being an orphan—I ran into Arishdenan market. And that's where I met Ev. I was terrified, hiding under a cart, and she gave me some thornfruit.

"It's stupid, I guess, that that's all it took. It sounds silly now. But I can't remember anybody else ever being kind to me before that. Iriyat was nice, but I always knew it was because I was useful to her, and that if I wasn't... the way I am, she wouldn't have kept me around."

"It's not stupid," Mala said, quiet but firm.

"I got chased out of the market that shift—had to dive off a bridge and swim out of sight—but I went back every week for the next ten years, looking for Ev. I could stand the crowd if I was looking for her. And she was always so easy to find. Especially because after a while, she started looking for me, too."

Mala said nothing for entirely too long. Then she asked, "Is she in love with you?"

Alizhan shrugged. "She thinks about me naked sometimes, or kissing me, and then gets embarrassed because she knows that I know. I don't care, though. People think about other people naked all the time. I know that's not the same as love. But it can go hand-in-hand, the sex stuff and the feelings. Although on the surface—I try not to dig too deep, since she doesn't like that—Ev mostly feels nervous and concerned and irritated when I'm around. But," Alizhan added, "in my defense, a lot of people have been trying to kill us."

Mala seemed to find this entertaining, and Alizhan had no idea why. It was just the truth.

Only a tiny fraction of the truth, really. Alizhan knew Ev's feelings ran deeper than that. But Ev didn't want her to know, and she certainly wouldn't want Alizhan to talk about it. And Alizhan didn't want to talk about it, either, and not just out of respect for Ev. Talking about it meant she'd have to think about it, and that would lead her to want things she couldn't have.

Alizhan often thought of other people's minds as houses. Her own mind had a lot of locked doors. A lot of closed-up rooms she didn't even like to pass by.

"And you?"

"And me what?"

"Are you in love with her?"

Mala was banging on all the closed doors and rattling all the locks. Alizhan wanted her to stop. "What does any of this have to do with you teaching me to control my powers?"

"Answer the question, and we'll find out."

"No," Alizhan said, because she'd told Ev not to get her hopes up. She'd told Ev that they couldn't ever do that.

And then Mala was silent for a long, long time. Alizhan couldn't tell if it was the kind of silence that invited more conversation, but she didn't care. She had nothing more to say.

The force of Mala's gaze withered her resolve. Finally, she admitted, "It feels good to be around Ev. Beneath all that worry and irritation, she's happy to see me, and I like the way that feels."

And that was all she was going to say about it.

"There," Mala said, with a note of vindication. "I ask you a question about *your* feelings, and you tell me about Ev's feelings instead. That's a problem. You'll never set your mind in order if you don't address it."

Who knew training was going to involve so much scrutiny and judgment? How was this helping her? Alizhan didn't want to talk about it, and she knew just how to change the subject. Mala might've shut her out for now, but she'd been a thief of secrets her whole life, and Mala had let her in. Their moment of mental contact had been more than enough.

"All this stuff about only relying on yourself, because some time in the future you might be alone," Alizhan said, as though she were posing a very serious question. "Is that why you haven't slept with Djal even though you want to?"

One side of Mala's mouth curved up. "Little shit."

"Me or him?"

"The both of you," Mala said, shaking her head. "Back to work."

Ev AND DJAL came back after half a shift, although to Alizhan it felt like they'd been gone for years.

"You found something," Alizhan said immediately.

Mala didn't move when they came in. She hadn't finished teaching Alizhan to meditate, and she'd only just started letting Alizhan practice touching her hand, but Mala couldn't possibly expect her to continue sitting around in this room now that Ev and Djal had found the house.

"We found your priest," Djal confirmed. "He wasn't wearing robes, but Ev recognized his face from a pamphlet she read. Anavik, she said. Mean-looking, shriveled-up old guy. There are other people in the house, too. I'm not sure how many, but definitely more than were in any of the surrounding houses. We were too far away for me to get an accurate idea, and it's likely there were a lot of people in the house who could shield themselves from me, anyway."

Ev hadn't known about the others. She was surprised, but not mad. They'd left Gold Street as quickly as possible without arousing suspicion, not wanting to alert anyone in the house that they knew about its real purpose. Ev was still a little breathless from their walk back.

She'd enjoyed it. Ev was happy. Alizhan usually liked it when Ev was happy.

"What next?" Ev said.

"We have to find Kasrik." Alizhan felt like that was all she ever said. "I'll break in and see if he's there."

"It's a place where they hurt—and maybe kill—people like you!" Ev said.

"They're not going to catch me."

"You don't even know how many people are in the house," Djal said. "Let us go back. We'll be more circumspect. We'll watch the house for a shift and get an idea of who comes and goes."

"I'm going," Alizhan said. She reached for Mala's hand, fixing her gaze on Ev and Djal, and then she squeezed. "I made a lot of progress. Right, Mala?"

She didn't expect any support. They'd barely gotten anything done.

Mala was looking down at Alizhan's hand in surprise. "Yes," she said, and Alizhan realized it was the first time she'd touched Mala without feeling the effects of her gift—this only happened when Mala was in control—or accidentally hurting herself. Mala's hand just felt like a hand.

Alizhan got so caught up in the sight and sensation of

touching another person that she forgot the point she'd been trying to make.

"We're not finished," Mala said. "I still don't think it's a good idea for you to go out into the city, and especially not into that house."

"I didn't say it was a good idea," Alizhan said, dropping Mala's hand and snapping back to attention. "I still have to do it. Kasrik might die."

Mala nodded, and when Djal saw that, he nodded, too. "We'll come with you," he said. "If there are children being mistreated, we'll help you get them out."

"You might be getting yourselves in a lot of trouble," Ev said. "You might be making some powerful people very angry."

"Two exiled criminals like us?" Djal said with a brightness beyond even his usual cheer, and Ev laughed. "We can take care of ourselves."

"We should watch during the busiest shift. It'll be easier for us to loiter if there are lots of people in the street," Alizhan said. "In Gold Street, that's probably Rosefinch."

"That gives us half a shift until we go back to the house," Djal said. "Mala and I have an errand to run. We'll meet you here just before they call the shift change."

Mala stood, and the two of them walked out of the room, and no sooner were they gone than Alizhan found herself blurting, "You're in love with him." Alizhan didn't even know why she'd said it, or why the words had come out in that tone. Was it an accusation?

Ev was very, very surprised, but also a little bit embarrassed, which meant Alizhan was right. Vindication wasn't as sweet as she thought it would be. Maybe she didn't want to be right.

Ev didn't say anything for a long time, which gave Alizhan an opportunity to expand on her argument.

"You kissed him!" Alizhan continued. "And you laugh at his

jokes and you were excited to meet him and you liked spending time with him, and you're always thinking about his *face*."

Ev started to laugh, which was absurd, because Alizhan was only stating the facts. Then she said, "Of course I think about his face sometimes. I'm a human being with eyes and a pulse."

"What are you saying, that I'm *not*?"

"I'm sorry. I didn't mean it like that. But... I don't know how to explain it to you. You know sometimes you look up from the city streets, and you realize we live surrounded by these majestic cliffs, and you see the way the sunlight hits the ocean, and for a second, you can't breathe because of how beautiful it is?"

"His face looks like the ocean?"

Ev laughed again.

Alizhan didn't. It was a perfectly logical question, after Ev had said all that nonsense.

"No. It's just... distracting."

"I'm *glad* I can't see his stupid face."

"Oh, Alizhan. Don't say that. I'd let you into my head just for the pleasure of seeing his face."

"It doesn't work like that."

"I know," Ev said. "But he's beautiful. And once I decided to trust him a little, he was good company. I'm not in love with him, I promise. It's like looking at a landscape. A very smooth-talking landscape."

That was a lot to think about. Alizhan closed her eyes, ran back through what Ev had just said, and focused on what really mattered. "You'd let me in?"

Ev shrugged. "Of course. Faces are nice. I wish you could see them. I'd share that with you if I could."

Why was Ev so eternally confusing? Alizhan could see into her head and still not understand her. "But you don't like it when I read your mind the rest of the time."

"You don't barge into someone else's house when the door is closed, right?"

"Yes I do."

"Bad analogy. You understand what I mean, right? Just because I want to close the door sometimes doesn't mean I'd never open it for you."

"Oh," Alizhan said, because something important had just happened, and she wasn't sure what. It was as if the ground had lurched beneath her feet—she had to find new footing, and she was left wondering if there were more tremors to come.

17

LYREBIRD SHIFT, 8TH TRIAD OF ALAKSHA, 761

I T WAS NOT HARD TO persuade Laalvur that I was grief-stricken—I was, of course, but not because of my parents. My long, severe period of isolation only heightened the public's pity and admiration for Iriyat ha-Varensi, beautiful forlorn eighteen-year-old orphan. So many people had lost family members to the wave; the tragedy brought us together.

They would doubtless have had less sympathy for Iriyat ha-Varensi, unmarried pregnant patricide, no matter how beautiful.

I hid my condition as best I could. This required cultivating a fiercely loyal staff, which I did with money and promises where possible, and with my hands, otherwise. You could interview my entire household right now, and every single one of them would swear up and down that I am a virgin. They would tell you how deeply religious I am, and how I swore never to marry after my parents' death. Iriyat ha-Varensi has no children. How could she? She has never been pregnant. Some of my staff genuinely believe all of these things. The rest of them are very convincing.

I spent those months of seclusion searching. The literal search for my mother was as fruitless as my figurative search for answers. I called priests of the Balance and priests of Doubt to

Varenx House to talk with me about what their faiths had to offer. After our talks, I was always careful to take their hands in mine and give them a heartfelt squeeze. They reported to their friends and colleagues that Ha-Varensi was radiant, even in modest grey mourning clothes, and that she had asked many probing questions about why the Balance allowed such disasters to happen. Then they would shake their heads, and sigh, and remark on what a shame it was that tragedy had struck such a beloved family, but that only in times of hardship is our true strength revealed. How admirably pious that young Iriyat was observing such a long period of mourning! How tragic that such a virginal young beauty had sworn never to marry!

These accounts were immeasurably helpful to my reputation.

Please do not think me entirely cynical. I also hid my pregnancy to protect you. The world was already so cruel, and I knew it would be crueler to a fatherless child.

My search for answers was genuine, as well. I prayed a great deal at that time, when I still believed prayer could bring me consolation. I prayed that all of us who had lost loved ones in the wave might learn to live with the pain. I prayed that those we lost might find peace in death. I prayed that a wave would never strike our shore again.

And I prayed that you would be like Arav, and not like me. I did not want you to bear my affliction.

Prayer brought me nothing but frustration, as did all my long talks with priests. Priests of Doubt only ever answered questions with other questions. Priests of the Balance took refuge in platitudes when faced with the hard truths of an unjust world. All things are contained in God's Balance—but perhaps some things shouldn't be.

I could not let you grow up in a world that would treat you as this world had treated me.

Long contemplation led me to two conclusions. In a just world, there would be no more waves. In a just world, there would be no more Lacemakers. Instead of being daunted by these two goals, I was invigorated. Here, at last, was a solution to my grief. No more lamenting the mysterious, random cruelty of the Balance. No more questioning why I had survived. Here was a purpose: fixing the world.

For you.

I had the political power, the wealth, and the motivation to accomplish what no one had ever dreamed of accomplishing. And I was still young; I had the rest of my life to devote to this work. There was a long history of attempts to predict or curtail the power of the ocean, all of which had been futile. I would need to use means that no one else had yet considered. And I would need to work in secret, preserving my reputation, since it was no small fraction of my power. Our world does not take kindly to ambitious women, and what is more ambitious than controlling the planet itself?

Finding the other Lacemakers might seem a trivial problem compared to the vastness of the ocean, and in those first few years, I considered it to be a separate and less urgent task. Finding one particular Lacemaker—my mother—was urgent, though, and I set about that right away. My mother had hidden herself well after her escape. She did not seem to be in Laalvur at all. I expanded my search, sending people to other cities to watch and listen, but she proved evasive.

Other Lacemakers were not so difficult to find. Neither were other people possessed of magical abilities. I soon discovered that there were many more kinds of magic in the world than Lacemaking, and I began to see connections between my projects where none had been evident before. In my hunt for Lacemakers, I discovered people who could calm or excite others with a touch, people like Arav who could intuit moods or thoughts, people who could aim or catch objects with uncanny accuracy, people who could acquire the knowledge of hundreds of languages with the barest of introductions, and people who could always guess the outcomes of games and wagers. It was these last few categories that interested me the most. It seemed to me there was a similar thread tying these abilities together, a sort of recognition of patterns that otherwise escaped notice. That kind of predictive power could perhaps be turned toward reading the signs of the ocean.

I could not kill the thing that had killed Arav, as he had killed the medusa to avenge his friends, but I could conquer it. I could take control of the waves.

As for these other people with magical abilities, I did not have such a visceral reaction to them as I did to my own kind. All magic is a product of the mind, but some magic is done exclusively with the mind. The other category, into which Lace-making falls, requires use of the hands. I think of them as sense-magic and touch-magic, not having found any other adequate terms. Both kinds must be carried in the blood, as they run in families, and truly strong ability seems to be rare regardless of kind. Magic has remained so reviled and so hidden in our world that it is difficult to find literature on the subject. I detailed all of my findings, as is my nature, but I doubt that anyone but you will ever see them. I need no monuments, no histories. Achieving my goals will be reward enough.

Over the course of years, it became clear that I would need access to the islanders. That their cultures persist on those tiny islands despite the waves is proof that they know how to protect themselves. The islanders, somewhat like the Adpri, are also far more accepting of magic. I began to suspect a connection: they had found a way to train people to predict the waves.

The other elusive secret of the islanders is their knowledge of medusa venom. Initially, I was interested in the venom for profit—this quest requires resources—and also as a convenient cover for my true goals. It was easy enough to persuade Mar ha-Solora and Prince Ilyr that this was the case last month, when I finally had the opportunity to take a step forward in this years-long quest.

It was only a few triads ago that I had word from Prince Ilyr that he is preparing a voyage to the islands. I wish him success.

Until I know what the islanders know, I will have to continue to buy venom. It has been tedious and expensive, acquiring it discreetly in Laalvur. But it is worth it.

Properly treated venom affects most people in a way similar to many intoxicants. It loosens inhibitions. It is useful for plea-sure and for managing pain. Venom in its raw form inflicts pain, as Arav's scars had taught me. It is a powerful substance. Most importantly, it dampens magical abilities. Venom might be the key to eradicating Lacemaking.

As my ancestors hid themselves and their craft, I also worked largely under cover of secrecy. But in many ways, I have also been hiding in plain sight. It was useful to stir up fear and suspicion among the people, that they might lead me to anyone manifesting strange abilities. I accomplished this primarily through the Temple of the Balance, although of course the priests all think it was their own idea. I founded an orphanage at the Temple, and desperate citizens began to abandon their chil-dren there. Many of them were ordinary poor children. These, I simply fed and housed until they were of age to make their way in the world. They left the Temple orphanage none the wiser about my real project, but filled with gratitude toward the beau-tiful, wealthy patron who visited them so often and brought them presents at festival times. Many have come to work at Varenx House over the years, and they are dear to me.

But not all of the children were ordinary. Perhaps one in ten manifested some kind of power. The orphanage numbers are no doubt skewed; people are more likely to abandon unruly children with abilities that make them impossible to control. Only two children with a calming touch have ever been left at the orphanage, but I suspect this ability to be far more common than that. When children with magic were left at the orphanage, they were discreetly moved to a townhouse on Gold Street at the edge of the Knuckles, not far from Denandar, a narrow little stone affair, one of many city properties I owned and had no interest in. There, priests watched over them and conducted studies of their powers. In exchange for food and shelter, the children went out into the city and sought more of their own kind. Occasionally, if they had abilities that made them useful to me, I had them do other work. I refused to let my own personal distaste for the use of magic hinder me in my ambitions.

I never used Lacemakers, of course. Their skills were of no use to me, being no match for my own, and it was dangerous to let untrained Lacemakers roam freely. The ones who came to us had undoubtedly already done a great deal of damage in their short lives, and I do not regret putting a stop to them. They had to be weeded out.

I expected trouble from the priests, but instead they were willing participants in my plan, having believed every word about the dangers of magic. Indeed, they had to be stopped from disposing of the other children, the ones who might still be of use. Still, they dug graves, and I dug holes in their memories. It was cleaner that way.

You may think me ruthless. Think instead of all the people who lived their lives in peace, whole and unharmed and alive, with their memories untroubled by my kind, thanks to these interventions of mine. That is what I do, and I feel no remorse at all.

18

THIN BLACK SCARS

A LIZHAN HAD GROWN FOND OF all the clothes Ev had bought her, which was stupid, because she'd had to crawl under some bushes to get to her perch and now her yellow tunic was torn and dirty. There were leaves in her hair. Things like that used to be advantages in her work—reasons for people to look away from her. But she'd never had clothes worth caring about until now.

Alizhan split off from the others. She hadn't liked the idea of waiting in Gold Street and watching the front door. Ev and Djal had already done that, and they'd seen that thin priest come out. He'd seen them, too, even if he hadn't realized what they were doing.

Could the people who worked in this house also read minds? It was just one more thing she didn't know.

Alizhan was looking down a steep drop into the back garden of the house, where the same care had been taken to cut back the vines growing nearest to the house. Most tactics meant to keep people out were also good for keeping people in.

She had to get inside. She considered her options: jump down, then try to open the back door or one of the windows.

Alizhan didn't have her set of lockpicks on her, but there was a chance not all the windows were latched.

Another option: go around to the front of the house, knock on the door, wait for someone to answer and then knock them out. The drawback to this plan was that it would weaken her, or possibly knock her out as well.

That was when she saw the face in the window. A small brown oval in the lower corner pane. Based on height, it had to be a child. Alizhan couldn't tell if it was a boy or a girl.

She also couldn't tell if she'd been seen. But either she was already in trouble or this was the opportunity she'd been waiting for, so she jumped down, landing in a crouch, vines rustling under her feet. Quickly and silently, she made her way to the window and touched the glass.

The child recoiled from the sight of her hand, but then remembered the glass was there and moved closer to examine her. Alizhan put on what she hoped was a big, reassuring smile and pointed toward the door.

The child disappeared. The door opened.

A bearded man strode out of the doorway with his sword drawn. "You there."

Shit. Alizhan would never get close enough to touch him with his sword brandished like that. The guard's thoughts weren't silent, but they weren't easy to read, either. Everything in his mind was distant and foggy: he was suspicious and hostile, but she already knew that. From the sword.

Did he mean to kill her? She couldn't tell. That, as much as the brandished weapon, chilled her. This man knew how to protect himself against her, and she knew nothing of how to protect herself from him.

Her heart, that deafening drum, wanted to burst from her chest. Her feet would not move.

And then the guard smiled. Alizhan couldn't tell what kind

of a smile it was—in books, people were always talking about whether a smile was cold or warm or bright or grim—but Alizhan only ever saw smiles as an upward curve of the lips. No matter how long she studied this language of the face that everyone else had been born knowing, she would always decipher it with difficulty. Still, smiling struck her as an odd thing for a wary stranger to do.

He said nothing. There was no accompanying taunt.

Just as Alizhan realized that his suspicion and hostility were fading away, she noticed the child from the window standing next to him. The child was at his side, in a position to tug at his sleeve. One small hand was wrapped around the bare skin between the guard's glove and the end of his sleeve. The guard closed his eyes. His body folded as she watched, crumpling to the ground with no resistance.

"He's sleepy," the child said.

Based on the child's short hair and neutral-colored clothing, Alizhan was guessing it was a boy. He was small. Six years old? Seven? She didn't know anything about children. She hadn't really been expecting this one to reappear again.

"Everyone's always sleepy," he told her.

Alizhan's heart wouldn't stop pounding. Even though she recognized that this child was like Mala—and he was *uheko*, possessed of touch-magic, like her—she still felt a stab of terror. No matter how serenely the guard had slipped into sleep, it shook her to see an armed man felled by a small child. Was Alizhan next?

You do the same thing, she reminded herself. *Other people are scared of you.*

They'd been scared of her since she'd been as small as him. Except Ev. What would Ev do? The boy didn't come closer. Maybe he could tell she was afraid of him. More likely, he was afraid of her. But they didn't have to be. Alizhan bent down to his height. She nodded gravely and then put a finger to her lips. There were probably more guards. "My name is Alizhan. What's yours?" she whispered.

"Zilal."

"How many kids live here, Zilal?"

"At least one hundred."

She couldn't feel everyone in the house, but that figure struck her as unlikely, to say the least. But the boy's answer definitely meant more than two or three. Maybe more than ten. Could it mean more than twenty? How could she get that many children out? Maybe she should make her way to the front door and let Ev, Djal, and Mala in.

But she'd come here for another reason.

"Have you seen a boy..." she started. What could she say about Kasrik? She could draw an outline, but she could never fill in the details. "A man. Taller than me. Skinny. Angry. He, um... he can read minds?"

"The one who spits," Zilal said, a solemn guess.

That was a better lead than she'd had before. Alizhan nodded. "Can you show me?"

Zilal stuck out his hand, obviously wanting her to hold it. Alizhan stopped. It was such a tiny little thing to be afraid of, a child's bare hand.

Her own hands were bare. She'd been prepared to hurt someone. She took a breath. She'd touched Mala earlier. Zilal had a similar gift, if he'd put that guard to sleep himself. It was good that he was gifted; his shields would be naturally strong and it would make things easier for her. Far easier than touching someone with no gift.

Alizhan took the boy's hand, bracing for a stab of pain through her temples. Nothing happened. Zilal stared at her and tugged on her hand until she followed him.

Alizhan had watched the back of the house while Ev, Djal,

and Mala had lurked in Gold Street for the past few hours. In addition to Anavik, the one Ev had recognized from the pamphlet, there were three others—two more men and one woman—who'd come and gone. Alizhan had checked with the others twice now, and they'd be expecting her again soon.

Four priests and at least one guard. There was likely another guard at the front of the house, which she'd need to keep in mind if she wanted to leave by that door. Probably another one around somewhere else, too. If she were in charge, she wouldn't leave "at least one hundred" gifted children in the care of only two adult guards.

She wouldn't leave them in the care of ungifted adults at all, since Zilal had just demonstrated what a bad idea that was.

He led her up a set of stairs and into a room with no windows. It was lit by the green glow of lamp light, and in the center, Kasrik was strapped to a chair.

"Kasrik."

His head lolled back against the wooden chair frame. Either he couldn't hear her or he couldn't respond. Alizhan let go of Zilal's hand and rushed to Kasrik, tugging at the restraints around his arms, heedless of touching him. She needed something to cut the ropes, so tightly knotted that they were digging into the flesh of his forearms. Alizhan turned to the table that ran along one wall of the otherwise empty room. Its surface was covered with tools—her stomach lurched—and glass bottles of some clear liquid, some with what looked like long, tangled coils of translucent string inside.

Her hand finally landed on a simple blade. She whipped back around to cut Kasrik free, and that was when she noticed his arms.

They were covered in long, thin black scars. No, not scars—something else. The skin was dead and flaking away.

Kasrik didn't flinch when she touched him. He barely moved

at all. Alizhan felt nothing from his mind, and very little reaction from his body. But he was breathing. He had a pulse.

She slid the blade of the knife between his arm and the rope and then slit the rope. When she freed Kasrik's left arm, it simply dropped from the armrest of the chair to hang at his side.

What would she do if he didn't wake up? He was bigger than her. She couldn't carry him out of here. Alizhan pushed that worry aside and cut the ropes at his ankles. Zilal was still watching her in silence.

"Do you know what they did to him?" Alizhan asked.

Zilal nodded once. "They made him scream."

Alizhan's breath caught. But just as she was about to ask more questions, she felt someone's presence in the hallway outside the door. Kasrik was unbound but unconscious, and there was no way she could save him, and Zilal, and herself.

A stocky young man appeared in the doorway.

She clenched the handle of the knife.

The man wasn't dressed like a priest, but he thought of himself as one. That was all Alizhan could get from his thoughts. Like the guard at the door, he'd learned to obscure his intentions. He gave off only a hint of what he felt, and it wasn't reassuring. The man didn't smell like the bright alertness that might precede a confrontation. Smug triumph sat heavy in the air around him.

"You want to know what we did to him?" the man said. "We asked him about you."

"THEY RANG THE HOUR BELL," Ev said. "Alizhan was supposed to check in and she didn't."

"What do you want to do about it?" Djal asked. "Should we look for her around back?"

Ev shook her head. Her quivering heart threatened to panic. Either Alizhan had been captured or she'd gone in alone. "There's only one place she could be."

The orphanage, remarkably similar in construction and style to all the surrounding houses, still somehow gave off a grim air of foreboding. Djal was saying something about making a plan, and Mala was agreeing with him, but Ev simply left them behind. She walked right up to the courtyard wall.

"What are you doing?" Djal said.

"Boost me up," she demanded. "And then toss my staff over. We should have done this hours ago. I'll let you in when I can."

He nodded, kneeling and lacing his hands together. Even as tall as she was, Ev couldn't reach the top of the wall that way. Instead, she had to sit on his shoulders, wait for him to stand, and then rise to a standing position on top of his shoulders, with one hand braced against the wall.

So much for subtlety.

She grabbed the top of the wall and pulled herself over, then dropped down into the garden. A few moments later, her staff clattered to the ground beside her. She picked it up just in time to swing it at the guard who came charging out of the house. She didn't hit him hard enough to take him down, but it was enough to send his sword toward the empty air instead of her torso. Ev stepped to the side, rearranging her grip on the staff so she could aim a sweeping strike at his legs. He went down hard, cracking his head against the cobblestone path to the door.

Ev rifled through his pockets and found a ring of keys. She shoved key after key into the garden gate, glancing over her shoulder, until one finally clicked. Djal and Mala came right through.

"You're bleeding," Djal said. He bent to pick up the guard's sword as he said it.

"But he didn't hit—" Ev started, and then saw that he was

right. It was the cut her mother had stitched closed after she and Alizhan had first been attacked. The newly healed skin must have split open. Once Djal pointed it out, the pain was obvious, burning along her side. But she'd ignored it before and she could ignore it again. She needed to focus to dull the pain in her side and to quiet the frantic and fearful trembling at the back of her mind that threatened to overwhelm her. "It doesn't matter. Find Alizhan."

The door was an imposing thing, heavy wood with many latches. But in his haste, the guard hadn't locked it. Ev opened it and walked in. The inside of the house, much like the outside, was unremarkable. Red tile floor and white plaster walls. Very little furniture in the first rooms. But men with swords didn't come charging out of unremarkable houses.

"You go up, we'll search this floor and the cellar," Djal said.

Ev ran up the stairs with no further discussion. At the top, she was confronted with the sound of conversation, and a stocky young man standing in the doorway of a room, blocking her view.

"We asked him about you," the man was saying. He hadn't noticed Ev yet. He was intent on something in the room, and one of his big, gloved hands was clamped around the neck of a squirming child. "But now that you're here, we don't need to ask him anything else. That's a good thing, too. He was getting more and more useless."

"Why do you care who I am?" That was Alizhan's voice. Strange to hear her ask a question. Either she was stalling, or she genuinely didn't know. Maybe both. Could this man have some kind of power?

"Where's the book?" he countered.

"What could you possibly want with a book? It's not like you can read."

"As opposed to gutter trash like you," he said, not rising to the taunt. "The lowest of the low. Ha-Varensi took you in and raised you like her own, and you threw it all away. For what? Mar's money? Or is he giving you something else? Are you one of his little sluts?" The man advanced on Alizhan. "You'll tell me where the book is and what Mar ha-Solora paid you to betray ha-Varensi once I burn it out of you. See your friend there? He had a real smart mouth until I got to him. And for him, it was only his arms. With you, I think we'll start with your face." He huffed with satisfaction, then looked down at the child, still writhing in his grip. "And you, little monster—you can watch."

If Ev attacked him, she might hurt the child. Maybe if she bashed him in the head with her staff, his hand would spasm and he'd let go of the kid. But the doorway would keep her from making a swing with enough momentum to do real damage.

"What *did* you do to him?" Alizhan said with what sounded like real interest. "I've never seen scars like that before."

"Pure medusa venom," the man said with a note of pride. "Those streaks are from the tentacles. You lay them right down on the skin, it burns like hell and never heals. Fixes your filthy kind right up. Stops you from working your witchcraft on innocent people."

"You've done this before," Alizhan guessed, as though they were both partaking in an intellectual exercise. Ev could never have sounded so detached from her own fate, especially not if that fate was imminent torture.

"Don't worry, I've had plenty of practice curing the deformed," the man said. "Now, since you've so conveniently cut all his restraints, push him onto the floor and get in the chair."

"Why would I do that?"

"Because if you don't, I'll snap this little one's neck."

The child gasped at that, and Ev heard movement, but still couldn't see into the room. It didn't matter. She didn't need a perfect plan. This man had threatened to murder a child and torture Alizhan, and she had to do something right now.

Instead of bashing him with her staff, she simply jabbed him sharply in the small of the back.

He whirled, but didn't let go of the boy, which had been her hope. Oh well. Kids were resourceful in general, and Ev was guessing this one in particular could take care of himself. She dropped her staff and charged the man, ramming into him with her whole body and sending them both sprawling to the floor. He did let go of the boy as they were falling, and the boy got away as quickly as possible. Ev pinned the man to the ground under her body, sat up, and punched him in the face. Hard. And then she kept punching.

"Ev, Ev, stop. There's rope in here. We can tie him up. We need him alive."

"I wasn't planning to murder him," Ev said between breaths, although in truth she wasn't so sure. Her knuckles were bloody. She wiped them on her victim's clothes.

"I was reminding myself," Alizhan said. "This room is evidence against Iriyat. Everyone in this house is evidence. We're going to need everyone and everything here to take her down."

"He's not going to say anything against her," Ev said.

"Maybe," Alizhan said. "He was talking like a true believer. But it's possible that everyone here has had their memory altered. Maybe everyone working for Iriyat has. I want to give them a chance."

"How can we possibly protect this many people while we wait for the Council to gather for a trial?" Ev asked. If they lost track of any of these people, Iriyat could swoop in and change their memories. It felt insurmountable.

"I think we just have to keep them here. We'll stay in the house."

"He can't stay in the house," Ev said, nodding at Kasrik, still barely conscious in the chair. "He needs help."

"You're right," Alizhan said. "Find Mala. She'll know what to do. If it's safe to move him, take him to Mar. I trust him to help Kasrik, and we need him to get Ezatur and Sideran on his side, because that's our best chance of exposing Iriyat. He'll have to work quietly. If Iriyat gets word that we're here, or that Kasrik got out alive, she'll come. If she comes, I don't know how we'll stop her. She could make us forget our own names."

Violence came to mind so quickly that Ev felt ashamed of herself. They couldn't just kill Iriyat. Beyond the problem of getting away with the murder of a beloved public figure, Iriyat had loyal supporters in the Temple, people who might continue this unconscionable work without her. No, Ev and Alizhan had to discredit her. They had to link her to this terrible place, and they had to do it in full view of the city. Her downfall needed to be seared into the collective memory so completely that even Iriyat herself could not undo it.

Ev took a deep breath. Easier said than done.

Ev LEFT Alizhan with Kasrik and their tied-up attacker.

The child in the room, a boy named Zilal, led Ev down the stairs into a large room packed wall-to-wall with cots. Djal and Mala were kneeling on the floor in the aisle between the beds, surrounded by children. There were at least a dozen—no, Ev realized after counting, there were nineteen, including the boy at her side.

There would have been twenty while Kasrik was living here. Had he been as miserable in this room as Alizhan would be? Had he spent long hours watching for an opportunity to escape?

"Alizhan says we need to stay here with them," Ev told Djal and Mala.

Djal nodded. "I found a guard sleeping on the floor near the back door, and I knocked out another one on my way here. Trussed them both up in the hallway. I'm sure there are more."

"Alizhan and I found one upstairs, in the room with Kasrik," Ev said. "And we saw four people go in and out..." She paused, uncertain which of those four people were out of the house and might be returning. They'd find out soon enough. She directed her gaze at Mala. "Kasrik is hurt. Alizhan wants to know if he can be moved safely. If so, I'll take him to Solor House and explain to Mar what we've found."

Mala nodded. "Let's go."

Kasrik was awake but dazed when they re-entered the room. Mala made a quick, efficient check of his vitals. Unlike Alizhan, who'd calmed under Mala's touch, Kasrik seemed to liven up. His eyes focused more clearly on her.

"I don't think I can heal him here, at least not in the time we have," Mala said. "His wounds aren't the kind we can see." Kasrik did have visible wounds—raw flesh where his wrists had been bound, and a black eye, to start—but there must be something beyond what Ev could see. Mala was enumerating things. "No broken bones, no gashes... I don't know if he can walk under his own power, dazed as he is, but I think if you go with him, he can get there."

Ev hated the idea of leaving the house and all its vulnerable children unprotected, but Mala and Djal would be here. And if Ev was being honest with herself—a difficult thing—what she really hated was leaving Alizhan.

"I'll take care of myself," Alizhan said quietly, and for once, Ev just nodded.

"We need Mar," she said, more to convince herself than anything else. They needed him to accuse Iriyat before the rest of the Council. They needed the resources his wealth could provide. Then she lifted Kasrik out of the chair and held him until he was carrying some of his own weight. Half-slouched against her, barely awake, he wouldn't be an easy companion to transport across the city.

Ev was spending far too much of her time carrying semi-conscious people across Laalvur. Kasrik was heavier than Alizhan had been. His eyes were open, but she couldn't tell how aware he was.

The trip was excruciating, but at least it ended easily enough. Ev didn't have to say a word to the servant who opened the door at Solor House. The man recognized Kasrik and ushered her inside immediately. Once, entering one of the Great Houses had been a dream, and she might have marveled at the high ceilings of the entrance hall or the elaborate carved stone screens on the Nightward side. There were white and blue tiles arranged in complicated mosaic patterns and rugs in every shade of blue. Ev couldn't put Kasrik down to remove her shoes. She'd never dirtied something so expensive, and that stray thought might have made her laugh if she hadn't been so frantic. The servant led her to a room with a bed where she could deposit Kasrik—the trip had taken its toll—so she did.

Just as she was wondering what to do next, she turned around and Mar ha-Solora was standing in the room. The thick carpet had muffled his tread. His clothes were wrinkled, his hair was mussed, and his eyes drooped with fatigue. Still, he made the space feel much smaller.

"Will he live?"

"I think so," Ev said. "Mala—a healer we know—thought it was safe for me to bring him across the city. She said his worst wounds are the kind we can't see."

Mar pushed past her and knelt beside the bed, gently examining one of Kasrik's bare arms and the black scarring that traced up and down his skin like a new set of veins. "What happened? Who did this? *What* did this?"

"We found the orphanage he told us about," Ev said. "In Gold Street. There were several people working there—we suspect they're priests of the Balance. At least some of them. Two of them might just be guards. They're keeping nineteen children in the house. I think—I think—" Ev took a breath, realizing that she had been talking extraordinarily fast, "—I think they might be doing experiments. With venom."

"Medusa venom?"

She nodded.

Mar frowned. "Now that I think of it, I suppose I'd heard somewhere that it left this distinctive kind of scarring. But what possible purpose could this serve? You can't be telling me that Iriyat is keeping a secret house full of orphaned children just to do cruel experiments on them? I know I underestimated her, but..."

Ev had no answers.

"There must be some reason," Mar insisted.

"Can you come up with a good enough reason to hurt kids?"

Mar glanced at Kasrik. His shoulders slumped. "I hate this." He sighed. "I suppose you came here so I could gather the other seven Council members to bring Iriyat to trial."

"Alizhan is still at the house with all the children," Ev said. "They can be witnesses. The house is full of evidence."

"What are we going to do with nineteen children?" Mar said. He rubbed a hand over his face. "Nineteen children who terrified their families into abandoning them."

"Don't say that," Ev snapped. "It's not the kids' fault. And their parents were probably terrified by all those sermons that priests of the Balance are always giving about the horrors of the 'Unbalanced' among us. But we'll figure it out. We'll find homes for them, or... people who know how to teach them, or something."

"In a city where no one believes in magic." Mar rubbed the bridge of his nose. "What a mess."

"Yes." Ev meant her reply to sound steadfast. She wanted to convey that they'd solve this.

Mar interpreted it differently. "It's not like Iriyat to be sloppy. I know the house was hidden in plain sight, and you might not have found it if not for... Alizhan. But employing so many people gets dangerous. People talk. And keeping so many children a secret. The more I learn about this, the more questions I have. This place must be a secret from most of Iriyat's servants, and also from most of the priests. How do we find out who's involved?"

"People might be involved without knowing it," Ev said. "But I suppose we should start with the ones who are in the house."

"Two guards, you said, and four others you think might be priests. What about that guard of hers who nearly killed Zenav in the Temple of Doubt? The gruff one with the beard? Do you think he knows?"

Ev had Alizhan's memory of hiding in the foliage outside Varenx House and eavesdropping. "He knows something, but not everything. I think he kills people for Iriyat sometimes, but he doesn't like doing it. He might not remember it."

Mar stared. "How can you possibly know—never mind, I know it's Alizhan. Fine. We'll assume he's involved, willingly or not. So that's seven accomplices at least. I have no idea how our courts will deal with someone who might have had their memories altered, but we'll get to that. I think you said six of these people are in the house, yes?"

"No," Ev said. Cold horror seeped into her gut. Anavik had left the house while they'd been watching, and they hadn't seen him come back. He could return at any moment. Worse, he might be reporting to Iriyat right now. "One left before we went in."

"That's not good," Mar said. "We need evidence. And that means we need to keep this secret from Iriyat for as long as possible. If she gets word—"

Ev already knew. "Call your Council. I'm going back."

She should never have left Alizhan alone at the house. Not alone, of course, but what could Djal and Mala do against Iriyat's hands? What could Ev do, for that matter? She didn't know, but she knew she had to get there anyway. If Anavik came back, he'd know instantly that the house had been compromised. Even if they could contain him, he might have mentioned to Iriyat or Vatik that strangers were lurking in the street—he'd given Ev and Djal a thorough examination when he'd left. Anyone working in the house would have a healthy sense of paranoia.

Why hadn't she planned for this? She should've known better.

Just as Ev had come in without looking at any of the elaborate decorations of Solor House, she strode right back out without another glance.

19

THE SOUL OF VIRTUE

D JAL AND MALA HELPED ALIZHAN carry the tied-up priest down the stairs into the room where all the children were staying. They'd also left the two incapacitated guards there—the one Zilal had put to sleep, and another whose hair was matted with blood—in addition to two men and a woman Alizhan had never seen before, all of whom were alive, but unconscious and bound. Zilal followed them down the stairs, quite cheerful for a child whose life had recently been threatened.

"Will we still live in this house?" he asked.

"I don't know," Alizhan said. "Do you want to stay here?"

The boy chewed his lip. The question stumped him, so Alizhan let it go.

"Can you tell me the names of the people who work here?"

He nodded. "Hakur," he said, pointing to the stocky young man who'd threatened his life and Alizhan's. Then he looked at the other captives. "Josik," he said, indicating the man he'd put to sleep in order to allow Alizhan into the house. "Okardas," he said, pointing to the man with blood in his hair. The two men and the woman, he named, "Lortseya, Ashtur, Osan."

"Is there anybody else who isn't here?"

"Anavik," he said. "And a nice lady."

"With yellow hair?"

Zilal nodded. Iriyat. Alizhan's stomach clenched at the thought of Anavik walking free. He might be reporting to Iriyat right now. All Unbalanced Hells, she hadn't intended to take everyone in this house hostage. She'd only wanted to free Kasrik. But what could she do now?

"We're going to look around the kitchen and see if there's food for all these kids," Djal told her. "Do you need anything?"

For Ev to come back. For this to be over. "No, I'm fine."

"Sure you are," Djal said. "We've got this. We just need your friend Mar to show up with the rest of the Council and then it'll all be over."

Alizhan glanced down at Zilal, who wanted so badly to know if he and the other children would still live in this house. It would be a long time before this was over. "I don't understand why she did any of this."

"Trials get people talking," Mala said. "Come on, I'll make you some tea."

It was less work than Alizhan expected to get all nineteen children to go to bed, and it horrified her to think about just why they were all so obedient. Djal took up a post by the front door, and Mala stayed in the room with the children, so Alizhan went to sit by the back door. The thought of that room upstairs, with its chair and its dozens of implements, chilled her. All those bottles. Would Kasrik recover? Could you recover from being tortured, or was it something you learned to live with, instead?

Would Iriyat have done that to Alizhan, if Alizhan had been less eager to please?

All those years of pleasing Iriyat. Alizhan had never worried about whether she was doing the right thing. Now it seemed clear that she must have done the wrong thing—many times over. She'd never even stopped to consider that. Ev would've thought about it. Ev would never do something just to get someone to like her. Ev had principles. Alizhan had come by her own principles far too late.

Her mind slipped easily from these bleak distractions into the darkness of sleep, and she woke up to the choking, unnatural darkness of smoke. Tears stung her eyes.

Then someone grabbed her around the waist, and the shock of contact seared up and down her body. She blinked away the blackness from her vision, but the hall was full of smoke. *Fire.* The house was on fire. Where was everyone? Her captor lifted her up and threw her over a shoulder.

Breathe. Breathe. Ground yourself. But her feet weren't on the ground and there was no air, only smoke. Still, if she couldn't ground herself, maybe she could read her captor.

Little ghost more trouble than she's worth, he was thinking. Oh, Hells. It was Vatik. *Should've killed her like the others.* Others? Did he mean the children? Had he set the house and fire and left all the children in it to die? Were Mala and Djal still alive? Where was Ev?

"Stop," Alizhan said, and it was more coughing than words. Vatik ignored her. "Put me down."

She kicked at his chest. It had no effect.

Horrible, Unbalanced place. The city'll be better off without these monsters. At that, Alizhan gasped and had another coughing fit. Vatik didn't think the children were monsters. He thought the priests were monsters.

He'd killed them. And the guards. Alizhan searched frantically for thoughts of Djal and Mala. Vatik hadn't found Mala, but he'd fought an Adpri man when he entered the house. *A man lying on the floor with a gash in his stomach. As good as dead.* Alizhan sucked in a stinging breath of smoke. Was that Djal? Had Vatik killed Djal? A scream died in her throat, suffocated by fire and ash. Not now. She couldn't think of that now. She had to find out more.

"Iriyat ordered you to kill the priests," Alizhan guessed. She was killing the witnesses. Burning the evidence. "Did you kill the children, too?"

"Why, is that what you were planning?" Vatik said, his voice a low snarl. "What are you even doing in this place, little ghost?"

"Taking down Iriyat. Saving those kids."

"You're even madder than she said," Vatik said. His voice had a note of pity in it. "Iriyat told me you'd gotten all Unbalanced and run off after some delusion. I always knew you would. But she loves you, for some reason, so here I am cleaning up your mess and taking you home. At least I get to shut this awful place down as a benefit."

"What?" Alizhan choked.

"I don't know how you ended up here, or what those bastards did to you, but you're lucky Iriyat was paying attention," he said. "As soon as she got word you were here, she sent me to rescue you and burn this place to the ground. It's her sleep-shift, but she's out there in the street rescuing children, because that woman is a saint beyond the Balance."

Iriyat. Street. Children. "Oh, Hells, she's touching them."

"I never liked you, little ghost. Never understood why she did. You're too strange by half. Don't make me drop you before we get back to Gold Street."

Iriyat would touch her, too, and Vatik, and everyone, and no one would ever know this place had existed. Nothing would stop Iriyat from making another place just like it, and finding more nameless children for her cruel experiments. Alizhan had to do something. But Vatik thought Iriyat was the hero, not the villain.

Hakur had known exactly what he was doing. He'd known he was torturing children with abilities. He just happened to think he was working in the service of some greater good, at

Iriyat's behest, at least according to what he'd said out loud. Alizhan would bet all the other priests knew what they were doing, too, and probably the guards as well. That was why Iriyat had asked Vatik to kill them. But in order to get him to carry out that brutal order, she'd had to convince him that they were people worth killing—criminals, torturers, murderers.

In this case, they were. But Iriyat had still lied to Vatik. She'd had to twist the story. And Alizhan knew it wasn't the first time Iriyat had needed her power to keep Vatik in line.

He wasn't like the priests. He didn't believe in whatever awful project was happening in the house. He had a code. He believed in right and wrong, like Ev.

If Alizhan could save Vatik, she could save herself, too.

"Your memory troubles are Iriyat's fault," Alizhan said. "She's destroying you."

He stopped walking.

"Yes," Alizhan said. "I'm the little ghost, too strange by half, an unnatural horror and a monster and a disturbance to the Balance and probably a witch, too, sure. But I *know* things. I know your memory doesn't work as well as it should. That's because of Iriyat. When she asks you to do something that you consider dishonorable, and you resist, she makes you forget your concerns."

"My lady Ha-Varensi is the soul of virtue and she would never—"

"If she's the soul of virtue, why does she keep secrets? What could she possibly have to hide?" Alizhan said. "How did Iriyat know about this house? You don't need a perfect memory to see that something is wrong here."

"That something is *you.* You're a witch and a liar—"

"But I'm not wrong," she interrupted. "Your memory has holes in it. We both know it. Think. Iriyat told you not to touch me. You're wearing gloves now. Have you ever touched Iriyat? Has she ever touched you?"

"Absurd. She's a modest woman, a woman of strong faith—"

"You must be losing time," Alizhan pressed. "Are there shifts you can't account for? Do you find yourself in places without understanding how you got there?" She could feel the uncertainty uncurling in his gut. His fear and horror salted the air. And then his thoughts gave her exactly what she needed: an image. "Or maybe you find blood on the blade of your sword without knowing whose it is?"

A silence. She had him.

"Soldiers live hard," he said. It was a last effort, an excuse, and he didn't believe his own words. "If we don't die young, sometimes we grow old before our time."

"Yes," Alizhan said. "But it's one thing to forget names or places. It's something else to forget whose throat you cut."

"You watch your mouth, little ghost," he said. "I might be listening, but I still don't like you."

"Listening is all I need you to do," she said. The plan would come. She just had to keep talking. Vatik didn't like her, but he wouldn't kill her, and she could work with that.

20

SMOKE AND FIRE

"SMOKE AND FUCKING FIRE," EV said, and it wasn't just a curse. Smoke was billowing through Gold Street, and a crowd of people pressed close to the house. The Vigilkeepers had parked their wooden cart with its cistern of water in the street outside, and they were spraying the house with water. A chain of people were also handing off buckets of water to put out the blaze. Others were shouting and crushing closer, but they didn't seem to be helping.

Ev pushed forward until she could see why.

A tiny woman, her blond hair uncovered and mussed, stood near the garden gate, ushering wailing, soot-smudged children out into the street. Unconcerned by the devouring fire so close behind her, she calmly knelt and embraced each child, touching their cheeks and directing them away from the fire. The children were running toward the Vigilkeepers, who were helping them into an empty wagon. Ev counted thirteen of them already huddled together.

She should help them. Separate them from Iriyat. Hide them somewhere. But how? They were in the middle of a crowd and the house was still burning.

"Stay low to the ground, cover your mouth if you can," Iriyat was calling. Smoke flooded the air, and yet instead of sooty and sweaty and scared, Iriyat was fearless and radiant, her burnished gold hair shining under the twin red-gold lights of Laalvur's ever-present sun and the blaze of the orphanage.

A heroic image. No wonder the street was packed with gawking onlookers. Ev was at risk of becoming one of them until she shook herself. Iriyat didn't need to touch these bystanders to alter their memories. Her performance was enough. But she was careful to touch each child before letting go.

Iriyat was destroying the evidence and covering her tracks. "Get them away from her!" Ev shouted, but no one listened.

She shoved her way forward. Where were Alizhan, Djal, and Mala? Were they still inside? But most of the children were outside already. Iriyat was urging the last few toward the wagon. They were safe from the fire, if not from her. Ev didn't see any of the priests in the crowd, but in the packed, smoky street, she could easily have missed them. She didn't see her friends, either. It would have benefitted Iriyat to silence them, which meant they might still be in the house.

In the blistering, flickering fire.

Ev used her size and shouldered her way through the crowd. As she got closer to the house, people began to let her pass more easily, since they were eager to be away from the blaze. The crowd parted just before she got to the gate, where Iriyat was standing in front of the bucket brigade leading into the house. People seemed to expect Ev to keep her distance from the ruler of Varenx House and the conflagration—any sane person would —so no one stopped her. And Ev didn't stop.

The air was scorching. A flurry of cinders swirled above them. Ev lifted her tunic so she could cover her mouth. Iriyat, unveiled, look right at her as she approached. They were so close that Iriyat could have reached out and touched her and ruined everything in one instant, but instead, she squinted at Ev in incomprehension.

They'd only met once, after all.

"You'll die if you go in there," Iriyat said, shouting over the sound of the fire. A warning to a stranger could serve as part of her heroic image, the kind of prop she needed to make people believe she cared.

"And they'll die if I don't."

The Vigilkeepers standing in the garden tossing buckets of water through the smashed front windows and the open door stared at Ev, and one tried to stop her. "Miss—"

"Did you get everyone out?" she demanded.

He opened his mouth, but Ev shoved him aside before waiting for his answer. No one knew how many people had been in the house except her.

The Vigilkeepers had taken an axe to the front door. Wooden remnants lay split on the ground, and Ev picked one up as she stepped over the threshold into the smoke, using it as a makeshift shield against the radiant heat. Her eyes watered. Her throat burned. She tried to match the impenetrable walls of smoke with her memory of the house from hours ago: there was an entrance hall, with a room on either side, and stairs to the second floor, which was where she'd last seen Alizhan.

Ev tried for the stairs, but halfway up, the heat and smoke were so thick that she could go no further. She backed away, hardly able to stand, and then went into the room where the children had slept. The fire roared and the house groaned around her, its walls buckling and straining. In the dormitory, the darkness was lit with an orange glow—the rows of cots were on fire.

Djal was on the floor near the doorway, with Mala beside him. She was clasping one of his hands, and with her other hand, she was pressing a wad of fabric against his abdomen. It was dark with blood.

"I can't carry him," Mala shouted.

But Ev could. She dropped her shield on the ground and bent to lift him. He was as big as her, an unwieldy and delicate burden, but she got one arm under his legs and the other around his torso. "Front door," she said, and Mala picked up her skirts and, half-crouched, began to make her way toward the door as fast as she could. As frantic as Ev felt, an eerie, slow calm had settled over her, and through the haze of smoke, her eyes were drawn to details: Mala's bare feet, the ripped hem of her patterned yellow dress.

Djal was heavy and unmoving in her arms.

Their passage through the open front door was not as much of a relief as it should have been. It was easier to see outside the building, but the air still burned. Ev carried Djal into the street, and the crowd parted for her again. In her peripheral vision, she saw the gold of Iriyat's hair as the woman began to move toward them. Ev tried to move faster without jostling Djal. Mala followed close behind. Out here, Ev could see the trails of sweat down her face and the red of her eyes.

"Alizhan?" Ev said.

Mala shook her head.

Two Vigilkeepers came toward them with a stretcher for Djal, and Mala and Ev helped them load him onto it. Mala kept a cloth pressed to his abdomen. His bloody wound might have come from the fire, if something had fallen on him. But Djal would have been guarding the house, and this fire didn't feel like an accident, not with Iriyat making her way closer to them with every passing instant.

"How did this happen?" Ev whispered.

"A man with a sword," Mala said. "I think he went after Alizhan."

Vatik. Could he still be in the house? Ev rejected the idea. He'd been looking for Alizhan. He'd probably found her. But where were they now? His orders must have been to bring Alizhan back alive. But Iriyat was here and Vatik and Alizhan were nowhere in sight.

"Oh no," Iriyat called through the crowd. "What happened to this poor man? Let me help him!"

"Get this man to a hospital!" Ev didn't intend to shout at the Vigilkeepers, but Iriyat's approach made her panic. Raising her voice had the intended effect. The two men carried Djal's stretcher toward one of their wagons.

"She'll have to go through me first," Mala said under her breath and then hurried after them.

"I'll find you later," Ev said. Had Mala even heard her? She was alone in the crowd now. Iriyat was closing in. Ev had to run, but where? The creaking, crackling house with fire blackening its stone walls? Iriyat wouldn't follow her in, but the house was a death trap. If Alizhan was still inside, there was no hope for her. But if Ev didn't move, Iriyat would touch her. Toward the house was her only option. Ev dashed for the garden. Her shoulders slammed into onlookers and Vigilkeepers in her rush. For one terrifying, hallucinatory instant, she made eye contact with Iriyat. Those ash-grey eyes narrowed. They were separated by one or two people—Iriyat's reach failed by the length of a hand. Then Ev was past Iriyat and past the crowd and into the heat.

Ev aimed for the foliage filling the narrow alley between the house and its neighbors. It was monstrously hot, and the branches scraped her arms and face, but she forced her way through the thicket at the side of the house until she was in the back garden.

Alizhan and Vatik were standing, facing each other. Vatik's arms were crossed, and Alizhan was gesticulating wildly and shouting. Ev couldn't hear a word over the sound of the fire, but she went closer. Alizhan had dropped her arms to her sides by that time.

"Fine," Vatik growled. "Say you're right. Say it's all true. The woman I've served all my life is manipulating me through some Unbalanced witchcraft. What can I possibly do about it? Run? I can't do that. I won't."

Alizhan blinked, stumped by his sudden acquiescence. Ev pushed her way into the conversation. "Maybe we could have this talk somewhere that's not on fire," she said.

"Iriyat ordered me to bring you back alive," Vatik said to Alizhan.

"Are you not listening?" Alizhan said. "You shouldn't go back to her, with or without me. She's killing you!"

"She'll know what happened if I don't go back," he said. "She'll come looking for me. Unless she finds my body."

"I'm trying to save you, not kill you," Alizhan said.

"What if Iriyat found your body, but you weren't dead?" Ev said. "What if it looked like we—or Alizhan, since Iriyat doesn't care about me—what if it looked like Alizhan overpowered you?"

Vatik directed an incredulous look at the skinny young woman in front of him and then a pointed one at his own powerful physique, as if to ask how Alizhan could ever hope to overpower him. Before Ev could explain, Alizhan interrupted. "If we do that, then Iriyat finds him and then he's still in her power, where she can alter his memory."

"She won't if I comply," Vatik said. "Or give the appearance of compliance."

Ev blinked. She hadn't expected any help from him. "Are you... are you offering to spy for us?"

"I'm not offering you two Unbalanced fools anything. I'm saving my own damn skin," Vatik said. "But if the little ghost is telling the truth, and Mar ha-Solora's on her side, then I'll only need to stay with Iriyat until the Council makes its move."

Behind them, a roof beam burst into flames and collapsed into the house, which groaned.

"Alizhan can knock you out," Ev said. "When the fire is put out, they'll find you back here. If we leave you far enough from the house, you shouldn't get hurt."

"How reassuring," Vatik said. Then he bent down so that his face was close to Alizhan's.

"What are you doing?"

"What are *you* doing?" he said. "Punch me already."

It was strange to hear a peal of laughter amid the thunder and crash of the fire, but that was all Ev heard before Alizhan grabbed Vatik's hand and he slumped to the ground. They left him propped up against the back garden wall, and then began the long climb out of the garden.

21

NOTORIOUSLY UNRELIABLE

"WELL, THAT WAS A DISASTER," Mar said. "Sideran and Ezatur now think I'm a wild-eyed conspiracy theorist who has it out for Iriyat. And I didn't have time to contact the heads of the five Lesser Houses, but I'm sure they'll hear the news soon enough—Mar ha-Solora wants to put Iriyat in prison for saving orphans!"

Mar was so agitated that Alizhan hadn't even entertained the idea of sleeping, although he'd offered her a room. Had Kasrik gotten any rest here, with Mar in this state? Ev had declined Mar's offer as well, so they were now sitting in his parlor, drinking tea as if it would calm them.

They hadn't heard from Mala. Alizhan didn't expect to hear from Vatik.

"Shouldn't Sideran and Ezatur be suspicious that the place you said was evidence against Iriyat burned down? And that Iriyat was on the scene right after it happened?" Ev asked.

"Of course," Mar said. "But they're not going to move against her without a mountain of compelling evidence. They won't take that risk unless they absolutely have to, and Iriyat just gave them an out. It doesn't matter what they believe in their hearts. Politics isn't about what's right. It's about what's convenient."

"So we get them some compelling evidence," Alizhan said.

"I don't know if you recall what just happened—" Mar began.

"We have Kasrik," Alizhan said. "We have Djal and Mala. We might even have Vatik, if he stays safe. Those are witnesses."

"How can we trust Vatik?" Ev said. "We'll never know if he's been compromised, because he won't know himself."

"Testimony from a street kid and two foreigners won't count for much with the Council," Mar said. "Especially not if Iriyat lets them know that Kasrik's been living in my house. I'd hate to see *that* pamphlet."

"We still have the book," Alizhan reminded him. "And somewhere out there are nineteen children who suffered in that house and who need taking care of."

"I saw the Vigilkeepers load them into a wagon. They must have taken them to the Temple Street orphanage. The kids can't stay there, though. If Iriyat knows where they are, then it's not safe," Ev said. "And they don't know that they suffered, because Iriyat got to all of them."

"You think taking away the memory heals the rest?" Alizhan said. She didn't know the answer herself, but she suspected it was *no*.

"I suppose not," Ev said. "I'm not saying we shouldn't help them. But I doubt they'll be able to testify, in any case."

"And I haven't been able to decode the book," Mar said.

"So you just want to *give up*?" Alizhan said, and when their surprise buffeted her, it occurred to her that she'd shouted. "Iriyat is hunting down children—people like me and Kasrik—and hurting them, maybe killing them. If we don't stop her, nothing will."

Mar and Ev said nothing, which was good, because Alizhan wasn't finished.

"If you'd like to withdraw your accusations against Iriyat because it's politically *convenient* for you," she said, and she forced herself to look into Mar's eyes even though the intensity nearly overwhelmed her, "then Ev and I will continue without you. I doubt Kasrik will want to stay here any longer, either."

Mar didn't say anything, but he didn't have to. She knew what he wanted: to be proved right in the eyes of his fellow Council members, to rid himself of the specter of having loved Iriyat, to stop the horrors they'd described to him from happening again, and to get justice for Kasrik. Ev might've thought less of Mar if she'd learned he wasn't driven by justice alone. Luckily, Alizhan was familiar with the gritty underside of human nature, and she didn't care about the purity of anyone's motives.

"We have Zenav, too," Alizhan said. "And probably some other people who were in the Temple of Doubt. Didn't you say there were pamphlets about it? We can track some down."

"Pamphlets are notoriously unreliable," Mar said.

"You wanted a mountain of compelling evidence, and I'm working on it," Alizhan snapped. "We need all the help we can get. We have to consider every angle."

"You're right," Mar said.

"Didn't you say there was someone—a 'ghost'—in Varenx House?" Ev asked.

Alizhan nodded. She hated to add a problem to their list, but they had to be realistic. "It's the same issue we have with the kids, though. I doubt he remembers anything that would be useful to us."

Ev was quiet for a moment, but her mind was sifting possibilities and weighing outcomes. She'd speak soon. Mar opened his mouth to say something, and Alizhan held up a hand to silence him so that Ev could talk. He was affronted, but he kept his mouth shut.

"You gave me a memory," Ev finally said.

"The first time we touched," Alizhan said. "But how does that help us? Even if we assume that I could figure out how to do it again, which I might not, I made you remember something that happened to *me*. What we need from these people is for them to remember things that happened to *them*. Things that I have no way of knowing. Things that have been removed."

"But what if they haven't been removed?" Ev said. "We don't know anything about how this works. What if the altered memories are just hidden? Or encoded?"

Mar was nodding. "If I may speak," he said to Alizhan, and she knew the words were some sort of sharp-edged joke from the way he pitched his voice so obsequiously but still emanated smugness, but she didn't care. "It's a good point," Mar said. "As far as we know, Iriyat takes things *out* of people's memories. And in one instance, you put something *in*. She takes; you give. I'm not religious myself, but it does make sense that the world might balance itself like that. If some people are born with the ability to alter memories, other people are born with the ability to restore them."

The idea that she might not be a monstrous aberration, but a natural, necessary part of the system of the world made a tiny bud of something—hope?—open inside Alizhan, but she crushed it shut. "I've never done what you're proposing, and I've only done the thing Ev is talking about *once*, and that was an accident that knocked both of us unconscious."

"Didn't you just shout at us about not giving up?" Ev said mildly.

"I'm sorry if this isn't *convenient* for you," Mar said, much less mildly.

Alizhan pressed her bare feet into the thick pile of Mar's

expensive carpet and took a deep breath. She took a sip of tea, too, but it was cold.

"Speaking of things that are hidden or encoded, we should talk about the book again," Mar said. "Just because I haven't been able to read it doesn't mean it's impossible."

"How modest of you," Alizhan said.

A vivid flash of desire, viciously repressed, from Ev. Ev had imagined elbowing Alizhan sharply in the tender place just below her ribs—a warning against baiting their single powerful ally—but they were both tired, and hurting, and Ev cared too much about Alizhan's wellbeing to do it, which made Alizhan smile.

"I might know someone who could read it," Mar said. "And it might be a good idea for the two of you to disappear for a while. Iriyat will be looking for Alizhan, and she saw you at the house, Ev, so it's a good bet she'll be looking for you, too."

"I'm not leaving until we know those children are safe," Alizhan said, because she could see the plan forming in Mar's mind.

"Ilyr," Ev guessed. "You want us to go to Nalitzva and find Ilyr."

"Yes," Mar said. He was surprised to hear the words coming from Ev, rather than Alizhan. Alizhan took pleasure in that. People were always underestimating Ev. "I'll pay your passage and arrange false papers for you. The faster we get you out of the city, the less chance that Iriyat will figure out what we're up to, and the faster you'll come back and solve this."

"What will you do here, in the meantime?" Alizhan asked.

"I've been on the Council for twenty years," Mar said. "I think I can manage a month without you."

"I might know a ship that would take us," Ev said. "But Alizhan is right—if we don't rescue those children right now, we might as well have left them in that house. They might not help us solve the case, but we can't just leave them at Iriyat's mercy. We have to hide them."

———

SLEEPING and eating at Solor House was grander than all of Ev's wildest dreams, and yet their breakfast of bread and honey on the terrace overlooking the ocean was shadowed by failure. Alizhan, undeterred, was talking as fast as anyone could talk while shoving food into her mouth.

"Zilal helped me slip into the house," Alizhan said. She paused to swallow. "He didn't know me then. He might be willing to talk to me again, even if he doesn't remember me. If we can get into the orphanage—which I'm sure we can."

"That's one kid out of nineteen," Ev said. What worried her wasn't getting *in*, but getting *out*. "How do we persuade the others to come with us? Why would they trust us? Why would they trust anyone?"

"It's scary to be alone," Alizhan said. She picked up a green *jiyar* fruit from a bowl of fruit on the table and shoved her thumbnail into the rind, squirting juice into the air. She began to scrape at the peel, scattering little bits of it over the table. "Scarier if people have treated you like a monster your whole life. But I think I can get them to come with us."

"You can?" Ev said. The chaotic way Alizhan was attacking the fruit almost made her cringe, but Alizhan handed the whole mess to her before Ev had even lifted her shoulders. Ev accepted the *jiyar* and methodically removed what remained of its rind in a single spiraling strip, revealing the pink inside. "I'm sorry. I don't mean to sound so skeptical. But we're talking about *you*, and, well, a crowd of strangers."

"I know," Alizhan said. She took a section of *jiyar* from Ev and popped it into her mouth. "But I learned from the best."

At that moment, Kasrik shuffled onto the terrace, barefoot and battered. Bruises ringed his neck and bloomed ugly and purple around both eyes. Sleeping two shifts had done little to heal him. His tunic had short sleeves, and his arms were still covered in thin black tracks. They showed no signs of improving.

He pulled out another chair from under the ornately patterned tiled table, and its metal feet screeched against the terrace. Kasrik collapsed into the chair, and then put both arms on the table and slumped forward like he was planning to go back to sleep right there.

"I'm guessing you don't feel any better," Alizhan said, observing this display. Then, checking with Ev, she said, "That's what that means, right? I don't like it when I can't read people."

"Me neither," said the pile of limbs and tousled black hair previously known as Kasrik.

"Wait, what?"

"I can't read *anyone*," Kasrik said. "Not her, not Mar, not any of the servants who've been in my room bringing me food."

Ev, who'd never been able to read anyone's mind, didn't grasp the problem at first. But it must feel like losing a limb, or even a sense. Going blind or deaf. When she thought of it in these new terms, she understood why Kasrik was so upset. Her instinct was to hug him, or at least to reach out and pat him on the head, but she didn't know him at all. Was he averse to touch like Alizhan? Or perhaps he had been, and now he wasn't. Ev glanced at Alizhan for guidance, but Alizhan was staring into the distance. Her usually mobile features were frozen.

"My name is Ev," Ev said. Strange that she'd never actually met Kasrik, since she'd spent so much time discussing him with Alizhan. "How are you feeling?"

"Bad."

It had been a stupid question. But Ev had more to ask. "Do

you think you can't read anyone because of what Hakur did to you? Because of the venom?"

Kasrik nodded without lifting his head from his arms. "He told me this would happen."

"I'm sorry," Ev said, because she was, and because Alizhan wasn't saying anything.

In the silence, Ev picked up a thornfruit from the bowl and split its brown rind open. She wasn't hungry, but peeling the *jiyar* had been the last moment of calm in her life. She put the peeled thornfruit on her empty plate and the husk on the table, selected another one, and began to make two neat little pyramids. After a while, when the air was scented with the tangy sweetness of the fruit, Kasrik sat up straight and took one of the peeled ones from her plate. Ev pushed that pile closer to him.

Kasrik had eaten half a dozen, and Ev had peeled a dozen more, before Alizhan said, "Iriyat wanted to fix me."

Kasrik whipped around to glare at her. "So *this*—like everything else—is your fault."

"It sounds to me like it's Iriyat's fault," Ev said, as gently as possible. Then she looked at Alizhan. "What do you mean, she wanted to fix you? I thought she was using you for your abilities."

"She was. But she hated that I was suffering. That I couldn't walk through the city like a normal person. That I couldn't touch anyone."

"She didn't give a damn about your suffering," Kasrik said. "She was exploiting you, and she was pissed that she couldn't get more out of you. What kind of shitty spy can't go out in public?"

"I think she did care," Alizhan said, but it came out soft and uncertain. "I don't know why I think that. It's not like I ever knew what she was feeling. I didn't know her at all."

"It's not your fault," Ev said. "Of course you wanted to believe

she loved you. And you thought she was a good person, because you're a good person, and it didn't occur to you that she might lie to you."

Alizhan hadn't stop gazing into the distance. "I'm not," she said. Her hand splayed flat on the table, and then her fingers curled in again. "I should have known."

"I don't care how bad you feel," Kasrik cut in. "That's not helping me."

Ev needed to redirect this conversation away from the subject of blame. "I'm sorry to have to ask this, Kasrik, but do you think this change is permanent? Or is it something more like a bruise or a cut that might heal with time?"

"I don't know," he said, and drooped back into his chair.

"Okay," Ev said. "We'll work on finding out. We'll ask our friends Mala and Djal when we see them. And Mar has a library. He knows other rich people with libraries. We can try asking at the Temple of Doubt, too. Right now, we also need your help rescuing the other kids. You knew them better than anyone. The Vigilkeepers took them to the Temple Street orphanage after the fire. We want to get them out."

Kasrik assessed her with narrowed eyes. "What do you want them for?"

It was a fair question, especially considering that Kasrik had just lost his ability to know the difference between her words and her intentions. All Ev said was, "I don't want them to suffer. And if any of them remember details of what happened, it might help us convince the Council to throw Iriyat out of power."

"And into prison, I hope," Kasrik muttered. "Okay. I'll help them. *Them*, not you. This doesn't make us friends."

"We also need you to convince Mar to house and feed some of these kids. Maybe all of them," Alizhan said. She couldn't read his mind or his face, so his glare slid off her like water

the scene made Ev's stomach hurt. She wished Kasrik and Alizhan could have met some other way. Then maybe they could've been friends.

Kasrik thought about Alizhan's request, and then he shrugged. "Mar likes me for some reason. He'll probably do it. He'll grumble about it, but he'll do it."

Ev hadn't realized this was part of Alizhan's plan until right now. "Are you sure they'll be safe here? Shouldn't we hide them?"

"You know a place to hide nineteen kids?" Kasrik said.

Ev shook her head.

"We also have to get them out without getting caught," Alizhan said. "There will be other kids and lots of priests at the orphanage, and Temple Street is busy."

"We'll do it right this time," Ev said. "We'll make a real plan. And you won't go in alone."

"I did what I had to," Alizhan said. "Kasrik was in there. And we got out just fine."

After the chaos Ev had witnessed—the fire, Djal's ugly wound, and Iriyat touching the kids—nothing was *just fine*. And it could all have been different with a bit more careful planning.

"Or we could have taken our time and planned meticulously and Iriyat could *still* have outmaneuvered us," Alizhan snapped. "And Kasrik would've spent longer in that torture chamber."

"Whoa," Kasrik said, surprise and unhappiness in his expression. He hadn't expected Alizhan to respond so fiercely to Ev's silent contemplation—another reminder of his lost ability. He glanced between Alizhan and Ev, both the unwilling subject of and witness to their argument. "Don't drag me into whatever this is."

"At least we caught her a little off-guard this time," Alizhan continued, ignoring him. "I'm sure it wasn't her plan for those kids to end up back at Temple Street, but she had to let the

Vigilkeepers take care of them, because anything else would've raised suspicions. I know they're not safe yet, but anything is better than where they were."

"Alright," Ev said. "Let's not fight. Let's go check it out. Maybe something will come to us on the way. Kasrik, you can stay here if you don't feel up to the walk."

It was the wrong thing to say, and his fourteen-year-old pride was clearly wounded.

"I said I'd help."

Kasrik walked with them into the city, although he was stiff and slow in his gait. He wore a determined expression and said almost nothing as he led them along the ridge of Hahim and across the city. Temple Street was in Denandar, a long way from Solor House, but Kasrik didn't bring up the distance, so neither did Ev.

They paused in Pachisar Fountain Square for Kasrik to catch his breath. Ev was sweating under the long, hooded overgarment she'd borrowed from one of Mar's servants. She wanted to remove the hood, but it was a poor enough disguise on its own, and they were a conspicuous trio. The chaotic intersection of three streets wasn't a square at all, but the space was coursing with people. In the shadow of her own hood, Alizhan had the determined set to her jaw that meant she was concentrating hard on blocking out everyone's feelings. Kasrik just looked tired.

Pachisar was so crowded that it took Ev a moment to hear the crier, and even longer to locate him. He was twelve or thirteen years old, standing on the low stone wall around the fountain with one wiry arm thrust into the air above his head, waving a stack of pamphlets.

"True story! Iriyat ha-Varensi saved orphans from a fire! Read it right here, only two kalap!"

So that was what this shift's pamphlets were about. The

news was already filtering into the city. A pamphlet about Iriyat heroically rescuing orphans was bad news for their cause. At least there didn't seem to be any pamphlets speculating about a rift between Mar and Iriyat yet. If Iriyat managed to turn the rest of the Council against Mar, there'd be no hope for a trial.

Ev watched the boy for a few minutes, and even without the promise of pornography, he sold several copies.

"Should we buy one?" she asked Alizhan. The story in that pamphlet had come from somewhere—or someone. There was a difference between spinning a tale from thin air and weaving one with threads of truth, and in this case, Ev had an unpleasant feeling that she knew who was pulling the strings. "Maybe it would be useful just to see what it says?"

"I know what it says," Alizhan said darkly, and turned away. Kasrik went with her, and they made their way out of the square.

After a short time, Kasrik slowed his pace, and Ev fell into stride with him. Alizhan was far enough ahead that she probably couldn't hear them.

"She feels really awful about everything," Ev said. "She's sorry and she's trying to make things right."

"What, now you're a mind-reader too?"

"No, but I know Alizhan. And I want you to know she's trying."

"She could tell me herself."

"You think she'd be better at this stuff, since she's spent her life feeling everybody else's feelings," Ev said, conceding his point. She wanted so badly to apologize on Alizhan's behalf, to defend her, to make Kasrik see how good she was. "But things have been hard for her, too. That's not an excuse, I know. I'm just trying to explain."

"You can stop trying," Kasrik informed her. He walked faster and was soon too far ahead for conversation.

When they arrived in Denandar, Alizhan picked a ledge

overlooking Temple Street and the three of them sat down on the low wall with their feet dangling. Ev positioned herself between Alizhan and Kasrik for peacekeeping purposes, although all three of them were exhausted and prickly enough to fall into an argument at any moment. Alizhan tapped her heels against the wall and drummed her thigh up and down. Their vantage point granted them a view of the flow of humanity through Temple Street, or at least the tops of everyone's heads. Alizhan had chosen this spot since it was right next to a ladder. Staying above the street kept anyone from touching her, but when their target came along, she'd be able to climb down and follow.

The orphanage wasn't as worn down and dirty as Ev had thought, at least on the outside. But it was Iriyat's pet cause and she'd poured money into refurbishing the ancient stone building, set into the cliff like all the others on the street. The massive wooden door was polished and swung silently on its oiled hinges.

Ev watched it open and shut many times in the next few hours. The orphanage was a busy place. It was mostly grey-robed priests who went in and out, but occasionally someone in more colorful clothes would enter. Only adults moved in and out freely. Ev didn't see any children.

Temple Street cleared. A diminutive, veiled woman strode into view. Her hair was covered and her face was difficult to see from this angle, but Ev knew only one woman who could part a crowd like that.

Next to her, Kasrik tensed. "Iriyat."

Ev couldn't blame him. She was clenching her teeth. If Iriyat glanced up and saw the three of them...

Alizhan said nothing. She was already moving, climbing down the ladder next to their seat so that she could join the crowd in Temple Street. She wanted to be closer.

"This is stupid," Kasrik hissed at Ev as she began to climb down the ladder. Ev agreed, but grabbing Alizhan now would cause a scene. People wanting a better look at Iriyat ha-Varensi was unremarkable—even as the crowd held back from her, it thickened with new arrivals hoping for a glimpse.

Thanks to her height, Ev had a clear view through the crowd. She tugged her hood lower and prayed Iriyat and Vatik didn't turn her way.

The orphanage door swung open and a grey-robed priest appeared on the threshold, a streak of severity in the colorful palette of the street. Her hair was also covered, but Ev would bet it was black with a few silver highlights, after squinting at her face. She looked about forty. Much taller than Iriyat, she squared her shoulders and gave her a decidedly cool reception.

"Who is—" Ev started, but Alizhan shushed her.

They waited in silence until the door had closed behind Iriyat and the priest.

"We need to go," Kasrik said, his voice low and urgent.

"We should stay and wait for her to come out," Alizhan said. Her voice was quiet, pitched so that only Ev and Kasrik could hear, but she was calm.

Kasrik whipped around. "Are you *insane*?"

"I want to listen to them again," Alizhan said.

Ev scrutinized Alizhan for signs of fatigue. Sweat at her hairline. Circles under her eyes.

"I'm fine," Alizhan said. "I'm breathing and focusing and paying attention to my body and everything Mala told me to."

Guilt rolled over Ev. They should have gone to check on Mala and Djal by now. She'd promised to find them. Was Djal recovering?

"Can we get back to the part where we leave before the woman who wants me dead comes out that door?" Kasrik said.

"Take Kasrik with you and go find Djal and Mala," Alizhan said. "I'm staying."

Ev hated that idea, but the door could open at any moment and next to her, Kasrik was ready to jump out of his skin. He deserved better than to be forced to stay here. He'd been through enough. "Promise me you won't do anything but observe. Don't go in there. If anyone notices you, you run."

"Promise," Alizhan said.

"If you're not back at Mar's in four hours, I will storm Varenx House by myself to find you," Ev said.

"I know."

KASRIK KEPT his shoulders hunched and said nothing as they made their way down to Arishdenan harbor. Ev's first thought was to check The Anchor, but Djal and Mala hadn't been staying there. Instead, she went back to The Red and Black, where Alizhan had first played cards with Djal. Inside, there were a handful of people drinking in semi-silence, and two people lazily tossing cards down on a table, but no sign of Djal and Mala.

Ev asked the young woman at the bar if she'd seen any Adpri sailors. The woman assessed Ev through her narrowed, heavily lined eyes for an instant and adopted a bored expression again. She reached under the counter, then dropped a stack of playing cards on top of it. Ev spread them out, perplexed. All five cards were Suns. The hand was called a Scorch, but she had no idea what it meant.

Ev wanted to turn to Kasrik and ask if he had any insight, but that would give away how lost she was.

Instead, she nodded as if she'd been expecting a cryptic playing card message. She could work this out. Obviously the bartender had been expecting her and had known her description, which meant the message was almost certainly from Djal and Mala. They'd remembered this tavern, too.

At Ev's nod, the young woman scooped up the cards on the counter, slid them back into the deck, and offered it to Ev.

Ev was supposed to leave a message in return. How could she express "we made it out alive" in playing cards? That was the most essential information, and it must be what Djal and Mala had intended in their own message. Just the fact that they'd left any message at all meant they were alive. The method itself suggested secrecy was more important than nuanced communication. Ev shouldn't leave a written note. She shouldn't ask around or go looking for them. They were hiding.

Ev selected a ten from each suit: Sun, Stars, Smoke, Snow. That conveyed "message received, we're alive too," didn't it? Ev scanned the cards one last time, then nodded at the bartender, who collected the cards and put them back under the counter.

After they'd left and begun their long hike up into the city, Kasrik said, "You have no idea what you're doing."

God, was it that obvious? Ev resisted the urge to cringe. "I thought you couldn't read minds anymore."

"I can't. I watched you," Kasrik said. "I watched the bartender, too. I don't think she knew that you were confused. You put on a good show."

"That was smart of you," Ev said. "You learned to read people in the usual way."

"It's so much work."

"Yes," Ev said. She didn't laugh, even though his amazement was charming. Kasrik had lost something. "And half the time, I'm wrong. Tell me, what did you think of the priest we saw at the door?"

"She didn't like Iriyat."

Ev nodded. She'd had the same impression. From Alizhan's

memories, she knew that was rare. Most people fawned over anyone beautiful, wealthy, and famous. Iriyat was doubly dangerous, with the tragic story of her parents' early deaths and her reputation for selfless generosity. A priest at the orphanage where Iriyat had given so much money and time ought to have been overjoyed to see her. "Do you think she suspects something?"

"Maybe," Kasrik said.

"Did you notice anything else about that priest, Kasrik?" Ev was fishing for confirmation. Now that she knew Kasrik could observe people in a way that Alizhan couldn't, she wanted his opinion.

"Yeah," he said. "She looked like Alizhan."

22

A TRICK OF THE LIGHT

"A SCORCH," ALIZHAN SAID WHEN she walked in the door to Solor House. Ev and Kasrik were sitting on one of the huge sofas in the first room after the entrance, with cards spread on the table in front of them. Kasrik was trying to teach Ev the rules to every game he could think of, in case she needed to leave more messages, but she'd been distracted, waiting for Alizhan.

Alizhan kicked off her shoes and came to join them. She sat cross-legged on the floor next to the low table and starting rearranging the cards so that all the Suns were together. With her features unmoving in concentration, her resemblance to the serious priest grew stronger. Ev pushed that thought aside as Alizhan fanned out five cards. "That's how Djal won when we played cards the first time. I called him Scorch because I didn't know his name."

"So it means what I thought," Ev said. "They're alive and recovering. And they'd prefer not to be found."

"That's my best guess, too," Alizhan said. She sorted the cards into the message that Ev had left: a ten of each suit. She nodded her approval. When that was done, she said, "I think we should talk to Eliyan Matrishal."

"Who?"

"The priest," Kasrik guessed. "The one who didn't like Iriyat."

"We just found a secret prison run by priests of the Balance, and now you want to *talk* to one?" Ev said.

"When Iriyat came out of the orphanage, so did Eliyan, and after Iriyat left, Eliyan went over to Arishdenan to buy some tea," Alizhan said. "I followed her for a long time. She's good, Ev, I promise. Some of them are rotten, but not all."

"They all think they're serving God," Ev marveled. This wasn't the old religion, with more than one god. These priests all served the *same* God. "The guy who hurt Kasrik thought he was carrying out God's will, and so does this woman who feeds and shelters orphans."

"Says more about them than it does about God."

Ev raised her eyebrows. She'd never asked if Alizhan believed in God.

"I don't want to. What kind of god makes a world like this one?" Then, like a priest of Doubt, Alizhan murmured, "But what do I know?"

"What should we talk to her about?" Kasrik asked.

"The truth."

"That's a far cry from breaking into the orphanage and sneaking out with nineteen kids," Ev said.

"We'll do that if Eliyan doesn't agree to help," Alizhan said. "But she already knows some of the kids who just arrived are strange. And she's uncomfortable with Iriyat, even though she doesn't know why. She'll believe us. We just have to show we don't mean them any harm."

Kasrik was nodding. "Take me with you. If she lets us inside, I'll talk to them." He yawned. "Next triad, though."

He got up and wandered out of the room. Ev was glad to see him planning to get some rest. She'd been worried that she'd have to order him to sleep. He'd been so determined not to show any weakness on their walk—except for the moment of Iriyat's appearance, and Ev couldn't blame him for that. She'd felt the same jolt of fear.

As soon as Kasrik was gone, Alizhan said, "She's not my mother. I know you talked about it and you both think I look like her, but she's not my mother."

"I know," Ev said. "It doesn't make sense." The resemblance was there—those thick, arched brows and that prominent nose. Eliyan's face was a little longer and squarer through the jaw than Alizhan's, and in the few minutes Ev had watched her, she'd held herself still and unsmiling. But the thought of Eliyan—a woman who'd dedicated her life to raising mother-less children—giving up her own child was absurd. The resemblance was some kind of accident. A trick of the light. "She loves kids."

"It's not that. She loves kids, sure, but she could have been forced into giving hers up somehow, if she had one," Alizhan said. "But I don't think she ever did."

Alizhan had glossed over a dark possibility—that Iriyat had stolen her and forced her mother to forget—with such speed that Ev was left lagging behind. "You think she never had a child? Why not?"

"She never thinks about sex," Alizhan said. "Most people do. Not consciously, but underneath the rest of their thoughts, there's a current. Someone attractive walks by, they notice. Not Eliyan. It never occurs to her."

"Maybe she hasn't seen anyone attractive in the hours you've been around her."

Alizhan shook her head. "I'm not explaining it right. You have to trust me, though. I can *feel* when people are... not necessarily that they're aroused or anything, but just... the possibility is there. She's not like that."

"Are you?" Ev hadn't meant to let the words out—her hand was halfway to her mouth, too late to slap it shut—but there they were. If Ev had kept silent, Alizhan would have ignored her thoughts on the subject, since it was exactly what she'd told Ev not to hope for.

Hope wasn't allowed, but Ev could be curious, couldn't she? Alizhan knew everything about her.

"Am I what? Like Eliyan?"

Alizhan didn't need that clarification. She was stalling. But Ev nodded.

"It doesn't matter," Alizhan said. "My point is that it's unlikely Eliyan ever had a kid of her own, even though she loves them. She just isn't interested in sex. I'm not saying it rules out your theory, but we should talk about more important things now."

"We almost got caught this shift," Ev said, accepting Alizhan's desire to change the subject. The hoods had been a good idea, but face veils would be better. "We'll have to be more careful next time."

"I don't mind wearing a veil," Alizhan said. "The world feels fairer that way—I can't see anyone's face, so why should they get to see mine?"

Fairer. Right. "You can *read minds.*"

Alizhan gave a lopsided smile, lifted her shoulders, and spread her hands wide. Despite her lingering frustration, Ev laughed.

"You're right that we'll have to watch ourselves. There's only the door in Temple Street and a back door on the other side of Denan. Eliyan won't be inclined to trust us if we go in that way, so we'll have to use the main door."

"You know we'd be endangering her by telling her the truth.

If Iriyat finds out about her involvement, she'll mess with Eliyan's memory. Or worse."

"That's always true. It could happen to Mar or Vatik. It could happen to me or you."

Ev had spent far too much time contemplating it already. Would it be painless, just a touch of the hand wiping away her memories? It would be like killing a small part of herself. As awful as it was to imagine her own loss, it was worse to imagine leading someone else into that danger. But they needed help.

"If we tell her truth, she'll want to help," Alizhan said. "You accepted the risks and so will she."

THE MASSIVE, metal ring for knocking on the orphanage door was huge and heavy in Alizhan's hand. The moments between knocking and the door opening hung suspended, stretching longer with every breath.

A man in grey robes opened the door. At the sight of two young women in face veils, one very tall and one very short, and a young man with his hood pulled low, recognition seized him.

Shit. Alizhan couldn't move. She couldn't give away that she knew what the priest knew. Iriyat and Vatik had warned him to watch for them. He'd send word as soon as he stepped away from them. By the time they left the orphanage, the streets would be full of Varenx House guards.

Alizhan's fingers twitched. She might hurt herself if she touched him. It might be worth it. Or maybe Ev could knock him out. He was only a little taller than Alizhan and the robes made it hard to tell, but she'd guess he was soft. How much of a fight could he put up?

Kasrik nudged her in the back. She didn't want to turn

toward him—too obvious. But she scanned the foyer beyond the priest and saw a child.

Not remarkable, to see a child in an orphanage. But this one was unreadable. And he was about Zilal's size. She ripped her gaze away from the child to meet the priest's eyes. She smiled at him, but from the wave of confusion that washed through him, she didn't do it right.

"Hello," Alizhan said as calmly as she could. "How are you?"

It was enough. The priest started to form a word, then his mouth went slack and his eyes rolled up and he sunk to the floor. Zilal stood behind him, still holding the priest's limp hand in his own small one. Alizhan hadn't seen or heard his approach —an impressive skill for such a young child, but one she wished he'd never had to learn. He stared up at Kasrik.

"Good work," Kasrik said. He crouched down. "You remember me?"

"No. Yes." Zilal made a face. "I don't like to remember."

"Can't blame you for that," Kasrik said.

"You don't have to remember," Alizhan said. Zilal didn't recognize her. "Are you hungry?"

Zilal scrutinized the three of them for a moment, and then nodded. Alizhan took a few steps toward him, and then knelt down and offered him something from the pocket of her tunic. A single thornfruit sat in the middle of her palm. Her hand was bare, but with one steadying breath, she reminded herself that he couldn't hurt her and she wouldn't hurt him. Her control was stronger now. Mala's tedious lessons in breathing had been worth it, since now Alizhan could offer this small kindness to someone else.

Zilal grabbed it and pinched the rind until it popped off, then ate it in one bite. Alizhan smiled and offered him several more, and he ate all of them. When he was finished swallowing, she picked up the rinds and said, "My name is Alizhan."

"Zilal."

"Oh my." The voice was low and female, and it came from the woman who was now standing on the other side of the foyer from them. Eliyan. "This isn't how we usually answer the door."

"Your new arrivals aren't usual," Alizhan said, getting right to the point. The other priest wouldn't sleep for long. He'd be sure to tell Iriyat he'd seen them when he woke, even if they got away. "Can we talk somewhere private?"

"Zilal, please go back to your room for a while. The rest of you, this way," Eliyan said. She led them through the cavernous main hall and into a small, sparsely furnished room divided by a curtain. On their side of the curtain, there was a chair and a desk covered in stacks of books and a lamp. The lamp, a tall column of glass filled with green fluid, was perched on the books. From Eliyan's thoughts, Alizhan knew the other side was where she slept.

Eliyan locked the door.

"I'm sorry I don't have more chairs."

"We don't have time to sit," Alizhan said. "You took in nineteen children after the fire in Gold Street—Zilal among them —didn't you?"

"Yes."

"The others are like Zilal," Alizhan said. "Not exactly like him, but they have unusual abilities."

Eliyan was nodding. "You don't have to dance around the rest. I've known children like this before."

"You have?" Ev was surprised. "Don't you believe all that stuff about how magic isn't real and people should abandon their Unbalanced children into the care of the Temple?"

"I grew up in the Marsh. We took care of our own," Eliyan said coolly. A few names and faces flitted through her mind, but one stayed longer than the rest. A brother. Eliyan had once had a brother with some ability. *Don't look*, she was thinking. Kasrik's black scars, only the raw ends visible at the hem of his sleeves, haunted her mind. Eliyan had seen scars like that before. "There were always whispers that someone was taking children. Especially certain children."

"Didn't it worry you that the Temple encouraged suspicion of anyone strange or different?" Ev asked. "And if there were rumors, why didn't anyone do anything about them?"

It bruised Ev's heart each time she learned of some new wrong. If only everyone could feel how badly they were failing Ev's hopes at every turn, the world would be a better, kinder place. At least, she made Alizhan want to work harder.

"We tried. I'm still here, trying. As for why we didn't report it to the authorities... Haven't you heard?" Eliyan asked, her voice bitter. "Salt-crusted, water-brained Marshers will believe anything."

"That's terrible," Ev said. "It still doesn't explain your choice to join—"

"I told you," Eliyan said. "I'm *here*, trying. I took this position specifically to protect these children. If anyone was trying to hurt them, I would know. And the Temple of the Balance is the spiritual home of hundreds of priests and thousands of worshippers. We're not all the same."

Alizhan didn't have time for this. She had to direct them back to the subject. "Someone is trying to hurt them. I know you noticed Kasrik's scars. You've seen scars like that before—on your brother's arms. You know what caused them."

Kasrik touched his wrists, but it was too late to hide.

Eliyan was only startled for an instant before understanding bloomed. *She's like him*, she thought, and her gaze searched Alizhan's face. Keeping her voice neutral, she said, "I don't, actually. I've seen sailors come home with scars like that after tangling with giant medusas." She turned to Kasrik, her voice softer, "But you look too young for that."

"He is," Alizhan said. "There's some kind of trade in medusa tentacles here in the city. They're still potent even after they're detached. There was a room full of jars in the house that burned down—a torture chamber. You can see what happened to Kasrik there."

No longer trying to hide, Kasrik pulled up one of his sleeves to expose the ragged black lines striping his forearm. "A priest of the Balance did this to me."

Eliyan went white-hot with rage. "Who?"

"A man named Hakur. He's already dead," Alizhan said. "But there are others. And they'll be looking for the children you just took in. That's why we came to talk to you. When Iriyat was here, did she ask you about them?"

"Of course, but everyone's talking about them. No one seems to know what happened, but the rumors are ugly." Eliyan was viscerally upset by the scars and their story. Her stomach was roiling. She was trying to calm down, reminding herself that she'd watched these three young people talk to Zilal. They seemed like good people. It wasn't their fault that they came bearing terrible news. At least they were speaking plainly.

"You don't like her," Alizhan said.

"We revere God's Balance in nature and we distort it in our communities," Eliyan said. "For Iriyat to be so rich, how many hundreds or thousands of other people must live in poverty? Her charity patches over something fundamentally broken."

Ev was trying not to smile, thinking of her father saying *rich people*. She liked Eliyan.

"You're right to dislike Iriyat. She's the reason children have disappeared from your communities for so many years. She's the reason the Temple preaches suspicion. We don't know what her goal was, but that house belonged to her. She'd been holding those children there, hurting them. She might have been studying them. Now that they're here, she'll look for a way to get them out again."

Eliyan went from stunned to skeptical and back. "How could she possibly keep all that a secret? And who are you, that you'd discover it?"

"I used to work for her," Alizhan said. "You already know what I can do. Iriyat can erase memories with a touch. Watch out for her hands next time she's here. And don't let her touch your skin. That power, combined with her wealth, is how she operates in secret."

"Say I believe this," Eliyan said. "What do we do about it?"

"We need to hide those children," Alizhan said. "It would be fine if they were adopted by people you trust, but if that happens, any evidence that they were here—or written records of where to find them—needs to go missing in a mysterious accident. And Zilal needs to get out *now*."

Eliyan had been preparing objections in her head, but the last sentence knocked her out of it. "Why Zilal?"

"Iriyat paid that priest who opened the door for us to inform her. He saw us, but Zilal interrupted our conversation. We need to be gone before he wakes up, and so does Zilal."

"I see," Eliyan said, unhappy. It was too much to ask, and too soon to ask it. She was willing to work with Alizhan, but she didn't want to be pushed into taking risks that might endanger the children. Instead of addressing the question about Zilal, she turned back to her interrupted train of thought. "Adoption is a long, slow process. It could take years for all nineteen of them to get adopted."

Alizhan was going to have to push her. "Then it's not safe. We'll have to smuggle them out. No records. As few witnesses as possible."

"Smuggle them out where?"

"I doubt we can hide them all in the same place," Alizhan

said. "But we need to get Zilal out this shift, and we'll have to work almost as fast with the others, so we'll have to get creative." Eliyan was wording more objections, so Alizhan continued quickly, "I've already told you enough about myself that you could easily report me to Iriyat yourself. You're not the only one taking risks here. I'm trusting you, too. You saw us with Zilal. He and Kasrik know each other. Let us talk to him. If he doesn't want to come with us, we won't make him."

"Fine. Let me bring him here, just to keep this as private as possible."

Before Eliyan opened the door to her office, Alizhan closed her eyes and focused on the space outside. Nothing but the quiet, confused mumblings of dreams. Zilal could put a man to sleep for a long time. "Don't let anyone see you."

Eliyan left and returned. She gently shepherded Zilal into the small room. Eliyan and Ev both worried about how thin he was, how unnaturally quiet and still for a child.

Kasrik was the first to speak with him, bringing himself down to the boy's height. "I'm sorry for leaving you in that place."

Zilal said nothing. It was impossible to know if he remembered the house in Gold Street at all. But he'd recognized Kasrik earlier, so that was something to cling to.

"These are my," Kasrik paused. He didn't have to spare Alizhan the truth. They weren't friends. He'd made that clear. Instead of finishing the sentence, he started a new one. "This is Ev, and that's Alizhan. We'd like to help you. We want to take you somewhere better."

If only she could read them! Was Zilal hopeful? Suspicious? What did he know of Kasrik?

"Where?" Zilal asked.

Kasrik was quiet. *Oh.* He was looking at Alizhan, waiting for her to say something.

She bent her knees, crouching flat-footed so that Zilal could see her face, whatever that was worth. "It's a good place. The people who live there will take you in and feed you, and they'll never hurt you. And they have dogs."

A note of surprise from Ev. She'd been expecting a description of Solor House. Mar didn't have any dogs. Alizhan had changed the plan at the last minute, but Ev had inspired her. She'd been thinking about how grand and unfriendly Solor House might seem to a child. Her parents' farm would be more welcoming. And hiding Zilal in Orzatvur might buy them time —Iriyat would be watching Mar, but she couldn't watch every farm in every little outlying village. And as much as Ev hated to put her family in more danger, they were already involved—and there'd never been any question in her mind that her parents would agree to help despite the risks.

"There's a striped one named Tez who needs a lot of attention," Alizhan continued. "It's a big farm. They have a cow and a donkey and chickens and a big garden where they grow food. They grow these." Alizhan reached into her pocket and pulled out the last few thornfruits she'd taken from the breakfast table.

Zilal took another one eagerly, letting its rind fall on Eliyan's floor. With one cheek full, he said, while chewing, "How many dogs?"

A shrewd negotiator. Alizhan tried to take the question as seriously as he did. "We'll have to ask an expert," she said, glancing at Ev. She offered Zilal another thornfruit and he accepted it. His hand brushed hers—and nothing happened. Just a touch.

"Three," Ev said. "And eight cats—six in the barn, and an orange one named Vesper and a grey one named Aurora who sleep in my room."

"You live there?"

"Yes, although I might... have to go away for a while," Ev said. "Will you take care of the animals for me?"

Ev always knew the right thing to say. After a moment, he nodded. Eliyan wasn't fully satisfied, but she'd keep her word. Alizhan couldn't blame her for her attitude. That skepticism might save her memory or her life. But maybe there was a way to address her fears.

"Will you be sure to write to your friends here?" Alizhan said. That would provide a way for Eliyan to watch over him. The letters would have to be hidden or encoded, but that could be arranged somehow. "Kasrik will deliver the letters."

Zilal nodded again.

Eliyan and Kasrik could do good work together, but they'd need a whole network of people if they were going to secret nineteen children out of Iriyat's reach. And Alizhan and Ev wouldn't be there to help.

"Kasrik, the other eighteen kids—are any of them like Iriyat?" Alizhan asked. "Can they alter memories?"

He shook his head. "No, no one like that ever came to the house."

There was a mystery to ponder. Was Iriyat's ability rarer than others? Or was she doing something else with children who were like her?

"Too bad," Alizhan said. "We could use someone like that. What about other mind-readers?"

"One besides me," Kasrik said. "A boy named Sorav. And maybe a girl named Orilan, but she never talks so it's hard to tell what she can do. Both of them are little, though. I'm not sure how good they are."

"You'll have to teach them to sense anything unusual or dangerous," Alizhan said. "Sneak back in."

God, there were so many ways this could go wrong. Alizhan had never done anything like this—and she'd never depended on other people before. Iriyat had made sure she worked alone. Could Kasrik and Eliyan handle this? Would they work together? Would they find other people to trust?

Luckily, Ev was already solving the same problem. "My father sells fruit in Arishdenan market. A big, tall Adpri man with a shaved head. He'll help you—smuggling people or carrying messages or anything else you can think of. He won't betray you. At least... not if he's in his right mind."

"You think we should just walk up and talk to him about this?" Eliyan asked.

"Of course not," Alizhan said. This part was easy to plan. And she already knew the schedule. "He's there on Estri and Chistri, always during the first half of the shift of the Rosefinch. Sometimes longer if he doesn't sell out. Start frequenting his stall. Develop a regular order. Next week, Kasrik can lurk around there and you can run into each other. Don't have a conversation. Just... bump into each other."

Ev was remembering the card messages at The Red and Black. Her thoughts fizzed with amusement. "Kasrik should steal some thornfruits. You can catch him at it. Make a little scene. That way, my father will recognize you."

"And if things go wrong, you should know that there's a man in Iriyat's guard who's... not entirely evil," Alizhan said. "He has one brown eye and one blue eye. His name's Vatik. Remember that—try to keep it separate in your mind. I can't guarantee he'll help you, but..." She finished her sentence with a shrug. It was hard to shake the feeling that she was assigning them an impossible task and abandoning them. But right now, her presence endangered everyone more than her absence. "We need to go. Iriyat's mole will wake up any minute now. There's a back door that will let us out into Arishdenan, right?"

Alizhan no longer sensed the quivering tension of worry from Eliyan. Instead, she was emanating a very particular, serene kind of focus. *Like one of Mala's breathing exercises, but where would she have learned that? Oh—praying. She's praying.* None of the other priests had felt anything like that. It lasted only a moment, then Eliyan stepped out into the hall decisively. "Follow me."

THE BACK EXIT of the orphanage was in the kitchen. Eliyan had said the door let out into a short alley where they dumped their refuse, which would give them a moment of cover before they went into the street. Ev's head kept brushing the kitchen ceiling as the four of them crammed into a passageway that served as a pantry, next to jugs of oil and sacks of rice, ready to rush out the door at any moment.

She watched Alizhan's hand hover over the door handle for two long minutes before she grasped it at last. But she didn't open the door. "The street is crowded," Alizhan said. "A guard from Varenx House—or someone working for Iriyat who had our descriptions—just passed by."

Mar had been right. They needed to get out of the city. Ev's stomach twisted. They'd been awaited at the orphanage, and there were people looking for them all over the city. It was a miracle they hadn't been caught already.

"We should split up," Alizhan said. "I'm going back to Solor House to retrieve the book and whatever papers Mar has had forged to get us on a ship and into Nalitzva. Then, after a while, Kasrik will go back—discreetly."

"I robbed Varenx House right under your nose," Kasrik said. "I'm stealthier than you've ever been."

Alizhan made a sound of frustration, but otherwise ignored this jab. "Just do what you're told. And remember, for now, you trust Mar and Eliyan and Obin and no one else."

"I'm not the one who trusted the wrong person to start with."

Alizhan turned toward him, nearly knocking over a stack of jugs in her haste. At the sudden movement, Zilal backed up into Ev and hunched until he was as small as possible. She wanted to offer him some comforting touch, but she really couldn't afford to fall asleep right now. She laid her hands on his shoulders, hoping his threadbare tunic was enough to protect her.

They'd already been speaking with lowered voices, and in her anger, instead of raising her voice, Alizhan lowered it further. "What do you want me to do, Kasrik? I am trying to fix this."

"You could start with 'sorry.'"

"Wait, really?" Alizhan said, her tone jumping up with surprise. "But isn't that obvious?"

Ev recalled her own version of this conversation, and she couldn't fight the disappointment that Alizhan hadn't figured it out by herself. But at least they were talking about it. She'd asked what he wanted. That counted for something.

"Not to me," Kasrik said. "Not anymore."

"You said you didn't care how bad I felt," Alizhan said.

"Yeah," Kasrik said. "Because you were making it all about *you*."

"Oh. Well. I'm sorry. I've been sorry this whole time. I didn't know I had to tell you. I'm sorry about that, too. Is this all you wanted?"

"No," Kasrik said. "You still have to do the other stuff. But it helps."

"This is lovely, but could we get back to saving ourselves?" Ev said. Zilal wasn't cowering quite as badly as he had during their argument, but his shoulders were still tense under her hands. "You two are going to Solor House. Zilal and I are going somewhere else, I take it?"

"Your trip is much shorter," Alizhan said. "You're going to the market."

To see Papa. Of course. She'd gotten him thoroughly mired in this. *One smoking hell of a mess*, he'd called it, and it had only gotten messier. But they could rely on him to get Zilal to safety. "Where should I meet you?"

"The Red and Black," Alizhan said. "Then we'll go find *Vines*. Djal said they were leaving on the twelfth of Alaksha. If you're not there by then, I'll have to leave with them. But if I'm not there, run or hide or whatever you have to do to save yourself from Iriyat."

"Fuck that," Ev said. "If you're not there, I'm sure as smoke gonna fucking look for you."

Zilal straightened up to his full height. "That's a bad word."

Ev's cheeks heated. "Sorry."

"Fuck," he said with more cheer than he'd displayed since Alizhan had last offered him food. At least he was resilient. He was handling this at least as well as any of them. He displayed more patience than Ev while they waited for Alizhan to slip out, and then again while Kasrik cracked the door open and peered into the alley and the street beyond for an opportunity.

When Ev and Zilal finally left, she had to fight back the urge to hold his hand as they joined the surging crowd in the street. She rested her hand on his shoulder instead as they made their way down to the market. The collection of carts arrayed in a half-circle at the innermost point of Arishdenan was a familiar sight. Ev breathed in the scents of the harbor, the people, the animals, the dirty city streets, the fruit, the cheese, the fish. It was easy to see her father, standing taller than everyone else.

Obin wasn't alone. Ajee was with him. Would he accept this task? Could she confide in him? Zilal batted her hand away from his shoulder when worry made her grip uncomfortably tight.

Before Ev got close enough to say anything, a shape shot out from under Obin's cart and a dog came bounding toward her. Tez jumped up and put his front paws on her stomach, panting with joy. No face veil could fool him. Ev scratched his head and ears and back, and a moment later, she was bending down to rub his belly.

"Can I pet him?" Zilal asked.

"Of course. This is Tez."

Zilal got to his knees on the dusty cobblestones and for once in his canine life, Tez met a human who had as much energy and enthusiasm as he did.

Ev let them enjoy it for a few minutes, and then said, "Hey. I need you to meet someone."

What could she possibly say to her father? And Ajee? She and Alizhan had come up with a way for Eliyan and Kasrik to reveal themselves to Obin without saying a word, but it would already be obvious to anyone watching that Ev knew them. Tez had taken care of that.

Tez jogged along beside her as she walked up to the cart, then flopped on the ground and demanded more affection from Zilal, who was happy to give it.

Ev didn't have to say anything. Obin hugged her as soon as she got close. "Bad news in the city of late," he murmured.

"It's worse than you know," she said.

As she was looking over her father's shoulder, her gaze connected with someone else's. One brown eye and one icy blue. Vatik was standing on the other side of the market, watching. Ev's breath cut off.

Her father's embrace loosened in response, as though he'd been hugging her too hard.

Would Vatik keep his word? Or would he report this to Iriyat? Worse, would he march over here and take Ev prisoner? He could make some loud, made-up claim about her crimes against Varenx House. Ev would fight him, and so would her father, but he had a sword.

Ev's eyes hurt from not blinking. But as she stared, Vatik lifted his chin in an almost imperceptible acknowledgement of her.

And then he turned away.

He wasn't coming for her. He wasn't even going to watch what she did.

That must mean he planned to keep his word. If he didn't know what she was doing, he couldn't tell Iriyat anything. If she dug through his memory, she might find the agreement he'd made with Alizhan in the burning garden, but she'd only go looking if he gave her cause for suspicion. Ev hoped he could play his part.

"Are you alright?" Obin asked.

Ev took a breath. "Yes. And this is my friend Zilal."

Zilal glanced up, deemed them boring, and went back to playing with the dog.

"Hello, Ev," Ajee said, his voice carefully neutral.

"Hi," she said. He chewed his lip, looking like he wanted to say something, but Ev's silence couldn't unlock it.

So she said, "I have to go away for a little while. I'm sorry I'll miss your wedding. I'm sure it will be lovely. You and Seliman will make each other very happy."

Ajee nodded, and then quickly, as though to spit out the words before he could reconsider them, he said, "I was wrong about you. I'm sorry about the things I said."

Ev was conscious of her father standing beside her. Would Ajee have apologized if Obin weren't looming over him? Maybe Ev didn't want to know the answer.

"Thank you," Ev said. Kasrik had wanted an apology from Alizhan so badly, and getting one seemed to bring him a measure of peace. Ev hadn't expected an apology from Ajee, and all she wanted was for this conversation to be over. She couldn't remember what it felt like to care about his opinion. That had been some other lifetime. "But you know what's better than an apology?"

Ajee looked wary, like she might say *a punch in the gut* next. "What?"

"Help," Ev said. She tilted her head down toward Zilal.

"You need help?" Obin cut in.

"Yes, but I can't talk about it here."

"Of course you can," he responded in Adpri. "Look around. There are maybe two or three people in this crowd who could eavesdrop on us, and none of them are close enough to try." He'd hardly spoken it to her since she was a child. She had vague memories of him singing lullabies to her. It was funny to hear her father talk without a foreign accent—an accent that ought to remind everyone that he was accommodating their inability to speak his language, rather than the other way around.

Djal and Mala had wanted to speak Adpri with Ev, and she'd demurred. She wasn't good at it, and she hated being unable to express herself with nuance. But now was the time to try.

And if the conversation happened to exclude Ajee, it was pure coincidence.

Ev explained, as best she could, that Zilal was in danger and he needed to be hidden somewhere outside the city. There were more children like him. They'd all been in the house that burned down and now they were in the orphanage. Sometime soon, while he was in the market, he'd meet a priest and a teenage boy he could trust. He'd know them when he saw them. She tried to fill in as many details as possible after that, but at least she'd conveyed the important parts.

Obin shook his head at her story about Iriyat, the Council, and the priests. "I knew they were all rotten."

"Not Mar, Papa," Ev said. She wanted to say *he's not pure and innocent, but no one is, and at least he's trying to do the right thing,* but instead she said, "Nobody's perfect. He tries."

"And you're going away?"

"Yes. We find someone to read the book," Ev said. She didn't know how to say *decode.* "Tell Mom sorry and I love her."

"She knows."

"Still."

"Of course I'll tell her."

"And you be careful with Zilal—he's nice, but he puts people to sleep with his hand."

"We might need him to do that on our way home," Obin said, smiling wide.

"Don't let nobody see you," Ev said. "Don't—"

"I was a smuggler before you were born. I know how to do this."

"I love you," Ev said. That phrase came easily to her in Adpri because she'd heard it so often. She didn't know how to say *And There Still the Curling Vines Do Grow,* and her father wouldn't know Djal and Mala personally, but she wanted him to know that he'd helped her. "We found your ship. We sail soon."

"Good. I don't know what they'll say about me on *Vines,*" he said, looking directly at Ev. "But I know you'll try to understand, because you always do."

"You could tell me yourself," Ev pointed out, switching back to Laalvuri.

"I wouldn't know what to say," he said in a tone that ended the conversation.

"We'll talk about this when I come back," Ev said. "Because I *am* coming back." And then she hugged him again.

"Hey," Ajee said, before Ev could crouch down to say goodbye to Zilal. "Don't leave yet." He didn't hug her, just stood awkwardly close with his arms by his sides. "I meant what I said about being sorry. I shouldn't have said any of that stuff to you. Obin and Neiran took me to task and it made me think about some things. You can still be mad at me if you want, but—tell me we might be friends again? Eventually?"

"Of course," Ev said. "Especially if you help." She grabbed him in an impulsive hug. An instant later, he hugged her back fiercely.

23

AND THERE STILL THE CURLING VINES DO GROW

AND THERE STILL THE CURLING Vines Do Grow was anchored in the deep water outside the narrow confines of Arishdenan harbor, so Ev and Alizhan had to take a rowboat out to the ship. Djal had wanted to bring them himself, but he hadn't fully recovered from his injuries. Instead, Mala met them in the harbor and Ev rowed. Mala conveyed Djal's wishes in her slow, musical accent. "He said, and I quote, 'I hope they beat the shit out of him.'"

"We didn't," Ev said, and from Mala's narrowed eyes, Ev guessed she'd been hoping for the same. "Vatik offered to go back and keep an eye out. We might need him later."

The captain was not in evidence when they arrived, so Djal took them to a cabin to wait while he searched for her. The few minutes of waiting stretched and stretched. Ev had no interest in studying the vibrantly colored cloth hangings decorating the cabin, or the pile of pillows on the bed, set into a niche in the wall. There was a chair opposite the bed. Ev was too restless to sit down. Alizhan sat and drummed her fingers on the chair arm.

The captain's arrival was preceded by voices outside.

"But Djal promised that this trip, I could help him. I don't want to spend the whole time babysitting two—" the door to the cabin opened to reveal a chubby adolescent boy and an older woman, and as the boy's gaze took in Alizhan and Ev, his eyes widened and the tone of his voice turned to awe as he finished his sentence: "—girls."

The woman didn't raise a hand, but she gave him a look like a slap. The young man hunched his shoulders, chastened.

Ev could hardly pay attention to him.

The woman towered over him. She was imposing, taller than Ev but more angular, and her skin was lustrous black. She was surely older than Ev, but time hadn't touched her face—only a knife had. A scar slashed her left cheek underneath her eye, a single flaw in her striking symmetry. Her head was shaved. The bright green fabric of her clothes was patterned with rows of gold circles. Papa rarely wore Adpri prints at home, but Ev recognized the design and its meaning: the sun, a symbol of strength. Two teardrops of beaten gold hung from the woman's earlobes, catching the light when she moved her head.

Ev had never seen a woman like her. She was beautiful.

"Girls indeed," the woman said. She appraised Ev, but her expression gave nothing away. "Show it to me."

Ev held out the ring for inspection, and the woman's demeanor changed entirely. She grinned and held up her left hand, wiggling her fingers so that her own ring caught the light. "How is it that Obin Umarsad's daughter came to have a name like *Evreyet*?"

Djal must have told the captain what he knew about her. Or perhaps this woman really did know her father. Ev tried to hide her concerns and appear calm. "My mother liked it."

"Yes, the legendary, fearsome Neiran."

The captain knew her mother's name. Ev had never thought of small, cheerful Neiran—who lined her eyes carefully with kohl after waking and who jangled about their house weighed down with jewelry, humming happily, her long braid swinging —as fearsome, but when she considered the description, it wasn't wrong.

"More importantly, how is it that Obin Umarsad doesn't write me for years, never comes to find me when I'm in the harbor, never invites me to his home, and then sends me his daughter to cart across the sea like a bolt of cloth or a barrel of lamp fluid?"

"I sent myself," Ev said. "And how is it that you know my father, again?" *And why did he never tell me about you?* she added silently. What would she have given to know that there were women like this in the world? Women who looked like her, women who cut off all their hair and hung swords from their belts.

"Djal and Mala tell me the two of you want to get to Nalitzva very badly," the captain said. She'd sidestepped the question. "Why is that?"

"We're seeking audience with Prince Ilyr," Ev said as seriously as she could. She'd never said "seeking audience" before, only read it in books.

The captain burst out laughing. "I bet Obin loved that."

He had not.

She shuffled through some pages in her hands. "I see someone—Djal said it was Mar ha-Solora, but I'm not sure I believed him until just this moment—has paid your passage and furnished you with letters of reference." She paused to examine the wax seals on all the letters. "Mar's keeping his own name out of it, but it all looks respectable enough. That's good. They register everyone who enters Nalitzva, and you'll never even make it out of the harbor without papers, let alone anywhere near the prince. Anything else you want to tell me about this surprise trip across the sea?"

Ev hesitated. How much Djal and Mala had shared? How much it was safe to share? She had a terrible feeling that the captain was relishing her silence. Djal and Mala trusted this woman, and this was the ship that her father had once worked on, and Ev had never met anyone so much like herself. Perhaps her reasoning was foolish, but Ev wanted to be honest with the captain. "Also, everyone in Laalvur is trying to kill us."

The captain laughed again. "Now *there's* a reason to go to Nalitzva. Lucky for you, I'm no stranger to that particular problem. As for your father and me, that's a long story." A brilliant smile. "But the short version is that my name is Ifeleh Umarsad, and you're my niece."

Ev tried not to let her jaw drop. "Papa's your brother."

"Half-brother, technically," Ifeleh said. She tilted her head to the side. "The bad half."

Ev's eyes couldn't get any larger. What else was she missing? Were there other family members? Why didn't Obin ever talk about his family?

"He didn't tell you any of this, I see," Ifeleh said. "Well, that's a story that requires more time than I have to tell, and it's waited twenty-some years, so it'll wait longer. I have things to do. Welcome aboard *Vines*. This is Gad. He's here to keep an eye on you. Try not to get in the way."

She left as abruptly as she'd arrived.

"Where'd you two come from, anyway? Are people really trying to kill you? That's the only good reason to go to Nalitzva, unless you're smuggling," Gad said. "Can't do anything fun there."

GAD PROVED A TALKATIVE, if not entirely credible, companion. Ev wasn't inclined to believe his claim that he'd seen "a *thousand* sharks," for instance. But it was nice to have someone to talk to, since Alizhan had holed up with Mala, and Djal and Ifeleh were occupied with their work.

As nice as Gad was, Ev was always looking for anyone else to talk to. One shift, Ev caught a glimpse of Alizhan and Mala strolling the deck together, with Alizhan wearing an expression of great concentration and holding Mala's hand. It was jarring to see Alizhan sustain such touch, and it stirred a longing in Ev's chest.

Even more jarring, Djal passed by and grinned at both of them. "Looking lovely and alive this fine shift of the Lyrebird, ladies."

"He thinks he's so smooth," Mala said to Alizhan.

"So do you," Alizhan said, guileless and cheerful, with no trace of the seriousness that had creased her face a moment ago. Mala looked heavenward and put a hand over her face. Djal burst out laughing.

"Thank you for that. Never could read this one," Djal said. "Now come here. I heard you've been practicing."

Practicing what? No one had said a thing to Ev, even though she was standing nearby. She felt as though half the conversation was in a language she didn't speak. Alizhan was hesitating, hanging back by Mala instead of approaching Djal, even though his arms were spread.

"You can't hurt me, little sister," Djal said. Alizhan steeled herself, then sprang out of Mala's arms and clamped him in a hug.

Watching the two of them, Ev was pierced with envy. She was Alizhan's friend first. She'd fought for Alizhan, left home for her, caught her when she fell. Ev ought to be able to hug her, at least. Then Ev remembered whose company she was sharing, and the strength of her reaction embarrassed her. It was too much to hope that neither Alizhan nor Djal had felt it. Could

Mala feel other people's feelings too? Smoke, that would be the only way to make this more mortifying.

"Ev," Alizhan said, breaking away from Djal and acknowledging her.

Mala looked at Alizhan and shook her head. "You're not ready for that."

"We'll talk later, Ev, I promise," Alizhan said, and then she and Mala were walking away. Everyone was always promising to talk to Ev later, never right now.

"You're alright," Djal assured her once it was only the two of them standing together. "Or you'll get there."

Ev frowned. "Thank you?"

Laughter came easily to him. "I like you, Evreyet Umarsad, even though you never relax. In Adappyr we call each other brother, sister, cousin, aunt, uncle, you know that?"

"Yes," Ev said. It warmed her every time he did. Ev wore her heritage on her skin and in her hair, but Adappyr itself was just a dot on a map. When Djal and the other crew members called her *little sister*, it connected her to a place she'd never been. "Can I call you *brother*?"

"Took you long enough to ask, little sister."

"Do you miss it? Adappyr?"

He nodded. "Some parts. It's complicated, like all places. I miss some people. I miss the food, too. I miss that bright, hot sunshine that you can't get anywhere else in the world. Laalvuri shadows are too long for me."

"But Adappyr's an underground city."

"We have skylights," he said. "How else would we grow food?"

"I'd like to see it," Ev said. Her father's mysterious homeland.

"I hate to tell you this, but we're sailing the wrong direction for that," Djal said, and grinned.

"What's Nalitzva like?"

"Cold. Grand. Imposing. They throw you in prison for spitting on the ground."

Ev felt like she was talking to Gad again, with his preposterous claims. "They do not."

"As good as," Djal said. "You look at somebody the wrong way, you're in trouble. Say the wrong thing, read the wrong thing, get seen with the wrong person, you're in trouble. Be careful there, Ev. Laalvur has its problems, but you've grown up with a certain kind of freedom, and you take it for granted. Laalvur's a mess—all different kinds of people, ones who want to help you and ones who want to hurt you—but it has an openness you won't find in Nalitzva. They got nice, clean, quiet, straight streets there, with no pamphleteers or pickpockets, but they paid for 'em."

"Well, we won't be staying long," Ev said, unaccountably chilled.

"Let's hope not, little sister."

"Djal," Ev said, because he was moving to end their conversation and get back to work. "Is Adappyr like that? Is that why you can't go back?"

"Something like that. There was a time—a short time—when Adappyr was free and just. But it didn't last."

"What happened?"

"That's something you'll want to ask your father," Djal said, and left.

Ev nearly rushed after him, but he clearly didn't want to give her the answers she sought. And Djal had never known her father, not really. But someone on the ship had.

Unfortunately, Ifeleh was busy all the time. The ship, as small and crowded as it was, felt perversely lonely to Ev.

Alizhan, in a rare moment away from Mala, sat with her in her bunk and said, "That thing Djal said is bothering you."

Ev nodded. "But it's not just that. It's also the things he said about Nalitzva. How can we possibly expect help from the prince of a place like that?"

"I met him," Alizhan said. "I liked him."

"You met him at Varenx House." Ilyr's connection to Iriyat troubled Ev. How could they trust anyone associated with her? Nothing Ev had learned about the man was reassuring. "And you think he's a good person even though his family governs a terrible place?"

Alizhan's gaze wandered over the worn, dark planks of the cabin. "People aren't good or bad. They do bad things and good things."

"Really? You, who can see into people's most secret depths, don't think anyone deserves to be called a bad person?" Ev said. "Not even Iriyat?"

Alizhan looked up at Ev, and there was one brief instant of clear grey eye contact, then she turned. "Especially not Iriyat."

Ev thought of Zilal and the other orphans, and Kasrik strapped to the chair, and Djal with a sword wound to his gut, and didn't feel so charitable toward Iriyat. But Iriyat hadn't raised her, so she said nothing. "And you think Prince Ilyr will help us?"

"I'm sure he's done bad things," Alizhan allowed. "But I don't think he's a bad person. I don't think your father's a bad person, either."

"Do you know what he did?"

Alizhan shook her head. "If a secret isn't on the surface of someone's mind, I have to go digging for it. And I didn't."

For Alizhan, that was very restrained and respectful. Ev might have appreciated it, except that she really wanted to know.

"Ifeleh knows," Alizhan added. "If she won't tell you, I'll find out."

"Thank you."

"But Ev."

"Yeah?"

"Have you considered that you might not want to know?" Alizhan said, and her light eyes glowed in the darkness of the room. "Sometimes not knowing is nice."

Ev shook her head. "I need to."

Ifeleh rarely slept, but she was usually in her cabin during the Rosefinch shift. Ev had to wait hours, but when the moment came, she knocked on the captain's door and then opened it without waiting for an answer.

Ifeleh didn't look happy to see her. Had she really been busy this whole time, or had she been avoiding Ev's questions? "I should throw you out," she said. "I might've been naked in here."

"Then you should have locked the door," Ev said. "I need you to tell me about my father, since no one else will."

"No. You came into my room. You tell me about your father first."

"There's nothing to tell," Ev said. "He runs a farm with my mother. We grow fruit and sell it in Laalvur. He's educated, and I know he came from Adappyr and he was a smuggler for a while, but he never talks about any of that. He hates the rich and powerful. He taught me to fight."

"Was he a good father?"

"Yes," Ev said. Dozens of memories of Papa—walking to the market, sparring in the barn, reading in the sunlight—flooded her mind. If Alizhan had been there, she'd have blinked and rubbed her forehead at Ev's sudden rush of thoughts. "The best."

"You're lucky," Ifeleh said, looking down at her hands. There was a book lying open in her lap, and she closed it and put it aside on the bed. "Not everyone has a good father."

Ev knew that. She'd met too many orphans. "He taught me to fight because the other kids in the village used to pick on me. They told me my father was a murderer," Ev said. "It made me cry. My mother always said he wasn't—she said everyone was just prejudiced against him because he was Adpri—but I could never get him to deny it."

Ifeleh huffed out a laugh, smiled sadly, and said, "Obin. Of course."

That wasn't the response Ev wanted.

"What do you know about Adappyr?"

"It's an underground city," Ev said, feeling as though she were reciting a passage she'd memorized in school. "It's the closest human settlement to Noon, and although it's still very far from Noon, it's too hot to live above ground there. It's also close to the volcano Adap, but people settled there to take advantage of a system of underground caves and a nearby vein of ore, which they mine and export."

Ifeleh waved a hand in the air. "Hurry up. You're encroaching on my sleep shift."

"Um," Ev said, not sure what exactly Ifeleh wanted her to say. "My father talks a lot about how everyone in Adappyr can read, and how everyone has enough to eat, and no one has to work if they're too old or too sick. And there's no religion. The people govern themselves."

"Ah. Is that what he thinks?"

"I never understood how or why a place like that would send its citizens into permanent exile so often."

"Adappyr used to be like that," Ifeleh said. "Although even when there was enough for everyone, the laws were still strict about violence, and the punishment was always exile. But the Adpri worked to make paradise, and as long as you didn't commit a violent crime, you could partake."

"What happened?"

"Many of us believed in these ideas, in this movement, and we were working together to make it possible. But we had a leader. A beloved, charismatic man named Usmam. He brought us together. If there were arguments about how to proceed, he settled them. He was just and considerate, and he worked his whole life to achieve peace and prosperity for his people."

The knots in Ev's stomach could rival any on the ship in their twisted tension. One good man who'd been the key to continued peace in Adappyr—a peace that no longer existed. It wasn't hard to guess what Ifeleh was about to tell her.

But there was a detail she hadn't foreseen.

"He was my father," Ifeleh said. "Our father."

Ev blinked. "But you said my father was your half-brother —'the bad half.'"

"So I did. I'm sure you've guessed by now what I'm about to tell you. Obin killed Usmam. Usmam was a respected, adored leader outside his own home, but inside it, he was sick with rage. He screamed at us and beat us. He killed his first wife, your grandmother, and he would have killed his second, and me as well, if Obin hadn't killed him."

Ev's heart stuttered in her chest. So her father was a murderer after all. All those schoolyard fights over his honor, all those tears, all those times he'd never been able to look her in the eye and say "of course I've never killed anyone."

All those years, and he hadn't just told her the truth. That stung more than anything.

"But Usmam was a pacifist who made violent crime illegal! Why wasn't he convicted and exiled?"

"No one believed us, niece," Ifeleh said.

Just like no one would believe Ev and Alizhan if they told the truth about Iriyat. "So my father killed him to save you, and then he suffered for it."

Ifeleh nodded and said, "So did many other people."

"You *blame* him? But he saved your life!"

"Is my life worth a city?" Ifeleh asked. She raised her hands, palms out, in a philosophical gesture. "I don't know. I won't ever know. Who can make that choice?"

"Is this why we've never met before? Why you don't come around?"

"It's complicated. You know, some people survive ugliness and it brings them together. Obin and I, we still love each other, but... we remind each other of the bad times. We wanted new lives, so now he has his and I have mine. But he sent you to me because he knew I'd help you, and I will."

"Thank you for telling me," Ev said as she left, but she didn't feel any gratitude. Alizhan had been right—sometimes it was better not to know. Ifeleh's story twisted her up inside, and two contradictory wishes warred in her mind: she wished he'd told her the truth a long time ago, and she wished he'd lied.

Most of all, she wished she'd heard from him—a lie, the truth, anything—instead of someone else. Why hadn't he told her? Didn't he trust her? Didn't he think she loved him enough to forgive him?

Did she love him enough to forgive him?

The answer was immediate and unshakeable: yes. Of course she did. But you could love someone with all your heart and still be very, very angry with them, and Ev went to sleep with her jaw and her fists clenched.

The next time she saw Alizhan, Ev had been thinking a lot about fathers. And aunts. But family was a delicate subject, and Alizhan had brusquely pushed it aside last time Ev had broached the topic. Maybe it was better not to bring it up. They were crossing the ocean together, going somewhere neither of them had ever been. They needed each other. They had to stay friends.

"You know," Alizhan said, leaning against the railing and peering down into the water. "The harder you try not to mention something, the more you think about it, and the more obvious it becomes to me."

"I know," Ev said, and sighed. She stood next to Alizhan and rested her hands on the railing. As they'd sailed farther from Laalvur, the sun had dropped toward the horizon and the sky had dimmed from its usual red-gold. The water still glittered in the low light. "I'm trying to be polite. I thought you might not want to talk about it."

"I don't. But if you're going to think about it all the time, then I have to think about it all the time, too. So why don't you just say it?"

"I know you're sure Eliyan's not your mother. But you also mentioned her brother. And she'd known people like you before..."

"You think he's my father and Eliyan's my aunt," Alizhan said. "But I don't want him to be my father."

"Why not?" Didn't she want to meet him? Hadn't Alizhan longed to find her family? Wouldn't this lay the mystery to rest? And wouldn't it be nice to gain Eliyan as a family member? On the other hand, Ev had recently discovered a new family member and found the answer to a lifelong question about her father, and it hadn't brought her much peace.

"Because he's dead, Ev."

"Oh." Nobody had mentioned that. Guilt settled in Ev's stomach. No wonder Alizhan hadn't wanted to talk about it. She should have guessed.

Alizhan dabbed at her eyelashes, then pulled her hand away and stared at her fingertips as if the wetness there were some dangerous alien substance. She dropped her hand down, leaning her elbows on the railing again and letting her tears drip into the sea.

Ev tried to bring up the silver lining. "We don't know it's him for sure, but that would mean he didn't—"

"I've been looking for him my whole life and he's dead." Alizhan bit out the words with force, but the beat of silence after her sentence was broken by a ragged breath. Ev stepped closer. Could she hug Alizhan without hurting either of them? She settled for laying a hand on her back. "He's not supposed to be dead."

"You'd rather have it be someone living? Someone who chose to leave you at the orphanage?"

"Living people can change their minds. They can fix their mistakes. The dead are just dead."

Ev had never seen Alizhan cry, and she wasn't sure if she was witnessing it now. Alizhan kept her face down, turned away from Ev. Ev stroked her hand down Alizhan's back, moving in big, slow circles. "Do you know how Eliyan's brother died?"

"The last wave." Eliyan hadn't mentioned it, which meant Alizhan had cared enough to search her mind for the answer. Alizhan scrubbed the back of her hand across her face. Was that a sniffle?

"I was three. You would have been a baby, or maybe not even born yet. That means that if he was your father, he didn't abandon you. That's important, right? You talked about people fixing their mistakes, but maybe he never made a mistake to fix. It's not his fault he died in the wave. He wanted you. He would have loved you."

"You don't know that."

"I do," Ev said. An instant later, Alizhan was clinging to her, arms clamped around her waist and face pressed into her chest. Ev waited an instant, but neither of them recoiled in pain or passed out. She put her arms around Alizhan. Smoke, she was so small. Ev lifted one hand to stroke Alizhan's hair. She let it run the glossy length of her braid. "You're allowed to cry, you know. You can be upset about this."

"I know," Alizhan mumbled. "I don't like it."

"Crying? Having feelings?"

"There are things inside me that I don't control or understand," Alizhan said. "I don't know what will happen if I let them out. What if I hurt someone?"

"You hurt me once and I'm still here."

That did make Alizhan cry. It was a long time before either of them said anything else. Ev sat down on the deck and Alizhan curled up next to her, knees bent and kept tight to her chest. Ev rubbed her back and let her cry.

Eventually, Alizhan's sobs slowed and she blotted her eyes with the hem of her tunic. "You're too good for me."

"Don't be ridiculous."

"You are. You deserve somebody who's better at this. Somebody who can touch you. Really touch you, I mean. Somebody who can see your face and appreciate it. Somebody who knows when to say sorry without being told. Somebody who wouldn't put you and everyone you care about in danger and then drag you across the ocean."

"I'd like to see you try to drag me anywhere," Ev said, poking one of Alizhan's wiry arms. "And you don't get to tell me what I want."

"But I know what you want," Alizhan said. "I see your dreams. I can't be that for you, Ev. I'll hurt you."

This was the constant refrain of their relationship—such as it was. Alizhan told Ev that what she wanted was impossible, that Alizhan couldn't ever, that Ev should stop wanting her. Ev's desires were always out in the open. When Alizhan refused them, she never said *I don't want to*. Only *I can't*. And she'd been upset to learn that Djal had kissed Ev. But every time Ev tried to learn how Alizhan felt, Alizhan shut down the conversation. When Ev had asked if Alizhan was like Eliyan—uninterested in sex—instead of saying yes or no, she'd said *it doesn't matter*. That was avoidance. Fear.

"Listen," Ev said. "If you don't want this, then say you don't want it. I'll still be here if that's how it is. But if you've been telling me it's impossible because you're afraid, well… You didn't hurt me just now. I know we weren't skin-to-skin, but it's still progress. And you've been on this ship with all these people this whole time, and you haven't been sick. You've been practicing with Mala. You're getting better. And I'm very patient." Ev squeezed Alizhan's shoulders. "Did you know I once waited ten years for a girl to tell me her name?"

Alizhan laughed—a teary, startled sound.

"It's possible," Ev insisted. "So stop thinking about what I want. Think about what *you* want."

Alizhan hugged her knees tight and buried her face in them. "That sounds like it involves feelings."

At that, Ev laughed. "Yes. Yes, it does."

EV TRIED to give Alizhan some space to think after their raw, revealing conversation. She didn't want to pressure her. So Ev passed a lot of time aboard *Vines* in a troubled, solitary haze. Ev kept away from the crew—did they think of her as the captain's niece, or as the traitor's daughter?—and let Alizhan spend her time with Mala. Gad tried to cheer her up with stories or distract her with questions, but even he eventually ran out of things to say.

There was a commotion on the deck one triad, which Ev ignored, because if there was a problem, she'd only be in the way of people with more wisdom and experience than herself, and they'd ask her to leave. But then Gad dragged her out of her berth, and he insisted on going to get Alizhan, too. Mala allowed it, and the three of them went up to the deck and stood by the railing.

"Look," Gad said, pointing down into the water.

A huge, translucent orb floated just underneath the surface, green as a lamp, with hundreds of finger-thin tentacles trailing after it like the train of a gown. A giant medusa. Ev felt her eyes go as wide and round as its bell.

How strange. It was so massive, so sinister, so threatening, and yet utterly silent. If none of the sailors had seen it, the creature might have passed beneath their ship unnoticed. Ev wondered how many other medusas had done exactly that.

"I wanted to go after it, but the captain said no," Gad said. "She said you need special training and equipment to do it without dying, and no prize is worth dying for, anyway."

The medusa was still drifting by, in no hurry to go anywhere. Did it know they were above it, in this ship? Was it *waiting*? She shivered.

Alizhan was standing curiously close to her. Her gaze wasn't pointed toward the creature in the water, but on the distant horizon. And yet she seemed to be concentrating on something. Was she afraid? How could anyone come so close to the thing in the water beneath them and *not* feel afraid?

Gad was still talking. "The captain said if you sail long enough, if you stop in enough harbors, you meet sailors who tried. The ones who lived, anyway. If they still have all their limbs, they have black scars on their bodies, places where their skin just *died*. That's how powerful the venom is. Sometimes it has funny effects on people's minds, too. But it sells for so much money in Laalvur, and it's all the rage in Nalitzva now. We could be rich..."

Ev had stopped listening. Alizhan's gloved hand had slid into hers. Ev wanted to grip fiercely and never let go, but instead she stayed perfectly still and regulated her breathing. Alizhan's fingers curled around hers, slowly, but with increasing sureness. By the end, Alizhan was holding her hand.

That answered Ev's question about what Alizhan wanted.

Ev's eyes were wet, but she wasn't afraid. She looked back at the monster in the water. "I'm happy to let it go. I don't ever want to get close to one of those."

"That's why I'm gonna be rich and you're not," Gad said. He grinned.

"Did you say something about black scars?" Ev asked.

Gad took off again, recounting the horrors of being touched by medusa venom: excruciating pain, black scars that never healed, stiffness in the affected limbs, and for some, a dullness of the senses. Ev looked at Alizhan, thinking of Kasrik, but Alizhan was now gazing directly into the water—into the dark emptiness where the monster had once been. Ev squeezed her hand.

"Anyway, before this thing showed up, *that* was what I wanted to show you."

Gad pointed. Rising above the horizon, blurred with mist and painted in the dim cool sunlight of the Nightward shore, was the white stone edifice of Nalitzva.

READ ON FOR AN EXCERPT...

Nightvine, book two of *The Gardener's Hand* and the sequel to *Thornfruit*, will come out in Spring 2018.

NIGHTVINE

Their cell was quiet, but Ev could hear the din of prisoners shouting, sobbing, and striking the walls of the other cells. That wasn't the reason Ev wanted out—*being in prison* was enough of a reason for her—but she had no intention of quibbling with Alizhan. "If I lift you up, maybe we could get to that window. Do you think we could work those bars free?"

The window was too high for Ev to reach all by herself. It was also so small that it was hard to imagine even Alizhan squeezing through it, and the metal bars were solidly embedded in the wall, but Ev didn't have a better idea.

"It's rude to plan an escape and not invite me," the other prisoner said, startling Ev.

He spoke Laalvuri. *Smoke.*

"It's rude to eavesdrop," Ev snapped.

She'd thought he was asleep or unconscious, and even if he'd been awake, he hadn't seemed interested in either of them. But he must have been listening. He lifted his head from his prone position, then sat up. With one hand, he brushed off some of the straw and dirt clinging to his clothes. He somehow managed to make the action look graceful, even regal.

"What's rude is you being so unbearably dull," he informed Ev.

Ev started to stand, but Alizhan said, "Wait."

"Ooh, the little one's in charge," said the prisoner. "I was picturing it all wrong."

What had he been picturing? How could he make Ev so angry and uncomfortable with just his tone of voice? Ev wouldn't have hit him. She might have loomed over him in a silent, threatening way, though. She missed her stick fiercely.

"Don't worry, Ev," Alizhan said. She wasn't even looking at Ev. Her eyes were still locked on the prisoner. It was fiery unsettling sometimes, having a conversation with Alizhan. She pulled things out of the silence with eerie accuracy. "He smells good."

Alizhan crawled across the cell and sat down cross-legged in front of the prisoner.

He laughed, a single flat sound with no humor in it, and directed his gaze at Ev. "There is something *tragically* wrong with your friend's nose."

Ev might have laughed and explained it to him if he'd been a little nicer. As it was, she was mystified by what Alizhan saw—or smelled—in him.

"He's sad. And hurt," Alizhan continued, addressing Ev as if the man in front of her couldn't hear her. "He's trying to hide it."

So he was hissing at Ev to distract her, like a wounded tomcat hiding in a dark corner of the barn? She would've had patience for the cat. Unfortunately for her cellmate, Ev's sympathies didn't extend to sharp-tongued strangers.

"He is not," the prisoner said. "He is in perfect health and would make a useful accomplice for any escapes you might be planning. In fact, out of an astonishing generosity of spirit, he will mastermind said escape plans for you, since your previous attempts have been so lackluster."

It was dim in the prison, but he didn't look or sound Nalitzvan. Despite speaking flawless Laalvuri, he didn't look like anyone Ev had ever met in Laalvur. His skin was a golden shade of tan, lighter in color than Ev's or Alizhan's, but not the milky shade of most Nalitzvans, either. He was wearing the same loose beige tunic and trousers as all the other prisoners, so his clothes gave no clue as to where he was from. He sat with his legs crossed. And since Alizhan had mentioned it, Ev noticed he was cradling his right hand in his lap. His black curls were matted with dust. A sparse scattering of stubble dotted his cheeks.

"You're an islander," Alizhan said. Ev wouldn't have blurted it out so casually, even if she had put it together. "How did you end up here?"

"An excellent question. Also rather rude."

Alizhan wasn't deterred. Good manners were not among her skills. She stopped trembling and focused all her attention on the prisoner. "If you're an islander in prison in Nalitzva, then how and why do you speak Laalvuri?"

"There isn't a good Laalvuri word for it," he said, which wasn't the answer Ev expected, although it was hard to say what she'd expected. Was he some kind of international criminal? Or was he like them, unjustly imprisoned?

"You know, we're not all the same. I don't go around calling you *mainlanders*. I know you're Laalvuri."

"Well, which island are you from, then?" Alizhan said, as if she were being very patient. "Tell me and I'll call you that instead."

"I'm from Hoi," the prisoner said. There was a note of amusement in his voice, which usually a good sign in people's dealings with Alizhan, but Ev didn't want to think well of him just yet. "And I'd very much like to get the watery hell out of Nalitzva and go back there, but first I want to know what you think I smell like."

"It's not always a smell," Alizhan said, unfazed by the Hoi's priorities. She waved a hand in the air, drawing a series of vague circles, in a gesture Ev guessed was supposed to be helpful and explanatory. "Sometimes it's a feeling. Or a color. A sound. An image. Words, maybe, if someone's really loud. Anyway, I can't tell much about you, which might be because you're in so much pain, or—"

Ev wanted to hear the end of that sentence, but the prisoner interrupted. "Well, prison is terribly hard on my complexion, you understand. I shudder to appear before you in this state, but I suppose it is a lesson in what life is like for those who haven't been graced with dazzling good looks."

Ev didn't have time for this. For him. She supposed under all the filth and bruises he might have been handsome, but she couldn't imagine a less important subject. She crossed her arms over her chest and tried not to tap her fingers with impatience.

"So I haven't been able to attend to my toilette as usual. And the beds in this place! Let's not even mention the food. Or lack thereof. A little ennui is to be expected. Anyway, clearly you're a mind-reader. I'd say 'why didn't you just say so,' but I suppose the answer is obvious, given where we find ourselves."

Alizhan nodded.

In a different tone, rougher around the edges, the prisoner said, "You're lucky these barbarians just threw you in prison instead of killing you on the spot."

"Lucky," Ev repeated. He knew about magic, this man. He wasn't suspicious or even surprised. He thought magic-hating Nalitzvans were barbarians. Maybe he could help them after all, even if he was glib and snide. Was he really in pain, like Alizhan said? Ev squinted at his hand.

"Yes, lucky," he said seriously. "In the same way I'm lucky that it was only one hand, and the wrong one, at that." With his left hand, he gestured at the hand in his lap. Now that Ev was invited to examine it more closely, she could see it was swollen.

Bruises darkened his skin. Some of his fingers were bent at unnatural angles. "We're all marvelously lucky, aren't we?"

"They broke your hand," Ev said, outraged. She felt guilty for all her uncharitable thoughts toward him. She didn't like him, but he didn't deserve to be maimed. And what could he possibly have done to incur such an inhumane punishment? What would the guards do to Alizhan and Ev if they couldn't escape? A frisson of fear ran down her spine.

"Beauty *and* brains," the prisoner drawled.

He was really testing the limits of her sympathy, this stranger.

"Why?" Alizhan said. "What did you do?"

"What did *you* do?" he shot back. Alizhan probably couldn't tell that he was glaring at her when he said it, since she rarely looked at anyone's face, but Ev could.

"Nothing," Alizhan said, unmoved by his tone.

There was a long silence, and finally the prisoner relented.

"Well, I wrote something," he said. "The guards are possessed of strong literary opinions and they took it upon themselves to end my career."

"What did you write? Was it libel? Did you criticize the royal family?" Ev said.

"Neither. It was both glorifying and truthful." A joyless smile. "But really, why talk about how we ended up here—a dull, trivial subject—when instead, we could talk about how to get out?"

"It's not right," Ev said. "We didn't do anything wrong. We don't deserve to be here, and whatever you wrote, you didn't deserve that. It's not like you killed someone."

"Yes, yes," he said. "I'm so glad to know your sense of justice is offended. Now, about that escape plan. I hear you need to get to llyr. To get to him, you need someone who can speak Nalitzvan and someone who knows the palace. Coincidentally,

this shift Mother Mah Yee and all your gods have rained bless-
ings down upon you," here he paused, and with his good hand,
the prisoner made a graceful, sweeping gesture, indicating
himself, "granting you the good fortune of meeting me. Get me
out and I will get you in."

"More of a trickle than a rain," Alizhan said, laughing.

"More of a drought," Ev muttered. Then she mentally
pushed aside all the nonsense he'd said, and responded to the
important part. "You know the palace?"

"And you speak Nalitzvan as well as Laalvuri?" Alizhan said.

"Naturally."

His words gave Ev pause. She hated his little reminder that
he'd eavesdropped on her private conversation with Alizhan
earlier. But it was more than that. What could he possibly mean
by "naturally"? His Laalvuri was perfect. Nothing about him
made sense. Islanders rarely left their home. Ev had never met
one in Laalvur, but she knew there was a trader who sold
medusa venom and products made from it. She'd assumed
Nalitzva would be similar. What was someone from Hoi doing in
prison here?

"Also, the window will never work. Alizhan, can you tell me
about the guards?"

Alizhan shook her head. "They're too far. There's too many
people." And then she added, "How do you know my name?"

"Ev and I had a chat," he said. "If the guards come closer,
could you read them?"

"Probably." Alizhan shrugged. Then she said, caught
between curiosity and suspicion, "Ev doesn't like to talk."

"She does," he replied. Ev didn't appreciate being spoken
about as if she weren't there, but the prisoner was already
continuing. "We have to distract the guards somehow. Get them
to open the door. There are almost always two of them, and we'll

only have a second. Ev can take one and you and I will take the other."

"Ev could take both if she had her stick," Alizhan said. As always, she had far more confidence in Ev than Ev did.

"Could she," the prisoner said, and for the first time, he really smiled. It flashed across his face and was gone. Alizhan smiled in return, a quick mirror. Ev felt very far away. How had they already come to like each other?

"That's good to know," the prisoner continued. "But as Ev does not have her stick, I won't assign her the task of taking out two very large men by herself. Once we get out of here, I'll direct you to Ilyr. You can probably even get your book back, whatever you want it for."

"Why are you helping us?" Ev asked.

"I should think it obvious. I want to get out of prison."

"Why are you helping us *with Ilyr*," Ev said flatly. The prisoner always slipped out of the way of questions. He hadn't said his name yet, he'd barely explained what landed him in prison in the first place, and he hadn't explained how he could possibly know his way around the palace. Alizhan's instinct wasn't enough for Ev to trust him.

"Oh, that," he said. "It's a long story."

"We're very busy, as you can see," Alizhan said, gesturing at the cell.

"I do like a captive audience."

Alizhan laughed. Ev stared at the prisoner until he began to talk.

ACKNOWLEDGMENTS

A whole community of marvelous, talented, brilliant, kind-hearted, good-looking people helped this book come into the world.

First among them is my live-in science consultant, who has answered questions about the physics of tidally locked planets, the chemistry of invisible ink, and the nervous systems of sea monsters that I invented—that *we* invented. With endlessly renewable patience, my science consultant listened to hours of soliloquy about this book, much of it overwrought in both senses of the word. (If you were faking the patience, thanks for that, too.) The science consultant also repeatedly predicted that I was, in fact, capable of writing a novel. His hypothesis has been confirmed.

I am grateful to my friends and fellow writers Lis, Kristin, and Ryan for beta reading and making suggestions, and most of all for every exclamation-point-filled or all-caps text, DM, or email live-blogging this book to me. Have you ever been so overcome with delight that you had to stand up and walk out of a room so you could clutch your face and remember how to breathe in private? I have. I hope to repay all of you in kind.

Thank you also to my parents and my brother, who are always, always willing to talk about books, even books they hadn't read and weren't allowed to see until after publication, like this one.

And to every fandom I've been in, where I learned as much about stories as I did in grad school, and to all the internet strangers and friends who crossed my path before this, thank you for teaching me that I could.

ABOUT THE AUTHOR

Felicia Davin's short fiction has been featured in *Lightspeed*, *Nature*, and *Heiresses of Russ 2016: The Year's Best Lesbian Speculative Fiction*.

She lives in Massachusetts with her partner and their cat. When not writing and reading fiction, she teaches and translates French. She loves linguistics, singing, and baking. She is bisexual, but not ambidextrous.

You can find her at feliciadavin.com.

 twitter.com/FeliciaDavin

CPSIA information can be obtained
at www.ICGtesting.com
Printed in the USA
FFOW02n0927190518
46643754-48720FF

9 780998 995700